THE ROADIE CARTEL

A NOVEL

phillip j kriz

HILDE
BRAND
BOOKS

Hildebrand Books
an imprint of W. Brand Publishing
NASHVILLE, TENNESSEE

Copyright © 2023 Phillip J Kriz

This book is a work of fiction, using research from public domain and free information readily available. All incidents and dialogue, and all characters with the exception of some well-known historical figures, are products of the author's imagination and are not to be construed as real. Where real-life historical figures appear, the situations, incidents, and dialogues concerning those persons are entirely fictional and are not intended to depict actual events or to change the entirely fictional nature of the work, with the exception of factual descriptions of the actions of said historical figures. In all other respects, any resemblance to actual persons, living or dead, events, or locales is entirely coincidental.

This book does not represent personal or political views. It was written for entertainment. regardless of race, religion, or country of origin.

All rights reserved. No part of this publication may be reproduced, distributed, or transmitted in any form or by any means, including photocopying, recording, or other electronic or mechanical methods, without prior written permission, except in the case of brief quotations embodied in critical reviews and certain other noncommercial uses permitted by copyright law.

Hildebrand Books an imprint of W. Brand Publishing
j.brand@wbrandpub.com
www.wbrandpub.com

Cover design by Phillip J Kriz and designchik.net
Developmental edit by: Desiree Yost
Copy edit by: Nancy LaFever

The Roadie Cartel – Phillip J Kriz - First Edition

Available in Paperback, Kindle, and eBook formats.
Paperback: 978-1-956906-76-9
eBook: 978-1-956906-77-6
Release date: December 1, 2023

Library of Congress Control Number: 2023916895

The Set List

In loving memory
Virginia D. Kriz

road·ie /ˈrōdē/

noun

a person employed by a touring band of musicians to set up and maintain equipment.

car·tel /kär'tel/

noun

an association of manufacturers or suppliers with the purpose of maintaining prices at a high level and restricting the competition.

good /go͝od/
noun
that which is morally right, righteousness.

e·vil /ˈēvəl/

noun

profound immorality and wickedness, especially when regarded as a supernatural force.

A Native American elder once described his own inner struggles in this manner: Inside of me there are two dogs. One of the dogs is mean and evil. The other dog is good. The mean dog fights the good dog all the time. When asked which dog wins, he reflected for a moment and replied, "The one I feed the most."

—George Bernard Shaw

The Band is Walking...

October 13, 2009, 13:35:00 **The Arena - Seattle, WA**

Sitting alone is something new to me. I sit in my production office, confused and angry, and with a loaded revolver in my lap. Outside these four concrete walls the world is spinning, but the rotation of my world is quickly slowing down. I have a tough decision to make, facing a pivotal point in my life. I am either going to face my demons or end it to join my father. Without a soul to turn to and with the odds against me, the idea of pulling the trigger becomes easier by the second. Simply adjust the barrel to the temple and apply slight pressure to instigate a final click. I need to escape the constant mental pain that has consumed me since his passing.

With the hammer pulled back and ready to fire, "I am sorry, Father," escapes my mouth in a whisper. I shut my eyes . . . I take one long last breath in and start to squeeze the . . . I suddenly feel pressure, a hand on my shoulder. I jolt around! Nothing. . .

Freaking out, I sit back in my chair as pictures of my father and reflections of how strong a man he was flash in my unhealthy, fragile and fucked up state of mind. Is this how he would want me to reach the afterlife? I am not sure if there is a heaven, but my father started to believe during his last years on earth. Would he accept my presence on his cloud of eternal peace with my brains trickling down my neck? Probably not. Besides, I may be alive because he has unfinished business that falls onto my shoulders caused by his untimely death. Barrel pressed to my head and the hammer pulled back, my thoughts shifted from a cloud in the sky back down to reality.

In all honesty, I am not sure if I will be ready for what stands against me, but my brains on the floor also sends shivers down my spine and tears down my face. Since it is in my blood to stand my ground and not run, pressure from my finger on the trigger softened. Though it is not removed, I sit and think of the battle ahead and it is not a choice when I fight. The freight train that is my enemy shows zero signs of slowing down, if anything, the fight has already begun.

I have only one weapon. And something I have used before. A nuisance, but a necessity.

It is time. I have waited long enough. I have to make a choice, like my father always said, "shit or get off the pot." Life or death. . .I close my eyes, slide to the edge of my seat and inhale as if ready to plunge into a deep, dark abyss. I hold my breath. I pause. The world around me stands still as I hear my tears landing on my jeans below.

One of my favorite photos of my father and me standing on the edge of a stage suddenly comes to mind. I must have been seven. We were standing with our backs facing the crowd, hundreds of thousands of screaming fans behind us; I was so scared that day. But he held my hand, and said, "look at me, don't worry about the crowd, one day I will be gone and only a voice in your head telling you to stand tall but today I will show you that you can move thousands with just one small action." Down on one knee he smiled at me and started to count down as the crowd got audibly louder, "THREE, TWO, ONE. . . raise your arms to the sky!" he shouted. The photo is taped to the wall of my road case; my father, my stuffed tiger, me and a sea of people all have our hands up. I think he would want me to stay and fight.

I force open one eye, closely followed by the other, and there it sits on the desk in front of me. A new beginning. With the gun still in one hand, I lean forward and pick up my new weapon. It is lighter. I press the button on the side. The screen shines against my face like a morning light. A vibration sends a rush of energy back to my soul, and a sigh of relief escapes my mouth. Holding this modern day sword, I run my thumb across the smooth surface and swallow firmly while my nerves strain to travel from my brain to my fingertips. *The cartel, will never expect an attack like this; they can't stop me now.*

I am less anxious with the revolver than I am with this new cell phone. A supercomputer. A "smart" phone. Who knew this would be my salvation? I slide back in my worn leather office chair and take a deep breath as I choose life today. I holster the revolver under my left arm in the shoulder strap that was gifted to me by a fellow roadie, Pie. He carries a bigger side piece these days.

I stare entranced at my glowing weapon and the array of tools at my fingertips. With clammy hands, I swallow my pride and prepare for a long and maybe pointless search for the one person who I was told can help me. As of now, he is a phantom for the public, and only speculation asserts that he is still alive and the only one who can take down the demon who is pursuing me.

My fingers feel like they are gliding on ice with each new gesture I make. Since the phone is practically twice the size of my former burner flip phones, I must use one hand to hold the beast and the other to swipe as I become familiar with the software. After fumbling through this innovative device for a solid chunk of time, I decide that I am no tech wizard, but am nevertheless comfortable enough to move forward. It is time I stop feeling sorry for myself and execute what I had conjured during my flight to the West Coast.

I navigate from the homepage to download a new video-photo application, a new wider reaching social media app, which allows me to tag my location at any time throughout the world. There have been social media apps before this one—that have connected people—but this was the first of its kind. It offered a live streaming function as well as long formatted videos to be uploaded to it. When I heard about such an invention, I was indifferent. Now, months later, my world is flipped upside down, and I am forced to use new technology to defeat my enemy. I catch myself smirking at the device, frozen in awe with the thought that I may change this cartel's future forever with something that fits in my pocket. But it has always been something they have feared ending up in the wrong hands and infiltrating their way of life before it could be destroyed.

I click the app icon, and it transports me into the setup menu. Something lighthearted needs to keep me sane, so I come up with a flippant screenname: *roadiekid713*. The app wanted to get to know me better; where are you from, male or female, what are your interests? But I opted to skip all and go explore.

In this new tech savvy world, I can open Pandora's box with a swipe and walk through the closet to reach Narnia. Everything fades away as I enter this new realm, and I am drawn to the first photo that appears when the app finishes with the prompt to conclude the signup process in settings. It is an image of people I have never met. Maybe a couple? They are both holding beers, smiling. I tried the zoom feature. In the background is the stage, to the show that I was taking around the world. I stop to think about what I am seeing. Am I connected to these strangers? No, I am not. I find myself confused, yet hooked and wanting to see more in the virtual world to which I now belong.

A quick "how to" arrow pops up on the screen to entice me to move on from this girl's image. As I touch the screen with my thumb, the photo scrolls upward. I feel an eyebrow raise as a new image appears of a dog sitting on a porch. I swipe again. This time, I am witnessing a club full of people with hands in the air, eyes clenched, mouths gaped with excitement. Again, I swipe. A group of girls on a beach. Then once again I swipe up. A boy with his grandfather on their family ranch with a pet cow. A 50th wedding anniversary. The people on the app look so happy and full of life. I pause and stare around my stale, glum office. It feels dead and without life. Those people do not share the same reality as I am living. My life reflects that of this old dressing room, empty and grim. Lies and betrayal sweep through my mind. Do I belong on this site? Do I want to poison the innocence displayed before me? Will they even allow my message on here?

With hope dissipating, I swipe again. A video for the first time. I watch a group of teenagers who are street fighting, and I feel relieved. Maybe there is more to this site than happy drunks and people's pets. With each swipe, I become more obsessed, noting that these upload-ed images have a story and location tagged to each one. And then I come across what appears to be a video diary. The building sudden-ly erupts with loud music from the sound check. From the plastic packaging that lies on my desk, I grab hold of new earbuds to listen closely. I adjust myself in my office chair and become aware the of the hard metal that remains pressed against my inner arm and ribs.

I snap back into my reality and force myself away from the mil-lions of people sharing their lives for attention. After my short practice run of working the record button, I chuckle to myself as I unintentionally flip the camera to face me. I see a double chin. *Woof.* Although this will be the position I use most often to record, I was taken off guard by my hideous complexion. My eyes resembled the great wild North American trash panda's and don't even get me started on the amount of dried salt plastered to my cheeks from cry-ing. I feel silly. Even in my sadness, my double chin and racoon eyes makes me laugh, but my smile cannot hide my sleep deprivation and nervousness. My time is running out. I need to flush out the one person who can help me. I cannot think of another way to send my message to the masses and find the man that can change my fate. At the end of the day, I may not be the smartest, but I know these social apps are bringing people closer than ever.

Here goes nothing. Adjusting the earbuds to ensure a snug fit, I begin my first video diary to share my life that has been involved with the biggest and most sophisticated cartel that is hiding right in plain sight in front of the whole world.

>>>START RECORDING<<<

This is, video diary #1 October 13, 2009, 13:55:00

Hi, social media world! My name is Wyatt Reznek . . .

and if you couldn't tell, I'm a little nervous about talking into this screen. This is my first time talking to something that. . .well, that can't talk back . . .

and . . . I . . . I . . . I

I have . . .

>>>PAUSE RECORDING<<<

I stop. I put the phone on the table. I shake my head. I look to the sky, hoping my father can provide courage to say it. He was, and in many ways, still is, my rock. "Shit, another self-pity party," murmurs in my head. I am already walking a road to a shallow grave, so fuck it, I have nothing to lose. I shake my head to get out my jitters. Inflate my lungs with some oxygen. Roll my neck side to side, tiny cracks but I feel better. I clear my throat. Pick the phone up and start again. . .

>>>RESUME RECORDING<<<

My name is Wyatt Reznek, and **I am** determined to bring justice to my father's killers. I will be posting every day until they come for me for sharing the tale of my family. My hope is that you can help lead me to the man I must find whose last known whereabout was in a small Mexican town south of Columbus, New Mexico. The police will only cause more danger and harm to the roadies around me. I implore you to listen to my story. I . . . I am putting my faith in technology and others who have been harmed by these men.

I have been blacklisted from people I once called friends and colleagues. I lost two people to men who falsely called me "family" a week ago and now want me dead. We are all slaves to this cartel, and—sadly—most don't know it yet. I feel like there is no escape, so—in a way—these videos will probably be the last anyone sees of me, but I'm willing to do so for justice. . .

Please. Listen. The local, and even federal, authorities are a major part of all of this. The cartel and the men who work for them are ruthless killers. Shortly after they killed my father days ago, they forced me back on tour with threats worse than death. I will do anything for my two best friends who are still alive, for now, and I will fight for them. Even when they sadly will not fight for me.

I must get my message out quickly. So, if you are out there, listen to the stories I am about to share. Time is of the essence. I beg of you . . .

Help me stop these monsters and what they are not only doing to me, but society. The evil empire must come to an end.

>>>PAUSE RECORDING<<<

Chills run down my spine during my last line in the video—a sensation much like those when my father said his last goodbyes. I force myself to shake off the bad vibe, focus, and stop being emotional. This is not the time to be scared or feel sorry for myself. I pull an earbud from my right ear. I sit and listen to the silence in the room. Even outside of my office, it is quiet . . . now, this is unusual when on a big tour like this. Nervously, I continue my journey into social media.

>>>RESUME RECORDING<<<

Look, the last few days have been long. My thoughts might be jumbled because all I can think about is what might happen if they don't get caught. The things they'll do to . . . they will do to . . .

>>>PAUSE RECORDING<<<

I took a long pause because suddenly I knew that what I was going to do by exposing these animals would ultimately hurt so many other innocent people in the wake of their ant hill being destroyed. I can't think about that right now, I have to think of the end goal . . . to exterminate the ants from the land.

>>>RESUME RECORDING<<<

. . . they will only continue to destroy and conquer and become more powerful. So, I must sacrifice my own life eventually to bringing them down.

It's ignorant to believe someone from the cartel won't come across these videos—it is showing zero viewers now—but I don't have any other way to do this. I am sure there is a tale somewhere about a hero defeating a grizzly and vicious military and if not, well I hope someone writes about me one day. So, I need you to be my eyes and ears—my army of insight—to find a cop that's from Mexico who my dad told me is the only one who has ever tried to stand up to these criminals and might still hold a secret on how to take them down.

>>>PAUSE RECORDING<<<

My eyes look down, again. Number of viewers: still zero. Without friends, how can I make this work? The reality of loneliness kicks in. Discouraging. But I know I need to push forward and hope my mission is not a disaster. With a small eye roll of annoyance with myself, I center my face on the screen, rubbing the dark bags under my eyes and move my hair out of my eyes. I place the missing earbud back into place.

>>>RESUME RECORDING<<<

I'm not your typical thirty-one-year-old. By society's standards, one could say I've had it all: money, worldly travels, and I have had fun in more airplane bathrooms than Zeppelin has number one hits. For almost two decades, I've been crisscrossing the globe as a production manager setting up some of the world's largest stadium and arena concert tours that have been produced. Hell, there are roadies who dream of having my job and punters—you know random everyday people—who have wet dreams about my life, but I didn't choose it, the cartel tour life chose me.

I've traveled since I was eight, with my father on his tours. I am what people call a roadie. And I'm a damn good one. From pop to rock to rap to country acts, I've been lucky enough to see it all—and I'm also cursed to see it all . . .

During those years, we have smuggled more drugs than anyone can fathom. Crazy part is, we, AKA the cartel, are part of your everyday life and that's what has made things easy. Most will say my life is amazing when they look at it from the outside. What no one sees, though, is that there's no chance of leaving the cartel when you work for them—other than death . . .

We're cocaine-moving slaves . . .

I was born into this family and didn't know better. I just wanted to be a part of the family business. Then . . .

Then my father's death made me question everything.

Before I go on, you need to understand . . .

This is the biggest (I spread out my arms as far as they could reach) **—cartel in the world!** No one messes with us. They hoped I would believe them when they said it was a rival cartel that killed my father. But how could I take that as a truth when there is no rival?

They messed with the wrong roadie. They took my father's life, and now I'm committed to take theirs . . .

If you plan to help me, do so with caution. It'll take a lot of shit to happen for this monopoly to fall apart after they've made billions through concert goers to cover their tracks. I will never be able to erase the damage done to countless souls, but I hope to make a change now.

They've been able to use their profits to pay off government favors without flinching. In the beginning, there were two production companies along with a couple management businesses that handled artists and their shows as separate entities. The founding fathers, my family, spotted a way into the industry and decided they could control the transit and routing of these bands, their gear, and even the crew members. All they needed was a full in-house system to cater to the pocketbooks of the artists. No middlemen. Eventually, they molded the culture of touring and even how fans attended shows as an avenue to boost the cartel's central system. From moving drugs to laundering money, they have figured out how to bypass flawed banking and government systems. The cartel chose the music industry because the ones in charge were weak and only looking to grow their pocketbooks, plus they can fly under the radar by using these famous names.

And if you don't like the system, they have a man to help "persuade" you to think otherwise. The one to really worry about, in fact, is the drug lord's righthand man nicknamed "The Butcher." He should be called "Death" and dress in all black to fit the part and to uphold the obsession of his trade when the boss orders him to procure a soul . . .

>>>PAUSE RECORDING<<<

I catch myself on the verge of rambling. This social space is addicting. There is so much to say, but I feel it best to continue tomorrow so I may be more concise. First, though, I share what is most important—and most dangerous.

>>>RESUME RECORDING<<<

I need to find Officer Michael Hernández. His exact last known whereabouts is hard to say, but he used to be the chief of police in the small Mexican town of Palomas. If I can manage to stay alive for a few more days, you can find me in my hometown of El Paso on November 6th, searching for him on my day off before our big show there in town.

>>>STOP RECORDING<<<

A little parched and on the verge of crying, I knew it was time to stop the recording that had been broadcast to the world. Slumping back in my chair for a quick break, I reached for a bottle of water and accidently nudged my computer mouse, the bright light from my monitor lit the room up.

"Damn, that was weird." I said out loud about the video I just made as I was getting up from my chair.

I unplug my headphones and slide my new phone into a hidden pocket on my tour jacket. My new weapon sits inches from the revolver, the thing I thought would help end my misery, but for now they both rest . . . it is time to go walk to the drug lab and check on tonight's shipment. Before walking away from my desk, I paused and smiled at an image of my father and me on my computer screen. Although he is gone, I know he is still here looking after me, like he always said he would.

November 5, 2009, 13:39:00
Production Office Before the Show - Phoenix, AZ

My days are so off lately. It has been a few weeks since my father's murder, and I am surprised that the cartel has not "replaced" me yet. It is also spooky because I have stopped caring about the show and the cocaine. I am still doing my job, but in no comparison with my past involvement. I still get the band to stage, I check to make sure the product is getting cut and packaged, but I yearn for the continuance of my video diaries.

I can assume that the band's manager has broken the news that they will lose me to another band soon—well that is what is being told to them—but production has been waiting for the upcoming break to make the swap to the new guy. In layman's terms, they plan to kill me.

I return from a stroll to the basement level of the arena, a place that even some of the most seasoned roadies never visit, and most do not realize exists. This is where most of the cutting and packaging of coke occurs. I sit back in my office chair, which leans so far back that I am practically horizontal, kick my feet up on to my desk and grab my not so new weapon, but my new favorite tool in my arsenal from my left pocket.

With a couple swipes and a tap on the calendar app, I realize I have been uploading my videos for longer than I had anticipated I would be. Swiping out of my calendar, I quickly open my video diary app. Just as I thought: only a handful of people who (I think the lingo is) follow me. Damn it. The worst part is that I believe at least one of these people are surely a cartel member simply because this specific follower does not upload their own material, but they watch each one of my videos.

I am starting to obsess over this social media app contraption. I never thought I would be so addicted, needing to know whether others have seen my videos or posts. It is true—I am oddly obsessed with opening this application and looking at the small icon at the top of the screen that lets me know if someone has viewed my page. Every time the icon lights up, I am hopeful it is someone new, but it is always the faceless profile. With disappointment, I set my phone down and reach for my backpack and grab my earbuds out of the top pocket to start a new video entry. My one fan is waiting. I scoff.

I have a gut feeling that once the break hits, my chances of bringing this cartel down is over, I am a goner. As I plug in my earbuds, I try not to worry about something I cannot control, and I remind myself of the power of words. The thing to do, then, is to continue my story. I gather my thoughts from where I had left off. I have to get this video out before the show starts and make sure this one is the most effective. This post is going to detail my last days with my father and what he told me to bring the cartel's game to light. I was never meant to be the target—well, at least I never thought I was—that feeling has shifted now that I have looked at this situation from the outside in. But in the end, I will wear a blaring bull's eye. When they saw my father and me together before they killed him, though, it is a no brainer that they must kill me too. "But they should have killed me that night," in a low not audible voice.

After my muttering, I insert the earbuds, open the app, and tap the red button on my screen.

>>>START RECORDING<<<

This is, video diary #17 November 5, 2009, 13:41:00

I kind of always knew this life would catch up to me, but I didn't think it would be from guys on the same team. We have all seen Scarface and The Godfather. We know that eventually someone comes for you. Hell, that is how this organization grew to the size it is. The founding fathers took over smaller, weaker, and dumber crime syndicates as I mentioned earlier. I have told you all of this already. This video is about my father and our last day together with the exact information he told me about his family and why they hunted and killed him that night . . .

>>>STOP RECORDING<<<

The culmination of the most intense story I have told online to date, I pause, and stop the video diary. There was only one thing left to do since this wasn't a live feed this time, I hit the upload button. I get a foreboding feeling—goosebumps and chills that run down my back to my toes. He is closing in on his target: me.

I hate to relive such memories, but they have to be made public.

As I finish the video, tears stream down my face. I am exhausted from telling this story. I believe this may be the last video I need to publish, hoping I bring this organization down while doing the right thing for once in my life. This is the first time I can say that I am over this gig.

"I am over it!" I scream. I sigh and slouch into my office chair. I hit upload on the screen. Sharply, I experience a deep, dark sentiment, and chills run down my back to my toes.

The swishing sound of the upload softly exits the headphone speakers as it completes its job of helping me put my life into the World Wide Web for anyone—hopefully everyone—but perhaps no one—to find.

There she is: time. She is a bitch some days, and it catches me off guard at this moment. I glance at my watch and realize I am late for the only thing I care about on the road now, the artists who my father loved. I need to reach the band's dressing room ASAP. Luckily for me tonight, I am only four hallways, two sets of stairs, and a service elevator away. Gotta love life when everyone is out to make your day suck. Although I hate doing my job for these criminals, I know that if I am still here standing on this earth, I still have a chance to win. Being a part of the system has allowed me to keep enough tabs on the activities around me. I realize that I am no superhero. I cannot hear and see it all, but I can perceive people better now that I have distanced myself to an extent.

"Okay, Wyatt. Remember your WHY," I say to myself. I walk out of my production office and into the first of many hallways. A line from the movie *SLC Punk* pops into my thoughts, which brings me hope. The main character says, "I could do a hell of a lot more damage in the system than outside of it."

Making it to the bands dressing room just in time to make what could be my last call on this tour. It was time to do a show and then load up a ton of cash, because we are heading home where this cartel started, in that west Texas town.

"The band is WALKING," I blurted my last call into my push-to-talk radio as we made that all so famous walk down the dressing room hallway and then out on to the stage.

CHAPTER 2

The Ride Home

November 6, 2009, 01:30:00. Post Show – Phoenix, AZ

Movies and interviews from old rock bands have painted the backstage area to be an orgy fueled by drugs and Satan, they are semi-correct. Sure, in the '70s, '80s and even into the '90s roadies were able to dabble in the fun, but they all had real jobs to do. Looking back on my life in this industry I have to honestly say the real action backstage was not the groupies or the bands' dressing rooms. No, the real roadies let the kids have their fun upstairs, while the main action was in the cut and cash rooms many floors below the dressing rooms.

A few weeks ago, I was sitting in the dressing room with two of my best friends, Axel and Wes, enjoying some after-show beverages and a couple of lines. We were going on about what we were going to do with our big end-of-tour bonus. This tour we moved tons of weight around North America and even Australia, so we knew there were going to be at least four zeros after a five, maybe even a seven. Now, I sit alone. I sip on a beer as I reminiscence the fun shit-talking days that I had with people who were a big part of my life. The more I think about how the cartel brainwashed them, I find it difficult to imagine the task ahead of me. I finish my after-show birthday beer with a sigh; on my way out of this cramped production closet of an office they gave me today, I grab one more beer and head to a dressing room to shower.

After showering, I sit in an empty hockey player's locker room with a towel wrapped around me, my chin resting heavily in one hand, a cigarette dangling precariously in the other. I realize that my old fears are gone; each night used to hold a different kind of eeriness when I was the last one on the bus each night. I am no longer worried about the bus rolling over while I lie in my bunk, no longer concerned about the wheels catching on fire and losing the brakess. Hell, even a case of deadly bed bugs or crabs killing me in my sleep used to cross my mind. But now I am busy with my videos, and I think about the cartel drawing closer each night. Like a game of Clue, will they come at me in the dressing room with a baseball bat? On the bus in the middle of the night with a gun? Or will they poison my room service at a hotel? The brain enjoys painting worst-case scenarios, and images of my death are what keep me up at night now.

I lift my head slightly and in unison with one hand move my long, wet hair back behind my ears and with my other hand, I take a drag of my cigarette. I tap the ash inside my empty beer bottle and check the time—1:30 in the morning. The clock that sits above the doorway reminds me of those old clocks that hung above the chalkboards at school. I stare with expressionless eyes at the slow, almost stuck-in-time second hand, a reminder that time is on nobody's side. My eyes move down scanning the tattoos that clothe my legs, hands and arms. My attention stops at a bleeding heart below the wrist of my right hand. Suffering and atonement. My eyes dart to the letters L-O-V-E, which are placed below each knuckle of the same hand respectively. I scoff at the irony. I stand up and look tiredly in the full-body mirror that is fixed on the bathroom door to study the art that covers nearly every inch of my skin. My tattoos are a reminder of my experiences, my memories, and my pain that I consider both tragic and beautiful. Over the past weeks I continue to ask myself if it was all worth it. If, the money, drugs and travel were worth losing the one man who gave me the world.

Looking up at that old clock above the door once again, I am left puzzled . . . 1:30? I turn quickly to grab my Rolex from my shower bag. 1:50! SHIT! The clock on the wall is broken and time is defiantly not on my side right this second. With no time to spare before the buses leave for El Paso, I throw on a shirt without caring whether it is clean. I drop my legs into a pair of shorts, slide my feet into my black checkered Vans without bothering about socks, and grab my bag as I head toward the door. I am not going to get oil spotted and miss my chance at getting my revenge on these assholes.

Running down the back hallway through the venue and out toward the bus for our new destination, I am sadly reminded by the fact that no one on that bus couldn't care less if I made it on. Those who had once loved to spend time with me, would now be happy to leave me like an oil spot there on that asphalt and let me deal with the consequences—all because they think I brought trouble and drama to the team—in other words, I was hitting a hornet's nest for accusing the cartel of killing my father. Sprinting to the bus, I can see the merchandise dude sitting in the jump seat, looking at his watch and occasionally glancing up with resentment. Out of everyone that I deal with, he especially hates me, so he turns to tell the driver it is time to leave once he spots my silhouette approaching. However, I win with enough time to throw my bag under the bus and get my feet in the bus door before our departure to our new destination.

Lately, I have hated getting onto the bus post-show. One of the worst parts of walking onto this bus is that I must walk past my associates who would rather not see my face. The saddest part of walking on to this bus is that I must walk past my two best friends, who don't speak to me either. Life can get lonely when you change your perspective and call out the bullshit when trying to do the right thing. Speaking of which, I need to drop a quick video, telling whoever may be watching of my upcoming stops. But tonight, I wasn't worried about them acknowledging me; nope, I rush past everyone and open the lounge door located in the back of the bus. It is empty tonight, so I decided to get it over with instead of doing the video from my bunk. I settle into the couch, pull my phone from my pocket, swipe up to unlock the screen, and open the app to record.

>>>START RECORDING<<<

This is video diary #18 November 6, 2009, 02:05:00

I'm on my bus right now, heading east on I-10 and should arrive in El Paso before noon. I'm then going to Mexico soon after to check out The Red Door restaurant in Palomas. I hear Michael used to hang there. If I'm unsuccessful in meeting this cop—or if those who want to help can't meet me there—I'll head back across the border to Linda's Cantina, which is at the end of the old highway road, close to the racetrack. Meet me after dark. If you're listening, be safe out there! Remember, the cartel is around every corner.

>>>STOP RECORDING<<<

I hit the "end" button quickly, grab my lighter, and instead of going to the jump seat like I normally would, I crack a window in the back lounge and start up a cigarette as the bus' tires hit the highway. I am still working out the details of my plan in my head, so I hope to have a chance at getting a lead at the little bar in Mexico because my father spoke of the cartel heads going to Linda's Cantina for drinks after watching the ponies run. If I cannot find this cop in Mexico, and if by chance the cartel is there at this cantina, I will take the law into my own hands and fight to the death. But, if I get ambushed, there or along the way, well. . . my road will come to an end finally. This is starting to feel like a suicide mission. One thing about this cartel is that they are stealthy and watch their prey like a tiger through the brush. When the helpless victim is off guard, they pounce straight for the jugular. They take their time to ensure a body is never found and leaves no trace. This is probably why they have allowed me to live this long; The Butcher is setting up a seamless kill. Hopefully my videos will make an impact one day, until that day though, I will keep fighting. The Butcher might get the better of me but one day he will get his.

Watching the cherry on my cigarette light up as it inches its way closer to the filter, I am left daydreaming about the fire in me. There may be zero method to my approach when firing off these videos into the wild west that is the Internet, but I know something is better than nothing. It is a long shot, but if I am putting slight pressure on this larger-than-life entity, by even a small fraction, then that means I am heading in the right direction. There is a chance to win but damn—this whole situation is fucked up. I need this living nightmare to be over, I need sleep.

November 6, 2009, 06:45:00
On the Bus, Highway 9, New Mexico

"Hello darkness, my old friend . . ."

The lyrics play in my head as I lie in my bed, gazing up at nothingness. On my back, eyes wide and with the curtain shut, I wait for sleep to take over. I don't think I am alone on this, but it is wild how my brain starts speeding up as it thinks about the past, present, and future when I need to rest. I begin to think about every move, trying to play out every step of my arrival in my hometown, then into

Mexico. Then, I imagine meeting this cop and what I would say. For all I know, he can tell me to fuck off and want nothing to do with someone who could end his career . . . if he still has one. Then doubt kicks in again. Am I doing the right thing by exposing this cartel? Imposter syndrome kicks in, I am no superhero. Deep in my soul, I feel like I have dug a deeper grave—that they have somehow hacked the system and made these videos unviewable. I have no idea how the Internet works, but I figure these guys are powerful enough to manipulate the system, hell I know they are. Reality starts to weigh down the blanket I am hiding under now. It is hard to believe that I am going to make a difference, especially when I have been pouring my heart out in these videos and have never heard a peep.

On a daily basis, relaxing is difficult in this line of work already, as we move coke alongside the roadie cover. There is a multi-million dollar show that happens each night, and everyone strives to be flawless for the performance. On top of that, we are packaging and moving a few hundred pounds of high-grade narcotics within each venue swap. I wish I could go back to when that was the only stress in my life. I truly wish I could go back to when I was just a kid, enjoying a tour bus with my father and other roadies, when there were no real worries in life except if catering was going to have French fries for dinner.

Suddenly, our bus swerves a little, it crosses the yellow line and the sound of the tires driving across the rumble strips echoes from below the bus. The morbid side of my brain kicks in. Would it be all that bad if our driver accidently drove us off a cliff? My bunk reminds me of a coffin. They look similar, and I imagine there is a homey feeling to both; I may find out for certain soon enough. I finally stress myself out enough to the point to which my body shuts itself down for me.

Deep sleep doesn't last long . . . as I drift in and out of sleep, I can hear the front lounge TV and my former best friends laughing. I hate the fact that we are no longer close, and I instead receive looks of anger and resentment for questioning the men that practically own us. Shit, you would think I kicked their dog, when in reality I am actually trying to stand up for us all. I have the urge to head up to the front, punch them both in the face, crank the music to eleven, and party until we reach our hometown where we continue to celebrate my birthday. Instead, I lay in my bunk wishing for a way to get them to see my side, but punches, music, nor my birthday will shift their views of me right now. . . they only have eyes for the money these days.

There is an ominous darkness as I drift off to sleep, but I try not to fight it. I feel the vibrations from the tires rolling across the heat-cracked highway as the wind sways the bus gently like a cradle. The black of night shifts to seas of red. Blood-soaked hands reach toward me. My brain jolts back to the sound of the lounge TV to steer away from the image. I make out voices talking, and it calms me.

Suddenly, I hear a violent noise like the slamming of a door. I shoot straight up in my bunk and crack open my curtain, which allows a glow of neon blue light from the AC panel into my bunk, but I can see nothing out of the ordinary. As I close the curtain to lie down again, I hear the same booming sound. This time, it sounds like a person pounding on the driver's side of the bus. Naturally, this cannot be the case since we are driving down the freeway. With a sudden jerk of the steering wheel, I hear the curtains flailing. Once again, the bus cabin is filled with the sounds of tires running on the rumble strips. Back and forth the bus rocks as it feels like the bus driver is trying to gain back control of his trusty steed. Is someone hanging out of a window in a car next to us causing this shit to happen?

I hear a scream along with a *tap-tap-tap-tap-tap*. "Someone shot me!"

It is then that I realize we are under FUCKING attack! Of course, they came for me here where it all began for me.

The gun shots moved forward on the bus walls, so, I yell for everyone to move to the back lounge. The gun fire intensifies. I jump from my bunk to the floor. The bus swerves violently followed by squealing, screeching, and screaming from roadies who have taken bullets penetrating the left side of our vehicle. I can feel the speed slow down and listen intently to the mass commotion from the front lounge. I instantly recognize two voices—my best friends—that are yelling for the driver to keep going.

Normally, we have small LEDs close to the floor that act as night lights, but they are not on this time. Figures. I follow my hand along the wall of bunks, searching for one of the light switches. My mind stops for a moment to question whether I should help these people who have shunned me. I hear roadies gasping frantically for their last breath as the bus's engine takes its last intake of air and slowly shuts down after crossing over the rumble strips one last time.

Everything about this moment points to an ambush. In the darkness of the bunk hallway, I imagine the bloody hands again. A chill runs down my spine, and I hear something like fireworks whistling by the front lounge. Our driver, KC, yells profanities as it sounds like he is trying to restart the bus. Roadies yell indistinctly at and for each other as I sift through the floor clutter for my gun and find it next to backpacks and random junk flung from the bunks.

"KC, what the hell are you doing? Drive! Run them over!" the security for the tour, Wes, orders harshly without success. I can hear my merch tech groaning in agony whose bunk is higher from the ground. I start to get up and then hesitate, realizing it is best to stay low and army crawl to a vantage point. I inch forward to the front lounge door. I can hear music emulating from the TV and a gurgling noise as fluid enters the lung of the merch tech that slowly drowns him. I close my eyes and feel saddened that our last encounter was not a friendly one. With no time to dwell on the sounds of dying roadies . . . then as if I was catapulted into a war zone, multiple blasts just beyond the door in front of me from a high-powered machine gun go off in succession. With time running out, I focus on my potential threats. I have fired guns before but never in the position I am in now. For one, I am on the floor in the dark. Secondly, I am potentially surrounded. I slowly pull back the hammer of my revolver and get to my feet, keeping one hand on the bunk doorknob, understanding that I am hiding behind material as protective as construction paper. As I slowly head toward the door, it comes crashing against me, torn off its hinges by a mighty kick from the opposing side, and my weapon flies out of my hand. Shit. I lie there stunned; it was like a horse kicked me across the whole front of my body. As I attempt to uncross my eyes and shake my brain into place, I pause and realize it doesn't matter, I may only have a few more moments to suffer anyway.

Still alive, I force myself off my back and onto one elbow so I could peer through the doorway. Expecting to find a demolition team emerging from that blast, instead, it is one man. The beast takes a step forward, and his shoulders barely fit within the entryway. He tilts his head to one side, his features like that of a ten-foot creature from my standpoint. Although I have never seen this man before, I know him, he is one of The Butcher's men. The dark-dressed military garb. Guns locked in his hands. A cigar hanging from his mouth through the bush of beard. The creases in his forehead and his piercing eyes express hatred and an invitation to hell. My life is over. As I lay back down and wait for the final gun shot to ring through my ears, I am warmed one last time by the blood from the dead roadies hanging from their bunks.

At this time there is no point in running and trying to squeeze my ass through the damn back lounge window does not seem like a plausible idea. So, instead, I smirk at him with disgruntlement.

His deep voice bellows, *"Donde esta la llave?"*

I do not answer. Fuck this asshole.

"Donde esta la llave?" he asks again with a tone that makes my heart sink. He takes my hesitation as a sign of not understanding and roars, "Where is the key, *puta?*"

I snarl, "I have many different keys. What can I say? I'm an important puta. How am I supposed to know which key you want? But wait, let me guess . . . You are too stupid to even know what key you are looking for, you fucking sheep?"

The brute hovers over me menacingly. He growls loudly, "Wyatt! De boss want de key now! Ju want me to do it de hart way, *puta?*"

Knowing damn well which key he wants, I continue to play stupid for as long as possible. "Look, the only key in this bus is in the ignition. Take the key, money, coke—whatever you want. I wouldn't fucking play around with you; you're too much of a sweetheart."

In response, he spits his cigar at me, pauses to crack his neck, and fires two shots before I had time to even blink. I immediately feel a warm sensation and lose my breath as the sound of Desert Eagle shots rattle my brain enough to distract me from the truth that soon lies before me. I blink firmly a couple of times and look down to grasp the reality of a bullet in each leg. My initial shock swings into an unbearable pain. I grip my legs below my knees, rolling my head back, screaming in agony. It is as if lava is searing my flesh, and the fire inside my legs intermingles with a sensation of razors slicing through the layers of muscle.

The behemoth holsters his guns, grabs me by the ankles with one hand, and yanks me across the blood-soaked floor. I feel sick and almost lose consciousness from the torture, feeling my left ankle dislocate and my right knee pop out of its socket. Through the small bus galley, he drags me effortlessly over to my best friends. He tosses me on top of them like a rag doll, and I feel their warm, lifeless bodies. In life, there are things that can prepare you for physical pain, but there is nothing compared to the emotional agony of lying on people who were once dear to you with a bullet hole in their heads. In a way, though, I feel relieved to have their company. We are at least in this together, finally.

Another man enters the front lounge area, but—instead of stepping over me—he uses my head as foot support, smashing my face sideways against the belly of one of the corpses beneath me. Without my dead companion, my skull would have easily crushed. I hear the stranger sliding a magazine into his gun. I go deaf again in both ears. Figures. I had just gotten all my hearing back. I realize he pulled the trigger of a fully automatic machine gun, unleashing its power into the bunks for whoever was still potentially semi-alive.

I would imagine war to sound much like what has been happening in the bus: a lot of screaming, guns firing off rounds, and when you hear people talk about the sound of death, I always thought they were full of shit, but it is a sickening melody. The silence in between the moaning, crying, and mutilated flesh truly makes you wish the song was over before the next round of terror signals the chorus.

I never took life seriously, and—in many situations—I thought I was invincible, but lying here shot and with death surrounding me, I begin to see my end. My hope of avenging my father's death is slowly leaving me as I look around at dead colleagues while the beast of a man stares down at me. I do not have much left in life, so I decide that if I cannot return gun fire at these men, I can at least go out knowing I gave them shit until my last breath. Knowing that I have what they seek, I figure I am ready to poke the bear until they get fed up looking for this key and just shoot me. So, I poked.

"Hey, big guy," I call as he looks down at me. "I have a few semi-truck trailer keys, two bus keys, some workbox keys . . . so which one do you and your boyfriend want?" Hissing through my teeth, my tone reveals that I am holding back the pain in my heart and legs. No answer from the beast of a man.

The fucker who had fired his machine gun until it ran out of bullets strolls toward the back end of the bus, reemerging from the bathroom as if he had not just shot and killed four innocent people. He casually zips his pants up before stepping on my forehead, nose, and left eye to make his way off the bus. As his footsteps trail away, I can hear new, louder steps making their way onto the bus and into the front lounge and more voices from outside the shot-out windshield. A new man starts to speak in Spanish, but I do not recognize the slang, so it does not get me far with deciphering what he is saying. Lying in pain from the gunshot wounds to my legs and the broken heart from the loss of my friends, I try to pay attention to the men, but my mind is a mess, and it is getting hard to concentrate on them. At this point in my night and life, I really want to be put out of my misery, so—once again—I cynically explain to the men that they will have to gut me to see if I swallowed this key. Followed by a few choice words about their mothers, I truly hope that my vulgar mouth will persuade them to finish me off. I do not have more to live for now that my friends have left this world to join my father. Hopefully, they are somewhere far away from this hell on earth that we have created.

Lying on my back, staring at the ceiling and belting shit out of my mouth when I can, I sense someone standing above me. The last thing I can perceive before my sight goes black is the butt end of a gun coming at my face like a Mike Tyson knockout punch. When I start to regain consciousness after my little nap, I realize, sadly, that this suffering has not ended. I have zero feeling in my legs, a few missing teeth, and it feels like I have multiple broken bones. It is safe to say that I am pretty beat up, but strangely still alive. I am doubtful that this is a good thing.

Where can I go with shattered joints and eyes practically swollen shut? The beast maintains a pressure on my head much like the force necessary for the earth's mantle to form diamonds. I slip in and out of consciousness. I feel a wild sensation as if gravity is pulling me closer to the ground and, at times, through it. I can only describe this feeling as smoking way too much weed, followed with a weed brownie, chased by a bong hit, after eating a hand full of magic mushrooms that is when you melt into the earth. Perhaps death has finally made his appearance at the party. I never believed the stories of people who would describe how their life flashed before their eyes during near-death experiences. To my dismay, much like a movie, the pictures from my life start to roll. These memories of mine flow like the waves of an ocean, one followed closely by another. The visions of my two friends alive crash into me as one fond memory. Then, thoughts of my father surface as if in real time—and moments we shared on tour barrel in. Memories of past loves come ashore. The faces slowly retreat as images fade to black. In an instant, I find myself lying on the bus floor that is crumpled below me.

I try to move. Nothing. My father used to say, "There are no co-incidences in life, no matter if they are good or bad." Silence surrounds me as I listen to the echoes of his voice in my head.

My mind drifts from his voice and I start thinking back to the video diaries I started a few short weeks ago. The stories I shared of my father and where it all started. Even about my great-great-grand-father. A legend in his own badass way. The second video I made detailing their journey to America and just how I ended up here starts to replay in my mind.

I might have been dead or dying at this point but there was one thing that was still fighting, it was my subconscious brain . . . maybe it was my body looking for inspiration to stay alive? Either way, I was having an out of my body experience and I was watching myself hit record on my second video diary . . .

>>>START RECORDING<<<
Video Diary #2 October 14, 2009, 07:13:55
Day off Portland, Oregon

My family's journey to becoming the world's largest cartel started in a sleepy town over five thousand miles away . . .

CHAPTER 3

The Reznik Kids

Video Diary #2 October 14, 2009, 07:14:00
Day off Portland, Oregon

. . . Ceske Budejovice, Czechoslovakia, was not the go-to destination for the rich or the famous—or really for anyone during the early 20th century. It was your typical sleepy farm town tucked in a surprisingly even more quiet part of the country away from all the dramas of the wars that had been plaguing Europe. The town was relaxed and nothing like what you would have seen in western European cities. It was built around a beautiful town square with a little church that bore a tall steeple located in the center. There were rugged, uneven stone walls and small brick buildings lining the main street that would lead you all the way out to the farmland. Trees dotted the quaint landscape. It was especially beautiful in the autumn when the trees changed from a bright lush green and started to give way to vibrant reds and yellows.

My great grandparents came to this town to start fresh and hopefully start a family away from the tragedies of war. This is not an easy task when you don't have much. But my great grandpa did have one thing . . . well, no—actually. He happened to have two things: one was drive and the second was a gold coin that he had found as a young man. He had kept that coin in his shoe, "the best place to hide something," he would have said knowing one day it would be useful.

>>>PAUSE RECORDING<<<

The sound of the merch guy calling for me over the two-way-radio suddenly interrupts. I pause, "should I answer," I debate in my head. . .

"Go for Wyatt"

"Not that you care but how many shirts did the boss need pulled for the guests in suite 24?" my merch guy asked with a heavy dose of fuck you in his voice. He clearly was not a fan of me anymore and each day he was out to make that very apparent.

"Nine and the guests will arrive at seven." I said with a smile on my face. For I knew this was a perfect little thing to add to my video diary before I continued with the story of my family.

>>>RESUME RECORDING<<<

Sorry for that interruption, but since I am being open and honest about this cartel in these video diaries, I will decipher that seemingly innocent little exchange.

When the merch guy asked how many "shirts" he was going to need to pull for the boss tonight, he was actually asking how many bricks of cocaine need to be packaged and leave the arena tonight. Cocaine over the radio is always referred to as suite 24 and the number of shirts represents the number of bricks. More on our codes later but I thought that was a perfect time to fill you in on some of the cartel's lingo.

OK where did I leave *off*. . .My great grandfather arrived in this little town with his dream and his gold coin, and it worked. He ended up being able to buy a nice piece of land off a struggling frail older farmer that he had met in town. Shortly after purchasing the land the old farmer's son came and left with the old man. They left in a hurry, leaving it all behind but a few items for the old man to wear. So, there was only one thing to do, my great grandfather started to dig his roots there with my great grandmother, a mule, two cows, and a goat that the farmer had also left.

Like most twenty-something-year-olds, my great grandpa had no clue as to what the hell he was going to do now that he had purchased this land. The only thing he had ever been really good at was butchering the meat his father would bring home from his hunts. Seeing that the land had a weathered barn, he decided—before he did anything else—that he had to fix their living situation. That didn't take long at all, it was mainly getting rid of some the old farmer's items that they couldn't mend or repurpose for themselves. Next, was fixing the barn up. He wasn't looking for fancy, no, he was hoping to make it a place where they could sell items to passersby during the day. Moving to any town is a gamble, even still to this day, but he would definitely be risking it all during that time. He did it anyway, and as he started to slowly establish his business, he was using the remaining seconds of the day to build the house that my family would eventually live in.

The unforgiving lifestyle of a farmer, especially before modernized equipment and techniques, created hard times for the two. The Reznik operation began sparsely, but—like all businesses that push forward—he gained more goats; then, chickens appeared; and, not long after them, a hog. The small farm started to not only make ends meet and keep food on the table, but soon they were also able to start selling the surplus.

I have been told, numerous times by my father, that mornings are a prime time to get a jump on most things in life: from running coke past a sleepy border agent to making sure the chickens, goats, and the hogs were fed, and the stalls were cleaned. This mindset must have been handed down from my great grandfather. Each morning, Adolf Senior, my great grandfather, would be out cleaning the stalls. My great grandmother, Olivia, would be hard at work in the kitchen getting the morning breakfast on the table for them to enjoy. After the daily morning meal, she would head right out to the garden they had been building, which was located on the side of the barn, to harvest the ripened veggies. Shortly after, she would then head off to the barn to get milk to churn and make homemade goat cheese. The lady put in a ridiculous amount of work by the time most of my friends and I would be rolling out of bed—extremely hungover—and dreading the walk to the kitchen for water. And that was just the start to my great grandmother's day.

Time passed and the house and barn were fixed up to their liking for work and down time and—wouldn't you know it? —their hard laboring started to pay off. The town people started to visit their makeshift "farmers market" daily. It was a dope little operation. They had veggies and cheeses alongside the one protein, eggs, at first. When a little time passed, they were able to offer meats on special days. Just like in the cocaine business, if you have good product, the word spreads and business booms. It wasn't anywhere nearly as successful as the roadie cartel's cocaine operation, but it was enough for Senior to afford a storefront in town. This was monumental because now he would be able to house more meat, cheese, and veggies with his visions of a refrigeration system that he had heard of.

No wonder my family was able to grow today's business to heights never heard of before; their genes came from an entrepreneurial mindset!

On a funny note, even to this day, I still don't think Europeans understand what a real refrigeration system is like, but I digress. Now, Senior was not thinking about giant walk-in refrigerators. No, no. He was thinking simple ice chests, but . . . for those days, it was huge. In addition to cured meats, his new vision of keeping products cold and selling his own products, Senior opened his doors to the other farmers in the area to help sell their goods in his butcher shop. This was how he became a local hit and really started to put our name on the map. The day came and written on the wall was "Reznik's House." Senior's dream became a reality, and the shop opened its doors.

There was still one thing missing. Not for lack of trying, they couldn't produce a child. They tried for years until Olivia became pregnant. Sadly, the baby never made it past a few months old. This happened to them two more times.

I question myself a lot lately and under different circumstances. But, do I have the same resilience my great-grandparents had, especially in the face of tragedy?

On the fourth and what would be the final time they tried for offspring, for the mental and physical demands were slowly killing them both, they had a healthy baby boy. I am not sure about emotions connected to childbirth, but I would assume they were freaking out with joy. It was a boy who could carry on the Reznik legacy. Adolf Junior was the light of their lives. Junior had an amazingly full head of hair for a newborn, but his brown puppy dog eyes were what would eventually melt my great grandmother's heart daily. All my great grandfather wanted was a son to carry on the name, the farm, and the business . . . a son who gave his heart like he did and embodied the values he and my great grandmother held onto throughout their lives.

My grandfather, Junior, was a quiet kid. He loved to be out in the fields and the garden, learning all he could about life on a farm. In my grandfather's day, there was trouble to get into. But, seeing that he started working at a young age on the farm, by the time he was done with his day, all he had time to do was eat and sleep. This was very handy for Senior because his only child needed to be fully committed to the farm and the butcher shop.

Once Junior got a handle on all things around the house and farm, Senior started to allow his son to come by the butcher shop to help clean and slowly learn the artform of butchery. Little did Junior know that this new trade was going to transform him into the rock star butcher of the town. This trade became even more badass to him than the farm tending ever would. He soon spent all day at the shop perfecting his new passions of cutting, curing, packaging, and learning the amazing art of being a butcher. He was a man who knew his meats and spices.

As time marched forward, Junior was becoming quite the talk around town and even the surrounding settlements. It was all about how great his sausage was. Everyone wanted it. They traveled miles (or kilometers, whatever floats your boat) to taste it. Throughout his teen years, Junior's passion for his father's shop only continued to grow regardless of whether times of business were good or bad. The one thing he probably took the most passion in was watching his father interact with the customers. He always treated them with kindness and respect. He never cheated them on prices and if you were not able to pay that week, he was always willing to offer an IOU.

Right around Junior's eighteenth birthday, his father grew quite ill and passed away later that year. This obviously wasn't easy on Junior and his mother. Even though he was a great help around the house and the butcher shop, trying to fill his father's shoes was going to be the undertaking of his life. Junior took on this challenge and soon was head of the household, farm, and butcher shop. He took on his father's dream . . . and over the next few years, he not only sold local farm products, but he also brought in meats and cheese from all over Czechoslovakia. Based on the stories I have heard about the man Junior grew up to be, I think he would be disappointed in all of us and where we ended up. We all chose a life of crime and spit on his passion for something he worked so hard to earn.

A year after my great grandfather passed away, the sadness took my great grandmother. They say dying of a broken heart is a true thing. I personally have never felt "love," so I can't speak on the subject too much. The one and only time I thought I knew what love was, I caught them red-handed fucking . . . anyways, let me just say that was the last time I dated or messed around with someone on the same tour as me. *C'est la vie.* Such is life. It was fun while it lasted.

Laying his mother to rest next to his father out behind the barn might have been the hardest thing he had to do as a young man without family to comfort him. It took a toll on Junior's state of mind. He was running the butcher shop full time and the only help he was getting out in the garden and stable was sadly now gone, but the saddest part of it is that he was completely alone. Some sacrifices people make during their time on earth are greater than themselves. Even though it was tough to lay both parents to rest in the same year, Junior at a young age had to look toward the future. He took a hard, honest look at what his father wanted, which was to continue and not worry about what he couldn't fix. He wanted him to succeed. Even with my skewed view of existence, I respected this man more than a lot of others because if he had not stepped it up, I would not be here.

Junior started his day much like his late father did. Every day was an early call time. He would head straight out to the barn for fresh eggs and milk, sit down for a quick breakfast, and then it was off to the butcher shop. Life didn't get easier, but it did get brighter for Junior each day since he took on all the responsibilities of the farm. He had even saved up for a small pickup truck that helped him with hauling meat for the business, and he didn't have to walk in to work any longer.

Summer had come in fast this year and with it brought a few new faces to the town. One morning, the butcher's sturdy old wooden shop door slowly creaked open. With the jingle of the bell hanging on the door, a gorgeous new stranger appeared in the entrance. She was out of this world and nothing like any of the other girls in town. Her long wavy blonde hair still blowing from the wind that followed her into the shop. Her eyes were a shade of blue stolen from a perfectly clear summer day. When Junior locked onto them, he got so lost in them that he tripped and dropped all the sausage he was carrying. After picking himself up off the floor, he couldn't help but pinch himself to wake from what could only be a dream with this angel in it. As he stammered to find the words to ask if she needed help, she beat him to the punch and started to help my clumsy grandfather pick up the sausage scattered across the floor. They spent the better half of the morning in the shop going over all the meats he offered . . . twice! But finally, she had to get home with a cut for dinner. As she was preparing to leave, he made sure to explain he was there every day and to come by whenever she needed his meat. As Junior turned red from his comment, she blushed and—wouldn't you know it?—she did, in fact, come back time and time again. In fact, she came back every day for a whole month. Maria loved to come in and talk. Junior learned many things about her that month. Maria and a few of her family members had come from an even smaller town to the east of Ceske, looking for bigger opportunities and a better life for the whole family. But first they had to get settled before the rest of the family followed.

Junior was enamored with this sweet woman, and every evening before she left to go back home, he would adorn her with fresh fruits, veggies, and herbs from the garden. Then, he would finish her basket off with a specialty cut of meat to go along with each garden offering. He was for sure trying to score brownie points in her diary, and it did.

Not long after their first month of talking, Junior decided there was no reason why they shouldn't just spend the rest of their lives together. Instead of spending the day inside the shop talking, they took a walk and when they reached the small church in the center of town, he asked for her hand in marriage. And she said *yes*!

Over the next few months, Maria began to help Junior at the shop. Junior's now-fiancée would wait for him to arrive and would then help unload the meats and vegetables for the day. Then one morning, as Junior was walking out to the barn, he saw her walking up the long gravel driveway with a basket snuggled against her waist. She said that she couldn't wait and wanted to come help on the farm too. Daily, she would now help gather the eggs, vegetables, and fresh fruits for the butcher shop while he handled the livestock and breakfast. They would then load up the little pickup truck full of each day's fresh picks and, like any couple in love and with a bench seat, she would scoot her butt as close to Junior as possible for the beautiful drive into town down the little two-lane road.

The morning help from Maria turned into staying to help close the shop and, of course, he couldn't let her walk home alone . . . even though there wasn't a bad soul in this town. Nightly, he drove her home and walked her all the way to the front door. Times have changed, chivalry isn't dead, but I would also not say it is something boys are practicing. But that is for another conversation, my grandfather was just from another time.

Even though I don't understand the idea of being in love, it was alive with Junior and Maria. One night, instead of turning down the road to Maria's house, Junior drove to his farm. When they got there, he simply stated that he never wanted to drive her to any other home except her new one with him. I am pretty sure you can guess what happened next. Get your minds out of the gutter, you pervs. They officially got hitched very shortly after that drive home. Adolf couldn't wait any longer to start a life and family with his beautiful woman.

In the summer of 1947, Junior and Maria welcomed their first born who would one day inherit the farm and butcher shop. They named him Adolf Reznik III, setting the family up for a long lineage. Adolf III was like every other male in the family when it came to looks. He was a handsome little devil with a full head of hair who looked ready to take over the world from the start. And take over he did! He instantly ran the household, and Maria was forced to devote all her time to tending to the overly needy baby.

This kid was different from a young age. He did not take well to anything outside and was constantly testing his mother and father's patience as a toddler. As he grew into an older child, he loved to spend his time inside more and more. Not only did he hate the farm life, but he also saw zero appeal in getting dirty with the other local kids. He did, though, love the coins his father would bring home from the day's take at the butcher shop and was caught red-handed multiple times, taking the change purse and hiding it in his room to play with later.

Junior hoped Adolf III would show more interest in the farm and butcher shop as he entered his pre-teen years. Junior would take him into town a couple days a week to hopefully spark interest in the family butcher shop. However, all Adolf III wanted to do was go down the street to a local grocery that sold newspapers and a couple of magazines. There, he would spend hours gazing at the ads and stories of wealth that he would find inside some of these publications. This was hard on Junior because this is who he thought would grow up to run the family businesses. Every attempt he made to get his son to join in and engage was getting harder and harder as time went on.

Adolf III's wild imagination was filling with dreams and fantasies of money, travel, and fame. Times were changing. Print was now more widely available, and even shows on the radio would stop him in his tracks, and he'd listen to them while in the town, which started to get racier for the young man's imagination.

In a last-ditch effort to engage the boy, Junior had his son help him kill a cow for meat at the butcher shop. Junior was not sure how his young son would react to this task, but he surprisingly took the gun without hesitation and put the cow down with a single shot to the head. At first, Junior was joyful that his son had been so enthusiastic to pull the trigger, but soon that joy grew into concern . . . not because of the speed with which he agreed to kill the cow, but because he told his father it was fun and asked if there was another cow he could shoot. Junior explained that killing was a small part of the bigger picture to being a good butcher. The point he was trying to make was to get Adolf to understand they did it to bring food to the town not to hurt the cow for fun. Junior explained to Adolf that the next order of business was to go clean and butcher the meat to be put up for sale. Upon hearing this, Adolf quickly lost interest but agreed he would go learn how to use all the butcher knives. After very little instruction, Junior was very taken back with how swiftly Adolf excelled at butchery. It was as if the art of butchery was in the boy's blood. He still could never get Adolf to show interest in cleaning up the butcher shop, but at least they found some common ground.

Adolf's imagination, urges, and desires grew for a lifestyle bigger than the farm and the little town could ever provide him. Adolf was far unlike his father and grandfather and even the siblings to follow. At a ripe young age, he loved harassing the town and causing trouble any chance he could. The rumors floating around town about the mischievous butcher's son slowly tarnished the Reznik name due to his wild antics. He had even become a petty thief, stealing from not only his father's nightstand and butcher shop but also from the local grocery store. This obviously was not how he was raised, and both parents were flabbergasted by the outbursts. They just prayed his bad behavior would not rub off on their other two children, Zora and Ivan (more about them later).

In time, Adolf found gambling to be his drug of choice. (This was mainly due to some of the hard drugs like coke not being available yet since they still hadn't made their way to this part of Europe.) He particularly loved the famous street hustle called the shell game. On a walk home from the corner shop, he was stopped by a group of older teenagers who had a little game set up on a makeshift table. Most have seen or been a part of one of the simplest and cleanest hustles next to a good old pyramid scheme that your friend from high school called you about. The game originated in Paris with street thieves trying to sucker the tourists out of their riches. It's exactly what you could imagine this game to be—a game for suckers, pawns, the young, the old, and my favorite: the drunks at bars, looking to get rich quick.

Here is a fast breakdown of the game if you have been living under a rock. I would set up on a street corner somewhere close to a bar where I know drunkards will be walking out soon. Then, I create a small scene with a pawn in the game, preferably one or two of my friends, looking to hustle at the same time. I have three cups. One has a wadded-up piece of paper or something that doesn't make noise under it. I then shuffle the cups in front of my accomplice, and—as I stop the cups—I give my guy a little wink as to which cup to choose, and bingo! My criminal friend wins the game. I would then give him his winnings, make a small scene, and hope a sucker comes along soon after. Once I do bait a big fish and his friends, it is fair game for me and my cronies to take full advantage of their wallets and whatever else these drunks have on them. And that there is a simple but highly effective street hustle, with now many versions.

Well, shortly after the day that little Adolf learned of such a hustle, he decided he wanted to be a criminal in life too, okay maybe that is a bit rash, but he didn't want a traditional career. School? That was for the real suckers in life. And farming? How the hell was he going to become rich off some chickens and goat cheese? On his walk back to the butcher shop from the corner store, he stumbled upon some older teens playing the shell game in an alley. He witnessed one of them stuffing his pockets with all the cash and coins. Adolf instantly wanted in after seeing all that kid's money he had won. It just so happens that Adolf was given money by his mother to go purchase some necessities for the family. "But who cares!" the little devil on his shoulder said something like. "Go use the money on the game instead, it will be fun." Adolf stepped up to the table for the first time. He was nervous like Shaq shooting free throws, but he was feeling lucky. I mean, he had just watched a kid from town win. Unfortunately, today was not his lucky day, and with the blink of an eye, all his money was gone. Muttering a few curse words, it dawned on him that his father's butcher shop was right around the corner. With empty pockets and the urge for payback, he headed right for the butcher shop. He was already acting like an addict in Las Vegas after a brutal pocket-emptying beatdown by the casino with the unrelenting mentality that "this is my time to win."

So, instead of doing the right thing and going home to fess up to his mother, little Adolf went to the butcher shop, and—after distracting his father with some questions about meat—he snuck up front and took money out of his father's money pouch. With money in his pocket and the option to run and actually get the items needed for his mother, he instead ran back to where the boys were, but they were gone. He had been hustled a second time when they said they would still be there. Although Adolf was frustrated, he loved the rush of the game and stealing that money added to the thrill. The addiction was on! He learned how to hustle everything, and he quickly learned that he loved to gamble with everyone else's money. As time went on, he started to win more and more often until it got to the point where he rarely ever lost. Instead of focusing on his studies, he masterminded countless scams during his time at school. Adolf's life turned into one big gamble. At last, he had found something he was good at and loved.

Though Adolf started to hustle at a young age, it wasn't long into his teenage years until the town folks were wise to his ways, forcing him to go find new marks and suckers elsewhere. So, he traveled to the neighboring big city where the newly renovated local brewery was located, but he was missing something. If he was ever going to hustle in the big leagues, he was going to have to put together a crew. Seeing that Adolf had never been good at making friends, he was fortunate to have two siblings. They were going to have to play with the little devil whether they liked it or not. He was going to try a new approach. . .one he hadn't seen before. He was going to need a girl to distract the men in his newest hustle. After years of being a one-man show, he decided he was going to make his sister, Zora, his partner in crime. Adolf knew they would be able to hit the road one day and go on to make hundreds—maybe even thousands—of dollars. He probably never imagined in his wildest dreams that one day they would be sitting on millions upon millions of dollars . . . but, then again, maybe he knew he would all along. Who knows what drove him officially, but I am going to say it was the feeling of being in power and control after a win. Maybe, the drug wasn't the hustle but it was power . . .

Zora was born only a year and a few months after Adolf, and she quickly became the family favorite. Junior was beside himself with joy and knew he was going to spoil her with all the gifts a father could provide for his new little tot. She was an all-smiles kind of child from the second she woke up to the last blink of her eyes before her father tucked her in to bed. Early on, it was very obvious that Zora was intelligent. She was book smart whereas Adolf was street smart. She was different from all the other girls in town. She was stunning, elegant, and graceful . . . especially for someone who came from this small farm town.

Zora and Adolf didn't speak much or play much growing up. He was always daydreaming about money, and she loved to read about all the different countries and envisioned herself traveling to them all. Junior always encouraged his little princess and would tell her made up stories of the adventures she would go on one day. The one place Zora wanted to see more than anywhere else was America, especially the Southwest with all the cowboys and their horses. Seeing Zora now, you would not think desert and horses; she looked more like someone who would be lying on a beach somewhere sipping on a margarita with one of those tiny umbrellas in it. She dreamed about as much as Adolf did as a kid, but she was dreaming of finding

Mr. Right, who would sweep her off her feet and onto his horse so they could ride off into the sunset together.

The final addition to the Reznik family (and who might have been last, but he was the biggest of the bunch) was Ivan. He was, for sure, a surprise in the summer of 1950, but he was the most pleasant of them all. Sure, the big boy nearly ripped his sweet mother in half on the table but soon he became the baby his father had been dreaming for. From the second Ivan could walk, he fell in love with the farm— from feeding the animals with his father in the early dawn hours to getting the mules back in the pens before dinner time. This meant he didn't really hang with the other two nor did he want to. Sure, like Adolf, he didn't want to go to school, but he also wanted nothing to do with crime or anything down that route. He was a little more like Zora in that he did enjoy learning and reading to some extent, but he couldn't bear leaving the farm. He would often tell her and Adolf they were crazy for wanting to leave such a beautiful place. Ivan was his parents' shining star, which divided the family. Of course, the other two were loved and cared for even in their moments of wanting to leave the farm, but Adolf and Zora soon gravitated to one another since they had other, bigger, and more dangerous plans that had zero to do with pigs and hens.

Ivan was, hands down, the biggest in the family, towering well over his father who was by no means short, and over the years he did end up finding one love outside the farm. And that was wrestling, surprisingly enough. In their small school, he stumbled upon a small group of men after school out on the grass practicing wrestling moves on each other and this soon became priority number two. As his love for animals and wrestling grew, so did the boy. He soon looked like a Greco-Roman wrestler rather than a farmer in his overalls. As big of a man as he was, he was a gentle man who loved everyone. Also, one thing to keep in mind, he was not some body builder with biceps that looked like balloons, he was just taller than the family and had a very muscular appearance. But then again, I am small, so next to him he is a giant.

As the three grew older, Adolf and Zora would find themselves engaging more with their youngest sibling, but it was mainly when they needed something from Ivan like his strength or sweet disposition. As their younger brother, Ivan still wanted their approval, so he would never question their motives. Based on his size, you would expect him to be a loud, mouth-breathing jock, but he was a gentle young man with a certain charisma. His charm is what the townspeople seemed to gravitate toward when he was working around the butcher shop. Junior was proud of his son's work ethics and truly saw leadership values in Ivan. He was someone you would trust to lead you into battle. I can even think about times in the busy cocaine trafficking life; Ivan still held on to his values of being a fair and kindhearted leader. He was known as a gentle leader on tours . . . and over the decades of being a production manager to the biggest names in the business, he soon became a legend among the roadies.

Ceske Budejovice was by no means a bad place to grow up as a teen. Okay . . . maybe you had more chores to do as a kid, and you had to kind of pull your weight around the farm . . . but there were honestly very few rules in the town, seeing that it was so small. Ivan was such a work horse that he would usually knock out his chores in the early morning and then have enough time to cover for his siblings who stayed out all night traveling to nearby cities to hustle the drunks and tourists. It was thankless work doing that favor, but he got accustomed to keeping the farm up to his father's standards for his own happiness. Throughout the years, Adolf and Zora grew further and further from the farm and butcher shop. Their mischief took them closer to the big brewery a town over to prey on tourists more often. It was not unusual for the pair to sneak off by train to further distant cities like Prague to perfect their hustles on larger crowds. This would irritate Ivan who would never want to join but was forced to cover for them with their parents. Oh, how Zora's and Adolf's ego grew! The more they took, the more they strutted around the little town. The only thing more overgrown than their egos now was their greed. The duo wanted to grow into something more with each passing day. The laws in these major cities didn't even scare them anymore.

One day, Junior caught the pair red-handed in his own shop. He couldn't believe they were stealing out of the register from him and hustling the customers he had worked so hard to build a relationship with as their go-to butcher. Even though it killed him to banish his own two children from the butcher shop, he could not let them damage the family name and reputation in town any further. Adolf took this the hardest and, at one point, had enough of being told what to do. A wedge had been driven between him and his father, and their relationship would never be the same. It was time for him and Zora to spread their wings, leave the country life, explore the new cities, and etch their names next to the great criminals of the world. They needed a plan, but they were going to need money most of all for their journey.

One night after running their typical hustle at a small pub in the bigger city just up the road, they saw a red sports car pulling out of the back gate of the brewery across the street. Seeing that red-hot sports car sparked a fire in Adolf. He now knew exactly where they were going to get their money as he stared at the car, trying to figure out where it was from. And bingo! He turned to Zora and exclaimed, "America!" He knew that car screamed money from the country that had the best slogan of all time: "the land of opportunity." Whatever that man had, Adolf wanted it and would stop at nothing to get it.

While on the way home, Adolf explained to Zora how this was not going to be like any small-time pickpocket scam they had pulled off before. We all love to think a job like this could get done so easily like we see all the time in the movies, but even Adolf's young mind knew it was going to take more than two people. Prior to them staking out this man, Adolf asked around the area who drove the red Corvette. Come to find out that this man was the new owner of the brewery, and all anyone really could say about this man was that he was not from the area and lived outside the city limits alone. This news was the green light that the duo was looking for. Some people get signs from God; the duo got their messages straight from, well, somewhere a little darker.

Every day and night, for the next month, their time was spent scoping the place out . . . you know, looking at how things were run, who came in and who left with what. Shit like that. Adolf started to see a trend happening every Thursday night after the main shift let out. The owner left out of the back doors and headed to the Corvette carrying one duffle bag and one briefcase. The duffle bag always got placed in the small trunk. He would then make his way to open the passenger door and set his briefcase on the seat. Finally, he would walk around the front of the car admiring the beast. The plan was set. The last thing missing was some muscle.

On numerous occasions, I have interrogated Ivan for details about what happened that night that they fled to America. I wanted to know what happened with that red Corvette and the man driving it. I grilled Ivan to tell me how crazy of a crime they had to have committed to leave his family's farm behind. I mean, come on! It was the one place Ivan loved and talked about the most. Ivan would let me carry on with all types of wild conspiracy theories until I got drunk enough to bring up how his parents must have felt waking up to an empty house. Then he would shut me up by changing the subject. The only thing I know is that the three left in the middle of the night with a one-track mind for the land of opportunity. Whatever went down that night outweighed everything else Adolf had done to the sleepy town and surrounding areas. This crime must have been far worse with punishments greater than what a father and a leather belt could do. That midnight run out of town was the start to the family crime syndicate that we are today. The actions that night sparked a devilish fire deep in Adolf that would now be the catalyst to a lifelong obsession with money, crime, and punishment to anyone who stood in his way.

With the little darkness that was left before dawn, the siblings quickly packed the bare minimum and made their way to the train station where they hopped on the first train heading west. Once they were settled on the train, they opened the duffle bag only to realize their heist didn't pay off the way they thought it would. The damage was done. There was no going back. It was clear to them all that the next few months of their journey to America were going to be rough. Zora, being the smart one, had done her research and knew they would not be able to afford flights for all three of them. She had remembered reading about an ocean liner that crossed the Atlantic out of France and landed in the Big Apple. This was a much better option then stowing away on a container ship, so Ivan and Adolf went along with the logical plan. I still get a good laugh out of Ivan when we board a private jet, and I complain about the jellybeans or gummy bears offered to us. My stupid jokes are usually met with a very generous slap to my arm or even the occasional flick of a finger to the back of the head for being so arrogant. Not sure if any of you have crossed the ocean in one of those new beautiful floating cities of the seas, but this crossing was not even close to that. It was like riding in the back of a cattle truck bound for some third-world country, or at least where their cots were located. Thinking about that . . . I will never complain about my coach seat again.

It is always weird for me to think of these three people in my life as my relatives who came from a farm. I wouldn't be here, and they could still be living that simple life if it wasn't for the decisions that they made on that fateful night. One day, Ivan was milking the cows and gathering eggs out of the chicken coop for breakfast. Next, he was crammed into what could be a sock drawer of a rich man's house with forty other immigrants and his siblings, trying to make it to America before the air runs out. That farm life was so honest compared to the life we live today. This cartel life is like looking into a fucked-up action movie at times. The guns, men, women, and drugs . . . the killing, laundering of millions of dollars daily . . . the blatant disregard for the general public. The Reznik family values have disappeared completely from what Adolf Junior's father had originally dreamt.

As the three made the journey across the ocean, they all sat in silence. There was no one to blame for what they had done but themselves, and this was the new life they had to live. Running away from life's problems is never the answer, but this was their chance to start fresh in the land of dreams and opportunity.

. . .But, sadly, like all vices in life . . . once you are hooked, it is a tricky road to navigate away from. Adolf had worked too hard at becoming a criminal, so there was no way in hell he would reach the land of the rich and not be the biggest conqueror of them all.

>>>STOP RECORDING<<<

I was pretty speechless after this recording. Sitting there blank and sad, thinking about just what a tragedy we had written up till then in the pages of time. Today is a new day so let's see if I make it out of this hotel room alive for one more day of slaving away for the cartel at tomorrow's show.

CHAPTER 4

No Red Carpet Welcome to America?

Show day - Portland, Oregon

I am still hesitant about this new phone and social media app. Then again, I am trying to get my message out to the world, so I don't have a choice. Most of the crew is grabbing a bite to eat for lunch in catering, so my production office is quiet. I pull the stylish earbuds from my bag, plug them in, and lean back in the office chair. It is time to dive deeper into how we went from the farm to an empire state of mind and then to a dusty west Texas town.

>>>START RECORDING<<<

This is video diary #3 on October 16, 2009, 12:22:21

Of all the cities in the world, my family chose the one that truly embodies the American dream: the Big Apple, the Empire City, the city that never sleeps, the city of dreams. I have been around the world many times over; I have had the pleasure of stumbling down the stairs at Geronimo's in Japan; and I have tried to make my way through a mosh pit in South America during a rock n' roll festival. I even sang "You've Lost That Lovin' Feeling" to a bride-to-be on the love ferry between Helsinki and Stockholm. But I'll never enjoy a place the way I enjoy New York City. Maybe it's because I have such close ties here with the mob and cartel. Maybe it's just written in my DNA. Maybe, just maybe I fucking love the pizza, but whatever it is that draws me in each time, there is only one thing I can say. Even after all the heartbreak, I love NYC.

There is and will only ever be one New York City, and Adolf knew that when he walked off that boat. There is a certain vibe one gets when walking the streets—the feeling of possibilities. My last time in the Big Apple ended in tragedy which is obviously fueling these video entries that I am currently sharing with you about my family . . . but, when they got there, they were about to embark on a journey in life that no one would have expected.

Let's be real. No boat ride across the Atlantic Ocean until the 1980s, was luxurious unless you were rich. The ride was long, and the accommodations were lackluster; the quarters were foul-smelling and agonizing to say the least. By the end of the journey, Ivan was so homesick and riddled with guilt for leaving his parents, wondering what would happen to them, that he was almost willing to stay aboard for a grueling ride back. What was the teenager to feel or do in this situation? Everything he knew was gone in a blink of an eye.

Zora and Adolf, well . . . they had a different perspective when running away from their home. The life Ivan loved had vanished, but it was time to start fresh. "Out with the old and in with the new" is all his siblings could tell him. They were clearly looking at the situation as if gold coins rained from the sky in America. The world can be a daunting place, and life in a big city can be very intimidating, so Ivan had to make a tough choice as a teenager: sink or swim. There were not many options for him now. The little boy within Ivan wanted to do only one thing when they landed on the shores of America, and that was to reach out to his mother and father. Could you blame him? Some days, we need our safety blanket. He wanted to let them know he loved them and would miss them, but Adolf and Zora told him they would end up in big trouble if he reached out. Even if Ivan was to sneak off to send a letter or make a phone call, Zora held on tight to what little money they had left from the robbery and boat ride over, so there was no hope to buy a simple stamp. Whatever Ivan could have said wouldn't have mattered anyway, he thought his parents would end up in jail, it wasn't worth the risk. They were in New York City, and it was time to grow up—and grow up fast.

Everyone deals with stress differently and the three siblings, for sure, had their different opinions on how they were going to handle this new bigger, louder, and more dangerous city. They disembarked the ship and set their sights on the island of Manhattan for the first time. Once in the city, Ivan stood stunned by the hustle and bustle of all the people while Zora and Adolf took to it as if they had prepared for that big city their whole life. Leaving home for the first time is not an easy adventure for most kids . . . and I use "kids" because that's what they were. Children. Picture yourself landing on an entirely different continent thousands of miles away from the only place you knew since the day you were born. Then stepping foot into a country surrounded by people who speak a language you barely know. To top it all off, the two people who forced you out from under that blanket are telling you to suck it up and stop acting like a child. Being overwhelmed and pissed at his two older siblings for calling him a child only built up more aggression inside Ivan as they made their walk uptown before sunset. Moping along behind the duo, he was reminded of a story his father would tell him about his grandfather's experience leaving his home at a young age, never to return. Growing up Ivan always thought of his grandfather as his guardian angel in tough times. The future was going to be rough, but he knew deep down that he would have to step it up if he wanted to make it in on these tough streets, but at least he had someone looking down on him.

New York City in the late '60s and early '70s was no kiddie playground. The city was riddled with drugs, prostitution, and real hardcore mobsters who ran the streets and unions. This city has produced some of the world's most ruthless criminals of all time. These mob guys were far from the baggy pants and basketball jersey wearing thugs from the '90s. No, these men wore suits, rocked gold Rolexes, and their gold chains got lost in their chest hair. But don't think for one minute these sharp-dressed men wouldn't feed you to the fish in the Hudson River for stealing a penny from their take.

But back to when the family landed in New York. When they arrived, Nixon was in office, the Vietnam War had just held the draft, and one iconic music festival was about to be held in the middle of a field for the first time. That same festival happened to be one of Ivan's first gigs that he worked. More on that later.

Most immigrants arriving in America come with a dream or are looking for refuge. The Reznik kids came seeking both. While Adolf and Zora saw dollar signs and the opportunity for luxury at every corner, Ivan played devil's advocate and would constantly remind them that they needed a plan for survival. The first few months were unbelievably hard. They would sleep in parks or shelters, go without food for days, and—if they were lucky with a half-decent score off the tourists that night—they could purchase a pay-by-the-hour motel room. Zora had an ace up her sleeve when times were especially tough. She would play the damsel in distress at an uptown pub and sucker a lonely man into letting her come "sleep" over. Usually, as they walked out the door, they would be met by giant Ivan who would then convince the gentleman that their party was a G-rated event that also came with two chaperones. This was rarely met with an argument, so the three would at least get a warm shower from time to time this way.

After a few months of living off the streets and working odd jobs here and there, the three of them started to get disheartened about the American dream that they thought would come easily. Most of their time was spent around the lower east side of town. This is where Zora and Adolf would work the corners and hustle for scraps. The big score days always happened when they would head uptown. The duo hated to share their take with Ivan since he would rarely participate, but they would still make sure he at least ate. Although Ivan would be hungry and mostly would do anything to eat, Ivan hated to hustle tourists for their money, but he would straight up ask for food. Most of the time, he couldn't bring himself to lie, cheat, and steal like his siblings. But some days Adolf, being the golden-tongued spawn of Satan, would manipulate Ivan into participating. There were days that Ivan would find himself parting ways with the duo and walking the city for hours to get away from this hustling life that he was now sadly living. Even after becoming one of the roadie cartel's main production managers, Ivan would still find himself wanting to escape the tour life by going on long walks to find a quiet bar where he could enjoy fine tequila alone with his thoughts. Once I was old enough to go on the road with him, I became one of the few that he invited on these special outings to sit and share life stories with.

There are not many stories Ivan tells about NYC that are happy until the night he was introduced to the music business. I can still remember him sharing these memories with me the first time he took me to that famous little club that also happened to be my first time in the Big Apple. I remember that day vividly. We started walking around midday after we departed the bus and checked into the hotel. I was finally of age and able to partake in the one thing every roadie loved on a day off, day drinking. On any tour, good or bad, day drinking is always a great start to any day off, but after a long bus ride, there is nothing like a cold beer and warm slice of New York pizza to help calm the jitters. We started bar hopping not far from Penn Station and made our way down to the area where this small music club changed our family's history—and the music industry—forever. Destiny had put Ivan in the right place at the right time many years ago, like she tends to do, but Ivan still fights me that it was his grandpa looking down on him. Up until his death, I stuck with destiny but with each day above ground, I have a feeling he is now looking down on me.

Okay, back to my point . . . on this special day, Ivan took me to this club and shared this story with me, Ivan was riding on a very nice buzz after downing enough beers that led to a storytelling mood. Once we arrived at the club, we decided to grab a cold beer at the pub across the street. As we sat outside, Ivan began to reminisce about the night he "walked" away from his hustling family members and ended up in the music industry. Out of all the things Ivan said to me that day, the one thing I remember the most—especially since I had never heard him speak about music, ever—was, "The sounds coming through the walls that night stopped me dead in my tracks. Hell, it sounded like an angel was playing this guitar to only me." Ivan stared at a photo of the club behind the bar in front of us. Up until that moment, I didn't think he knew what a guitar was . . .

>>>PAUSE RECORDING<<<

I suddenly realize I am getting sidetracked from the story with fun memories that Ivan has shared with me, but as these old images dance around in my brain, I cannot help but remember his poetic moments, which were few and far between. He was a man of a few words most days. I pause to take a sip of energy drink and readjust my earbuds.

>>>RESUME RECORDING<<<

Being a kid from a small town in Czechoslovakia, Ivan had no idea what music was besides the traditional local music played at a day parade or the Christmas shows that happened in a town close by. That fateful night, after parting ways from his brother and sister, Ivan started walking in a direction he had never taken before. Ivan told me that he saw a blinking light on a building that reminded him of a star his father would tell him was his grandfather checking in on him. So, even though it was red and much different from the bright star in the dark Czechoslovakian night sky, he followed it anyway. Ivan would say, "I needed something to believe in that night." He followed the blinking light until it disappeared into the New York City skyline where all the tall buildings that surround you have lights that blink, twinkle, and shine brightly like the stars in the sky. While Ivan was stopped, looking for the light, he suddenly heard the rich and even sensual tones of an electric guitar for the first time. Unfortunately, he didn't have any money to get into the club, so he did the next best thing. He posted up by the backstage entrance to get as close as possible to this new ear candy he had stumbled upon. With a few rolled cigarettes that he had taken from Zora, he stood there until the music died out, and all that was left were screams from adoring fans. As he turned to leave and find his way home, Ivan was surrounded by fans leaving the venue who flocked to the backstage entrance for one last look at the band. Confused but interested in all the commotion, he soon had a new group of sounds and people to focus his attention on. And it wasn't just the adorning fans. No, these long-haired guys started to make their way through the gaggle of screaming women with graffitied covered cases. The straggly men all had on very similar attire—denim jeans and a faded black t-shirt. Some had visible tattoos like they were part of a biker gang who had stopped to help the band with their luggage. (It would take time for him to adjust to the proper term "road case.") Still not sure what was happening, Ivan took notice of a man playing traffic cop and directing everyone who was bringing stuff out to the alley to the bus and small trailer. The bus parked close to the backstage door resembled a badly renovated school bus that the band and their gear traveled in. Ivan had no clue why they needed a bus. Hell, he still had no idea why New York had so many yellow cars! The traffic director was ruthless when telling these hoodlums where to put the boxes on the bus and in the trailer, while at the same time yelling at the girls to get out of the way and go home. This man was cracking Ivan up. For the first time in a long while, Ivan smiled; it was amusing to witness backstage antics.

Near the backstage door, Ivan was caught off guard by a larger, well-fed stagehand—another term he learned later—lost control of the tall road case labeled "fragile" across every side that he was pushing out to the alley. The case almost toppled over, but Ivan jumped in with his massive build to help in time. This was a huge moment for the kid! He didn't know what he had just done, but the man directing the backstage traffic ran over and thanked Ivan for preventing the main guitar amps from hitting the ground. A little intimidated by this man, and trying to not show it, Ivan stood there nodding and smiling with no clue what an amp was and why this man was so excited about it. After thanking Ivan, the man turned to leave, but Ivan reached out and tapped him on his shoulder to ask if he could help finish whatever they were doing. It looked fun. With a few questions and one last drag off his rolled cig, Ivan hopped in with the stagehands. Being a giant of a teen, he outpowered most of the stagehands immediately. He might not have known what a road case was or how to stack one in the trailer properly, but he was a natural when it came to his work ethic.

Once the last road case was on the bus and the trailer was secured, the tour manager approached Ivan with a big smile, a handshake, and an invitation to join him in the bus. The man's name was Pie. Yes, like the dessert. To this day no one knows his real name or last name. He is the guy who pioneered the idea of what a roadie does for the bands they work for. Pie was known as the premier production manager in the business. On this tour, though, he wanted to relive his days of working in clubs and smaller venues. I am totally fucking kidding, he took this gig to move up in, at the time, the smaller world of touring. He wanted to become the tour manager for larger bands and this one was going to be a catalyst for that dream. But for this particular gig it also meant he was now wearing one too many hats for this up-and-coming artist. On top of getting the sweet tour manager title, AKA the bands babysitter, Pie was also the band's production manager, the stage manager, and he also had to mix the sound for the band on nights when there was not a house sound engineer. The man was getting pulled in too many directions; he needed a guy. Pie spent the next few minutes asking Ivan about his background and what he was doing in the big city. He was pleased to find out that this giant kid's schedule was wide open, indefinitely. Pie needed help; he was a little desperate to fill a stage manager position. Even though Ivan knew nothing about the road, Pie saw potential. With a tense look on his face, Pie reached out, grabbed Ivan by the back of his neck, and shared some advice. "Some of the greatest road guys I know started with only great work ethic. The rest comes with experience," Pie said as they talked in the front lounge of the bus.

Pie told Ivan all about the road life . . . how you get to see the world, meet new faces, and live life with few rules. They were playing a festival the next day on a farm in New York, and Pie really needed help. There were rumors that the festival was growing, and all hands needed to be on deck to get the band up on stage and off site before it got too wild. Sitting on the bus with the guys, listening to every word, Ivan's eyes were as big as cue balls. He imagined a better living situation as he witnessed real work—no hustling. It was hard for Ivan to turn down the job offer. With this gig, he wouldn't need to swindle with Adolf and Zora anymore (at least for this weekend). And how could he pass up food and a "bed" on the bus?

Although Ivan remained fairly upset with his two siblings, he couldn't just up and leave. He was too considerate to do that. So, he asked Pie, like one would ask an older sibling or even a parent, if he would be able to run back to the shelter where they had been crashing to leave a note. Pie, the most badass roadie in the world at this time, paused. Ivan, for the first time in his life suddenly felt small. He was in the presence of a man who in reality was not much older and not even as tall, but he was someone who commanded so much respect already in life. So, like a deer in headlights, Ivan was still as Pie stared at him and with his deep, raspy and smoke worn voice said, "Bus leaves in thirty minutes, so don't be late or the oil spot will be the only thing left here when you return." Pie added one last thing before Ivan ran off and that was to bring all his clothes; he had a feeling the kid was going to end up going for a long ride. Not knowing what an oil spot was, Ivan nodded his head in agreement, bolted off the bus and sprinted toward the shelter.

Blowing down the street and into the shelter like the Tasmanian devil on a Sunday morning cartoon, completely out of breath, he ran right for the spot in the back corner that they had been provided for the week. There he found Adolf and Zora divvying up the night's take. With little time left, Ivan tried to explain that he had to leave, but not one coherent sentence was made. His siblings looked at each other quizzically and followed Ivan around and between the three cots, attempting to understand the excitement that was spilling out of the youngest Reznik child. While packing his belongings, Ivan managed to explain that he had found a job and would be back at some point. Adolf and Zora had more questions for Ivan than he had time to answer, so they simply slipped him the number to the Italian restaurant where Adolf had just found a part-time job and told him to call when he could. As they hugged each other goodbye, Adolf leaned in and whispered menacingly into Ivan's ear, "You better not be going back to the farm. I will come find you and bury you and anyone else with you there." Throwing the pillowcase full of clothes over his shoulder and with no time to give Adolf's comment the time of day, Ivan sprinted back to the tour bus for his first true "bus-call."

Peering out the front window of the bus while standing on the stairs with the door open, Pie glanced at his watch and sighed with disappointment since time was almost up. Then to Pie's utter amazement, with only seconds to spare, the kid came tearing around the corner and up the stairs to the bus. An unwitting spectator could only assume a rabid dog was chasing him.

"Nice timing, kid," Pie said with a smirk.

Out of breath and with his pillowcase in hand, the young Czech smiled and sunk into the bus steps as the driver hit the door locks and put Ivan's new tenement on wheels in drive.

Little did Ivan know that this weekend journey was the start to what would be a very successful life as one of the most respected men in touring history. However, as he joined the others on the bus for the first time, he was fresh meat—the newbie. Like any situation when you're the new guy or even girl for that matter, everyone sizes you up, looks you up and down, and asks you stupid, repetitive questions about where you're from, who you worked for and *blah, blah,*

blah. Since he was clueless, Ivan was the butt of the jokes as he took up the bartender role, but he didn't care one little bit. He was finally free from his older brother's hold on him.

Maybe it was the idea of the band and crew getting ready to experience a historical event the next day—a never-done-before festival experience. Maybe it was because Ivan was so nervous to ride his first tour bus. Whatever the case, he decided to partake in all the fun that everyone was having. For the first time in a while, he was around people who weren't forcing him to be a liar or a cheat; they just wanted to get him a little more fucked up than Ivan had ever been before. After drinking a few beers—at least that's what he told me—and hitting a joint for the first time, Ivan fell victim to something that every roadie has done at least once. His eyelids became heavy as the weed kicked in. He passed out in the front lounge.

Now, I am not sure if the unwritten laws of bus etiquette were around yet, but I always hoped to find a photo with his face covered in permanent marker penises.

When his eyes reopened, he stared perplexingly at the bus ceiling, forgetting where he was for a few moments. Dazed and confused, Ivan closed his eyes and tried to rub the hangover away, hoping he would begin recognizing his surroundings. You know it's a wild night when you don't remember falling asleep and find yourself with one shoe on in the front of a tour bus the next day.

Ivan's memory clicked. He rolled off the couch and heard a crowd cheering and music playing. He was backstage at his first real gig.

The bus door flung open. Pie entered to check on Sleeping Beauty and to remind him that they had to get the gear on the stage and do a show soon. After getting dressed and making his way toward the front door of the bus, Ivan looked out the big driver's windows. He had never in all his years seen anything like what he was witnessing. He saw the massive crowd. His eyes widened—and he realized he had no clue what a roadie does. It's not like there was a "Roadie 101" course for this Czechoslovakian kid. Instead, experience taught him the ways of this world.

After a healthy couple glasses of water, Ivan headed to meet Pie in one of the most mysterious and elusive places still to this day, backstage. Standing back there smoking a rolled cigarette, Ivan and

Pie talked about what was going to happen that day. While walking up onto the stage, Pie turned to Ivan with an encouraging smile and said, "Time to sink or swim, kid." Ivan chuckled as he realized he had said the same thing to himself not long ago. With nothing to lose, he did exactly what Pie told him to do. Not once did he want to deviate from his new boss' plan.

It was go time, and Pie watched Ivan like a hawk. Ivan, in turn, showed Pie that he was serious and a strong work horse. From loading the band gear onto the stage, to helping Pie get the band to the stage in time for their set, to then taking all the gear back out and putting it back on the bus and into the trailer . . . oh yeah, and they would do it all again the next day in Boston. Pie left that little nugget out when he first recruited Ivan for the gig, but it didn't matter. Ivan was relieved he wasn't living as a scumbag like his siblings.

Before Ivan could blink, the show was over, and they were back on the bus. No matter what you do in life, there is something very rewarding in enjoying an ice-cold beer after a job well done. Pie would say that often to Ivan in the early years. Once they were all back on the bus and rolling toward Massachusetts, Ivan sat across from Pie, amazed by this man's greatness. Ivan was shocked to find out that Pie had already been in the game for over ten years now—and still hadn't reached his twenty-fifth birthday yet. Finally, Ivan was able to look up to someone other than his father or grandfather. Little did Pie know that he would become a mentor to a seventeen-year-old kid looking badly for direction. Sitting there, reminiscing about the day's hard work and awesome music, they both smiled. When you share a smile, brain wavelengths are at an all-time high. The room buzzes with energy. And the future—well, the future has endless potential.

>>>PAUSE RECORDING<<<

I stop to light a cigarette. The production office is so quiet that the sound of the paper burning can be heard on camera as the smoke rolls elegantly off the tip of the red-hot cherry after taking a long drag. Two thick streams of used tobacco smoke shot from my nostrils like a dragon shooting fire at the knight who is after his gold.

>>>RESUME RECORDING<<<

Ask anyone who has ever traveled for a living. In the beginning, it is like a drug, and Ivan fell in love with his new life on the road instantly. Touring allowed him to see the world firsthand. And, thanks to his luck of crossing paths with someone like Pie, Ivan gained freedom from his oppressive brother and sister that he had been stuck with for what felt like an eternity. Keep in mind—not every day on tour is spent gazing at the rushing waters of Niagara Falls or experiencing the sheer size of the Great Wall of China. Some days, you are trapped inside the concrete box that is the arena. But, again, Ivan was far from the troubled duo who, in his mind, could go to hell for guilt tripping him to leave home for their botched crime.

Ivan was never a mischievous tyke growing up, but this new road life he had adopted felt risqué for him and, boy, did he love it! Name one teenage boy with raging hormones who wouldn't love a good backstage party—hell, any party!—filled with half-naked women and all the booze you could drink. Out of all the things Ivan pictured himself doing in his lifetime, not in a million years did he think it would be riding on a tour bus across America for the next few months setting up this band's gear. His workdays on this first tour were very labor intensive, and he found such a life extremely satisfying, reminding him of a hard day's work on the farm.

Even though he was surrounded by all these wild adventures, Ivan was a good kid who never took advantage of a situation. He also missed his family, a lot. Ivan was a family man and even though he couldn't stand his siblings somedays, he would always find time to call his brother so he could update Zora. Ivan enjoyed calling the Italian restaurant more than Adolf liked receiving them at his new job. Even though they weren't close, Adolf would let his excited brother ramble about the great sights and the mundane details of everyday tour life such as the trucks, buses, truck stops, hotels—and all things in between. And on some days, he would wander alone for a moment to think of home and his parents. Ivan just wanted that family dynamic back more than he probably ever let on.

Not long after Ivan hit the road, Adolf and Zora were able to afford a tiny one-room apartment not far from Little Italy. It was a dump, but it was close to Adolf's job at this Italian joint called Plinio's Pasta and Pizza, which was run by the mob and when I say "the mob," I mean the biggest one to ever walk the streets of New York City. The Three Ps dealt in the fine art of pasta-making, but the family's main business was extortion, neighborhood security, gun running, cocaine dealing and they also had a laundry business right next door for—you guessed it: money laundering. Adolf was the newest member of this multi-generation Italian mob family restaurant as the new dishwasher. This brought in constant money, Adolf and Zora would hustle on the side merely for fun now. Another perk to Adolf's job was that he could take home as much spaghetti and stale bread as he wanted at the end of his shift. After a while he was able to also bring Zora home half-drunk bottles of wine the mob wives would leave behind.

Adolf might have the best looks between the Reznik boys, but Ivan had clearly won in the job category. At times, Ivan would be tempted to rub his good fortune in his brother's face, but he knew better than to anger the already choleric Adolf. It wasn't long before the owners and the front of house staff took notice of the younger European male in the back washing dishes next to a prominently South American kitchen staff. He was strikingly good looking, but the other thing that got him noticed was his smart mouth. Adolf would take shots at the kitchen's butcher who was notorious for messing up the choice cuts of veal for dinner service. They quickly took notice of the punk who knew a thing or two about cuts of meat, but would he be able to take on a new task in the kitchen without getting himself into trouble?

Not long after the dinner rush one night, a big lasagna-eating mobster walked up to Adolf with slick black hair, a nice suit, and a toothpick hanging from the side of his lip. In a thick New York Italian accent he said, "Hey'a kid, yous'a wanna be my food'a delivery kid tomorrow?" The heavy-set man's eyes closed a little as he stood a little taller, adjusted his pants and tilted his head up a little before finishing with, "the otha' kid . . . well'a, he didn't work out, let's'a say."

With little hesitation, Adolf stepped out from behind the wash rack and agreed to the new position without asking what exactly he would be running. But hey, at least he would not have to stand in a pool of dirty dish water most of the night. With a grin, Adolf went to take his apron off and leave when the big mobster stopped him and reminded him that the job started tomorrow.

We have all seen the movies about mobsters and the businesses they run. The Three Ps wasn't much different. Adolf now worked for one of the premier drug running, money laundering, and neighborhood protection (even if you didn't ask for the protection) Italian mob families on the East Coast. The restaurant that Adolf worked at was the main hangout for this Italian family and so many other Italian immigrants. They had other random businesses, but this one was best known for its "Mamma Mia special." This might be hard to believe for some, but if you wanted coke back in the day, you couldn't just text your local drug dealer. No, you had to pick up the phone or go find "the guy" working the streets. So, Three Ps would take your special order right over the phone like any other order; then, their new slick-looking delivery boy, Adolf, would run that special right over to you. Hidden inside was a surprise for the buyer. One of the most exciting parts of the drug game, to me, is the challenge of being clever. Most people aren't in the mood for a cold cut Italian sub when they are ordering a bag of cocaine or a few rocks of crack, but this was Three Ps' way of transporting the substance around. If you got stopped or if any snoopy cops decided to swing by the restaurant, everything looked legit. You had to look legit if you wanted to make it as a drug business operating as an Italian joint. If you were going to outsmart the crooks in the government wanting their free cut, then you had to dot the i's and cross the t's and have extra funds set aside for high-paid bribes.

One more important part to the drug game is the team. You don't need lowlifes helping you. You need criminals. They are two very different types of people. The lowlife will simply do up all your junk, make up excuses as to why he doesn't have your drugs or money, and then skip town before you can kill them. The criminal wants more money. Sure, you have to watch your back around them—but, hey, it's not like you are going to find a nun willing to move your coke . . . or maybe you will. Some of the nicest people I have ever met are muscle bound, tattooed, one-percenters that will baby talk to a cat, but you better never lie to them or you and your cat will find yourselves skinned, and we all know there are multiple ways to accomplish that task. In the drug business, you have to test your men for this exact reason. Are they a crook or a junkie? Not because you are looking for the hardest criminal on the block, but because you are looking for the most honest and loyal one. Someone who isn't going to steal from you. Family doesn't always mean you have to be bound by blood. In this cartel and mob world, you can be anyone, but if you cross them, they will kill you and find a new YOU! I always thought that blood would mean a little more in the game, but it doesn't. Sounds harsh, but that's life. When you are the boss, you don't have time to worry about some "Johnson" skimming another eight ball off the top to take home and share with his stripper girlfriend. There is only one worry, how to make MORE MONEY.

With dishwashing a thing of the past, Adolf came into work a new man. As he walked in confidently and cocky one afternoon, there stood the Italian mob boss and his two cronies. The kingpin stared into Adolf's eyes, and softly—almost a whisper—he said, "Look'a here kid, there is a very expensive thing at the bottom of that box on the table. Don't look at it. Don't even breathe on the box. Deliver to this address on the paper. And don't be a minute late!"

Without saying a word, Adolf glanced at the address. He grabbed the box off the table, turned, blew through the double doors at the front of the restaurant, and started to run down the street. One thing about being a criminal is that you get sudden bursts of adrenalin when doing something unknown, especially something that might get you thrown in the trash like the last delivery kid. As Adolf was sprinting down the street, he realized he got a rush much like he felt the night they had to leave Czechoslovakia. This was the first time he had felt alive in the Big Apple.

Out of breath, Adolf arrived at the address and walked through the door of an old brownstone. Sitting at a table, waiting with a fork and knife, was the old Italian boss with slicked back jet black hair and a jacket draped over his shoulders. "Good, you made it. I was hungry," he said in a subtle tone. Adolf stood stunned, surprised at the effort he exerted when that old man could have simply eaten his lunch at the table back at the restaurant.

The old man looked up at one of his cronies and nodded his head. Adolf never did find out what was in the bottom of the box, but he made the old man happy. As a broke kid without much going on except the drive to make a name for him and become rich, this was a step in the right direction. And, like that, Adolf started to run "the daily special" every day for the mob. On top of the pay, he also got to take home some nice tips. Things were looking up at the Italian joint for everyone, especially the Czech kid.

The big boss started to acknowledge Adolf as a new member and a part of the bigger picture. There was a lesson Adolf was taught one day when coming through the back door of the kitchen: remember, everyone is replaceable in business. The old butcher wasn't cutting it any longer, and as Adolf walked into that kitchen and saw the old butcher being wheeled into the walk-in freezer with tape over his mouth, he knew something was up. In a blink of an eye, the two main thugs for the boss closed the door, dropped the locking pin into the handle, and pointed to Adolf, saying, "Da boss said you's are up tonight to cut the meat." For a guy who never liked school, nor did he even finish it, Adolf was moving up the mobsters' corporate ladder as if he was holding a degree from the university of hard-knocks.

Saturdays usually started quietly for Adolf and the cooking staff. Adolf was at his new cutting station, prepping choice cuts for the dinner rush. On the other side of the kitchen, Latin music played loudly as the others completed the food and drug prep. Unexpectedly, one of the mob boss's head cronies walked in, shut the radio off, and walked over to Adolf in a way that made everyone think that there was about to be a position opening for another butcher and deliverer. He told Adolf that he needed to take the car out front and drive to west Texas to pick up a large package that was very important to the boss. Even though he didn't even have a driver's license or know where Texas was, he had no choice. The head crony explained that there was a map on the front seat and all the contact info was in the glove box. There was not much more said as he tossed Adolf the keys and a roll of cash.

Adolf hung his butcher apron on a wall hook, grabbed his smokes, and headed to the car. He felt the need to tell Zora about his undertaking since he (who had maybe five total hours of driving time in his life) was about to drive across the country. After getting into the giant boat of a car, the crony gave Adolf one last message and a "friend" to keep him company. He threw him a bag of blow and told him to be back in a week. If there was any trouble, he could find a gun under his seat. I don't know how many of you have had to drive across the country and back within a week, but to make that deadline, Adolf was going to need every speck of that booger sugar.

Driving across the United States is a feat. Driving across it and back in one week is not a situation I would ever want to be in, especially when having to pick up a package for a very intimidating boss who happens to run part of the Italian mob in New York. What concerned Adolf the most was the consequence if he were late. Would he be given a little slap on the wrist, or would he be fitted with a pair of cement shoes for a late-night swim in the Hudson River? With these mob guys, it was probably the latter. Adolf knew there was no messing around with this guy's deadline. As Adolf, the car, and the blow made it out of New York and hit Pennsylvania, he decided to make a quick pit stop. After filling up on gas and taking a quick piss, he got back into the car and took a giant snort of the devil's dandruff. With his new manufactured self-confidence, he quickly felt around for the location of the gun. After a quick cracking of his knuckles, he pulled back on to the interstate toward . . . El Paso, Texas. Adolf had no clue what he was going to get into, he just knew it was time to push on the right pedal and get back as fast as he could. During this era, Adolf didn't have to worry about fancy speed traps and facial recognition. So, if he could keep it between the lines and not draw much attention to himself, he would be fine.

Hours into the grueling drive, Adolf started to have those moments one gets during long coke binges when paranoia kicks in and everything around you starts to look suspicious. The long drive was playing tricks on his brain; the white stripes became lines of coke, and the semitrucks began to look like giant razor blades. He decided it was time to pull over for a quick break and splash a little water on his face. As he pulled off the road to find a safe resting spot and a place to drain his bladder, Zora—who was still back in New York—received a call from her baby brother. A week before Adolf left for his surprise trip, he was able to have a landline installed in their apartment, so Ivan didn't have to contact them through the Three P's Italian restaurant. Ivan had some awesome news. He was coming back to town for a show, and he would have a day off in the city. Ivan was a little sad to hear that his big brother wasn't going to be able to see him in person, but he was also relieved to know he would not have to deal with his older brother's antics.

After shutting his eyes for an hour, it was time to hit it again and make up for lost time. Adolf was back on the road. With his heart rate back to normal, he started wondering about the mystery men he was going to meet. Were they nice? How did they meet the Italians? It was difficult for a kid who had never seen the world—let alone deal with mobsters at a level of the Italian family—to really compile an accurate assumption. So, with more driving to do, Adolf did the logical thing. He reached into his little magic bag of powder, snorted a giant gagger, and off he went without hesitation.

Adolf drove for two days and into the next morning. With a beautiful sunrise coming up over the horizon behind him, the anticipation was building in the young man. Adolf was finally on his last leg of the long push to reach El Paso. There were mountains and desert filling his eyes now; these were sights he had never witnessed in his young life. Even in his coked-out state of mind, Adolf was speechless as he approached the majestic Franklin mountains that are a staple in the region that splits El Paso in half. Driving through the east side of the mountains and with the desert surrounding him, Adolf felt like a cowboy riding into town looking for T-R-O-U-B-L-E. As he got closer, he could see El Paso's bigger sister city, Ciudad Juarez, Mexico. Like a distant mirage, the two cities form an image of one to the untrained eye in that desert heat.

Running on fumes from the last cup of coffee, the little bit of coke left in the baggie, and the adrenalin, he pulled the map out one more time to check the address. He turned off the interstate and pulled into what can only be described as a parking lot, full of cars. Adolf slid the boat of a car into the first open spot and stepped outside. He looked around at the hundreds of empty vehicles, shiny, new and some with prices written on the front windshield. Confused, he scanned the area silently until he unexpectedly heard his name shouted in the distance. Adolf turned to find a very sharply dressed man with masculine features and a voice that was authoritative but friendly and with an accent similar to men that worked in the kitchen with him. The man extended his hand and with a very firm hand-shake completed the greeting with, "Hola, amigo. Welcome to El Paso. My name is Juan," while still gripping the young Adolf's hand, he smiled and winked, "Juan Ladrón."

This was not the name the Italians had provided Adolf, but he was more worried about using the restroom and freshening up with something other than coffee or coke. Juan led him into his office and offered him water followed by a cold beer. He began the conversation by complementing Adolf's timing; he figured the Italians wouldn't make it until the next day or even next. He then explained that his father had passed away not long ago, so Juan was the new business connection that Adolf would be dealing with. With hesitation, Adolf commented that he was only there to pick up a package and needed to get back as soon as possible.

"Nonsense. You are here with Juan now," the sharp dressed Mexican man said as he extended his arms. "I will show you around, and I will make sure to tell your boss you are here making him proud." Juan's grin reached from ear to ear. Adolf's eyes quickly fixated upon one gold tooth that was in Juan's upper teeth, entrancing him like Medusa's eyes.

Adolf paused to contemplate Juan's legitimacy. Why wouldn't Adolf want to party with a new friend who is offering a free beer and breaking up cocaine on his desk? Adolf felt comfortable and asked to use the phone. He told Juan that he needed to tell Zora, his sister, he'd be staying an extra day.

"Why didn't you bring your sister? We could have shown you both around my ranch." With a chuckle, Adolf promised that if the Italians sent him again, he would love to bring Zora; she has always wanted to visit the Southwest and meet a cowboy.

Zora didn't have much going on back in New York and was waiting for the phone to ring. She knew Ivan would call after his last show before heading to New York City. She was worried that she hadn't heard from Adolf but soon enough received the call that he made from the dealership. Once she knew both of her brothers were safe, she felt at ease and excited to see her little brother the next day. She was taken aback that her baby brother had a very wild request. Ivan had asked her to score him and his road friends some cocaine . . . but life was changing and so was her roadie brother.

The next day, Ivan rolled into town mid-morning from the show the night before. Once you start touring, you really get into some crazy, maybe even slightly psychotic, habits. For example, you wake up, sometimes hungover, and roll out of your bunk. If you are on the top bunk, you may find yourself making a slow, ungraceful climb down the bunks, avoiding hands and other appendages that may be hanging from fellow roadies' bunks. Once you are up and moving, there are certain routines each roadie has. Some roadies go pee. Some make coffee. Some light a cigarette. Smoking in the bunks is now frowned upon, but it used to be acceptable (kind of like smoking on planes used to be cool). But Ivan ran to the front window of the bus like clockwork every morning to see the view. Each day brought a view for him which he could never—and still can't—get enough of. The bus pulled into the Big Apple like it had many times before. This time, Ivan was standing in the jump seat position next to the driver, waiting to leap from the top step into his sister's arms when they arrived at the hotel. Even though they didn't always see eye to eye, Ivan was still closer to Zora than he was Adolf, so there she stood with her arms extended, waiting for the bus to completely stop. He was so excited to see his sister for her company and because she was also holding everyone's little bundles of fun. As the door blew open, Zora was bombarded by the band and crew in need of a party. Fortunately for them, she knew another cook at Three Ps that could help her out since Adolf was gone. Like Ivan had told the band and crew, Zora did not disappoint them. Today was a great day for them all. Ivan was home with his big sister. He was about to take her out on the town and show her the new Ivan (the one that likes booze now) and spend some of his money he had been saving up just for a night like tonight. Ivan's famous words that afternoon, which haunted him later, went something like, "Oh, look an Irish pub! Let's go have a couple cold ones and see where the night takes us."

Back in El Paso, Adolf and his new friend Juan were already slugging back beers and snorting lines like a couple of frat boys heading to a big kegger. At a certain point in anyone's life, the words "I am never drinking again" get spewed from their lying mouths like word vomit. Why do we say it and why don't we stick to that vow? Adolf was all in and ready to party the night away with. . .

>>>PAUSE RECORDING<<<

I felt a buzzing in my pocket . . . oh this isn't going to be good.

>>>RESUME RECORDING<<<

I have to go!

>>>STOP RECORDING<<<

I want to go into the story about Juan taking Adolf to Mexico— and Ivan taking Zora out on the town, but my cartel cell phone just buzzed. From the looks of it, I am wanted down in the coke lab, NOW.

CHAPTER 5

A Tale of Two Hangovers

>>>START RECORDING<<<

This is video diary #4 October 18, 2009. Boise, Idaho

Hello, Internet, my new escape, and the few followers joining my video diary. Or vid-iary? Video-log . . . ? I can't remember what the correct term is but HI.

>>>PAUSE RECORDING<<<

I roll my eyes at my attempt to sound relevant. Does it really matter? Is anyone listening to my story and pleas for help? I have to stop this pity-fucking-party, I must push forward, regardless. I shrug my shoulders and continue.

>>>RESUME RECORDING<<<

Oh yeah, *Vlog*! There it is. Now I sound like I am someone who should be here . . .

I am still on the road, and my closest associates slowly continue to distance themselves from me. They sometimes talk to me, but I have noticed that my closest two friends show doubt when I speak of the crimes committed against my father. I am outside the venue making this entry today because—well, I don't feel welcomed inside the building or the production office. I will never know when the cartel will turn on me and kill me, but I will continue to tell the stories of how it started and what I have seen until my day arrives. Now, I was not in either of these cities the night the cartel off-shoot was born, but this is what I was told had happened simultaneously . . .

Adolf and Juan, well they were basically long-lost friends. They hit it off almost instantly once he made it to Texas. The adrenalin and cocaine started to wear off, and Adolf started to look like a grandpa after a big Thanksgiving dinner on the couch. If you know anything about blow, the drop from a long high, emphasis on high, is brutal on the body. He was awake, but each time Juan looked outside the window at the car lot, Adolf took that moment to close his eyes and enjoy a moment of rest. He couldn't fight it any longer, and just as he was about to ask Juan if he could take a quick nap on his couch, his new sharply dressed friend turned from the window and slid a mirror from his desk to Adolf, and on that mirror sat a small ski resort of coke.

Even though Adolf's body was screaming at him to sleep, that little devil on his shoulder woke up and handed him a rolled-up hundred-dollar bill to snort that line and continue the party. Sure, Adolf was tired, but standing before him was the kind of man Adolf wanted to impress. He was everything the young man from Czechoslovakia wanted to be. Adolf was willing to do whatever possible because Juan was the definition of cool—a young man with style, class, money, and, most importantly, power. His charisma instantly hooked Adolf. Considering that Adolf didn't have a single friend other than Zora (and sometimes Ivan), he was enamored by this stranger, talking to him like they had been friends since birth. Sleep could wait; tonight, he was hanging with, for lack of better words, the man he would kill to be liked by.

Being in his late twenties, Juan had it made, but he too had a hard time keeping friends. There was a slight age difference between the two men, but he was enjoying his company with the young man from Czechoslovakia. Juan instantly took an interest in his stories about coming to America and his dreams of making it rich here. Juan asked him about his family and where they were. Adolf explained that his one brother ran around the country setting up concerts for music artists, or some shit like that, with other guys on some bus. His sister Zora—well, she was pretty and had a talent for hustling men out of their money. Adolf pulled out a photo capturing the three of them from his wallet. Juan smiled and nodded with respect.

The men sat in Juan's office with a beautiful panoramic view of the mountains in front of them as they chatted, sipping on beers and snorting lines of fresh powder. Adolf told Juan that he still had no idea why the Italians sent him, but he was here and ready anytime Juan wanted to send him back with the package. Juan had another thing in mind. Juan paused after Adolf's short story with his hands interlocked and pressed against his lips, in deep thought. While never taking his eyes off the young Adolf, he suddenly dropped both hands, stood up with a loud hand slap to his knees, staring the kid straight in the eyes and smiled. A little freaked out at the sudden jolt of energy, Adolf wondered what would happen next; Juan walked to a large wooden cabinet just to the left of his desk, opened one of the doors, and reached in. Adolf shifted further back and braced for the worst. Then with a smile that spread across his face, Juan pulled out the most beautiful black ceramic bottle with hand-painted red vines scrolling from around the neck of the bottle, down and around its base. Juan explained that this was some of the finest tequila in all the world and since there was going to be a celebration tonight, it was time to open the good stuff. While pouring the men some drinks, Juan shared that he also owned this tequila operation down in Mexico. Second largest imported beverage into the states. Adolf was enamored. Juan sat a three finger pour of this fine tequila, in a beautiful crystal rocks glass down in front of the young man.

As Adolf tasted tequila for the first time, his eyes watered, and he coughed up a bit of the fiery brown liquid. And by no means was it bad; he had to adjust from cheap gin and vodka. After swallowing forcibly and catching his breath, he asked Juan about his origin and how he got into the states. Slowly, he explained to Adolf that he grew up in a small town in Mexico that was right along the stunning Pacific Ocean. Life was simple there. They had a big ranch not far from the water with various animals but primarily the land was used for other styles of farming.

"But why talk about farming, I will show you the land one day!" Juan said with a wink.

Adolf smiled, knowing that a huge boss like him had also come from a farming background. Juan went on to explain that the family ranch was significant in maintaining small businesses and the one church in town but also it was the epicenter to the bigger family empire. Once his father passed away, Juan was in charge of running all the family businesses.

Naïvely, Adolf asked Juan, "Like more car businesses and farms— oh, and tequila distilleries in Mexico?"

With a devilish chuckle chased down by the rest of the fine tequila in his rocks glass, Juan stood up, headed to the window, and explained that, sure, the dealerships were part of his family's success. But his grandpa funded his first dealership with money he had made during the prohibition era, running booze north into New York and other eastern states. He went on to tell Adolf, how it was his father that truly took things to new heights. With some of the connections his grandfather made through booze distribution, Juan's father started to run bigger money items up to the Italians in New York; guns, cheap labor and some drugs, mainly weed. And with that money Juan's father took over Mexico, with factories, pharmacies and farms. On a trip to South America once he met a man who told him about importing cocaine into the states was cheaper. This was the start to his multi-billion-dollar, multi-drug trafficking organization, named the Mexican cartel. All the farms, factories and pharmacies became part of the drug network. The United States had no idea what was hitting them, the shipments were coming across by the truck loads, thanks to all the Mexican factories Juan's father owned who were supplying the states with all sorts of products. He went on a bit longer about how the initial operations worked, but Juan ended with, "We are now in a battle with not only other cartels seeking to gain power by undercutting us but internally we are struggling to keep up with transportation, distribution and high manufacturing costs."

His father's cartel had been slowly fading, so it had been a rough start for Juan as the new head. He had had a more challenging time than expected with trafficking products into the states. The Italians were one of his father's key distribution partners for the northeast and even over towards Chicago. Still, since Juan had taken over, they had slowly been trying to take advantage of some of the verbal contracts Juan's father had set in place years prior. Juan explained that when he first met Adolf, his blood boiled because it felt like a slap to the face that the Italians would send the lowest member on the payroll to talk business. However, the more the two men chatted in the upstairs office, the more Juan's anger subsided. Being a businessman, he looked at this meeting as something more significant. He started to see something special in this kid who was high on life—and high on a lot of high-grade coke.

Unbeknownst to Adolf, he could be Juan's golden ticket to help with transportation needs to the East Coast. Juan was not just being polite and having a friendly conversation. He was genuinely interested in hearing more about some of the men that Adolf crossed paths with daily in New York City and his brother who traveled around The United States. Adolf didn't understand Juan's intentions, reminding him often that he's a simple delivery boy that may get into trouble with his boss for taking up Juan's time. Every time Adolf brought up his Italian employer, Juan chortled. He once said in a low, sarcastic laugh, "I am sure you will be running that town soon enough, amigo." Uneasy with this bold statement, Adolf stood to thank his host with the urgency to return to New York, but Juan again laughed. He instructed Adolf to head downstairs where a driver would take him elsewhere to shower and change.

This would be one of the last memories of the day for young Adolf.

Day drinking—for me, at least—always ends with waking up like Adolf . . . when the date, time, and place are unknown. Much like a movie, the young Czech found himself in a strange room next to two naked women the next morning. With a rush of endorphins all waking up in tandem, his mind jumped through hazy memories, and his eyes quickly skimmed the room. Back and forth and back and forth. Lavish decorations surrounded him; the ivory bed posts were inlaid with gold swirls, and the bed size seemed larger than three of his New York City apartments. He did pause a couple times and was particularly impressed by the giant gold-framed paintings of bullfighters on all the walls; the intricate crown moldings looked as if they were straight from a Roman cathedral. A stuffed grizzly bear in the corner made the young man think he was in a king's room. A tiger rug, head and all glared at him. He tried to analyze what appeared to be a wildly fun and naughty night between rubbing his eyes and looking at the girls and then back at the bear, then down at the tiger and then back at the girls and so on.

He started to get anxious about being in a place he couldn't afford and perhaps didn't belong. Trying to piece his shattered mind together, he scooted to the end of the giant bed when something caught his eye. In disbelief, he stared at blood-soaked pants and a shirt lying near the foot of the bed and a few feet from the giant white tiger's teeth. He wondered if the two girls next to him were even alive. With both hands, he quickly checked for a pulse. When both girls stirred, Adolf released a sigh of relief.

Seriously, the mind is wild . . . how things can ignite emotion or flip the switch of your memory, that switch just flipped for him. Under Adolf's fierce eyes, there spread an evil smile. He made himself comfortable beside the two women, snickering at his success. I will say one thing about Adolf; after his one second of worry for the two girls, he has never again shown an ounce of regret or sympathy regarding something he has done. The man is the definition of wickedness . . .

>>>PAUSE RECORDING<<<

As the words leave my mouth, a long but slow chill runs down my spine. It reminds me of my last day in New York before I saw my father. I pause to stretch, arch and crack my now tense back. As I am looking at the camera, I am frozen. My mind takes me on a quick dark ride with Adolf and his horrible, unspeakable acts of violence he has committed over the years. I shake my head. . . I had to disconnect from the intrusion of rage and death.

>>>RESUME RECORDING<<<

About a thousand miles away, as Adolf was getting ready for his night out with Juan, Zora was about to have her first encounter with some new roadie friends of Ivan. They were like no one she had met before. Like any group of characters we encounter, humans get stereotyped one way or another. Roadies are no exception. A roadie, however, does tend to live up to some of the hype that follows the stigma. Which is always funny to me when people find out I am a roadie. To society we are: Wild. Fun. Loud. Promiscuous. Drunk. Crazy. Nomadic. Pirates . . .

Okay, we could go on for days about the long list of roadie stereotypes, but this part of the story is how Ivan and Pie showed Zora how hard roadies love to party on days off. But it also details how they became bonded before anyone knew about the rollercoaster ride they would undergo together.

Unlike Adolf who was lying with his two Mexican beauties after his wild night with Juan, Ivan's morning was not starting on a high note. Like hitting the perfect windows in time when trafficking drugs, touring runs on a very tight timeframe also, hence why we work so well together. So, to be late on tour is a BIG no-no, and Ivan, by this time was missing his big load-in. Time is money. For instance, a domino effect happens if you have a late start for a Friday night show and it's hard to make up for that lost time. The tours of today deal with labor bills skyrocketing, the drivers running the risk of hitting overtime, and there's a chance that the Saturday show will be late. With that said, something as seemingly simple as the crew leaving the hotel on time is vital for the sake of the show. The concept of time hadn't faltered since the '70s when Ivan missed his first and last bus call.

Eight o'clock in the morning and no sign of Ivan. The bus pulled away from the hotel to head to the venue, leaving Ivan oil spotted. There is no worse feeling, especially when you realize you're late, missing out on a free ride to the venue, and now labeled "that" guy. The only thing that could potentially save Ivan's ass now was if Pie had missed the bus too.

Although he was out with Ivan and Zora most of the night, Pie managed to be downstairs in time for the lobby call. As seconds ticked away, Pie did what any tour friend would do before the bus departed; he asked them to call Ivan's room from the front desk (because there were no cell phones then). Every minute he had them re-call the room. He hoped Ivan would wake up, stuff his clothes in a bag, and save himself from embarrassment but it was not working. The famous walk of shame into a venue is nothing you want to experience as a roadie—especially in New York City. I guess this instance is where Ivan got one of his main rules for being out on tour with the roadies: everyone can have one "oops" moment. After that, it was a Greyhound bus ride home in the backseat next to the shitter.

In life, I have three people who I will try at all costs not to piss off. Number one is a Mexican mother wearing a pair of sandals. She will throw a chancla at you with ninja-like precision, which will hurt you. Number two is the heads of the cartel. They do not play nicely when mad. Number three would have to be a production manager.

Now, I have only had one production manager until I became one myself, but the times I angered Ivan, he made me pay with tears and humiliation but that was a lesson he had to hand down as not only a father figure but the manager. I would have rather taken a physical beating than the mental ones dished out on some of those early tours.

Bam-bam-bam! With a loud pounding at his hotel door by security, Ivan jumped to his feet into a lukewarm puddle. In dismay, he looked down to discover that he had managed to land in vomit, hopefully his. With a glance over to an empty side table where the clock and phone had been last night, his heart dropped when he saw them tangled in a broken mess by the hotel door. Late is late in the music business, but Ivan's three-hour delay was insane. He began the wild dance of panic packing, cursing in Czech with an intermittent American "Fuck!" for good measure.

Inevitably, you will forget something of great importance when rushing. And every minute that ticked past Ivan's call time meant his day would be more brutal once he finally arrived at the venue; he had witnessed the treatment of unpunctual band members and roadies. After Ivan threw his whole life into his suitcase, he sprinted for the door and down the hotel hallway, searching for the elevator. Of course, the elevator was not where he had left it the night before. He ran frantically in various directions until housekeeping could point him toward a successful escape route. With forty or maybe a hundred and forty incessant pushes of the down button, the elevator magically turned into the slowest moving contraption in North America. With time not on his side, he contemplated the stairs; a light jog in a sketchy New York hotel stairwell might sober him up.

Making his way down the five floors to the lobby became a nightmare. The bag that weighed thirty pounds the day before somehow was well over a thousand and seemed to enjoy finding every snag on the wall to slow Ivan down. He was finally at the front desk, and—to pour salt on an open wound—there was a line longer than the one at Ellis Island when the Rezniks first stepped off their boat.

After a brutal wait, Ivan was checked out and standing on the street corner, trying to hail a cab. His nervousness caused his stomach to twist into one big knot, and a recipe for disaster was brewing inside. With a hangover starting to kick in mixed with anxiety, he got into a taxi that smelt like it had been soaking in fake pine tree scent, armpit sweat, and cigarettes. This mixture of off-putting smells would make a sober person want to puke, so Ivan held back what felt like a round of rocket thrusts igniting in his guts. He reached his hand into his back pocket and realized he had forgotten his wallet in the hotel room. Speeding down Broadway in the foul-smelling cab, Ivan had one hand on his mouth and the other on his bag for an immediate exit. The cab came to a screeching halt when they finally made it to the venue. The door flew open, and Ivan bolted out of the cab. Ivan found a sparkle of hope when he discovered a five-dollar bill in the front pocket of his jeans. He wadded up the bill and threw it in the passenger window of the cab as he screamed, "Thanks!" and sprinted for the backstage door. Now in the venue, Ivan tried his best to play it cool.

As Ivan snuck into work in New York, Juan had work waiting for Adolf in El Paso. He had laid in bed with his two lady friends for as long as he could, but a hangover on par with a Category 5 hurricane required booze to keep him going. Laying there not wanting to move, his memory slowly led him back to the last shot of fine tequila the two new friends had in Juan's office before their night on the town.

It's crazy to think how Adolf transitioned from a fucked-up farm boy to a chauffeured drug cartel lackey. He was in heaven, sitting in the back of the stunning limousine. There was a tiny TV, a radio, and a minibar for him to enjoy. He touched every button twice, stuck his head out of the sunroof, and opened every compartment to peek inside, twice. Everything sparkled: the gold drink stirrers, the crystal glassware, the mirror-lined ceiling nestled within a crystal rim that cast beautiful rainbows from time to time on the leather seats, dependent upon the sunbeams playfully jumping off different surfaces. This was Adolf's childhood dream coming to life.

Adolf sipped champagne while the driver approached a palatial chateau on top of the mountain. After passing through the massive, gated entry and pulling into the circular driveway lined by yellow rosebushes, two men with machine guns were at military attention as the car stopped. As if a foreign dignitary was expected to exit the vehicle, the two men stood guard as a third appeared from the entrance to the mansion to open the car door for Adolf. Standing there in silence, he was in awe of the villa in front of him. The man welcomed him to the estate, directing Adolf to a guest suite and to dress in the robe located in the guest bath after his shower and that the tailor would be in shortly afterward to fit him for a suit. Once inside the enormous marble bathroom, Adolf found the robe, slippers, a bottle of tequila, and a pile of coke the size of a baseball. Passing on the party momentarily, he needed a shower and shave before any more blow found its way up his somehow still functioning nose; it wouldn't take long as you could imagine. Stepping out of the bathroom and into the bedroom, Adolf sighted Juan speaking to the tailor with a glass of fine tequila in one hand and a mirror on the table next to him with a large "A" written in cocaine. The tailor chuckled as he pulled the tape measure from around his neck and let Adolf finish his long line of blow. After all the measurements had been taken, Adolf asked where his clothes were, and Juan explained that he had his men burn those ratty things. He went on to say that if Adolf was going to go in public with him, he needed to fit in with the rest of his entourage. There was no room for a "food runner or bus boy." Juan was looking for a young, charismatic go-getter who wanted to help take over the world, one brick of coke at a time.

At the same time Adolf was getting his first tailored suit, Ivan and Zora were living it up in the New York City nightlife. By the way . . . you are missing out if you have never experienced the nightlife in the Big Apple. It's best to avoid the touristy places while visiting. Luckily for Ivan and Zora, they were not in a fancy dinner or a show mood but rather in a trashy bar and hot dog mood. Ivan had never experienced a bar until he joined this tour, and the other roadies started to take him under their wing to show him the ropes of the road. So, what did he do? He tried every bar he saw while on his first tour—and I mean all of them: fancy, gay, straight, small, large, club, after-hours club, stinky, sticky, X-rated, smoke-filled, smokeless, fire bars, ice bars, and even the swim-up style bars. (Okay, maybe that last one wasn't a thing yet, but you get my point.) But his all-time favorite to belly-up at were the real dingy, hole-in-the-wall type places. When they were kids, Ivan never drank, so now that he realized he liked it, it was on, sort of. Back home, Zora only knew him as the good son, the sweet one who was more interested in farm life.

So, when they sat down at the bar and he ordered a few drinks, Zora was pleased to see him coming out of his shell. She was shocked, though, when he chugged the beer and immediately knocked back the shot. Her innocent little brother was not so innocent anymore.

Any day off on tour for a roadie—rain or shine, you knew there would be a gathering. Usually, by mid-day, there is a drunken bar crawl started by a group of roadies somewhere in the world (that are never planned of course). This day was no different. It began as a casual hang between brother and sister until Pie showed up with his bag of blow and cash-filled pockets. Then in walked the next roadie, with his bag of blow, and the next until it was a full-blown party in the middle of the day. Remember there were no cell phones then, roadies just instinctually knew where to find the best party in any town. Before the cartel was even a thing, road crews have always come into a city, whether for one day or ten with a couple things in mind: taking over the local bar scene, running pool tables and snatching up all the loose women in town. Being a roadie came with an unofficial title to be a real-life land pirate. Kind of living up to the stereotype everyone pictures.

Back in El Paso, Adolf was having a quick flashback to child-hood. As a kid, he used to stare at himself in the family's one mirror and always wished his farm clothes would magically switch to an eye-catching three-piece suit. The new friends made their way out of the mansion to the limo, but before exiting the front door, Adolf caught himself in a mirror, the size of a two-story building, for the first time since arriving in Texas. He stopped and paused in awe at what he saw; he was in the black suit he had always imagined, but he never thought it would come true this quickly. Adolf had always wanted to be rich and powerful. So, seeing himself looking the part of the man in the suit he had always dreamt about being for so long made him realize he had a shot in hell. The limo pulled out of the driveway just as Juan started to pass another bottle of exception-al tequila around. Tonight, the men were heading to one of Juan's many clubs he owned in Juarez, Mexico. Crossing the border was usually not a hard thing for Juan. So, as the limo approached its exit for Mexico, it was speeding southbound like a bullet heading right for the narrow toll booth looking border crossing station.

Juan asked his young compadre for his immigration papers, but Adolf smiled and shook his head side to side. The whole limo went silent. It was a scene of a movie when all eyes turn to the guy in the back of the class who says something super stupid when asked for the answer. Then all eyes redirected to Juan. Juan's face shifted from cheerful to straight-faced, and he squinted his eyes. "You don't have your papers, *cabrón*? How the fuck do you expect us to cross?"

Adolf's face mirrored Juan's as he sat speechlessly. Juan clicked his tongue three times with annoyance as he looked over Adolf's shoulder to yell at the driver, "*Andalè*! Run them over if they get in the way." Juan glanced back over at his new friend, smirking. "Don't worry, amigo, we will get you across."

As the white limo came closer to the border-crossing booth, Adolf braced himself as he watched surrounding cars slow down. The limo swerved to an unoccupied lane blocked by small traffic cones. Adolf's face lost its color while Juan took a swig of tequila straight out of the bottle to keep it from spilling. Adolf caught the view of a border patrol agent holding a high-powered machine gun defensively, so the Czech dug his fingernails into the leather seating, waiting terrified for the bullets to pierce through the car. But, to his surprise, the agent lowered his gun and gave a quick wave of his hand as the limo blew into the neighboring country. All the men in the limo were in tears as they watched Adolf almost fall to the floor after inching himself closer to the edge of his seat in readiness for gunfire. Adolf soon realized that Juan loved to play practical jokes; he got a kick out of watching people shit themselves, literally.

As the sun was setting over the desert towns with Adolf and Juan in Juarez, the moon was starting to make its slow, long drive up into the heavens on the other side of the country with Ivan and Zora. Everyone knew it would be a wild night as the moon passed the skyscrapers and eventually took over the sky. The beers were going down quickly; the whiskey was smooth and fiery. This was a recipe for disaster. The group of roadies grew and was soon joined by a band member. They all wanted to meet the only woman Ivan had ever talked about, his sister. While a roadie's workday feels painfully slow, time off feels like it is running at triple the speed of sound. The second you sit at a bar in the afternoon, you order a beer and a shot. Then order your second round. Before you know it, it's last call—the saddest moment of an adult's life out at a bar.

There is one thing that can keep the party going for a roadie when "Last call!" is yelled in unison by the bartenders and bouncers. Usually, we have tour buses full of free booze where we can continue drinking our faces off. Sadly, New York City doesn't offer the luxury of accessible parking so buses were on the other side of the river till morning. Alternatively, if you know the right people, you can find a late-night bar in the city, but as those famous last words to get out were called, Ivan had a plan. He wanted to visit his brother and sister's apartment down the road; besides, Adolf was sure to have some cheap liquor under the sink. Now, this may sound like a safe bet, but you may find yourself traveling down a rabbit hole when you walk too far away from your hotel and temptation is at every corner. This is where Murphy's law kicks into gear, and all things will inevitably go belly up, especially after 2am.

Zora and Adolf's apartment was a little red-bricked building that offered residents a cozy Skid Row vibe as junkies and trash littered the stairs. Once inside the building, the paper-thin walls merely kept your neighbor from peering into your apartment. The roaches were of comparable size to the rats caught scurrying around the outside dumpsters and walking upright down the halls. But there was booze and more cigarettes—a must for anyone as drunk as Ivan. Zora, her very drunk younger brother, and a girl who had latched on to him at some point made it into the apartment. This was Zora's first time partaking in an all-day drinking marathon, so she was done and fading fast. With no one left except this random girl, Ivan decided they could have a better party back in his hotel room with Adolf's half-empty plastic bottle of cheap vodka that was missing the cap. Here we see a critical error in Ivan's thought process—the perverse mentality that he could make it back to his hotel room, have relations with this chick, and then somehow be ready for a lobby call. After a night like this, only the backline techs would be successful because, well, they don't have to be up as early as the remaining crew. The kid got greedy.

While Ivan was trying to get his new female companion back to his hotel room, Adolf was in a different bar scene, seemingly worlds away. Over the years of hanging with our cartel brothers, we've learned that roadies and the Mexican cartel guys love the same shit. We may dress differently and not have as many kills (or any), but we love booze. We love beautiful women and men. We love to have a great time at the expense of our livers and relationships. Juan and crew got escorted through the club's back door near the kitchen. Once they were seated at the VIP table, Adolf noticed everyone was staring at them. He leaned over to Juan and whispered curiously, "How powerful are you?"

Juan laughed and simply explained that this was his nightclub and kind of a big deal in Mexico. Adolf still didn't understand what it really meant to be hanging out with the head of one of Mexico's largest cartels, who was also a Robin Hood figure in the community to most. He was a savior in considerable ways to so many who looked to him for protection and money to survive.

By the time more of Juan's men showed up, the tequila and cocaine couldn't be slowed down; the servers and dancers surrounded their table like seagulls who smell fresh fish at outdoor markets. Even though many of Juan's entourage were at the table, he took a real liking to his new gringo friend who he kept close. They spent most of the night talking about Adolf's desires and discussing how much he enjoyed this new adventure in Texas and Mexico. Of course, Juan would tell him things like, "Well, you know, you can always have a home here with us if that is what you desire," and he would emphasize, "We would take much better care of you than those Italians do if you and your sister moved here."

Juan was attention-grabbing, fascinating, and said precisely what Adolf wanted to hear at all the right times. Juan had Adolf locked in with his tractor beam stare and was increasing the power with stories and visions of grandeur. He and his men oozed power and testosterone; Adolf admired their jet-black hair, the guns on their hips, gold watches and their alligator shoes. Adolf felt like he was part of a family, sitting with top generals and even some cartel sicarios—although he had no clue at the time.

The conversation shifted not long after a few more of Juan's men showed up. While Adolf expected to party the night away, Juan wasn't a frat boy president looking to snort coke and play grab-ass until daylight. No, Juan and his men were all there to decide if they would keep going down the same path of trafficking or move in a new direction. They began talking about expanding and moving more products around the states. There is no room for lying or stealing in the cartel business, and you must hold up your side of the deal. Juan had a zero-tolerance policy when it came to these matters. The conversations were in Spanish for the most part, but Juan was doing a great job of keeping Adolf in the loop. Juan directed the topic toward Ivan's career on the road with bands. When the last of the cartel showed up, Juan turned to Adolf and said, "In business, there is one rule when it comes to money and friends: keep them separate. This is not 'friendness'; it is business. No one gets special treatment. No one."

Adolf was shattered. Extremely drunk. The man was running on unhealthy amounts of sleep and cocaine. This bar normally had a very strict policy for patrons but tonight it was a little more relaxed than some of the ones Ivan and Zora had experienced in New York. Seeing that Juan owned this place, anything at Juan's table was a go. The more blacked out Adolf got on booze, the more cocaine was brought to the table to sober him up. Then more shots. It was a vicious cycle for the young man, but Juan needed him that way to finish the deal that he was about to sign in blood.

Juan was a smooth, calculated man who knew how to get what he wanted in life. With millions of dollars and a golden tongue, he could charm men and women with his incredible Spanish swagger. Adolf was eating it all up. Juan saw something in Adolf that he didn't see in the Italians anymore. That was a drive to win at all costs. He also saw dollar signs regarding Adolf's brother being in the music industry. The music business was not a new source of money for people around the world, but the touring side was an untapped goldmine waiting for someone to capitalize on its infancy, no-rules lifestyle and zero regulations. In other words, Juan saw a lawless society ripe for the picking. This night was the catalyst that sparked the start of one of the most significant drug trafficking and money laundering schemes of all time. One that spanned all fifty states and would eventually move into some of the world's biggest countries.

I think about the old saying that it's always darkest before dawn—

though kind of not true—the point was, that it's going to get worse before it gets better. Buckle up, cowboy. This statement would ring true for both men once they woke up. Ivan's hangover was not helping his memory as he paced one of the concourse bathrooms, trying to figure out where he had left his wallet. The last memory he had before laying his head on that comfy hotel pillow was a blurry silhouette of a woman standing at the foot of the bed in his room. Did it fall out of his pocket while packing? That couldn't be because he always kept the wallet in a shoe when he slept. So, it was gone before . . .

Then it hit him. That girl robbed him. That sweet, lovely girl had played him all night. She was on him when he took out that cash from his wallet at the first pub. There was no time to cry over lost cash; he had bigger issues like finally talking with Pie.

There is no way to sneak into work when you're late. It seems like the one person you do not want to cross paths with is the first person you inevitably encounter. With no wallet nor tour ID laminate, Ivan swallowed his pride and went to find Pie. Ivan was strong and knew he had messed up, so he was the first to admit that; it felt as though he had disappointed his father. After their conversation, Ivan had to suck it up and finish his duties on tour. Unfortunately, sobering up requires the hangover process. It was a full-frontal assault as if Armageddon was transpiring in his skull. There was no hiding, sleeping, or taking a break. Everyone made sure of it. That is how hangovers on the road typically go. You rage till the sun comes up, stumble into work, and get mentally abused by coworkers until you eventually climb into your bunk and pray to the roadie gods for a better day tomorrow.

In Texas, Adolf hung his legs over the edge of the bed, head in his hands, staring at the blood-stained shirt and pants. A knock at the door interrupted his thoughts, and a piece of paper was slipped under it. "On the cart in front of your door, you will find some fresh clothes and black coffee to help with the headache. Come downstairs when you are dressed, and I will have my butler waiting for you," the note said. The clothes on the cart were a more southwestern Mexican cowboy look. There were boots, a nice button-snap denim shirt, and a fresh pair of Levi's. After getting dressed, Adolf went downstairs and met the butler who escorted him accordingly.

"Hola, gringo!" Juan shouted from his poolside table in the courtyard. Juan stood up and greeted Adolf with a welcoming that took him by surprise. The two men sat for a quick bite of food and talked over some new business and what Adolf would say to the Italians once he was back in New York. This was not what he expected on his trip, but he was now on Juan's payroll by the sound of it. Adolf was all ears as he tried not to stare at Juan who was strapped with two revolvers in holsters under his arms. Adolf had a few more questions about the drop and where he needed to go once he had made it back to New York City, but Juan had moved on and was too busy discussing the two girls that Adolf came home with. Juan went on and on about the night and how great it was to have fresh blood on the team. He reminded Adolf to set up the meeting with Ivan like they had discussed the night prior. Confused, Adolf merely nodded his head. He knew there was no room for negotiations at this point. He was like those two revolvers tucked under his arms; Juan owned him and would use him how he saw fit.

It was getting late in the day. If Adolf wanted to get a jump on the long drive back, he would need to leave soon. With a few more chuckles and a big handshake, the new boss had one recommendation for him. He needed to move to El Paso sooner than later. Adolf coughed while trying to sip his coffee and just shook his head up and down. Not long after finding out he was now a Texan, Juan had a couple of the cartel members walk Adolf out to his new car that he would take back to New York City. One soldier dropped a big bag of blow into one of Adolf's hands while the other gave him his pistol just in case of any trouble. It was time for the long drive back.

After a nice drive down the mountain, just before turning onto the highway back home, the newest member of the Mexican cartel gazed into the rearview mirror, and memories from the wild night hit him. Sweat started to bead up on his brow, and he was hit by a wave of adrenalin. He had not felt this way since the first time he had helped his father kill an animal. Taking a deep breath in and exhaling slowly, Adolf smiled, and his heart rate decelerated. He smiled because he remembered why his clothes were drenched in blood. The night started to reveal its darkness in his mind. The vision of the man entering the club and his smirk was unforgettable. As it all played back in Adolf's mind, it made sense why he was Juan's new guy. He had murdered Juan's top man who dealt directly with the Italians in New York.

About a few hours into the drive and moving relatively quickly, the night started to take over the sky. With the sun setting behind him, Adolf reached for a cigarette to take the edge off. Then, a set of blue and red lights interrupted his peace. Adolf searched under the seat for a solution. He was going to have to kill again. He knew Juan would come after him if he got busted by the cops. Just as Adolf was slowing down to pull off to the side of the road, the state trooper hit the siren a few times . . . then accelerated and blew past him on the left.

Adolf thought about the plan regarding Ivan. How would he get his younger brother to help him start trafficking dope across the country for Juan? How was he going to get the Italians to cooperate with his new role? Driving east toward New York for what possibly could be the last time, the blue desert sky was shifting to beautiful hints of purples and deep reds that saturated the sky as dusk set in, and slowly the night faded into the black darkness much like the heart of Adolf. Adolf's rage and obsession with money and power grew with each mile marker that passed him in the night. He had gotten a taste of everything he had longed for since he was a young boy, and Juan was holding the key to unlock his deepest, darkest desires . . .

The Big Apple didn't know, but a storm was blowing in from the west.

>>>STOP RECORDING<<<

I lit a cigarette and wished I could stay outside all day, but sadly the band just arrived. Time to go in and get back to work.

CHAPTER 6

The Return to and Departure from NYC

A day off in another hotel room

Sitting near my hotel room window, I notice a slight hole in the wall above the bed. Most people would think nothing of this, but I know I am being watched. Most of these hotels are operated at some level by the cartel. Sometimes it's the staff cleaning the rooms and sometimes it is the manager running the whole operation. Only one, maybe two, at the very top truly know how big the cartel's reach around the world is. Maybe this is what got my father in trouble. He knew the extent, and someone got nervous. For all that it is worth, the cartel I work for is like a new-age-hybrid-super-society, we are everywhere. All who are part of this ever-growing subset of people are weaved right along normal everyday people. We just live, breathe and answer to the internal government Juan has created. The people in this cartel are brainwashed and this mini society is fiercely loyal to the hand that feeds them, even if they have never seen where the hand gets its food. But more on that later. Before I continue, I decide to dig around the room and see if I'm being paranoid at this point or whether today is when these pricks finally come for me.

After a decent sweep of the room, I find nothing. So, I pick up my phone, plug in my earphones, and hit record . . .

>>>START RECORDING<<<

This is video diary #5 October 19, 2009. Salt Lake City, Utah.

Hello, Internet. What I'm about to say is going to sound crazy but hear me out before I get into the story again. This is what I have to do every time I get into a new room . . .

[I spin around to capture—the make-shift bunker—that used to be my room with my phone camera to show the disarray.]

These hotels aren't safe because most of the ones we stay at during tours are cartel owned and operated. It is one way to kick back more money from the artists to the cartel but it also helps the roadie cartel members have a safe place to communicate to the heads of the operation. So, to ensure my safety for now, I have to practically ransack the place and barricade myself in for the night. I construct a bed in the middle of the floor and sit here with my gun ready to go so I'm not sleeping in a typical spot. I never know if bullets are going to fly through the mattress. Look, I know my days are numbered. I'm just trying to get as many video entries out to the world as possible before that day, so I go to these extremes now.

Alright, enough about my hotel room adventures. We'll get back to my family and how we got into the cocaine trafficking business. Let's see . . . I left off with Adolf driving back to New York City . . . right . . . yeah, he was on his way back.

During his long drive back to the city, Adolf had nothing but time to spend thinking, scheming, and dreaming. One colossal emotion kept coming over the young Adolf that had nothing to do with coke or women or a night of partying. No, this was the first time he felt like part of a family in his life now that Juan made him feel like he belonged—within forty-eight hours mind you!—opening the door to all of Adolf's wildest fantasies about power, money, and what he thought life was truly about. Aside from Zora and a few Italian mob guys, no one knew Adolf existed, so he was a very small goldfish in a big pond of koi fish. He was sick of being a nobody. Not this time and not in what would be his second "family." He was ready for his time in the spotlight. To be a true go-to man for this organization.

In life, we tend to meet someone who gives us courage. Juan was that guy, and the kid that left New York was returning as a man. Adolf was ready to defend his new boss's cartel to the bitter end with blood still embedded in the corners of his nails. Visions replayed in Adolf's mind of stabbing one of Juan's right-hand men in the neck with dull ice tongs in the limo. When the tongs finally did penetrate the skin, he was leaking so much blood from his face that it didn't matter that Adolf finally found the jugular. All this was happening while they were driving out to a ranch in the middle of the desert where they had the kid take the lifeless body from the limo and do the one thing he was great at. While Juan and his men stood by feeding his ego and pumping the young Adolf with more booze and dope, he butchered the corpse and threw his body parts into a steel drum full of acid. The last thing Adolf could remember that night was sealing it and rolling that barrel into a pit where a dozen or more sat piled on top of one another in the Mexican sand.

At breakfast, before Adolf left, Juan tasked him to return to the Big Apple to execute with the same passion like with Juan's long-time friend and business partner. Juan reminded Adolf that he was family now, and family helps each other out . . . and you never take from the hand that feeds you. Sounded pretty straightforward to Adolf. Get to the city and give that Italian mob boss the special treatment Juan thought he deserved for trying to take advantage of him.

Look, we know what it is like starting a new job. We tend to be over-achievers to impress the new boss before settling in. The difference in Adolf's case was that he didn't have a choice; I'm sure you can guess where he would end up if he chose not to help his new family. It didn't take long for Adolf to feel like the Italians had set him up for failure in Texas when meeting Juan. They were probably betting on him getting killed down there, but Juan read that situation and flipped it on them the second that kid drove onto his car lot. So, Juan did the most logical thing anyone would do in that position; he sent a very pissed-off man back to wreak vengeance upon them. Then Juan could hopefully take back control of the money flow and cocaine trafficking to the north. People forget what loyalty will bring you in business and life, and the Italian mob boss didn't realize the impact Juan would have on this kid. Plus, Juan had done one thing the Italian mob didn't. He gave Adolf respect and money— cold hard—*cash in hand!*—and a lot of it.

Adolf was coming back to New York City with more money than the mob would ever pay him in a lifetime. Juan didn't see him as a disposable lost soul. He saw him as an investment to the cartel that would not be swayed from his new direction. And while Adolf knew Juan saw something special in him, he was driven by a force greater than happiness or love or even friendship. Adolf was driven by power and money. With a deeper, darker, richer sense of energy, Adolf would be willing to do anything to please the man who could pave the future with golden roads, leading the young man to eternal abundance if he did what he was told.

With the big city lights on the horizon, the little red needle of

Adolf's car was now pointing to empty, but he wasn't worried. He was topped off with premium Mexican coke and only blocks away from his first stop. One of the cartel soldiers instructed him to drop the car off at a junkyard out in New Jersey, where he would meet a man that goes by Bobby (pronounced Baah-be). Even though Adolf's reason for going to Texas was to pick up a "package" for the Italians, Juan made it clear that there was never a package, but a set up for the kid. So, Juan did what Juan does best. He made a few phone calls, and before Adolf paid a visit to his soon to be ex-boss, he was tasked with a small payment drop off. Much like the food Adolf once delivered to the Italian mob boss, he knew it was not his business to ask why he had to go see Bobby first, and he sure as hell didn't ask what was in the trunk for the guys at the junkyard.

When Adolf pulled into the entrance of the old junkyard, there sat an old man, haggard and tired looking. The man was sitting under a single yellow incandescent light bulb, eating a sandwich dripping with mayonnaise while reading a newspaper. He was listening to a rock n' roll station, which was playing on an old beat-up silver radio in his little security booth. The man and his hands were as greasy and as oil stained as the window he sat behind. Adolf rolled down his window to explain who he was, but before a word came out, the security guard told him to follow the road to the back of a large building toward the end of the property not far from the water; there, Adolf would find what he was looking for.

Adolf was surprised but didn't argue; he just pulled through the entrance and followed directions. He took a short cruise past some beat-up cars, heavy equipment, and a machine with dinosaur-looking teeth that could tear a body into a thousand cubes if one "accidentally" fell into it. After a slight bend in the road, Adolf found what he was looking for behind a car press that was having a ball turning a full-sized station wagon into a television-sized cube. Standing by the trunk of a long four-door sedan stood two men. Pulling up slowly, Adolf stopped a few feet from the men and asked if they knew where he could find Bobby. The plumper of the two fellas spoke in a very thick East Coast accent. "Right heeah, kid."

Adolf didn't take long to realize that Bobby was not Mexican and didn't speak or act like any of the cartel members he was hanging with. He unconsciously shrugged his shoulders. Juan said to find him, so in his mind, he hoped that this wasn't a bigger set up or another test from his old mob boss. Bobby walked over to the kid, and after a very manly handshake, he then introduced Adolf to the manager who would harbor the car. As someone who does what he is told, Adolf turned to Bobby and said, "I was told to make sure you got what was in the trunk. It's a bag, I think, but I didn't look inside, I swear."

"I knows ya didn't look, kid," Bobby said to Adolf. He shook the manager's hand and then turned to Adolf once again. "Now go get into the back of that black car. We gots business that needs tending to."

Adolf was relieved to give the car to his new driver, but he knew he wasn't done for the day as he climbed into the back seat per Bobby's instructions. The next stop was to pay the Italians a little visit at the restaurant. As the two pulled out onto the main road from the junkyards' dirty and semi-muddy roads, Bobby grabbed something from his bag that he had pulled from the trunk before they left. Not sure what was happening in the front of the vehicle as he watched Bobby dig around the bag, Adolf was a bit uneasy and pushed back into his seat when Bobby's big arm flew toward him.

"WHOA! WHAT THE . . ." Adolf blurted.

Bobby snapped back instantly, "Kid, don't 'WHOA' at me. I ain't no horse, and I ain't gonna shoot ya. Here's a little somethin' I was told to give ya." Bobby handed Adolf an envelope. Inside was a handwritten letter. The letter read:

YOU MADE ME PROUD THIS WEEK. GO QUIT THAT SHITTY OLD JOB IN STYLE, YOU KNOW, JUST LIKE WE TALKED ABOUT. BOBBY HAS MORE GIFTS FOR YOU AND YOUR FAMILY, SOON YOU WILL GET SOME FLIGHT INFO TO COME START YOUR NEW LIFE IN TEXAS. BRING YOUR SISTER AND BROTHER. SEE YOU VERY SOON. -J-

Adolf smiled and perked up because he knew this meant it was his turn to test his old employer to see their reaction when his face came walking back into that restaurant. The kid was back, and Little Italy had no idea what was about to shake the foundation that district had been built on. The black sedan pulled up outside the Three P's Italian restaurant. Bobby got out of the car to open the door for Adolf, but he was too slow; the back door was left open, and the seat was empty. Adolf was heading for the front doors with a one-track mind. With each step closer to the front doors, he could hear the cheesy Italian music he hated hearing every time he walked in for work. To put it in perspective, the Italians weren't going for three-star Michelin dining but more of an old Hollywood movie set . . . you know, so that way everyone knew it was an Italian joint. Their Italian ancestors were probably rolling around in their graves, but then again, this was just a drug front.

Adolf paused, placing one hand on the door and the other on his gun holstered the same way as Juan holstered his. The kid's delay was long enough to where Bobby had caught up and almost had to nudge him. Adolf took a deep breath to calm his . . . A LOUD CRASH, then the sound of glass shattering rang through the building as Adolf flung open the door, causing the handle to shatter the glass that decorated the wall. He steered through the staff members who were running for the front door. Adolf found the mob boss sitting at his usual dining table.

Before the mob's two security guards could react, Adolf had his gun out and pointed it right at the head honcho's forehead. It was like they were staring at a ghost. No one at that table expected to see this kid again. He was standing taller than ever, with his brown eyes now drilling holes in them all. He was getting ready to deliver something to them that he had let boil with rage deep inside him on that long drive back. With nowhere to run, Adolf explained to his old boss that their little operation now belonged to Juan and his cartel. He then went on to state that whatever money they owed to Juan must be paid in full by the end of the week and that there would be no more buying drugs or guns from anyone other than Juan's cartel. The Italians also were forced to make a choice: turn over the men they were getting drugs from so they could be dealt with accordingly, or each mob member's family would be visited and turned into food for the wild ranch hogs and coyotes.

Juan was fed up with the Italians and had decided to place a heavy tax on all their businesses; he would take a cut, or there would be hell to pay. They had angered one of the world's largest and oldest cartels who were making a comeback, and Juan with his new bulldog Adolf, was ready to flex on anyone standing in his way to world domination.

Adolf had fire in his eyes he was so mad. This wasn't an act he was performing to throw a scare into the Italians. No, his blood boiled with each word that came out of his mouth. He wanted revenge for their actions of sending him down to Texas to get killed. So, to rub salt in the mob boss's open wound, he forced him to get on his hands and knees and beg Adolf for forgiveness. This was one of the biggest insults he thought he could do to the old man sitting behind his chicken parmesan. The old man stood and threw his napkin onto the table, paused, looked at Adolf with hostility, tilted his head up, and in his soft Italian voice, said,

"If you ever talk to me like that again, you little f . . ."

One shot rang from Adolf's revolver, leaving a hole in the old mobster's forehead as his lifeless body went down to its knees before eventually lying like cooked spaghetti drenched in marinara sauce. As the two goons sat with their mouths open in shock, two more shots rang out. Without a pause for a single breath from the two—*bang, bang!* Brushing off the splattered food, wine, and blood that had hit his new denim pants and shirt from those mobsters hitting the table and flinging food everywhere, Adolf turned and pointed his gun at each person left in that building. As he looked at the kitchen and bar staff, who had crouched under tables for safety, he smirked and reminded them they answered to a new god. And like that, Adolf calmly holstered his revolver and walked out of his first job in the big city.

In any business, legal or illegal, power can shift in the blink of an eye, much like a CEO who is caught inside-trading and jumps to his death. (However, it may go down, there is always someone gunning for your seat.) The move Juan pulled off through Adolf set the tone for who was about to run the show until the next heavyweight took a swing at the champ. Who holds power in the Americas regarding drugs, guns, and money is significant. And not just to the holder, obviously, but to the government too.

(I took a very brief pause and gave a big wink into the camera.)

After taking control of his father's failing cartel, Juan had one vision: to have possession of all the cocaine in North America—not only with transportation but also distribution around the states and cities. The Italians had long held control of many areas, but with a heavy tax on them now, they were just the start of a long list of organized crime syndicates about to pay dearly to Juan. Juan wanted to set the bar so high that no one, not even God, could touch him.

Riding in the sedan to return to Zora and his apartment, Adolf thought of what Juan had said to him over the last couple of days. Taking on the responsibility of helping Juan rebuild his cartel wouldn't be easy. Some of the biggest struggles recently in the failing cartel were loyalty, corruption from within, and the lack of support coming from government agencies. The time had come for Juan to clean house. He was a sinking ship with sharks surrounding the boat. Initially, Adolf didn't see himself as the cartel's savior, but it was worth a shot. It would come with a heavy price: Adolf's life and his two family members. By signing his name in blood, he now had to be willing to do whatever Juan asked of him. To Adolf, this was a game of life and death where he was clearly in control, and if you crossed him, you ended up in a fifty-gallon drum of acid somewhere in the Mexican desert. The three siblings would soon, once again, never be able to go back to life as they knew it.

Pulling up in front of the apartment, Bobby told Adolf that living in a dumpster would be a step up from this place and asked if he was ready to kiss it goodbye. The kid from Czechoslovakia had finally made some money by going to work for Juan, and leaving this apartment was a surreal moment. He had dreamt of riches and was excited to share the news of his recent wealth. On top of the money he now had in his pockets, Adolf was just as excited to tell his siblings that their new home would be in Texas. Adolf didn't have any words for Bobby's original question as he sat in the back seat, inching closer. He just stared at his old life waving goodbye as he took a giant step into the darkness that was his future.

Before the car could come to a complete stop, Adolf exited the sedan and sprinted for the stairs up to his soon-to-be former apartment. Blowing through the tiny shoebox apartment door, he realized it was empty. The house was a mess, and it looked like someone had gone through Zora's belongings. In a bit of panic, Adolf asked Bobby if this looked like the work of the Italians. "Could they have gotten to her that fast?" Adolf screamed as he started to ask so many questions that Bobby eventually had to slap him to calm him down.

With everything finally starting to go right in Adolf's life, this was the last thing he needed. Where the hell did she go? How would he ever start to look for her? Maybe he could go to her, "job," kind of hard to find someone who hustles people out of money unless they work in the government. Or here is an even better idea . . . Adolf could call the cops! Yeah, that would go over really well with Juan and all his new associates. Pacing the floor and talking to himself, Adolf was actually worried about something outside himself for once, maybe or maybe he was just worried about his new lifestyle having a hiccup.

Suddenly, Adolf and Bobby heard footsteps approaching the front door. Both men reached for their guns and pulled the hammers back on their revolvers. The footsteps stopped short of the paper-thin door and then . . . nothing. There was an eerie long pause, one that allowed both men to split to either side of the small room and draw their guns. The door slowly started to open. A sweet and soft whistling began as the handle slowly turned. The door opened; it was Zora. She screamed so loud! Zora was so startled by the guns pointed at her; she dropped the brown bag she had been carrying. Adolf sighed with relief and put his weapon away; Bobby quickly followed suit. As the two siblings shared a hug, Bobby was nice enough to clean the spilled contents of the bag. Thinking Adolf would arrive home the upcoming day, Zora had picked up a bottle of cheap vodka and a couple of chocolate bars to surprise the road warrior on his valiant return.

While the Reznik kids talked and caught up, Bobby went to work. See, Bobby had been working for Juan for a while and in many roles over the years. Cartel security was one for a while, so his mind had instantly figured one of the kitchen staff informed the mob upon finding out what Adolf had done to the boss. So, like any good mob faction, they would retaliate quickly by taking a hit out on Zora.

Chuckling to himself, he was obviously relieved that this was not the case . . . yet. So, he did what any great head of security would do. He called for reinforcements and had a few of his top New York thugs help keep an eye out on the siblings while they made their way around the city. At times, Adolf acted like a young alfa male lion in the wild, and Juan had already seen that and knew how to handle it. Hence Bobby's arrival. He was so critical to protecting Juan's new golden ticket, not just from Adolf's ego trying to cash a check too big, but clearly, he was already going to have an enemy or two looking for him in the city. So, Bobby was Adolf's babysitter for the next few days until they left for their new lives in Texas.

There was one goal. Adolf and Zora needed to be in El Paso so Adolf could broker a meeting between Ivan and Juan to start rewriting the drug trafficking game. The old game had been played out and it was time to expand. After Bobby cleared the broken glass and had his little chuckle, all-business Bobby went into full-dad-mode Bobby. He told the two they had a few minutes to grab whatever junk they wanted to keep and, "kiss their rodent friends goodbye; it was time to scram." He worried that the Italians would eventually return for them. Zora chimed in and explained that she would be hearing from Ivan either that night or the next day, and they would need to stay to explain and give him a new number to reach the siblings. Bobby, a quick thinker, went to the phone on a corner table again, and in a brief couple of words, he got another one of his thugs to come and sit by the phone until Ivan called.

It had not been more than ten minutes, but Bobby was ready and told the duo it was time to go. Juan had arranged for them to have a suite off Fifth Avenue until their home in Texas was ready. This was huge for the siblings—particularly Zora since her only real adventure in America had been when she saw Ivan and his roadie friends. She was happy to have Adolf back in town, but she was also not pleased with how much more selfish he had become. During the car ride, he only cared to talk to her about this new man Juan and how they were now part of some group out of Mexico. This annoyed her because anytime she tried to tell him about her time with Ivan and his roadie friends or how this move was going to affect her life, Adolf would interrupt her. He was continually inserting how they would be a part of this gang or mob and how they would be rich beyond belief. Bobby smirked a little as he watched them through the rearview mirror argue back and forth.

Finally arriving at the hotel, Bobby told them to keep it down as they entered the lobby. It's one thing to speak about the cartel in the back seat of a car. It's a whole other thing to talk in public about it. They didn't listen. Like any "father" would, Bobby separated the two bickering siblings until they got to the suite. The suite was beautiful. So beautiful that the two had all but forgotten what they were mad at each other about. It had multiple bedrooms, multiple bathrooms, multiple places to sit—it had multiple everything. Zora expressed that it was three or four times the size of the little apartment they had been living in. She might have been most excited that they each got their own bathroom equipped with a shower and a giant soaking bathtub. Coming from a small farm town where she only dreamt of luxury like this, Zora was almost in tears with all the amenities. Plus, she didn't have to share them with anyone. The main luxury the two had never had before was room service, which was crucial since Bobby instructed them not to leave under any circumstances. The Italian mob, by now, knew the fate of their longtime mob boss. So, they would look for the kid who once delivered for them. Not long after they settled into their new penthouse lifestyle, a few of the men Bobby had called arrived to add extra security to the ground floor entrances and the top floor where the two were staying.

At one point in the conversation, Bobby mentioned that the room service manager was one of Juan's Mexican cartel family. This instantly perked up Adolf's ears; his statement sparked great curiosity. He asked Bobby what the man was doing working that job if he was in the cartel making so much money. Bobby laughed and, without going into the complete story, explained that Juan's father tried to spread his cartel across North and South America, his dream was to cover the globe with cartel members and their families. He did this in the hope of getting members into day-to-day jobs that ranged from cops, food servers and mechanics, all the way to government officials and even the clergy to help facilitate the cartel's needs over the years. Adolf didn't understand the full scope of just what this meant, but he nodded his head in agreement and remembered Juan explaining something similar in his office. Impressed but also hungry from his long journey into town, he then asked more about the actual room service menu and what he could order. I guess a long drive into a mob hit, really sparks an appetite.

Life changed instantly for the siblings. Ivan was the only one who didn't have to watch his back yet, but that target would eventually come for him. Next, Bobby explained to the duo the phone rules. Under zero circumstances were they to say anything business-related over the phone to anyone, not even if Juan was to call, which he would because that is what he did, he checked in on his investments from time to time. This was obviously just to ensure information about them, and the cartel couldn't be leaked to anyone. Bobby said slowly, "Stay here. Don't leave," and added sarcastically, "or I'll be killin' yas myself."

With Bobby gone for the night, Zora's calm and semi-cool demeanor quickly flipped, and she lost her shit on Adolf. There were no punches thrown that evening, but she verbally assaulted him with questions for the next couple of hours. What happened in Texas? Who is Juan? Why is there blood on your clothes? Why do you have all this money? Who the hell is Bobby? Why are we prisoners in a hotel now? And what in the world is a cartel? The volume and intensity in her voice rose as each question flew at Adolf in her native tongue. Watching Zora pace between the two rooms, Adolf told her to calm down; this was the rich American dream they had always talked about back home in Czechoslovakia.

"I never dreamt of being in a . . . Mexican boys club!" Zora barked in a bitter sarcastic child's voice as she flung her hands into the air.

"Cartel," Adolf replied mockingly, and Zora dispatched a harsh glare that irritated him into a raging bull. "You. Want. Money!" Adolf snapped. "Now we have a chance to make unlimited amounts of it. So, grow up and be a fucking team player." Adolf pointed to the door, and—in a dark and evil voice she had never heard before—he said, "Or you can slum in the streets if you don't want this life that I'm offering you." He knew deep down this would cut her to the bone—even though she had always been a team player—and seal her fate as his accomplice for life.

Adolf described how Juan wanted them to be part of this new generation of cartel members to take over the states . . . and the world when the time was right. He also buttered his little sister's imagination up with short quips about Juan's lavish lifestyle and all the amenities at his houses. Zora, though seemingly sweet on the outside, was even more greedy than her big brother. So, after rolling her eyes at his offhand comments about her living on the streets again, her tune changed. Her smile grew again at the thought of easy money, fancy cars, fine-cut clothing, and gold. But when Adolf couldn't explain how they would actually pull this new gig off other than it would fall on Ivan to get these bands and the touring industry to comply with transporting the coke for the cartel, Zora's smile instantly shrunk. She reminded Adolf that he had dragged them halfway across the world, and she wasn't confident about moving again for a half-ass plan involving Ivan and his long-haired friends. All she wanted was the payout of a lifetime. With a little more persuasion, Adolf finally got her to believe this cartel scheme was going to work. He just had to speak to Ivan . . . who was at this point a ghost to them. Zora squinted sarcastically and then raised the corners of her lips; it was kind of a smile, but it more stated to Adolf that his conversation with Ivan was going to have to be a good one to get him on board. Otherwise, she threatened, she was going to kill him.

This was not a typical contract deal between Juan and the siblings, but their commitment was signed in blood long before Adolf made it back to New York. There was no time to waste arguing about what had happened or even how Adolf decided he should put all their lives in his hands again. The two had been going at each other's throats for hours once Zora brought up Ivan, and how Adolf needed to be nice when he asked him. They were wasting valuable time that they needed to use for planning and executing how they were going to pull this gig off. Juan was not a man that took kindly to being lied to, which Adolf knew firsthand. So, there was no going back on their deal; therefore, not much more could be said that night. Zora was still fired up from a long night she did not see coming. As she retired to her room, still angry that Adolf had signed her up to be a "cartel" member, she was relieved that she would not have to share a floor or old mattress with him for the first time since the farm. She had a bed. And a big one at that, with the most comfy sheets ever.

The mind and self-doubt can be an evil, dark twisting road, where anyone can get lost and so many never return from that unforgiving place. I have been there recently and soon Zora's brother was going to go there.

Laying in his own room, staring at the ceiling and the lights dancing in his peripherals from the street below, Adolf started to question if he could actually help Juan rebuild his cartel. He realized there was more to this cartel life than just moving drugs. What if they couldn't move the amount of drugs he promised that night in Juarez? Hell, he can't even remember the amount. Would he and his siblings now become the drug mules carrying the product back and forth across the country? Who were the drivers going to actually be? How much could Ivan even load into his truck? Are these big trucks like I saw on my drive? Are there multiple trucks? How would they hide it? What amount of cocaine does Juan actually want to move monthly? All night, he lay there thinking about the what-ifs and as hard as he tried, he couldn't remember any of Ivan's multiple rambling phone calls about work. As the morning light crept through the blinds of his spacious room, so did thoughts of death. The joy of being Juan's new guy was gone. Now a slight panic started to set in as he lay next to the imaginary list of "what-ifs." Little to no sleep will take its toll on any man, especially one who is nervous about his new boss potentially not liking how he has handled things so far. Every creak caused paranoia, and with images of torture dancing around in his mind, he felt the room close in on him. His gun was not far from him. Adolf's eyes were now fixed on the gun as his mind started to play tricks on him about death . . .

Just before Adolf went into an anxiety-driven meltdown, Zora entered the room. With the thought of some crazed maniac busting down her door all night, she didn't get much sleep either. As she slumped into a chair in the corner of the room, she started to ramble to Adolf in her sleep-deprived state. She was quick to jump right back into the conversation from last night, but this time it was not about how stupid Adolf was, which surprised him. It was how the hell they might start to pull this hustle off. Zora described some men (roadies) that Ivan had been hanging around when he came through New York City just a few days earlier. She noted them moving gear from city to city with a large bus in the still of the night; she mentioned this because this was their life. They moved stuff. What stuff she could not comment, but it was big and required many of them. The men had told Zora there were at least ten more groups of musicians and roadies doing the same thing as Ivan at any given time around the country. Why not just get those guys to jump in on the fun and make some extra money by transferring Juan's coke?

Okay. Sure, this sounds simple and easy, especially for two people who now know their lives are on the line. I guess most people in this situation who had a family member who was a roadie, might think the same, the job really is a mystery to most. Plus, they are preemptively signing guys up to do something highly illegal and still have zero clue as to how the touring industry works.

The two had their theory drawn up: if we get roadies to move drugs, we can move more drugs. But how? How do they make them, the roadies and even the musicians, do something illegal like this? And for what price would they do it? Adolf and Zora had never run a business, been on tour, known a single thing about the wild world of cartels, or even dealt with the logistics of moving, but they at least had a plan to start with. They both agreed it was time to ask some questions. The only person they felt they could trust who knew a thing or two about crime and, almost more importantly, info about Juan, was Bobby.

Bobby had been a longtime associate of the cartel. He was the one who told Juan that the Italians had something fishy going on and that they were sending some young punk to handle their business. He also was the one who tipped Juan off regarding his friend stealing from the cartel. Was he a snitch? No, he was just a man who was treated very well by Juan's father and was probably keeping an eye out for his son as a favor. Adolf and Zora needed to pick Bobby's brain on what the cartel and Juan expected from them. Hell, maybe he knew, or perhaps he didn't, but everything at this point was worth a shot. Once Bobby showed up, the siblings wasted no time with question after question. Bobby, being a fun-loving criminal at times, went into story hour but for criminals. Remember, Bobby was a New Yorker through and through, so there was a certain cadence—an ebb and flow to how he spoke to you. Storytime went on for a good while with Bobby sharing very personal encounters with Juan's father, the Mexicans, the cartel and answering some of the questions they had about Juan. Although Bobby thought it was brilliant having the roadies move drugs with buses, they were missing a few crucial steps in the process. He wondered if they had asked Ivan how this operation could run the smoothest. How many trucks are on a typical tour? Do these trucks and buses pass the same city every so many days? Was the touring industry growing or would they eventually run into logistical issues with size requirements? The two sat there speechless with blank stares, looking at the man who put a kink in their water hose. "Maybe you should ask him," Bobby said as he got up and walked over to fetch some cold French fries off the room service cart.

Ivan had been gigging like crazy, so he missed his usual calls with Zora to keep her in the loop that he was alive. So, the answer to Bobby's last question was a big "no." They had been in limbo waiting to hear from him, so even if they might have, it was a moot point. Ivan was the missing link; he held the knowledge of what it would take to get these roadies to move drugs for Juan. At this point, they could only daydream about it, either working out or . . . not working out. There was no real nice way to put it. Hell, Ivan still had no idea he was not only going to be working for a band as a roadie, but soon he would also hold the title of a drug trafficker. Welcome to your new family, little brother!

In the world of drug trafficking, you have no set amount to move, but you should want to move more than one eight-ball across the country at a time. Bobby hinted multiple times that Adolf needed to start thinking big and then multiply. . .for example, you should be moving more than one tour bus or truck at a time heading in different directions with (in Bobby's words) "a fuck'en shit ton. Like, I don't know that in numbers, kid, but that king-sized bed in that der room ova there stuffed like a turkey on Thanksgiving is a pretty gooood start, kid."

As the meeting continued, Bobby filled in the duo with how much the cartel was moving north to the Italians monthly. If they wanted to stay on Juan's good side, that number would need to double in quantity and frequency. The day had flown by, and there was still no call from Bobby's guy informing them about Ivan reaching out. So, Bobby gave his guy a ring at the old apartment to ensure that he was still alive, too. The guy confirmed there had been no call from their brother. With no call from Ivan and not much more to answer, Bobby called it a night and told the two he would be back tomorrow. He reminded them they needed to leave the hotel tomorrow and go across town for new clothes and a few accessories to keep them safe.

Adolf and Zora were not tired at this point but more determined to get this hustle started. They had dialed in on the key items to make this work: Juan, cartel support, buses or trucks, and roadies. The two decided they had to focus most on the roadies and transportation. They knew Juan had their back for now with cash. Zora told her brother that a man named Pie, who was a heavy hitter in the world of touring from what she could tell, had mentioned at one point how the live concert business was starting to take off and that he and his roadie friends were busier than ever and looking to gain more roadies each year as tours were, in his words, "ramping up." This was huge, not only because roadies were being hired more than ever, but they already had an in with someone as connected as Pie thanks to Ivan. After a few more hours of the same talk, Adolf started to rub his eyes and yawn but with each blink, his eye lids became heavier and heavier. His old friend exhaustion came knocking and it was time for Adolf to exit the room for a little shut eye. He stood up from his seat on the couch, turned, and headed for his room. Slipping into bed, he repeatedly said two words as he felt sleep creeping in. Roadie, cartel. Roadie, cartel. Roadie, cartel. It was like counting sheep. Exhaustion is a strong ass force, and it had locked its talons into Adolf.

Fast forward a little and two days had passed since Zora had seen Adolf come out of his room. He was long overdue for a good night of sleep—hell, he had needed sleep since he arrived in El Paso—and in dire need of a good detox from all his new adventures dabbling with the white lady. In this interval, Bobby had come and gone several times. He had taken Zora shopping for new clothes, a nice purse, and even a sleek little revolver she could keep in her new purse for protection. Zora had never shot a gun, so, Bobby being Bobby, he knew the perfect spot. He drove her out to the junkyard, and she got to put a few dozen holes in the side of an old '57 Chevy rust bucket that sadly had seen better days. Zora might have looked like a pretty little woman out of eastern Europe, but with a few tips from Bobby, her aim started to narrow, and before she knew it, she could hit most things Bobby pointed at to shoot.

Two more days had gone by, but still no sign of Adolf. They knew he was alive from the barely picked at food that would be placed back outside his bedroom door. Zora was busy with Bobby running around during the day, but at night she would have to return to something she had never experienced before. Adolf was having night terrors so severe that she would sit in her room with that new revolver pointed at the door in case something straight out of hell's gates tried to break in and attack her. There was a new Adolf that Zora didn't know much about, but with each night of painful screams from his room, she knew a new person was coming to life there. A person she wasn't sure she wanted to know.

After some semi-sleepless nights due to Adolf's night terrors, Zora had one more thing to worry about after Bobby had informed her that Ivan had called the old apartment phone line. Originally this was good news, but that was over a day ago, and they still had not heard from him at the hotel. This worried Zora because Ivan knew his brother was into some shady dealings with people Ivan would not normally associate with. So, potentially, Ivan might have contacted the police in a state of terror, worried that something had happened to his sister and brother when another man's voice came across the line. Zora was now going into complete freak-out mode, thinking that not only would the cops be looking for them, but also these Italians Adolf had angered. Bobby, doing the logical thing, splashed his glass of water in her face and told her she needed to take a deep breath and sit down. He told her the guy who spoke to Ivan said that he took the news of the new number to call just fine; maybe he had just misdialed, so they just had to give it a little more time.

A little while later . . . like a volcano in the middle of the Pacific Ocean sitting dormant for years, suddenly, an eruption happened. Adolf blasted out of bed and into the shared living room of the suite where Zora and Bobby were talking. But no one was in there. Reenergized and ready to go, he spotted Zora's door was closed. It blew open with one giant leap and a slight kick to the door. Zora jumped from her bed directly for her purse and her new revolver.

"Well, good afternoon to you too," Adolf said in a snarky tone.

With a small exchange of expletives, they finally calmed down enough for Zora to ask why he kicked his way into her room. He had accomplished what the two had not been able to figure out together a few days earlier. Adolf had put his dreams to work for him and created a plan over the last few days in his sleep. He had somehow remembered almost every detail down to how he would approach Juan, Ivan, and even this guy Pie, with the plan. Not caring if his sister wanted to hear the ideas at that hour, he started detailing the new hustle. He first explained that they would start their own offshoot of Juan's cartel to keep the road crew answering to someone like Ivan or this guy Pie she talked about. Okay, that was a solid first idea. No need to force these guys to work with someone they may not like. The next big thing would be to use multiple crews running all days of the week. This would speed up getting the product up north and across as many states multiple times a month. Another solid idea was to ensure Juan was happy with the quantity leaving Mexico.

As the two started to run down the list of things in his dreams, Zora did raise one question. How did Adolf plan to get all these guys to sign up to start moving drugs? Well, that was a tough one. They both paused as Adolf scratched his head. They would soon find out that roadies, much like pirates, love money and adventures and maybe drugs too. And would do just about anything for them.

"No idea, but I will wine them and dine them the same way Juan did to me," Adolf said as he looked out over Fifth Ave. He added, "Hell, some might need a good old fashion extortion or beat down to get on board." He smiled and winked; the roadies had no option at this point in his wicked mind. Adolf's multi-day slumber was the inception of what would become "**The Roadie Cartel.**"

Ivan had still not given them a call since he had gotten the new number to the hotel. Zora was still worried he had gone to the cops, but no one was busting down their doors yet, so all they could do was wait. They were waiting for Ivan and for details on their ride to their new home; hopefully, Ivan called before Juan did. The hotel did have some friends of the cartel working there, so they had a great system of not letting cops walk through the front doors without an alert, but there were still moments of worry for the two. Although waiting around did suck, this provided plenty of time to figure out how to get Ivan to come back so they could talk.

It was Bobby, who decided it would be in the cartel's best interest if Adolf and Ivan had their meeting in person. The last thing they wanted to do was spook him; in their minds, he had run away to live differently than his older siblings, and even though they knew he would oppose this new hustle, they still had to get him back to the city. No need to jeopardize the plan by speaking about it over the phone. After hours of standing by, late one night, the phone finally rang. Since no one else had their number, they knew it was the call they were waiting for.

Ivan started with a typical hello, but soon gave them excuses as to why it took so long to call until Adolf called bullshit. He came clean that he had lost his calling card after a long night out drinking with a new lady friend he had picked up at a local bar in Georgia. Ivan did what any teenager would do when invited by a woman to go spend some time alone. He did and she ended up following the tour around for the next week or so, having fun with Ivan every chance they could. Adolf was pissed Ivan was off fucking around with some chick and not checking in, but what could he do? He was trying to get Ivan to go along with his deal, so he couldn't be too mad at the kid. Eventually, the siblings calmed down, and Adolf started the conversation over. To his delight, when he asked Ivan where he would be in a few days, Ivan's reply brought a smile to the scornful older brother's face. Ivan's tour was up. He had two more shows and would be on a flight back to New York City. His time in the city would be brief because he and Pie were already booked for another tour with a new and bigger band. Seeing that he would be face to face with his brother in a few days, Adolf got the info on where and when to pick him up and then said bye and hung up the phone before Zora had a chance to even speak to her baby brother. Adolf didn't like to chat, especially about shit that didn't interest him.

The next few days dragged on, waiting for Ivan's flight to land in New Jersey. The planning continued anytime Adolf and Zora were awake and in the same room. They were also greeted by a lovely phone call from Juan, who had the pleasure of speaking with Zora for the first time. Of course, he used his golden tongue to dazzle her a little over the line. With red cheeks and a smile, Zora handed the phone to Adolf, who was given a quick run-down of a few moves they would be making that upcoming week.

Adolf looked at Zora and said, "We have a house ready for us, and we can leave anytime we want." This was huge. Adolf started in on how Juan is a man amongst kids, someone he truly is aspiring to be, and how the west Texas town of El Paso offers everything they need. Zora was excited because she had always had a thing for cowboys and the desert, especially since she had never actually seen either in real life—only in magazines and books as a kid.

The day had finally arrived. The pair headed to the airport in their sedan to pick up their missing piece, their baby brother. This was a big day for them all. Ivan flew on a plane for the first time. The siblings were going to get some much-needed brainstorming time with their kid brother. Plus, Ivan would never have to see the apartment he hated so much again. With a small sign Zora had scribbled together on some paper the front desk had given her, they waited outside his gate. There is no missing Ivan. He was a hefty young man, but Adolf almost looked right past him because he now had a small mustache and his hair had grown longer since he had left. The Burt Reynolds look gave them all a good laugh on the way to the car.

Pulling into the hotel, Ivan was a little confused about who this Bobby guy was and why they were staying in one of the nicest hotels in the city, but he couldn't stop smiling over the fact that he didn't have to go back to that shit-hole apartment. He must have asked Adolf a dozen times on the ride back how he met Juan and why they needed to have a talk about buses and the men he worked with. Adolf kept replying, "I will tell you when we get to the room." Finally, as older brothers do, Adolf reared back and slapped Ivan across the face saying, "Did your ears break while on that plane?" The mood had shifted a little after the altercation, but it was time to get to business once they reached their room.

Time was ticking once again for the group. Ivan informed them that he would leave for the West Coast sooner than he had initially thought. He would meet up with Pie to get the new band rehearsals up and running over the next month. Adolf started with how he thought Ivan was the leader on the road. This is when Zora almost slapped Adolf as he had done to Ivan since she had already explained that Pie was high up in the tour industry multiple times not Ivan. Instead, she rolled her eyes and grumbled in her native tongue quietly.

A light bulb went off in Adolf's brain, and his eyes widened as he explained to Ivan that he would fly to stay in Los Angeles with him, because he needed to set up a meeting with Pie immediately about some work.

"Why . . . you don't know any bands or have work for him as a street hustler?" Ivan stated suspiciously.

Adolf laid it ALL out for his kid brother shortly after that comment. He told him how he wanted to use the tour's transportation and crew to traffic and distribute the coke. This was met with instant resistance from Ivan. "Absolutely not. I'm not asking anyone to sell drugs, Adolf." Then Zora started in on Ivan. She explained how the night they were out together, she noticed the roadies loved to talk about money, drugs, and travel. Then she filled Ivan in on the crucial detail Adolf had left out; without talking with anyone, Adolf had signed the family up for "another" ride of a lifetime. He had given all their lives to Juan and his cartel.

Staring at his brother, Ivan asked, "Just what would the cartel do if I don't want to be a part of it?" And then shouted, "And why the fuck do you need me and my friend!"

Adolf turned and said, "You don't want to find out. I suggest you listen to how this hustle will go down and what role you will play. Got it?"

Ivan listened to the plan for the next hour or so before he finally said—strictly just so he didn't have to hear his brother speak a second longer—"I'm in, I'm in, but I just want to be a minion in this scheme. I like the road. I like what I do now. I'll get you in touch with Pie once I get into Los Angeles but leave me out as much as possible."

Being the youngest, he was once again suckered into doing something he didn't want to do, but he also knew he didn't have a choice. Sitting there listening to the other two talk of the money and riches coming their way, Ivan was missing the road and his old home. They were the only two places he wished he could be and escape his siblings; at least, for now, the road was his true escape. The next day, Ivan woke up early and headed out for a walk like he had done before on the road on his days off. This time he wanted to revisit the club and see the building that changed his life. Maybe he even went there hoping to find a new tour that would take him away from having to go see Pie now; he didn't want his family to ruin one more relationship of his. It didn't work that way, and he found his way back uptown soon enough and, in the room, talking with his brother and sister about the plan for his arrival in LA. They had also been given a number for the house in Texas where Ivan could reach them.

The dawn of a new day could not come quickly enough for Ivan. He was morally torn. In a few days, he would be faced with introducing his brother, the man who had stolen his innocence once before, to the one thing he had found in America to bring him joy.

Ivan met Bobby outside the hotel in the sedan. On the way to the airport, Ivan contemplated many things, one was jumping from the car and running, but he knew he had no place to run. Adolf would be so mad at him that he would just turn into a running target for his brother. Before he could do anything, they arrived at the departures area of the airport. As he was getting out of the car Bobby rolled down the front passenger window for one last bit of advice for the young Ivan. "If I was you, kid, I would get that idea of running out of your head. Make sure you and that Pie guy are in Los Angeles ready to make some moves." He rolled the window up without a goodbye.

Ivan was crushed by what he was about to do to his friend and an industry that he saw as his new more loving family. He already felt like his actions ruined his first family. The airport in front of Ivan offered many things, none of which were going to be happiness, or so he thought. His mind raced as he could hear Bobby's sedan still idling behind him. He wanted so badly to run. "Ok turn and run on three," he said to himself in a whisper. With his eyes closed, Ivan started to count, "one, two, three." But when he opened his eyes and turned to run, a strong breeze hit his face, followed by a single sun beam. It was then that Ivan knew running was not going to solve anything. He was going to have to face this dragon head on and on the beast's playing field. It was time for his inner light to drown out the darkness that had been trying to take him captive.

>>>STOP RECORDING<<<

I didn't have much more to say after that comment, plus I was starting to get pretty tired. Tomorrow I will pick up on the big move to Texas.

CHAPTER 7

Texas and Mexico

>>>START RECORDING<<<

Hey.

This is video diary #6, October 21, 2009. Reno, Nevada.

We are doing a show in a very small arena in the "Biggest Little City in the World" [as I pan the camera so anyone who watches can see the urinals that surround me.]

Today, I am doing the video in my quaint and cozy personal production manager office—you know, the shitter or water closet—there is a first time for everything. My old road crew are making it very clear lately they want me gone, they still can't handle the facts that I share when I am in the room with them all. But I digress, in all reality, it doesn't matter where they put me. I am here to do what I can while I'm still on the inside of this criminal organization. I think they have me right where they want me and I have them right where I need them but moves like this one only fire me up more. I want to expose these men and women for who they really are, so I'll take any day alive, even if it means I have to spend my day in a shitty shitter smelling urinal cakes.

Now that I have been on this social media app, I can see where most people's priorities sit. And most people aren't worried about Juan, or Adolf, or anyone else tied to this cartel. Hell, most of the world wouldn't know who these men were if they came across their TV in the middle of their favorite show. But you should care and hopefully these videos one day will make it to the mainstream media or to anyone who can help broadcast them further than I am currently.

Let me tell you—anyone who says a roadie life is glamorous has blinders on and only see the momentary glitz of their artist's fame. But behind all the stories and lies I used to tell people our roadie life is run by a cartel who is only in it for themselves at the end of the day. Don't get me wrong. I get it. Up until just a short time ago, I drank the tropical-flavored Kool-Aid of travel and money, but it was all for their pockets, not mine. Sure, I have made plenty of cash but nothing, NOTHING compared to the men at the top. Sitting here in this echo chamber that is my office, talking to my screen, I am reminded about Ivan stuck in his own shitty situations created by his brother and sister, and it makes me think "what if?" And we are all guilty of the "what ifs."

In this specific case I think about Ivan's life, but what if he had followed his gut and didn't go get on that flight after Bobby dropped him off? What if he had just stayed away from New York or disappeared into the distance like a cowboy riding his trusty horse like an old Western movie? What if he had just taken the money after that first tour and gone home. Anyway, there is no reason to derail this story with a bunch of what ifs. Sorry, I can't help thinking about it all being different at times.

Okay, back to where I left off . . .

New York all in all was remarkable for the Reznik kids. It was the first spot the family got their feet wet in the big league of organized crime and the music business. I would like to think Czechoslovakia was the place that changed their lives forever, but it actually was the Big Apple. And like all great things . . . the NYC chapter of their lives was over and done. Now it was time to leave for new adventures awaiting them in Texas.

Here's a little side note. Hell, it's more than that. Adolf became a legend on the East Coast after it came out some young gunner took a shot and killed one of the heads of the Italian mob. There is even a rap song written about Adolf, and we ended up working for that artist years later, using their tour to transport tons—and I mean tons—of coke! And they never had a clue that man was probably in the same building as them on a few occasions. Look, I say that because life is made up of so many full circle moments. So, even though they were saying goodbye to this city, it wouldn't be the last time they'd see her bright lights.

Getting ready to leave their hotel brought out a few emotions in Zora, but it was nothing like the last time they ran from their home in the middle of the night. Although sad for a moment, Zora snapped out of it quickly as she threw her new purse and luggage onto the bed to finish packing. Thanks to "money bags," Juan, they had more clothes to pack that would go directly into new luggage. Although she was anxious about getting acclimated to a new city, she did find time to bug Adolf with questions about how many cowboys would be out there and if they were all super rich like his new friend. The only answer Adolf could give was snarky. "I don't know! I didn't ask around when I was there. I was kind of busy landing us a new life." And then he added, "Just pack your bags, and let's get the fuck out of here."

Once they were ready to leave, Bobby showed up with a few men to escort them to the sedan like a couple rock stars and drive them to the airport. And with the closing of the sedan door, the siblings were on their way to The Lone Star state.

Leaving the city was easy and, honestly, the last thing on their minds now that they were about to enter a tunnel with the big sky-scrapers in the rearview mirror. Their only concern was the upcoming flight. Neither sibling had ever been on a plane. To see one up close for the first time a few days earlier . . . the big, loud flying tubes can be pretty intimidating. Seeing is one thing. Soon it would be time to board one and then fly in the air without freaking out. But as they passed the only airport they really knew, the siblings were left more confused than scared. If they weren't flying from there, then where? At this point, if Adolf could be pacing back and forth in the black sedan, he would be; he seemed more shaken up than his sister. Zora was too busy going between things she had heard about big airliners crashing and rich cowboys out west to even notice Adolf sweating bullets in the seat next to her.

After a short ride, they arrived. Zora, hands and face stuck to the window like a stuffed Garfield toy, was wondering why the car was being allowed on the airfield. They didn't do this for Ivan when they went to pick him up. When they pulled around to the back of the building, a sleek looking all-black private jet with a single red pin-stripe running along the side sat waiting for them. Adolf went from slumped back in his seat to peeking around the headrest. Both of their eyes lit up at the sight of the aircraft. Juan was about impress-ing people, but this wasn't for his new friend Adolf; he was already trained like a lap dog. No, this was strictly a power move to im-press Zora. Since Juan had only talked to the young woman a couple of times over the phone and once saw an outdated photo, he still wanted to make sure he impressed her. You know, just in case she was something he might fancy a date with. All flirting aside, Juan couldn't risk his little lap dog's life on a commercial flight. For the duo, they were a little less shaken and mentally ready to take the private jet wherever Juan wanted them to go now more than when they first departed the hotel.

During this time period, there were rich people with private jets, but they were much less common than today. And Juan was not just rich. He was buy-a-new-fucking-jet-each-week-if-he-wanted-to-kind of rich. Juan had money and loved to use it to his benefit. Sure, some went to lavish gifts and parties, but he mainly loved to have his money make more money for him. I tell you this because it is important to know just how much money this man pockets each month. There were guys like Elvis, who had a jet, and then there were very few men like Juan, who had a fleet. This was not just a flex, yes that is a real word I learned on this site the other day, but a time saver for the man. For the two siblings who were crammed into a closet just a few months earlier with about fifty other immigrants on their cross Atlantic voyage, this ride was going to be one they would never want to forget.

Adolf and Bobby chatted at the back of the sedan briefly while Zora told the men which were her belongings to get packed in the jet. Bobby explained to Adolf that if he was ever back in New York City to make sure he looked him up. Adolf was confused because he thought he would be back sooner and more frequently than Bobby was making it sound. Bobby smiled, shook his hand, waved at Zora through one of the plane's small windows, and said to Adolf, "Kid, you'll do big things with Juan. I've got your back here, so enjoy the ride. It's gonna come at ya fast."

When you think of a cartel, mob, or any other criminal gang, looking at them from the outside, you are usually under the impression that a criminal can only be evil. And sure, evil can be part of the game, but many of these groups are a brotherhood, filling a void for some people who never had a family. Adolf came from a good family, so to explain why he needed another family is beyond me, but Bobby cared for the kid. I think Adolf took that as a badge of accomplishment to have these high-ranking men pay attention to him. Bobby was—and will always be—a piece of shit in my book for some of the things I have heard him do to people, but if it wasn't for him showing support for Adolf's half-cocked plan, I wouldn't be here spilling my guts about the cartel. So, for that, I'll give that cocksucker a half-ass golf clap.

With a final wave to Bobby from the stairs of the private jet, Adolf ducked his head and made his way to his luxurious seat. Next stop: El Paso, Texas.

The plane took off from the little private airfield heading southbound out of New York air space in a hurry; the pilots knew they had some precious cargo on board, and Juan wanted it delivered ASAP. Juan's pilots were a couple of knuckleheads that used to be Navy pilots turned lawbreakers. For what it was worth, they were mini-celebrities in and around the cartel. They were known for some pretty impressive high-speed maneuvers, and they also liked to give the guests a memorable ride in and out of the Mexican ranch. Now, I'm not sure who tipped them off that it was Adolf and Zora's first time flying, but the pilots were going to give them a flight neither would soon forget. About an hour in, one of the pilots came to the back and explained that they probably were going to skip landing at the international airport there in west Texas. Juan hated dealing with the cops that hung around the El Paso airport, so the pilots always avoided it. They explained that Juan had a hanger on the west side of the mountain—close to Mexico and out in the middle of the desert. If by chance Juan ever felt spooked, the pilots would head even further south into Mexico. Although it was a long drive to the ranch, this was always the safest airport. Both Adolf and Zora were a little puzzled by this news, for they thought they would land and go straight to their new house up on the mountain. But, in unison, they shrugged their shoulders; they were on Juan's time now. And Juan's time was some very important time, so there was no getting out from doing what he wanted you to do and when he demanded it to be done. Before the co-pilot made his way back up to the cockpit, he explained that they would enter the flight pattern into the international airport but divert when close to landing, so the siblings would feel a sharp turn. This turn took the plane over the mountain top and then after crossing the ridge of the Franklin's the pilots would bring the jet down closer to the base of the mountain. There, they could fly low enough across the west side to look like a small Cessna making its way to Santa Teresa's airport. This tended to get a little bumpy depending on the jet's speed. As newbies to flying, Zora and Adolf simply smiled and nodded yes.

At some point in the flight, the two siblings fell asleep with their heads resting against the window. It isn't hard to fall asleep on most planes with their rhythmic sounds coming off the jets and the smooth, dimmed lighting setting the mood. The same goes for these private jets, AKA the Rolls Royces of the sky, but there is one big difference here. You don't tend to wake up with your seat neighbor hogging up the armrest or sipping down the last half of your Jack and coke.

Darkness engulfed the sky. Edge to edge of the dome displayed deep hues of black with hints of rich plum where sun mixed with moisture in the air. The only light the eye could pick up when looking out the windows were the stars sprinkling the night sky. The cabin was illuminated only by the wings' blinking lights and the wet bar at the front of the plane. As the jet made a turn to the south and slowly descended, flashing lights called to the pilots in the distance. You could see El Paso's international airport lights flashing when suddenly the plane dropped in altitude—and fast. Zora was woken up by the feeling of her stomach touching her throat and a sickening sense that the plane was going down. Jolted awake by her obnoxious shriek, Adolf let out his own terrified choice words as if those were going to help the situation. The co-pilot opened the door and yelled, "We are being chased by the United States Air Force! Take cover in the bathroom in the rear of the plane!"

As the two ran to a safer spot, the pilots now had free reign to let the fun begin. They turned toward the southwest to land at the little New Mexican airfield, but before it was time to land, they took that plane on a little international joy ride across the Mexican desert. They dipped the nose of the plane down a few hundred feet and then returned to its altitude. A few sharp turns later, they yelled back one more time that they were coming in for a landing, and they need not make a peep and stay hidden.

Huddled together in that cramped bathroom, their arms wrapped around each other and Zora practically having to sit on Adolf's lap, the wheels touched the ground. They had made it, or so they at least thought. Zora, who at times can be mean, decided this was the perfect time to free one of her hands and slap Adolf across the side of his head, "you said there was nothing to worry about." Adolf, eyes wide, plainly said, "I was under the impression Juan was going to have this flight cleared much like the time in the limo when we crossed into Mexico." He mumbled, "This can't happen—not now! This can't happen. Why is this happening? Not now . . ."

The plane came to a hard, fast stop. There was a long pause. The siblings could only hear the engines winding down. Then the sound of the cabin door opened, and they heard footsteps heading their way through the cabin of the plane, like out of a horror movie. All they could do was cower together in fear. Adolf quickly reached for the door handle, but the door ripped open, and there stood the two pilots. Seeing Adolf and Zora crammed together on the floor, they couldn't help but bust into a cackle. Come to find out, the two pilots had a huge bet with Juan that if they could finally scare someone into hiding in the lavatory, he owed them new Rolex watches and a weekend in Cabo. I sadly never got to fly on the "Midnight Express," that was the name of the plane, with Ace and Big D. Those pilots were eventually shot down over the desert of New Mexico when the feds were tipped off about a flight picking up a high-ranking cartel member from a skiing trip in Colorado. They should have listened to those F-14 pilots.

It took time for the pair to pick themselves up from the floor of the tiny water closet after being shaken, bounced, and rattled in between the sink cabinet and toilet. Once thinking straight again, Zora was most excited to look out one of the many windows and see the desert, but she instead observed what looked like a small army. A whole entourage of men parked close to the runway, standing in front of trucks and other off-road style vehicles. With a deep breath and still a little shaken up, Adolf told Zora he would exit the plane first to double check if it were a setup. Unless you are Rick "Wild Thing" Vaughn, the Pope, or a president, having a group of men standing outside your flight waiting for you, is not the best feeling unless you know it's your boys. The pilots snickered as they passed Zora and Adolf on the way out of the cabin door, with one even re-assuring Adolf that it was just a bad joke.

Once Adolf made it to the ground, he shielded his eyes from the car headlights and was able to see a familiar face, it was Juan approaching. Some friendships do not take long to build. Watching them interact, you would swear they were brothers. Adolf gave Juan a hug and expressed how happy he was that they weren't the feds. Zora made her way out of the plane and toward the cars. She could see the two laughing and carrying on as Adolf made hand gestures acting out the drama on the plane moments ago.

Even in the bad lighting and from a distance, Zora could see why Adolf was so excited about his new "friend." Juan was Adolf's idol that he had spent years dreaming about meeting as a kid. Adolf smiled from time to time back in the day, and today was one of those rare days. He had a smile of sheer joy as one of the world's richest and most powerful men was engaging with him about his plane story. They were in somewhat of a schoolyard banter like best friends. Surprisingly, Juan did make it easy for most people to interact with him. If you didn't know him, he seemed like a well-dressed rancher out of Mexico at the end of the day. If you did happen to know who he was, he was the world's most intimidating cocaine cowboy who would still charm you out of your pants. Being the head of the cartel gave him certain confidence most men only dreamt of having. One second, he could be eating chips and salsa at a table enjoying margaritas with you; then, the next moment, he could order his men to tie you up, throw you in the back of a pickup truck, headed to the middle of the desert to kill you and your family. He was the man Adolf had always wanted to be.

The two had gone on long enough with their sweet little bromance, and Zora . . . well, she had had enough and needed attention. She wanted to know who this Juan guy was in those Wrangler jeans, tucked-in button snap shirt, and hair that was perfectly styled. Now, remember Juan was no stranger to women. Usually, he had them running down the streets to get a piece of him with little to no effort required on his part. But he had never met this feisty Czech woman. With a bit of attitude, which she must have picked up while shopping with Bobby, Zora came strutting right between Juan and Adolf. Without introducing herself, she handed Juan her bag, flipped her hair at him, and made her way to the first truck she spotted with a door open. And like that, a light switch had been flipped, and the friends' bromance was cut short. Juan had his eyes on something else, and Adolf would just have to wait. Paralyzed would be one way to describe Juan's first reaction to Zora. He was hooked like a bigmouth bass. See, the thing was, the photo Adolf had shown Juan of Zora was from a few years back, so to Juan, he assumed he'd be meeting a young, average farm girl who was of age now. The cartel playboy's opinion quickly shifted when Zora strutted her curvy adult figure in front of him.

"Are you two love birds going to sit there all night, or are you going to pour me a shot of this tequila I keep hearing about?" Zora shouted out the window of Juan's truck.

Dazed by this woman talking to him like that, Juan turned and looked at Adolf. Adolf smiled, shrugged his shoulders, and said to Juan, "I would like to introduce you to my sister Zora."

Juan's smile widened. He turned back toward the trucks, looked over at his men, and swirled a hand up in the air. Tilted his head up to the sky and leaned way back as a good old-fashioned Mexican party whistle escaped his lips. He darted back to his truck not long after that. Adolf stood in a dust cloud left behind by Juan and was relieved his friend had a good sense of humor . . . because that could have ended way worse. Picking up his sister's bag as he headed to the truck, Adolf knew the night had fun written all over it. Juan fired up his off-roading beast of a truck and revved up the engine to excite his fellow cartel members as Adolf hopped in. Juan jammed on the gas pedal, and like that, it went speeding off like a bat out of hell into the dark desert night.

Look, all boys, deep down want to drive a race car at one point in their life. Actually, put most anyone who likes motorsports behind the wheel of any vehicle, and we will take it down a back dirt road faster than a mouse escaping a feral cat in a dark alley. Drive it like you stole it! This was precisely what Juan was doing. He showed Zora and Adolf what it was like to be in the Baja 1000. The more Zora squealed with joy or freaked out, the more Juan pushed to the max. Mind you, Adolf was in the back seat, shitting bricks because it was not like it was daytime, and his boss was blowing through the desert like a hurricane hitting a small island in the Atlantic. Juan was teetering out of control on that drive back, but he loved that Zora enjoyed every jump and sideways sliding with every unnecessary sharp turn. Juan was having so much fun making his new lady friend's night memorable that he did not notice that his entourage, who had been following him, were now distant specks of light in the review mirror as they headed toward his ranch in the Juarez desert.

Being the son of the head of a cartel and then taking over that job from his father, Juan was never alone. He was guarded day and night by heavily armed men, since birth practically. He was watched by a set of personal bodyguards with their own guards keeping an eye out on them. There were many rings of security to this system Juan had. Because of his status, the Mexican military was stationed at some of his properties. Keep in mind . . . Juan was not only a multi-million-dollar playboy with his property portfolio and investments around Mexico and elsewhere. This man also had one thing many "rich" men don't have: cold hard cash, diamonds, and gold at his fingertips. These resources were worth hundreds of millions and moving fast to the big "B"–Billion. So, he was able to afford some of the most lethal civilian and ex-military and even military personnel money could buy.

The truck came to a very abrupt stop where a single red marker stood a few feet tall. Juan paused as his crew of cartel gunners and some of his security detail caught up to them. Together, they continued forward with a sharp turn down a narrow dirt road heading toward a small desert plateau. Juan commented that he had missed his marker to the property before, which made for a long detour. If you didn't know what to look for, you would pass that red cactus in the blink of an eye.

Juan's ranch land stretched over hundreds of acres, but you would never know by looking around; it's the desert, for crying out loud. At the time, Zora and Adolf didn't realize just how special they were; Juan never took people out to the ranch. If he did, they were usually blindfolded and in the bed of a truck. As the mansion came into view, Juan pushed the truck harder down the narrow dirt road. He was ready to party with his two new guests.

The brother and sister didn't know they were being watched from the top of the small mountain, either. This mountain was manned all day, every day, by a team of snipers with an assortment of high-powered rifles waiting to take the shot if needed. Luckily, they were with Juan, and the crew in constant patrol knew it. I often think about being overly protected. It is a nice safety blanket to the outside world, but it also leaves you very naive to an inside threat. And sadly, I feel I've missed my window to kill Juan myself!

The desert is a big place where things happen and although these security measures sound a bit much, Juan isn't just trying to hide a few Rolex watches and a gold coin or two. So, he understands some trespassers are not always trying to cause harm. Some people just get lost out there in the desert. But unfortunately, those lost souls don't get out alive, Juan can't afford to have the ranch's location revealed. Juan had many houses scattered about the world; some were more special than others, but the ranch chateau was his favorite. I think anyone who had the pleasure of spending even a day out there fell in love with the view and the property.

Before you were allowed to step foot on the property, Juan had each guest searched head to toe for any weapons. This was Juan's father's tradition. The man didn't want to end up buried next to some of the guests that were found with a gun hidden in their pants. He did love the view, hence why he built the mansion in that spot, but he also built this mansion in the desert for another reason: to hide bodies.

I'm kidding. But not really. Either way, it was beautiful out there.

The three came screaming past the last guard shack and into the main driveway of the house, just off to the side of a beautiful fountain created in the likeness of the St. Michael statue in Paris. The figure was eye-catching in the night sky with lights adorning the angel's sword and majestic wings. Even the crystal blue water and gorgeous river rocks added a bit of love to this desert property. Juan had one of those statues at each property. "I need someone I truly trust to watch my back. Everyone here is a sinner," he said with a wink and a devilish grin.

Now that Adolf had gathered himself from the wild ride and had both feet back on solid ground, he soaked up the scenery, stunned that this property was more magnificent than the one where he had woken up with bloody clothes and that place was a palace of its own. Zora locked her eyes immediately on the stunning two-story Spanish-style estate. It felt as though it were out of a magazine with its red roof and white walls. Bottom-lit Spanish palms lined the perimeter for an opulent look Juan loved. The long walk up to the fourteen-foot-tall front double doors was staggering. This was the siblings' first time ever seeing a house like this.

Seeing that Zora could never get her drink down her throat during that wild ride to the house, she popped off to Juan again in broken English and with extra sass. "So, Juan, are you just going to keep showing us how much money you have, or are you going to pour me some of that tequila so we can finally get the party started?"

Once again, this was a power move. Zora was inwardly astounded by the extravagance surrounding her, but she knew not to lose her poker face and give away her hand. Adolf simply smiled and went along with whatever plan Juan had in his mind. And right now, his goal was to show off his mansion.

The massive staff loved Juan and looked at him as if he was the prince of thieves, a Robin Hood archetype, who saved them from poverty. So, they were ultra-loyal to the man from the time he walked in the front doors and even when he was away. Zora joked that she was moving in, but once the staff started waiting on her, she was in love and would have to be dragged out in a few days if things didn't go their way for her or Juan. Wink, wink. While Juan looked through the flavorful agave liquid he kept only for his closet associates, the staff hauled luggage to designated rooms.

This newly-formed trio bonded quickly. As they settled into one of the main living rooms with full glasses in hands, Adolf started with stories from a few weeks back of his and Juan's wild night out on the town, but Juan's interest was detained by Zora. As Adolf talked alone, Juan continued to lose his concentration as he flirted with Zora. He had a slight habit of pouring shots without hesitation, so Zora was in for a night of fun and booze. Since she was new to getting "Juan" drunk, it did not take long for the shots to kick in. As the night went on and conversations filled the room, Zora started to lose the battle against the prized fighter, tequila.

What does one do when the booze starts to win? For these three, they turned to a magical little friend. Mr. Toot Toot, uncut Mexican cocaine, is always a crowd pleaser for a little pick me up once the liquor shots kick in. But Zora had already faded into the night by this point, so, like any good big brother, Adolf checked to make sure she was alive, then left her at the mansion's indoor bar for the staff to clean up. They would help her find her bed better than he could anyways. Adolf was impressed and relieved that she made it this far in the night and that their new boss enjoyed their company.

>>>STOP RECORDING<<<

I had to take a second and let my goosebumps settle. I had one of those very realistic moments where you remember a place as a kid but then your brain catches up very quickly and reminds you of the fucked-up truth or darkness behind the once fond memory you held there . . .

>>>START RECORDING<<<

With the men left standing, it was time to talk business . . . and Adolf was curious about the rest of the villa; so far, the siblings had only seen a fraction of the property. Leaving Zora passed out on the main bar, they walked through one of the massive wings of the mansion that leads out to a private office or study of sorts that Juan left for only the most special guests. On the way, they passed everything from stuffed exotic animals to priceless paintings, some of which he explained he took as forms of payment from those that couldn't pay a debt. As a fellow gambler, Adolf was getting a kick out of hearing how Juan won some of the paintings by making pretty outrageous one-of-a-kind bets against wealthy men worldwide. In Juan's world, it was not always about taking cash. No, some days, it was about taking what a man loved most or could never get again.

They walked through the study and into a secluded lounge Juan kept for himself to sit in the nights he wasn't out on the town. This was a cigar-style sitting and reading room. The walls were finished in rich mahogany and were lined with bookshelves that, funny enough, didn't have a single book on them. There was a grand fireplace tall and wide enough to fit a grizzly bear. Above the fireplace was a hand-carved mantel fit for a king's palace. In front of the massive fireplace sat two sturdy handmade chairs for Juan and a guest to enjoy only the finest tequila and the world's best cigars. From any angle, your eyes are drawn to a painting above the fireplace that fills every inch up to the ceiling. Juan told Adolf it was a painting of his great-grandfather, one of Mexico's most decorated bullfighters. The man looked just like Juan. This man was standing tall and proud, with his sword pointed toward a dark fiery sky and one foot on the slain bull as if his grandfather was about to lead men to war. This room was full of opulence, beauty, and testosterone.

What happened next was not only surprising to the drunk Adolf; even a sober man would think this next move of Juan's was extraordinary. Juan set his crystal glass of tequila on the table and walked to a globe next to the bookcase. He opened up the globe, splitting the world at the equator with the turn of a key that hung around his neck on a gold chain. Inside the sphere was a set of skeleton keys that fit a series of locks hidden behind a faux wall panel. Juan twisted, turned, pulled, and even pushed the skeleton keys in a series of maneuvers that no one could duplicate, at least not without many months of straight practice. With one last quarter turn from the biggest key, the floor-to-ceiling bookshelf unlocked. With a simple pull, Juan opened a safe—and I'm not talking about your grandfather's gun safe. It was a giant bank vault, so big that even Fort Knox was a little jealous of it.

Lights began to illuminate the massive vault as the door was pulled open. One big beam of light broke through the darkness and lit Adolf up like a Christmas tree. The view from Juan's perspective was almost like a sunbeam sneaking through the clouds on an overcast day, and there stood Adolf in that single beam. Adolf had never seen that amount of cash, gold, and assortments of fine-cut gems, rubies, and diamonds . . . and so much more. With Adolf's jaw dropped and eyes the size of silver dollars, he stood speechless, gazing at something only found in cartoons and dreams. To the left inside the vault were bale-sized piles of cash from all the major countries around the world. The bundles of hundred-dollar bills were stacked so high that even a basketball player couldn't see over them. Each pile was longer and wider than a full-size truck. On the opposite wall were gold bars stacked waist high; there was no end to their depth. He had piles of stuff everywhere, from priceless paintings leaning against the wall in one corner to one-of-a-kind watches lining drawer after drawer of a custom dresser. On the back wall sat a few things you don't see every day. There was an assortment of gold-plated guns. While Adolf was spinning in circles, Juan pulled out a diamond the size of a fist to show off. He underhand tossed the jewel like a baseball coach to a player and then pointed at a crown lying next to a painting.

"I took that from a prince who lost a bet to me. Instead of embarrassing him in front of his whole country, he gave me that and asylum if I ever need to hide out. For now, I just dock my yacht there when I need a getaway."

Juan wanted his friend to see what this cartel life could bring. Not like Adolf needed more incentive. One would think all of these riches would make a man happy, but Juan explained to Adolf that he was feeling more broke than ever. Adolf tilted his head slightly, glancing around the room, scratching his head as he continued listening to Juan describe how he wanted to expand his drug operation.

There was a long pause as Juan let Adolf look around the room a bit longer, but it was time to chat. No, it was time to have a "come to Jesus" talk about how things needed to go down over the next few months and even years. Juan and Adolf had briefly spoken one morning before he left for New York. Other than a couple of phone calls to the hotel, they had only discussed business at that breakfast in El Paso. Juan knew that Adolf truly had something special with his brother and the fact that Ivan had connections in the music industry. Juan knew Adolf was his but was very worried about his brother Ivan not wanting to join in on the fun. So, Juan knew he had to massage the situation to get exactly what he needed. Amid the vault's riches, Juan walked over to an off-white phone you would find at grandma's house, very out of place for the room, and dialed one of the housekeepers. Within minutes, a man with a big smile showed up with a bottle of fine tequila and two more cigars.

Sitting on top of hundred-dollar bills with his legs crossed like a pretzel, Juan reiterated to Adolf his main goal was to move more cocaine using Ivan and find a way to start a new business to launder his dirty money. With excitement in his voice, Adolf was finally able to give his new boss the very first update; Ivan would be in Los Angeles with the man who really knew everything about the touring transportation industry. Juan was thrilled with the news. Without hesitation, he walked back over to that ugly white phone on the wall, rattled off a few quick sentences in Spanish, then hung up. In seconds, the phone rang, and with a couple of grunts of understanding, Juan hung up and informed Adolf that he would be flying to Los Angeles in the morning. Adolf sat there with no response and looked down at his tequila. Before he could set it down to get some sleep, Juan splashed more of the light brown, fiery substance into his cup.

The main objective, above all else, was to get Ivan and Pie to understand that they worked for the cartel now and that they would be answering to Juan, whether they wanted to or not. The next order of business was to concoct a real plan with Pie and Ivan as to how they would traffic cocaine across the states more efficiently. Lastly, since his night out with Adolf, Juan toyed with how he could levy a heavy tax on these bands who were going to be unknowingly helping move coke across the U.S. This was a way to generate money from these bands who had money rolling in constantly—or so Juan assumed—when they were on tour or off tour. Juan's vision saw money coming in even after the coke had been moved and tours were over. He wanted to own the band, their music, and whatever else he could get his hands on from these artists.

"Tax the bands?" Adolf asked.

Juan laughed and explained that there was so much the young Adolf had to learn about crime. You can extort money from basically anyone if you pose a threat or a problem to them, then turn around with a solution on how to oppose that threat or fix their new problem. A little too drunk to fully take in the conversation, Adolf smiled and reassured Juan that the two men would be fully on board by the time he left Los Angeles.

The men drank into the early morning, and it was soon time for Adolf to hop on a jet to the City of Angels. Juan told Adolf that whatever he wanted in cash was his. He should also take enough to bribe

Pie; Juan had a funny feeling about this guy.

Zora was still not up from the wild night. As Adolf's call time edged closer to wheels up in the jet, Juan told Adolf not to worry about his sister. He would feed her some menudo, get some tequila in her as they lounged by the pool, and she would be back to normal as they headed for Cabo in a few days.

Juan slid Adolf a piece of paper with a number on it to contact him in a week down in Cabo. With a brotherly hug and one last line of coke for the road, Adolf headed for the truck waiting to take him to the private jet.

"Enjoy my favorite hotel. The view by the pool is magnificent," Juan shouted from the front entrance as he waved good-bye.

In the back seat, Adolf's mind went numb as his dreams of riches slowly transformed into reality. He had a grand task ahead: rebuild a failing cartel.

>>>STOP RECORDING<<<

I sat back for a moment and thought about how wild it is that I am a part of this cartel, and how incredible that it all started because of an idea from a fucking ex-dishwasher. I guess that old saying, that "anything is possible" is a real thing." I laughed to myself a little as I slid my phone into my pocket and wrapped up my ear buds.

CHAPTER 8

Cabo and LA

I sit alone in another cold, stagnant arena that smells of days-old beer and body odor from last night's show that came through this dump. I hate it. I hate this place. I hate this cartel. I hate this fucking life I have to live now. "I miss my fucking father," I scream in pain.

Silence. At least in my room.

I wait. Before I hit the record button, I am left pondering for a minute. I wonder if I am making the right choice by making these videos. Should I just run? If I start now, I will at least have a chance to catch a flight out of the country. Okay, run to where? If I stay, do I have a chance in hell to put up a half-ass real fight? Sure, I am trying to fight now with my videos but they will come eventually, with guns. Some days I wish they would just end me now, like burst through the fucking door and just waste me! As I look up into the ceiling, I ask the guy my father seemed to have some faith in, "okay, 'God', if you are there, I will take one of those signs you like to send to others on what to do . . . like for real . . . any time now!" Looks like He has moved on. I am either spending the rest of my life here in a perpetual hell or maybe luck will finally kick in and the cartel will make Swiss cheese out of my body sooner than later.

"Fauuuuuuuck!" I scream internally as both hands land upon my face in disgust with my thoughts. "Get out of your head; think about your father!"

I do not understand the brain, but I want to know why I am having a fight between warring emotions where neither emotion can help me decide my future. I am in a very weird place in life, stuck between death and life. I feel torn, I love helping the roadies on this tour, but hate still having to help the cartel. I used to find pleasure in helping out our merchandise tech with tour shirts after they came back for the *hydro-caine-i-zation* process down in the lab. Now I can't even bring myself to say hello to the guy in fear that he will lose his temper on me, for things I have not even done. Let's just hope the new guy that will eventually replace me gets here fast. I am not sure I can hold back from pulling out my revolver and getting rid of a few at the top myself. But will that really solve or fix the actual problem . . . anyway, time to get the rest of this story out into the world-wide webs.

>>>START RECORDING<<<

This is video diary #7 October 22, 2009, Sacramento, California.

Looking around the load-in earlier today, I thought back to the stories of men writing the playbook of putting on a live show and touring the world. Live music has changed a whole lot since the days of four Brits with bad teeth in suits—or that one girl demanding some respect—or the chubby guy in rhinestones. One minor adjustment is the road and the bands' destinations. Over the decades, tours have loaded their gear into cars, trucks, vans, trailers, semi-trucks, and buses and traveled every inch of North America. The formula worked. Get the artist from one city to another, cram as many fans' butts into the seats as possible, make some money, and then pack it all up before it's off to the next city. Rinse and repeat for a few months. I am sure the first traveling bands were able to cram all their junk into a Cadillac trunk back in the day. Now, twenty-seven semi-trucks, another twenty-plus luxury buses, and a plane get the gear from city to city as needed, and that is just one tour. There are hundreds big and small tours all happening right this second. The road life is fast-paced, and the first roadies like Pie are still writing and amending the rules they once wrote with a Sharpie on the walls of some U-Haul many moons before I was born. Pie is the roadie at the top of the food chain. He is someone who most in the industry admire, so what he says is law. . .and will live on for generations of roadies to follow. Adolf knew, deep down, that without this man, his idea was just dust in the wind.

Ivan has only had two jobs in his whole life. After the first one was ripped out from under him, "roadie" was the next title he was handed after he met Pie. Ivan loaded gear onto stages, packed the bus and plugged-in cables. Pretty easy, right? It may seem like any blue-collar job that some smart chimp in a lab could do, but these guys were figuring out all the details back then. Everyone's journey is different when getting into the music business; some are rejects, while others are savants with an instrument.

Ivan was lucky; he was in the right time and place when coming into touring. He met Pie at a low point in his life and at the right time for Pie. He got lucky that he had the right mentor to help build him up in a career where your name is your resume. Fast forward a couple decades, and Ivan wears the hat Pie once wore as the big-time production manager. And he's not just any production manager; he became the go-to person in the industry for getting the show down the road. Ivan was also the greatest at moving cocaine. It's one thing to safely move the show, plus an eight-ball of blow a couple hundred miles down the road, but it's even more difficult when you're carrying a couple hundred pounds of high-grade, south-of-the-border boom-boom powder. Pounds versus ounces is what separates the men from the boys in the drug business. Ivan was good, but it all started with Pie showing him the ropes of the music game first.

Ivan was a unicorn in the touring world of being a roadie. Most people who sign up to be roadies have some connection to the stage or the band. Some love to do the tech side, some just want to work for their rock-star friends, and, well, some are trying to get their own music career going. But Ivan fell in with touring by complete accident. He stayed because he loved to work. Since he was a kid on the farm, he loved to labor. It was a simple formula for him at first. He would wake up, move road cases out of one place, do a show, put road cases back, and then sleep. Life was moving upward since planting his two feet on land from that long, horrible boat ride. Before his return to New York, Ivan had thought he had escaped his brother's lifelong reign of terror on him; but, like so many times in his life, Adolf reared his ugly head back in.

This offer was no different. Adolf would present a highly illegal scheme to Ivan and Pie in Los Angeles, and in Adolf's defense, it would also be the first time all parties involved could potentially make money off one of his obscure ideas. Although he got on his flight to Los Angeles, Ivan was on the fence about involving Pie with someone as rotten as Adolf. The worst part was Ivan knew Adolf would show up no matter what he told him, and Ivan knew he would bring the heat when it came to being persuasive. Pie and Ivan stood no chance of refusing to do what Adolf wanted, which was a sad reality for Ivan. Once again, he would have to bend to his brother's will, but this time, he would lose his soul no matter what side he chose, Adolf would make sure of that.

Juan and Adolf knew absolutely nothing about the music business, other than lots of money exchanged hands, let alone what it would take to be successful in the touring industry. Like most people who enjoy music, Juan had a slight infatuation with that lifestyle, but his desire went further than most. Juan knew the artists had money. He had always wanted to break into that business to exploit their addictions and insecurities and reap the untapped profit. Surprisingly, he just never had the "in" to that network of people. Juan knew a few big Mexican stars, but until Adolf, he only dreamt of one day getting his foot in the door of the Hollywood music scene. Much like a farm girl from Oklahoma would dream of LA, Juan wanted to be part of the contagious "music scene." What a crazy vision that Adolf probably never knew—that the kid who dreamed of meeting a "Juan" was actually the one who would help a man who had everything, live out one of his fantasies. Juan would be lying if he said he didn't think it was a stupid plan at first, but there was something about Adolf that made him continue to believe that this young man from Czechoslovakia could pull this off. Even if the plan did choke and go down in a blaze of fire, Juan would lose a few or a hundred million. Chump change to the playboy. See for Juan, he would go on living his life until the next cartel came to dethrone him or strike a deal. For the Rezniks, they would not be a part of this world anymore if Adolf's plan didn't work out accordingly. Fortunately, Juan really did see this plan taking off, but it all rested on one man. This man was Pie. He held the key to the success of this adventure into the touring world.

Flying into Los Angeles, Adolf started daydreaming about what one of the buses looked like. He had seen a brick of cocaine before and was trying to wrap his brain around where one would even hide one—or hell—several hundred of these bricks. Adolf had the heavy task of making sure they got the first conception of this offshoot from Juan's cartel done right. Pie, Ivan, and Adolf's first discussion—if everyone was on board—was how they would get buses and trucks running coke back and forth across the U.S. Secondly, how in the hell do you repeat that multiple times, simultaneously on different tours, and all of them doing what Juan expected most–move more product? This was the first of many hurdles Adolf would have to face as a leader in the roadie cartel.

There was no room for error. It was not like Adolf could repeatedly try and fail and expect to be on Juan's good side. Being a leader is hard, and this was why Adolf knew he needed Pie more than Pie needed him. Ivan was strong and somewhat smart, but Adolf needed Pie's street and roadie smarts. "No" was not going to be part of Adolf's dictionary this week.

Trying to understand the system was starting to hurt Adolf's brain, so as he rubbed a glass of iced tequila on his temples with one hand and two fingers with the other, trying to relax, he had an epiphany. As Ivan had told Zora in New York, roadies love money and work tirelessly to get it. They also crave power, which we all know is as addictive as cocaine when given to the right person. Gazing out of the window of the private jet, Adolf could see the Pacific Ocean. As the aircraft made a sweeping turn, his reflection appeared in the window. Staring back at him was a man who had given up childish hustles and was ready to take over the world as one of Juan's top guys, no matter the cost.

The music business and the cartel follow the same mantra: the hungry dog will find a way to eat. It's not exactly moral or fair, but at the end of the day, in both businesses, the person willing to go the furthest will come out on top, mainly because they are willing to do what others will not. Adolf knew this, and over the years, his hunger grew, so all he had to do was harness that energy into making others abide. Sure, sounds easy, but you have to really dig and find out who someone is and what they want in life. And the one thing most people want over anything else is money. Not many people in the music business will walk away from money for moral reasons. Remember, some people who desire riches will sell their souls to the highest bidder. So, Adolf also had greed on his side when it came to wheeling and dealing.

The roadie cartel has extorted not only artists over the years, but we have gone after some of the biggest managers and other music executives for our own gain. Look, they profit from the deal too.

That's how we can pull off all the hustles we do. It took time to extort on the level we do today, but the cartel started to write the playbook on how to win in the drug trafficking game, even from that first artist we taxed.

Adolf didn't waste time once the wheels of the jet hit the tarmac. His driver took him directly to Ivan's hotel. He was not in the mood to dilly dally; he stormed toward the hotel, ready for answers about how in the world tours would take Juan's drugs from city to city.

Like a manager that's pissed off before the shift has even started, something had set Adolf into a rage. His blood was at boiling temperatures as he entered the lobby. Maybe seeing himself in that window, knowing he could never be a child again, hardened his heart . . . or maybe the lines of coke mixing with the tequila got him pumped up to start making moves. I personally think it was both with a healthy dose of Juan will kill them all if something big doesn't happen. Luckily for the front desk, he didn't need to bother with them for his brother's room number; Ivan was sitting in the lobby enjoying a beer like a roadie might do on a day off. Adolf yanked Ivan out of his chair, which was a feat like no other, because on a normal day, it would have looked more like an ant trying to pick up a steak. When coked up, the smaller-framed brother became a fire-breathing dragon; he snarled and kicked his sibling as they headed for the elevators to take them to Ivan's room, nostrils flaring and teeth grinding.

On the way to Ivan's room, Adolf shoved and slapped his younger brother down the hall, making it very clear that Ivan had to get Pie on board. And, NOW! Time was of the essence. Ivan could have crushed his brother, but he loved Adolf deep down and wanted them to be a family—something he's always wanted. The only way to ever get his brother's love, or so he thought, was to go along with him and his crazy ideas. That's my take on it, at least. Ivan was a kid and missed his parents and his siblings. So, Ivan went against his gut feeling by dragging his new roadie buddy into the mix for family's sake.

After Adolf calmed down (the rush from all the blow subsided), they sat and started to discuss. What in the actual hell did Adolf want from Pie? Even though Ivan had learned quite a bit from Pie, but was still new to touring, he had trouble explaining the deeper logistics of rolling a show down the road each night. Sitting at a little table by the window, Ivan explained to his brother that Pie was moving into a tour manager role on this next tour, so he would be helping Ivan transition into his old spot as production manager. At first, Ivan was met by silence; this momentous moment for Ivan meant nothing to Adolf. Ivan added that he felt nervous about the next tour because Pie let it slip that the band was having money issues and wasn't sure if they would be adding the extra roadies and transportation to the show as previously thought. This would just make for longer and tighter truck packs.

People, and from what I saw earlier, say there is no God and miracles in life, that it's luck. But, as though he had won the lottery, Adolf jumped to his feet. Ivan watched him, puzzled. It became apparent to Adolf that Juan could manipulate any situation much like a chess master making a calculated move on a chessboard. Before he left for Los Angeles, Adolf had questioned Juan about why he had to take so much money with him. With the mantra in mind, Juan guaranteed the band or, any person in fact, would be willing to break some ribs squeezing through the neighbor's fence to get to that steak they were eyeing up. Juan loved to use hungry animal references when it came to the dirty, fucked-up side to life. He truly believed we all reverted to some of our basic instincts when going after something we desired so badly, and the true monsters were the hypocrites who would say, "Oh, I could never." Adolf sat back down slowly, amused by his superior, and stared intently at his brother as a sign to continue.

Ivan shared something he overheard Pie explaining on the phone one day. Pie wished there was a reliable bus and trucking company out there that understood the demands of concert touring. "I would just start my own fucking truck company," Pie has said multiple times. "Then I wouldn't have to put up with knuckle-headed fucking sheep haulers and perverted old city bus drivers."

Pie was right. This wasn't simply hauling chickens and hogs across the country. A couple companies had a few trucks and buses, but they were all beat up, and most were just midnight freight companies looking to make a buck between their next pick up. With the industry growing, it was inevitable that a new face would show up to answer the demand to move more tours but who and when.

"Does Juan have enough money to buy some trucks and buses with drivers?" Ivan asked.

Adolf, unsure how to answer, stared blankly at his brother. "Your friend should rent trucks and buses to this artist, who would then unknowingly transport his coke from city to city," Ivan said bluntly and then continued. "This way, Juan would make money instead of paying to transport coke and then Pie could help and not be so pissed about drivers all the time." Adolf tilted his head to the side and nodded slightly in agreement; he was impressed that his younger brother had such insight, but he kept a poker face.

This was not going to be an easy sell to Pie. He was the ideal crew member for any artist paying for a roadie in those days, because he was one of the most honest men in the business—at least from what Ivan had seen since they had met. Forcing your brother to join the cartel was one thing. Getting Pie to join and move product under his artists' noses . . . well, that was the issue at hand. Even though Ivan would try to talk him into it, he knew it would be a hard sell.

Trying not to upset Adolf, Ivan suggested that the roadie cartel should plan for the next tour Ivan or Pie was working. Adolf didn't have that kind of time on his side, unfortunately. Juan had made it clear that Adolf was not to leave Los Angeles until he could prove that the cocaine could be transferred using this new method and soon. So, Adolf was ready to move on the plans and go to Pie's room.

Ivan intervened delicately. "It would be better to set up dinner and drinks for the night because Pie's a big fan of food and a good stiff drink. It'd be a fun time for us too." Adolf's mind wandered back to his night out with Juan in Juarez at his club. He conceded that this would be better than busting through the door, threatening Pie into joining a cartel.

Adolf understood Pie was not a twenty-something-year-old immigrant looking to become rich. He was a young adult with a well-established career. This would be a game of finesse, for sure, or else the plan would backfire. So, Adolf concluded that if Pie didn't take the bait tonight and Adolf couldn't land the hook at dinner, there was always Juan's money to throw around for a couple of days to keep schmoozing the veteran roadie to join the cartel. Then, there was always the last resort, which no one wants to turn to . . . but let's face it, there are no rules in the cartel world. The second you say to someone you want them to traffic coke for you, there is only one acceptable answer: yes. But if they happen to say no, you don't try asking anymore; you turn to violence. Again, once some- one hears your pitch, they can never unhear it. If they get stupid and say words like "cops," "feds," or "jail," well . . . then it's goodnight for them. No one likes a snitch.

This might sound a bit one-sided, with everything riding on Adolf and Ivan, but before they came into Juan's life, the cartel had already wanted to expand. They just hadn't thought of a new solid and pos- sible way. When it came down to it, Juan wanted to traffic cocaine throughout every inch of the globe; worldwide dominance in the coke game would be huge for Juan's pocketbook and his ever-grow- ing ego. This would not come without the threat of competition. Plus, taking over the North American market would be a transportation nightmare, but Adolf's plan in the club that first night brought light back to Juan's vision of a global cartel. Adolf was the mad scientist who could power the table for Juan's Frankenstein. Juan had toyed and brainstormed with his father's master plan for a few years be- fore crossing paths with Adolf. The single transportation idea the young man spoke of was just the answer Juan needed to hopefully fulfill his father's dream, disbanding the struggles with the distribu- tion of his cocaine once it crossed the borders.

Juan was not a city planner by any stretch of the imagination. Still, when his father left him in charge, he decided all the ma- jor cities in America were missing a little something from their infrastructure. One of his greatest ideas slowly implemented was taking over the cities' government offices, businesses, and the surrounding suburban areas, emphasis on the suburbs. Juan wanted to fill these areas and positions with hard-working car- tel members who would blend in with the culture. This process would not fully happen overnight. He had been recruiting men, women, and children to move into these cities, receive education, and move their way into jobs that would allow Juan to call in fa- vors. This sleight-of-hand trick was substantial. He was placing these families into these towns to keep watch over the cartel from authorities and help receive, deliver, and sell cocaine. He was just missing that final link in the chain, which was transporting the blow into these cities he had been funneling his people into.

Before Pie had a chance to run for the hills, Adolf was already divvying up positions for the three men. Pie was the key and would hold the know-how to develop a solid transportation plan; Adolf would handle the money side of the roadie cartel; and Ivan . . . well, he was back to being the little tag-along brother after he got Pie to agree to dinner. There was going to be a need for great trustworthy roadies to move the coke too. But of course, Adolf had moved on before he could give Ivan an ounce of credit.

Adolf, a master manipulator and the Ph.D. daydreamer of the family, was now ready for his big dinner date. He always wanted to be the mystery man at a dinner with a large sack of money, prepared to make a deal. What started many years before in a young farm boy's imagination, Adolf's dreams of being the villain were becoming reality. Ivan who was once in, was now on the fence about going to dinner, especially because he didn't want to see his brother run his mouth, but then he thought of the trap he led his roadie friend into and decided it'd be in his best interest to go. Maybe he could, at least, keep his brother from harming Pie if he did say no in public by giving Pie just enough time to escape with his life. Unlike their sister, it didn't take long for these two siblings to get ready. Besides, Ivan didn't have an assortment of clothes to choose from, it was jeans and a black t-shirt. The two brothers went down to the lobby to meet Pie for their night out on the town.

I've only known Pie by his nickname. Apparently, he was a career roadie who had been around the music business his whole life; literally, since he was a kid, he toured with his hippy mother. By the time Ivan ran into Pie outside that music club, he had already been around the world a couple times working for various bands. Pie, much like Ivan, was a big man who could put back some booze, eat half a cow, and then load a whole truck worth of band gear like it was nothing. Since Pie loved liquor and was also known to enjoy a line or two, Adolf had some wiggle room if the conversation started to go south. This sounds very Miami or Hollywood, but you can always turn a party from a four to an eleven with some high-end booze and cocaine. Pie started his life on a farm like the Reznik kids, so life was always simple for him. As the two brothers made their way out to the front of the hotel, Ivan reminded Adolf that money wouldn't impress the guy. Adolf shrugged his shoulders, smirked and flipped Ivan off, "Everyone loves money. Everyone! End of conversation."

As Pie walked out the front door, Ivan and Adolf made it to the valet booth. As the men stood around, shaking hands, and making small talk, the car pulled up from around the alley that ran alongside the hotel. It was a beautiful black Dodge Challenger that sounded like she had been built to win the Daytona 500. While Ivan glared at his brother for showing off the sports car, Pie smirked and walked over to the passenger side door. As he opened it to get in the back seat, Adolf exclaimed, "No, no! Guests ride up front! Ivan in the back!" Adolf turned to give his brother the death stare.

Adolf took pages out of Juan's playbook and decided to take them out for a steak dinner and unlimited drinks. Adolf slipped into the driver's seat, and after giving the gas pedal a few pumps to let the exhaust sing under the hotel's front entrance awning, he dropped that baby in drive and smoked the tires all the way until they locked up with the street, and they were gone into the LA night. Pie let out a generous, "*hooooot*" out the open window as the car raced away from the two trails of rubber left on that California road.

At some point in life, we will inevitably be in a situation with a new acquaintance who tries too hard by showing off. Pie's happy moment didn't last long. It became a real nightmare when Adolf turned off the radio to the car to discuss investments in the transportation business. "I am having difficulty finding someone to help run the logistics for this new trucking business my friend and I are starting, you see." He chuckled with arrogance. "I can pay top dollar to get what I want, what our company needs, but—" Adolf glanced over at Pie as he raised his left eyebrow a time or two, "I need someone who is capable of making the behind-the-scenes magic happen."

Once at the restaurant, Adolf told his guest that he had cash to make moves at least a half dozen times. Although Ivan had told his brother to keep the tour's financial issues discretionary, Adolf thought he was smooth like Juan, assuring Pie that he could make his financial troubles disappear. In reality, it was like watching a car slide on ice; you know it'll stop by hitting something eventually, but until then, it makes you cringe with anticipation.

Throughout dinner, Pie got a few words in, but at one quiet moment in the conversation he began sharing with Adolf that the demand for live shows was expanding, so yes, the need for transportation of gear and the crew was growing. But with each business pitch thrown at Pie about how Juan was ready to get into that business, Adolf couldn't get the ball over the plate for Pie to hit; each toss continued to come up a bit outside for him to take a swing. Pie wouldn't engage about tour transportation logistics other than admit there was going to be a demand for it.

Flustered, Adolf rambled about the money he was willing to spend on an adventure with the roadies. Since Pie wasn't interested, Ivan's glare burned holes into his brother, trying to tell him to shut up and move on to a different subject. It was like Adolf was on a bad date and couldn't take the hint. Adolf's second moment of silence was just long enough to take a bite out of the warm bread that had been placed in front of them; he took a drink and glanced over to see his little brother's facial expressions. Adjusting the chair and clearing his throat, Adolf switched gears as he recalled Pie's reaction to the Challenger.

"I have met a fascinating person—a secret partner who loves cars. As a country boy, I never thought I'd have a chance to drive anything but a boring farm truck in my entire life."

This sparked Pie's attention. "I wanted to ask about the Challenger, but I didn't want to be intrusive—did not want to offend you by asking, you know, too many questions about the beast," Pie said as he straightened up and leaned forward till his chest almost touched the table.

There it was. Adolf had finally sunk the hook into this big fish and turned him into a small lake bass with his weakness for cars. Now it was Pie's turn to talk as Adolf and Ivan sat back and listened closely to every word flowing out of his mouth.

"I found a beat-up Corvette down south, and I was just about to buy it when suddenly my mom got sick. I've always wanted a car to build from the ground up. For many years, though, my mom and her medical bills have been my main concern. She's better now, thankfully, but I–"he rolled around the melting ice in his almost finished scotch and took a sip, "I'm kind of embarrassed to say this, but my bank account has seen better days . . . hence why I tour practically year-round."

Adolf and Ivan were both surprised that Pie opened up to them suddenly about money. Ivan had placed a bet with himself that Pie would be asleep if Adolf had talked for another five minutes; he never expected his friend to share such personal information with him for the first time in front of Adolf. This was, for sure, not the same Pie who went out with Ivan and Zora. He was coming around; Pie was ecstatic to talk about something he enjoyed.

When dinner ended, the men made their way out to the car, full bellies and all. Adolf made the executive decision to skip the strippers and blow party he had initially planned. No, they needed scotch, cigars, and more car talk . . . okay, and some blow. Pie and Ivan had no idea where they were off to, but a few times, both chimed in about missing their turn back to their hotel. Adolf would simply smile and nod his head in agreement but kept driving. It was like he was finally getting into the groove of how to properly wine and dine a client. They pulled into the valet area of a magnificent hotel in Beverly Hills; Adolf gave them their room keys and numbers and assured them that the rooms had already been paid for.

In life, nothing is ever free. Adolf knew this tactic would be a way to show off the money game and get the roadies out of their typical environment. It was a smart move, on his part, to show Pie he had the money to solve financial woes. Before the men exited the vehicle, Adolf explained the catch; they would need to continue the party in Adolf's room if they wanted to enjoy a view of bikinis by the pool in the morning. After peeking toward the backseat for Ivan's consensus, Pie also decided a nicer hotel room with poolside fun in the morning sounded like a good deal.

Back at the hotel, the three men sat at a glass table held together by a polished gold cast metal frame with detailed rope design located in the breakfast nook of Adolf's suite, surrounded by windows that provided a view of palm trees and mansions up on the hills. Adolf did the honor of cutting up lines on the glass top as they conversed about cars of all kinds. Pie did most of the talking about cars; Adolf and Ivan knew about as much about fine automobiles as Zora knew about what a real cowboy does out on a ranch. Whenever Adolf tried to steer the conversation toward roadie transportation, Pie would shift back to something outside the touring world. This was more of a challenge than Adolf imagined it would be. He thought he would be shaking hands, handing over cash by now and be in business with a few trucks ready to transport the dope around the country. It wasn't that simple. I can't blame the guy for thinking it would be easier; not many people realize what goes on logistically in the touring world and Pie had enough on his plate.

Before Adolf could brainstorm a new tactic, Pie called it a night. If he was going to make it to work and see girls in bikinis down by the pool, he must get some shut-eye. Once Pie and Ivan walked out of his room, Adolf snorted the last bump on the table and banged the glass irritably with his fist, catching white residue on the side of his hand. He slightly twisted his arm, licked the powder off his skin, and stood up to make himself another drink.

Early the following morning, Juan rang Adolf's hotel room to check how things were going. Juan and Zora were at the hotel in Cabo and might not be around much, so he would send a guy with more cash for any purchases Adolf might need to make. Adolf picked up a peculiar tone in Juan's voice. Though there was laughter in the background, Adolf could tell Juan was expecting more results from him—and soon. To appease Juan, Adolf told him he had a guy coming over that morning to discuss business regarding vehicles for the tours. That was a total lie, but at least it bought him a little more schmoozing time with Pie. Adolf could hear Zora in the background, insisting Juan let her brother know she was loving Mexico much more than New York City; the conversation ended shortly after her energetic outburst.

It didn't take long after Juan had hung up for Adolf to feel nervous about fulfilling the promise he had made to Juan. In a typical business, you might get away with being a little late or missing a step, but when it comes to a cartel or a tour, there is hardly room for error. Much like a live show, no one cares to hear your excuse as to why it didn't work or what held up the show. No, the cartels and artists want to be able to go to work, execute their job flawlessly, and leave as if they were never there. Adolf felt the pressure that Juan's time and money mattered, and he would need results fast.

Pulling himself together after the chat, he prepared to close the deal, hoping to make Juan proud. Not one to back down from a challenge, Adolf knew this would be the last time he would turn on the charm with Pie. After that, things would have to get ugly if he wanted to keep his promise to Juan.

Adolf slowly proceeded downstairs to the hotel pool to visit Pie and Ivan as he held a glass of iced vodka against his head, trying to reduce the coke-induced pulsation in his forehead. He looked over to find his companions sticking out like a sore thumb, wearing the same clothes as the day prior. (You know you're a roadie if you're sitting by a pool in jeans, a black t-shirt, and sunglasses, sipping on a cocktail.) They sat at a table by the rear of the pool, scoping out the stunning, rich women of Beverly Hills as they soaked up that deluxe California sun. After whispering orders to a nearby staff member, Adolf swung by for a few minutes to ensure the guys were taking care of their little hangover because Adolf wanted to do it all over again that night after rehearsals. He had something up his sleeve, so with a bit of small talk while finishing off his drink, he checked what time they would be leaving, and then scooted out of the pool area with a purpose.

After a couple more hours near the crystal blue water and a satisfying lunch followed by a few cold beers, Ivan and Pie decided it was time to get going. When they walked toward the exit, a bellhop stopped them. He informed them that their bags had been brought over from the other hotel for their continued stay. "Wow, he really did put us up here," Pie said amusedly. I mean, they were staying at one of the finest hotels in the whole world for over a month on Ivan's brother's tab. Confused, but in no place to complain, they got ready for a long night at the mansion where the band they were working with now was rehearsing for the upcoming tour and enjoying some heavy drugs while writing new music.

Pie was curious why Adolf was being so generous, but how do you say no when you're getting all the things you have always dreamed of having? Roadies make a nice living; some might even live a rich lifestyle, but they will never be super rich. They might act hard but dangle the idea of extra money in their pocket, and most will jump on the chance. Hell, that is most people in life, but if some rich dude was stuffing your pockets with gold coins in some swanky hotel as you sipped fine tequila by the pool, at what point do you stand up and ask what needs to be done in return for all this fun?

When Pie ran into Ivan waiting for the concierge, Pie nonchalantly hinted to Ivan that, whatever Adolf was up to, it would indeed be nice to live like this one day. "Unlimited money to afford lunches by the pool, luxurious suites . . . and people to drive you around in a nice muscle car . . . sounds pretty nice . . . and take care of my . . ." Pie stopped as two more beautiful sun-bleached blondes walked past him and smiled, causing him to spin and lose the rest of the sentence.

There it was. Ivan finally heard Pie's desires. Adolf now had Pie on the hook. It was only going to be a matter of time before his sleazy brother started reeling him in.

Pie's eyes saturated in opulence much like Adolf that one morning in El Paso. Pie described how he would spend his money if he had millions in the bank as the men waited outside the ritzy hotel, witnessing beautiful people strolling and an abundance of stunning cars to add to the eye candy. I have never seen Ivan care about money, so he just listened and smiled, much like a fisherman's first mate holding the net as his brother lures a big fish into the boat. In the short time they had been there waiting for the valet to bring their rental car around, Pie had laid out to Ivan the exact destinations he would travel in the world. Where he would buy up real estate. He even went as far as to say which country club he would become a member of and golf all day. That one seemed odd to Ivan, but what can I say? Maybe, roadies loved golf for some reason.

A distinct roar and purr joined their presence and perked up Pie's ears immediately. There are only a couple things in life that purr. Cats and Ferraris. Men tend to get excited about the latter of the two, so when a Ferrari is near, you can bet your paycheck that there will be a man or two ready to ask to hear it *PURRrrrrrrr*. The sound echoed behind the bushes leading up to the hotel's front entrance. A beautiful cherry red Ferrari appeared with camel brown Italian leather, drifting slowly to a stop in front of the two men. The two men stood quietly in awe of the splendor.

In Los Angeles, one could expect a sixteen-year-old movie star's kid or some business tycoon or even some rich housewife in the driver's seat. The red Italian beast passed the two men, but the driver was hidden by the sun visor. The door opened slowly, leaving the men in anticipation. With a smile, the valet popped out and said, "Mr. Pie, your vehicle is ready."

Pie stopped, sputtered unrecognizable noises out of his mouth, then paused again. He stammered, "*Umm* . . . that . . . is, *umm, umm* . . . that's not . . . not mine. I, *umm* have *aahh* . . . a, a rental thing . . ."

"Mr. Reznik knew you would say that. He told me to tell you, 'Welcome to the club and see you tonight.'" The valet held his hand out for a tip.

Like fishing with explosives, Adolf's ammunition created a devious advantage. The situation flustered Pie. Some important affairs on Pie's plate included Ivan's acclimation to being a production manager and taking on a more prominent tour manager role, so he had no extra time for a "transportation business," even if it was with his friend's brother and his rich friend. That's why—whenever Adolf brought up the topic—Pie shut it down and changed the conversation. Soon though, Pie wouldn't have that option. Soon, he would learn that those treats he thought were acts of Adolf's kindness were collateral for his knowledge. One thing about Adolf that some tend to forget—or don't care to see because he has such smooth, devil-like qualities—is that he is a hardened criminal who will kill, steal, and set fire to anything in his way. He is a selfish, man-eating individual out for his and Juan's gain.

Silence took hold of Pie and Ivan as the two men stood staring at the beautiful red curves of the car in their possession. Pie walked around the car, examined her lines, and even got on his hands and knees to check the undercarriage. He stood up to look at Ivan playfully before opening the door to experience the interior. Once Ivan settled in the passenger seat, Pie revved the engine to draw attention from the on-lookers in the valet area. In a situation like this, there is only one possible thing to do next. Pie stomped on the gas pedal as if there were a spider on it, and they were gone! Leaving only rubber from the tires on the pavement in the valet area where the red prancing horse once stood, they were off to see the band.

Speeding up Laurel Canyon, Pie realized he should not be in this car. He couldn't afford it if he wrecked it, and it was way out of his league, but his smile said something different. Ivan was already in deep with Adolf, and although he still didn't understand everything about the cartel, its reach, or how dangerous it was, he felt conflicted. He stared at his friend's enjoyment debating if he should tell him to run before it was too late. Ivan was standing on a knife-edge. Who was he to tell this man not to deal with his brother? Maybe Juan was a reasonable guy, and Pie could make enough money to save his mom and retire on a golf course like he wanted. What if Ivan was to give him a heads up? Would Juan see Ivan as a potential snitch down the road if he joined the cartel? Ivan ultimately decided Pie was a grown man and could choose his destiny. With that moral dilemma settled, the two rode through the hills, windows down, shades on, and smiles upon their faces as the two big men were crammed into the small exotic sports car.

Pulling up to the mansion, they saw the sexy black Challenger that had escorted them last night, and in front of the car stood Adolf. He was standing with an apparent neighbor admiring the car and smoking a cigarette with him. Pulling into the driveway in the red-hot beauty, Pie exited the vehicle and headed straight to Adolf, deciding he had to stop taking bribes. With good intentions, ha, like those have ever gotten anyone far, he tossed the keys to Adolf and let him know it had been fun, but it was time to get back to his non-fantasy lifestyle where he rides in shitty rentals, yellow cabs, but not Ferraris.

Adolf had a Grinch-like smile when he was up to no good, and it spread from ear to ear as he tossed back the keys and a black duffel bag to Pie. Adolf told Pie there would be more if needed, but plenty of cash was in the bag to get his head in the right mindset for their meeting tonight regarding the new touring transportation business. Adolf turned, got in the car, and like that, the black Challenger made its way out of sight. Ivan made his way over to Pie, standing alone in the street, holding a black duffel bag full of cash and keys to a car he wished he had never gotten into. The two stood in silence, staring into their future. It was as if a portal opened on that open road and both men need not say anything because they knew that no one's lives, especially theirs, would ever be the same from that second forward.

In a wholly different and far-off land where time did not exist, Zora and Juan enjoyed their lives in Cabo. They had laid by the water sipping margaritas all day and sucking down fresh fish tacos while life in Los Angeles for Pie, Ivan, and Adolf was taking a turn down a moral highway that resembled a treacherous dirt road to hell more than anything else. One thing that Zora couldn't get enough of was the mariachi band playing close by as they sunbathed. Even with all the excitement, she asked Juan if he had spoken to Adolf. She was worried that she was not helping enough and asked if she needed to go to Los Angeles. Juan's witty comments and charming demeanor never gave her an answer; he changed the subject to place her mind back in vacation mode far from her brothers.

Juan was obsessed with attention, so he did not want this European woman's mind wandering. He called over one of his men and whispered a command into his ear. Shortly after the quiet exchange, two men ran off and headed for the hotel. Clearly annoyed with the chatter about work, Juan announced to Zora that they would be dining on his yacht in the Pacific tonight. Call the move cunning to get a beautiful woman alone on a yacht out at sea, but I call it a little creepy, seeing that they were not an item.

When Juan is in the mood to drop a grip of money on something ridiculous and over the top, there are two things he likes to spend it on: tequila and wine. He loved to show off his knowledge of fine wines and expensive taste. This night, he made it all about Zora. He had a team of men run and prep the vessel for a voyage if they chose to set sail that night. This, of course, was up in the air depending on how Zora took to the boat. Once they finished with their time by the water, they headed up to the suite, and Juan told Zora to gather her belongings; they were moving to the yacht tonight.

That little surprise was huge for Zora. She had never been on a yacht and didn't really understand what one was, but she knew it had to be something nice if Juan was going. Sure, she came over on a boat from Europe, but that was a cruise liner. On the car ride over to the dock, Juan emphasized that his yacht, Athena, was made for royalty. "Pilgrims ride on cruise liners, people like us, we travel in style, Zora," Juan said with a wink as he poured a little champagne into her glass.

The goddess of war was longer than a football pitch and as wide as a city block. In Athena's day of super yachts, she was the sexiest thing on international waters. Zora and her host made their way through the elegant boat to the main deck, where tequila and a table for two were waiting. They sipped refined tequila that night under the moon, and as dinner ended, Juan started to paint a mental picture for Zora of his hometown along the coast of Mexico. He told her that he would love to show her the small village and the people of the nearby town. Secretly, Juan also needed to get back down there to attend to some serious business. Zora had come this far and was still alive, so what was a few more days away from her new home in El Paso? It was not like she had much going on there anyway. After a smile and a simple nod of her head, a tone of youthful excitement filled the Pacific air, Juan called for the ship's captain to set a course for the West Coast of the Mexican mainland. Juan wanted to go home. Popping open a new bottle of champagne, the two were off into the night without the slightest care about Adolf's meeting. Juan knew Adolf would listen to his ultimatum. "Just make it happen. No excuses."

Driving away from the band's house that night and heading for the hotel, Ivan and Pie didn't speak a word. And not in a good way like the Ferrari pulling up, but rather in an eerie way that caused uneasiness. There was a strange cloud hanging over Los Angeles that neither of them had felt, but the dark presence suddenly grabbed hold of them not long after the black Challenger pulled away earlier in the day. It is not a dim or dark city either; usually, there is electricity in the air, but as they pulled up to the hotel, there was a feeling of overwhelming weight saddled on them. They parted ways, Ivan to his room—and Pie made his way to Adolf's suite a few doors down from his own. Pie had to give back the money, the car, and the dreams of riches. He had too much happening in life to help someone he barely knew start a new business.

Approaching the entry to Adolf's suite, Pie could hear a distinct laugh he had heard before. He shook it off, thinking he was crazy. But he heard it again. With his ear pressed to the door now, he undoubtedly recognized this laugh from his past, but whose was it? Who did he know in Los Angeles that would be at this hotel? Who did he know in Los Angeles also attending his final meeting with Adolf to explain there would be no deal?

As Pie raised his fist to knock on the door, it opened, and there stood two men that looked like Mexican cowboy ranch hands. Each man was wearing jeans, boots, and a pressed flannel button-snap shirt. They both looked rough, like two men with whom you wouldn't want to find yourself on the wrong end of a bar fight. The most daunting part was they were brandishing revolvers strapped to their sides. Pie realized quickly that his day was not going according to plan, and that foreboding cloud lingering over LA was chaos. Darkness had now taken over his life.

Evil can take many forms, sometimes in ways that can't be seen or heard. In other cases, it can appear directly in front of you, a tangible presence that reeks of wickedness. Pie entered the room, hearing Adolf's voice telling a guest he would be back. As Adolf slithered his way into the main foyer, the smile on his face was something of pure evil. He told the two gun-toting men to stay put and invited Pie to join him. The two walked through the large living room and into the parlor by a grand window. As Pie rounded the corner, he locked eyes with the lady he could hear laughing from the hall.

"MOM!" Pie shouted as he ran to hug her petite frame that had become fragile with age and sickness. He studied her with loving concern. "Why are you here? How did you get here? Are you okay? He didn't . . ."

Turing toward Adolf, Pie asked protectively, "Why is my mother here in your room?" Adolf's smile did not change as he remained silent.

With Pie's assistance, his mother sat in a nearby chair with a soft grunt. "I was home when two men knocked on my door. They told me you had been working long hours, and this would be a surprise party in your honor." She coughed into a handkerchief clasped in one hand that trembled as it reached her lips. "What mother would say no to such an invite? And this sweet gentleman," as she pointed a gnarled finger toward Adolf's henchman, "took me for a nice drive up the coast in a beautiful car, so I could be your surprise after working a long day with your new band." Her eyes glinted with pride as she gazed affectionately at her son.

There was obviously a grander, more sinister plan lurking in the shadows, but would Adolf really hurt this lady if Pie didn't do what he asked? Not willing to chance it after all he had gone through to save her life, Pie bowed his head in defeat. He looked back at Adolf and nodded solemnly.

Pie grasped his mother's hands gently to lift her to her feet. She shuffled next to her son, her hands now clutched around his arm for support, as they made their way to his room, the timeworn woman unaware of her residential prison. I would like to think Pie saved his mother's life that night, for Adolf is not someone who shows a gun for fun. He would have plans to use that gun later. With Adolf's first conquest under his belt, he headed for the balcony to enjoy the dark night sky with a cigarette in one hand and tequila on ice in the other. It was time to make the move that would change how roadies operate on the road today.

>>>STOP RECORDING<<<

CHAPTER 9

It's A Yacht Life, But You Two Get Back to Work

Sitting in my office chair and spinning around and around, I was left thinking about the next pivotal part in the building of this new faction inside of Juan's already established, but dwindling, cartel. I know, the story is long, and you are ready for the big reveal, but it is necessary for the couple viewers on here to know the exact scope of how big this entity is. As my mind began to wander down all the stories my father told me about these men, I was starting to realize just how great roadies have it these days. Sure, work is hard and days are long but most guys backstage look bored out of their minds. Now it is also hard on the body and touring the world does take a certain type of person but Ivan, Pie and the rest of the first batch of roadie cartel members were a fierce breed of humans.

As the chair slowly ended its final rotation and I came to a gentle stop, I am left dizzy and bummed out. Here I am, in another concrete box on a beautiful day in sunny California missing a whole life outside the arena doors—and for what? Soon, I will be dust again and worst of all, I have nothing, and no one left in my life. If somehow, I do make it out of this ordeal alive and justice is brought to these killers . . . then what? Run my whole life? Witness Protection? *Hmmm. . .* maybe I can open a pizza joint in some sleepy Amish community in the middle of Pennsylvania, ha, yeah that sounds like something that would make me happy.

Annoyed, I take a deep breath, swipe my phone's screen to the social media app, this time I don't even look at a single thing a soul on there is doing. I hit record . . .

>>>START RECORDING<<<

This is video diary #8 October 24, 2009. San Jose, California

So, Pie finally saw the crazy side to Adolf! And as much as Pie wanted to dwell on the hand he was dealt, he didn't have time. The world of touring just got a little more interesting. Though there were tours out and shows happening, nobody, and I mean nobody but Pie, was ready for what these men were about to unleash. All Pie could think of doing was to run, but the crazy thing was, deep down he knew the industry needed this. And he was the only one who could see the bigger picture of what it could grow into, a multi-billion-dollar cash cow. I know that sounds fucked up and backwards but this was the shakeup that got the wheels of this mammoth we see today moving. Pie knew the industry could use this bump in transportation and, more on this next one later, also with merchandising. So as much as Adolf needed Pie, the concert business needed him too.

Big productions and full-scale tours, in-general, were a very new concept when Pie and Adolf crossed paths. In its infancy, Pie was, for all intents and purposes, the go-to man in the industry. He was the one writing the "unofficial, official," never-written book "the laws of touring with an artist or band around the world." Like any industry, there was bound to be a Joe Billy Bob Johnson out there in society claiming he did it first, but Pie dictated how to move gear around the world most efficiently first. It was plain and simple. Pie might not have been the first roadie, but he was the man when it came to big tours. Sure, Adolf could have taken a stab at the touring transportation business with Ivan leading the way, but Ivan was still too much of a newbie and a goodie-two-shoes to do Adolf's dirty work, even if he was forced into it. Pie, on the other hand, had the hookups. He knew the lay of the land and had the mental toughness to do the job, even if it sucked and he hated the guy cracking the whip behind him. This was the mentality Adolf and Juan needed to bring this sinking cartel afloat. This was why it was in Adolf's best interest to make sure this man became part of the roadie cartel, whatever the price would be.

Back in his room and with his mother safely sound asleep, Pie knew he couldn't run, and there was no way for him to go to the police if he and his mom wanted to stay alive. Even knowing what had to happen, he sat on the edge of his bed the whole night, contemplating his next move. The conscience is a fucking pain in the ass somedays and Pie's was no different. All night he fought himself, even though he knew the answers . . . Join this guy Adolf, who just threatened his mother's life, or run and die . . . or live and take this rich man's money? Do the right thing and die, or live as a slave to a man who, for a lack of better words, was the evilest man he had met to date?

When you are between the metaphorical rock and a hard place, doing the right thing gets lost in the darkness as the pressure narrows one's vision on the riches that potentially lay before you.

He was exhausted and mentally drained from standing guard over the room like a dog all night and battling the unanswered and answered questions in his mind. It was time. Pie had to make a move. But could he truly stomach working for someone so vile to keep his mother breathing? To keep himself breathing, too! Call it noble or stupid, Pie chose to step into the dark to keep himself and his mother alive. This was a gamble because they lived by a different set of rules to which only the cartel had the key. Pie figured if there was a chance of dying at the hands of Adolf, he might as well grab as much money and power as he could until that day came.

Pie justified joining Adolf as he sat, gazing at the sun's rays that peeked over the Hollywood hills. He had a few terms he needed to work out with Adolf. He lumbered over to the sink to splash his face with cold water from the faucet. He looked into the mirror and, with a deep breath and a couple quick slaps to his cheeks, decided it was time to visit Adolf. In Pie's mind, there was only one goal: to keep his mother alive. Unfortunately, this was the only way to do that.

As a production manager for many years, Pie knew how to read and deal with people, for the most part. And although he had great negotiation skills, he wasn't sure how to handle a seemingly crazy man who felt his business was more important than the life of others. Does one walk in and start to demand a better working environment or pay from a man who threatened the life of your mother? To be frank, yes. Pie was not an educated man, but a piece of paper doesn't make a criminal ruthlessly intimidating. No, it's the sheer balls to stand up for something, even if that something is considered illegal.

Approaching the door to Adolf's suite, Pie noticed the two men still standing guard. Pie didn't even stop at the door to give the two men a chance to ask why he was there. They followed Pie into the suite to keep a close eye on him, but they knew the reason he was back. There Adolf was, sitting in a chair on the balcony, sipping tequila while lighting another cigarette with the one he just finished and what appeared to be coke residue spread across the table.

"I stayed up all night worried about you . . . *ha*, I had a feeling you would come to your senses," Adolf said sarcastically.

Pie didn't hesitate to mandate his mother's safety above all things. To his surprise, it was so easy of a victory that Pie doubted Adolf's intentions. "Last night, I was under the impression you would hand me a long list of demands before you let me and her live."

Playing the big boss for a few days while in LA, Adolf said confidently, "I do have a list of demands, and neither of you is safe from Juan or me. Ever. But the more you do for us, the more money you make and the longer she lives. The roadie cartel will be built with you steering the boat, so I suggest you send your mother home. Let's start planning our world takeover."

"Hold on, so, what you're saying is that you want me to design and run this . . . cartel? I have to be the one that moves all product for this guy, Juan?" Pie asked to make sure he was hearing the coked-up Adolf correctly.

"Yep." Adolf nodded and took a slow sip from his rocks glass.

Pie interlaced his fingers and placed his hands atop his head as he sat down. He took a deep breath and grabbed the tequila with his right hand, taking a long pull straight from the bottle. Staring out into the beautiful southern California sky, he thought about cartels, letting his mind wander to the dark stuff first—you know, "the killings, prison and the product." As his eyes panned the room, he thought of potential positives like money and power and more money. It was hard not to see all the luxuries sprawled out in Adolf's suite. Juan had many tricks up his sleeves for getting his way.

"I don't think you are seeing the other side, Pie," Adolf chimed in. "Ever thought about building a community with jobs for the tours, the arenas, and eventually the cities." See the thing is, Juan used humanitarian tactics to influence the people and built large-scale businesses to breed winners who started with nothing but their shirt of their backs. As Pie tried to daydream of positives, he suddenly recollected a vacation that he took down to South America a few years ago after a tour ended in Mexico City. Upon his return home,

Pie joked with a few close roadie friends about how cheap cocaine and other drugs were down south. The real kicker was he even told one friend that whichever roadie figures out a way to hide the drugs in road cases will become the richest man in the world. He was stunned that this memory of a joking comment was on its way to becoming true. A smile started to grow on Pie's face because the one thing that would truly keep any roadie from attempting this massive feat, was a shit-ton of money to fund such an operation.

Lifting his head after his long silence, Pie reached over and pulled a cigarette from Adolf's pack and lit it. Pie ran his free hand through his hair, smiled, and said, "If I'm going to be running this show, I need to know what this cartel wants me to move, how much, and how many days I have to get it to and from each place. And when it comes to my pay, I am going to think on it. Just know . . . I am about to make us some rich sons-of-bitches."

Pie could see the potential of making money. This was their Microsoft moment, where two men on a mission were about to set out and change the future of band and gear transportation on tour and just exactly how the concert industry was going to operate from this day forward. I know that sounds insane to us now, trying to think about completely changing an industry into something it has never been, but thirty years ago, there were no rules and there sure as shit wasn't the industry you see today. There were no accountants on tour checking the books, there were no money managers—or, even better, not a single chemist working on tour or in an arena—touring in those days was the wild, wild west.

Now that Pie knew what they wanted from him, he had the upper hand for some of the negotiations he was about to start with Adolf. A big one right from the get-go was he wanted in on every decision made dealing with the roadie cartel's side of the logistics. He would deal with every transportation and logistical movement of these tours down to the truck trailers they would use, who would drive them and who would unload them. With a chuckle, Adolf sat back in his chair and agreed that he could have that nightmare because he knew nothing about it. Pie's quick mind then shot back to his rate for pay. Considering he would be doing all the hard work, he told Adolf whatever the cartel was paying him, he wanted ten percent more plus bonuses when they moved big loads. Adolf laughed again and told Pie he could discuss the bonus with Juan, the one they all answered to. Pie went on to state he could get them moving in no time; he just needed a few days to make some calls and cash for equipment. The last question Pie had for Adolf was where Ivan comes into this plan.

"That is for you to figure out. I am now the muscle, Juan is the bank, and you . . . well, I guess you are the mad scientist with the genius plan," Adolf said in a snarky voice, "better get to work."

After the men shook hands on all the terms discussed and enjoyed more tequila, followed by a cigar, Pie started to second guess his abilities. Maybe it was the booze or maybe it was the idea of dealing with men who don't take very kindly to losing money and the word no. There was no doubt in his skull that what they were doing was highly illegal and came with some serious consequences from both sides of the fence. But like any professional in their field of expertise would do, Pie had to shake it off. He got out of his mind and decided his choice was too big to pass up.

Pie is a roadie god to many for all the innovations he brought to the table over the years that weren't illegal surprisingly, but his biggest gig started that morning in a Los Angeles hotel room. The two men sat down to start pulling apart Adolf's transportation idea so they could rebuild it and make it doable. They started with the "how much cocaine needs to be moved" and "when does the first truck need to leave by" questions. This led to "where does the driver take the coke and drop it." This was super valuable information for Pie. During their discussion of the "plan," Pie realized that Juan had already set up a few small infrastructures of cartel men and cartel families from his hometown throughout the United States to handle the influx of coke from Mexico. Smart is an understatement, but his big concern was how do these drivers meet up with these cartel members.

"Do we know these cartel members exact locations?" Pie hastily asked.

Sadly, the infrastructure the Mexican cartel had worked so hard to build in the states sat in wait while Juan and his men cleaned house from the bad seeds, causing corruption from the inside. Not only were there cartel members waiting in the north, but all the coke farms in the south sat on hold, ready to ramp up production once they gutted and slaughtered the snitches plaguing the transportation nightmare the cartel was in. Now, Adolf knew a little but he really didn't know how to fully answer Pie's logistical question. He was only able to share the facts Juan had given him. The one thing Pie did have on his side when it came to logistics, was that Juan had started to clean house in hopes of this major addition helping the transportation run smoother than ever.

Suddenly a light bulb went off in Pie's head, and he blurted out, "We could manipulate the bands' routing for upcoming tours to distribute the coke to these locations Juan has established." This was perfect because Pie was preparing for an upcoming tour he was helping promote. It was brilliant. They could take this band and the one Ivan was about to production manage and route them to distribute the drugs. Since Pie had an "in" with a dozen more promoters at the time, it would be easy to expand the business into the promoter world as well.

There it was—the who and some of the dates. Next, loyal truck drivers. Finding a trucker who doesn't snort blow is like finding a Texan who doesn't think their state is the greatest country in the world. Another pressing issue: how do we get the profits from the coke sales back to the cartel? Pie started spitting out ideas, like having another tour pick up the cash to be laundered back home. Although most touring details went over Adolf's head, he thought that was a good idea. Basically, roadies would collect money to take to a drop-off point where tours crisscrossed the states. What started as a wishy-washy plan in a Mexican nightclub was growing legs pretty rapidly in this Beverly Hills hotel room.

Much like the routing ideas, Adolf found the production and touring lingo to be a little out of his league, and Pie could see he was getting exhausted, but they couldn't stop now. Pie's mind was cooking up some great ideas. There were a couple new trends that popped up into the conversation. First, bands were starting to tour more frequently, almost year-round. When one artist would finish one tour, another band or artist would start a new one. It was a good thing for the cartel because they could move product non-stop.

That trend then sparked another. Bands needed money to write, produce, and then tour once a new album dropped. Of course, that money didn't appear out of thin air. It came from their record labels in some sort of cash advance. Now, at first, this doesn't sound like much, but Pie had an idea for later down the road that would make the cartel the bank for these record labels. They would upfront the money to the bands, and then they could control the band and label. Booking and promoting would be under their thumb too. If they can at last control the management somehow, they then control the payout back to the band, who then owes the management company, who then owes the cartel money. Pie's mind was racing around and seeing gold coins everywhere, like in a video game and he wanted them all.

It sounds like a lot—and more on this later. Just understand, Pie was in the game so it allowed them to be able to play the game for the cartel and himself to win. In the beginning, Pie wore many hats as he was floating this massive ship into uncharted waters.

Okay, so now they had one major component somewhat settled regarding how they would at least set up a schedule of runs and route the tours. The next big question was, who would run these tours? The artists still had to have roadies setting their gear up daily in different venues, but I highly doubt the cartel had highly trained, cocaine-cutting, fader-pushing, guitar-tuning roadies on call. Each tour would need its own set of "roadie cartel" members to run the show and look after the blow. Thankfully, Pie already had a network of roadies who would be willing to do some shady things for some extra cash, and they were trustworthy for the most part. Now it was discovering whether they would be down to do some "extra" shady and highly illegal shit for money.

The industry we know today is massive (thanks to us) and full of men and women who are technicians with backgrounds ranging from electronics to computer networking, catering to accounts, and all the way up to band managers and CEOs on boards running major music venues. Back in Pie and Ivan's day, it was more like a bunch of nomads and vagabonds, hell, some could be considered the rejects of normal social standards. So, in all reality running some drugs for money would be one more thing to add to a resume of debauchery.

Although the touring industry is a very tight-knit group, where everyone kind of knows everyone, Pie took the roadie cartel family and made it even more exclusive. Once you were invited in, you just didn't talk about it. Sure, there are other tours that will never have heard of what a roadie cartel is, but that is how we like to operate, everyone in the dark. Including us! We bring in only the roadies who . . . let's just say, show signs for wanting more out of life. Not every roadie can make a good criminal and not every criminal can make a good roadie. So, we had to be choosy and picky. We also had to use some good old-fashioned blood in and blood out mentality when searching for prospects. Plus, the pay was so good, it was hard to turn down. But once you were in . . . there was no getting out.

Knowing the ruthlessness of the cartel, Pie used that firsthand when initiating new roadies into the roadie cartel. Even the ones Pie trusted from the start were put through something similar to what he went through to make sure they knew there was no turning back. I believe Pie's famous line went something like, "Are you sure you want to know? Because once you know, there is only one way out for you and your family." This usually kept them in the cartel and quiet. There have been and always will be a few that decided they didn't like how we operated, but you will never hear that from out of their mouths, ever, if you know what I mean. The roadie cartel will never apologize for how they got to the top. Why would they, winners write the pages of history, right?

This wild idea about tours toting blow in the gear from show to show became a reality with every new idea the two men talked through. The most amazing part in Adolf's eyes was the fact that Pie was actually getting into it. His greed was taking over, and soon he had idea after idea flowing out of his mouth. At this point Adolf was taking a back seat and letting Pie drive the whole plan. Who cared? Pie had all the hookups in the music industry. When it came to the venues, he knew everyone from the front-of-house staff that dealt with tickets to the back-of-house staff that ran the stages and the loading docks and even a couple lawyers in LA who weaseled their way into a paycheck from these artist.

Getting bored with the details, Adolf was concerned with what he should order from the room service menu and how much money they could make. The amount of cocaine Juan was looking to move monthly was a pretty hefty load, which was nice for the pocketbook considering the cost of trucks, buses, and equipment.

"How do we make money off all these trucks and buses?" Adolf asked in a confused and curious tone.

Pie stared out the window and said slowly, "Well, first off, we will charge a rental fee. Obviously the longer you take it, the better of a deal you might get or not. Secondly, we will only send all of our services out with our own roadie crew. We get to add more fees and can even throw on a tax for extra services rendered; no one reads the fine print anyways. Most deals are still word of mouth, so just leave that part to me; I got a guy."

"Brilliant!" Adolf shouted, followed by a drunk hiccup.

Lastly, the time frame. How long would it take to get money together to buy trucks and buses? How long would they have to move more Mexican cartel members and families into more key cities? How long did they have to get two roadie teams together to be the first test rats in the roadie cartel's drug trafficking and money laundering system? Pie was a roadie and he lived by a very specific time frame day in and day out.

Adolf reassured Pie that Juan was busy. He was not in any way, shape, or form worried about getting drugs moved this week, but soon. So, the two schemers decided it was important to focus on crew. They needed to place the right people in charge of these first two tours. The first tour would be leaving in a little over a month, and Pie without hesitation decided that this would be Ivan's baby.

Pie's mind was racing around at speeds only Formula One drivers were familiar with. Questions started to fly out of his mouth at warp speed toward Adolf mainly because he was the only one in the room. Adolf was a little too drunk and high to actually answer coherently. Where do the trucks dump the drugs? Who will be in charge of pulling said drugs out of cases, and how the hell were they going to do this on loading docks in the middle of a busy concert load-in? Adolf rolled onto his back and sighed in frustration at how much work this would take. But Pie was on a mission.

The day was fading into night as Pie and Adolf sat drinking beers now and snorting lines while running through every possible scenario regarding how they were going to run these drugs, while also running the show. The principal was there. Pie even had a way for the cartel to operate completely on the artists' money, but they were still missing a few details. For example, what was actually going to happen before and after the show with the dope? Both the load-in and the load-out were key to making sure the drugs moved from city to city. They also wondered where the tour trucks would go to make their pick-ups for the new shipments entering the states. The more coke Pie inhaled, the deeper the conversation went and the more detailed he became. This was not a petty robbery job they wanted to pull off. They were looking to extort bands, traffic drugs internationally, and launder millions upon millions of dollars daily. They couldn't fake their way through this job; they had to make sure they were fully loaded in every aspect when it came to moving Juan's products and using his money until more started to flow in. So, they had to keep digging deeper with how they could pull this off without a hitch.

Pie had left Ivan to fend for himself those first few days up at the mansion in the hills with the band, while he and Adolf chattered on like a couple schoolgirls planning out their homecoming. Getting details out on the table for discussion and, more importantly, getting some money ready for the operation was required. Like any relationship in its infancy, you tend to spend hours getting to know the other person. Even though things seemed cordial and friendly, Pie still knew this man had a dark side. There were also moments when Pie had to put on his tour manager hat with his new partner who loved the booze and blow a little too much when work needed to be done. Seeing that Pie had never met Juan and only knew that his life and his new bank account were on the line, they had to focus on the end game. There was no way they could rely on Adolf to do much more than keep Juan happy by playing middleman and selling the idea.

The Roadie Cartel was official. They knew the road would not be easy, but the greatest part was they did not have to play fair. They could rewrite any rule to make the roadie cartel come out on top unlike other companies trying to come up in the industry then. This was again thanks to Pie and his influence in touring. Pie was ready to take this on with the same passion he had when moving up in touring, bouncing from club bands to national acts and even worldwide touring bands.

It was stressful times for them all. Ivan was on edge, who at this point still had zero clue what his brother was scheming, but there was some fun mixed in for Pie and Adolf, at least. In between planning world domination via music business, Pie was able to see some of his most vivid fantasies come to life in the distance: speed boats, cars, island vacations, and a nice home for his mom. And Adolf's fun has always been the hustle. This cartel is all one giant hustle that gave him power over people, and ever since he was a kid, power, control, and money were Adolf's playground. But like all fantasies, they had to stop and get their ass back to work if these guys wanted to turn thoughts into realities.

Roadies are a different breed when it comes to executing tasks. They come in under cover of darkness and some days pull off the impossible without being seen. Building up this cartel would be the ultimate show, and Pie needed to pull it off without a hiccup. What things would set this cartel apart from the others? Juan and his father had many tricks over the years when it came to trafficking drugs. The obvious ones were humans, boats, cars and even the occasional donkey, but old tricks die fast. Okay, maybe not all tricks. They were still going to have to use humans and vehicles, clearly. But was there a way to stockpile the ingredients separately and then manufacture state side?

Pie needed a place where trucks could drive in under the cover of darkness. While the products are dropped and the product is picked up, new coke is manufactured and cut. This front had to be big, though. Big enough to hide semi-trucks—those tractors and trailers can average about 70-plus feet—in plain sight where no one would question why there would be a few of them just sitting. Where could they find a giant warehouse that was on the beaten path, close enough to the venues where they held concerts—a place where, even if the cops walked in, they would assume it was a normal warehouse, that housed . . . "what are we going to house?" Pie snapped at Adolf.

"You pick, that is why we pay you the big bucks now." Adolf retorted with raised eyebrows.

Pie in a sarcastic tone, questioned if Juan would ever think of buying an arena or a small music venue. Adolf had no idea what the hell an arena was or what they would do with such a thing. Pie rolled his eyes and then flicked his cigarette past Adolf's head. Pie went on to explain what an arena was first, then he helped paint a picture of what a typical venue would look like. Once inside with the gear, no one looks around and if they do, they have no idea what most of that gear is anyway. And no one looks in the darkest corners of these establishments. People just want to hang behind the stage and in dressing rooms from time to time. Hoping to see their favorite rock star.

Pie stood to his feet and said, "I fucking got it! We can be an all-in-one stop shop for receiving, cutting, and distributing cocaine. And the absolute best part is we can clean the money through the venue too. Trucks can swing through and pick up money if it was that time or they can pick up blow or drop ingredients off at any time."

Juan had more money than he really knew what to do with, and, like any boss, he wanted more. So, here was his solution, own a multi-purpose arena. There was only one problem both men could think of. The man with all the dough was still on his yacht, miles off the coast of Mexico with Zora. This is what Juan told Adolf to do. He wanted to change the game of moving drugs, not only in North and South America, but eventually the world. Pie was dead set that this would be the game changer Juan was looking for.

"He might kill us all," Adolf muttered as he walked to the room's opposite corner when he heard the potential cost of an arena, but Pie reminded him that this was an asset to control how, where, and when the drugs and money get touched. A hockey or basketball arena is better than a warehouse off a major highway because these venues have it all. Land, space, offices, concession, loading-docks, plumbing, heat, AC, fences—and, the most essential puzzle piece, big basements that no one ever sees. So, for someone looking to load and unload something highly illegal, what better place could you name? How about a place that generates revenue that can then be pumped back into the cartel without creating a fake revenue stream? Again, name me a better front. I'll wait . . .

Now picture this:

A concert goer buys a ticket. That's an easy concept—money in. This funds a few things; the band is a big one. The band has to use some of that money to pay for the trucks, gear, and crew. But since the cartel is the owner of the venue, they first take a quick cut from the ticket. The cartel is also the artist's management; therefore, since the roadie cartel management company helps secure the show *Bam*, another cut! And don't forget: the artists would be using cartel trucking and other services . . . for a small cost, of course. One more cut.

My point is this, the cartel has figured out a way for money to come in, then "leave," but come right back through multiple business funnels. Now, this didn't just happen overnight; there have been hostile and non-hostile takeovers of management companies and arenas and other companies necessary to make this syphoning highly effective.

Pie was on a roll at this point. Juan could staff all his venues with people from Mexico the same way he was filling in the cities. Slowly fill jobs around town with people to look out for the snitches and keep an eye out on his product. It wasn't hard then to find an immigrant from a South American country willing to move north for an opportunity to make more money and sell them on the idea; it's less risky than honest labor there in Mexico.

But some legalities must come into play to make the front look legit. Consequently, Pie talked Adolf into hiring a lawyer buddy who was into some real shady shit to help them on that end.

Once the building and staff are secured, there's a lot that can be done. Rent the venue out to concerts to make money off them. Sell merchandise from the sports team to make money off them. Sell tickets for sports, music, and other events for more money. Food and beverages during events equals money too. So, instead of opening a chain of hippy head shops selling water bongs, Juan can fork over some real big-boy cash to make some real money on the back end.

While these concerts and events occur in the arena, roadie cartel teams would be cutting coke and packaging it in the basement. Buying more arenas would eventually lead to his network of trafficking hubs, which in turn move more product, making Juan—and Adolf—more money and powerful.

The funny part was, while these guys were sweating how much this would cost, Juan couldn't have cared less what Adolf was doing with his money at this point, for Juan was smitten. While Adolf and

Pie planned the cartel's next moves, Juan focused on his chance with Zora. Far from the common folk at the resorts pool, they spent their days on the beautiful Athena. Although it was an impressive vessel, Zora was enamored more by the ocean. Sure, the dinners and other luxuries were nice, but she had never seen the ocean so vivid blue, so gentle at times, and so very grand.

Juan was the Mexican playboy of his time. Women loved him, and men wanted to be him. So, it was hard for this man, who had never heard the word "no," to try so hard to get the attention of this European maiden. As they sat out on a couch toward the front of the boat talking about their dreams, Zora slowly started to come around and show Juan she appreciated his kindness by showing her something so beautiful. She thanked Juan for these amazing adventures; her eyes would have never dreamed of seeing in ten lifetimes. From the moment she stepped off his jet, Juan knew he wanted to take her to his hometown to meet his mother and sister. This would be the true test. Even if all the riches and gifts in the world made Zora fall head over heels for the man, if his mother and sister disapproved, there was no hope to go further in the relationship.

I still laugh when I think about this man who just so happens to be one of the world's most notorious criminals ever, yet there he is floating on his multi-million-dollar yacht, nervous to take this woman home to meet mom. If you aren't familiar with a Mexican household, the mothers—and grandmothers—are people you should fear. They have a stare that will make you stop dead in your tracks. The Mexican mother is also crazy accurate with her deadliest of tools: her chancla (better known to the world as a sandal). This is used to grab attention, break up family fights, and discipline disobedient kids. You might be laughing, but this is true and one of the many reasons Juan was sweating bullets like a line cook going in for a drug test. There are rumors that a Mexican mother can hurl a chancla at speeds in excess of sixty-nine miles an hour. Okay, so maybe this is a little far-fetched, but Juan was scared to go home with this white girl who for all intents and purposes would probably make him very happy, but it wasn't his place to choose his happiness. Family business can be a rough environment, then add in an illegal family business with millions of dollars on the line, not just anyone walks into this household.

After buttering Zora up with a little more champagne, Juan finally dropped the news that the trip was not just a getaway but a trip to see his mother for business and a specific personal reason. Zora was more curious than upset about the surprise visit. She even suggested that she could go home if he needed to spend time with family. She wasn't sure how her two siblings felt about home at this moment in time, but she was missing her mother and father, a lot. This was it—time for Juan to come clean about his little crush. Juan went on to tell her how he knew Adolf had a sister from the photo he showed off, but that was not the same girl that walked off his jet that night. He was instantly shaken up by her beauty and originally planned to be in Los Angeles with her brother to keep an eye on all his money, but something about Zora's eyes buckled him at the knees. She captivated the man who at this time was an escape artist from all relationships prior. As a reaction, Zora got up from the deep couch the two had been sharing. She walked over to the bow of the ship and quietly stared out into the darkness as they floated in the middle of the ocean a couple miles from shore. Those are always hard moments when you are waiting in anticipation for the other person to show emotion, good or bad. Juan waited while Zora was clearly mulling something over in her head. Then like a little Mexican jumping bean, she jumped! She had turned and hopped right into Juan's arms and smiled a shy little smile, and as her cheeks turned red, she whispered into his ear, "I always wanted a cowboy to ride off into the sunset with. I just thought it would be on a horse, not a boat."

Now with the cat out of the bag, they could relax and not act like a couple nervous high schoolers at their first dance. What better place to connect than on a beautiful yacht floating under the stars in the sky? Who can blame Juan for his earlier extravagant displays? The man had never had a real relationship and only knew that if he showed off his cash, women's panties would hit the ground faster than a Mike Tyson opponent. Zora was very interested in why the playboy of Mexico was falling for her, for one, and secondly, she was super intrigued by Juan's past and family. It was easy for Juan to be a promiscuous cartel boss' son, but random girls may cause turmoil if his mother or sister had anything to do with it. This is because they were so protective of the family's cocaine business, farm and countless other businesses that his father left Juan and his sister when he was murdered. Juan went on to explain that he waited for the right one to come along, but as time passed, he got the impression that he would never meet the right girl, so he continued to play the role he knew best, the rich cartel bachelor.

Juan told Zora stories about his father and mother. He explained his mother is still pretty normal since his father's death, but his sister is super protective of him and the family business. His sister is known as La Reina, which means the queen. She is called the queen because, next to Juan, she is the boss in all of Mexico, but she changed after their father died. His sister had always been a little controlling and had a bit of an anger problem, but now she is darker and trying to be highly competitive in the drug trade, especially since new cartels have slowly made their way into the competition. Juan could only take so much of her, so he spent most of his time at the Juarez ranch or the car dealerships, or even in Cabo. The stress of keeping his sister happy is enough to drive any man crazy.

One thing Juan was not so honest about with Zora was how ruthless his sister could be. He skimmed over the fact that his young sibling had a violent side as well. La Reina was a merciless killer in Mexico and had been known to slay entire families if she thought you were stealing from her cartel family. There was a story I heard as a young adult about how one officer pissed her off so badly that La Reina forced him to watch his whole family die, sparing his life so he would live with that pain day in and day out. Even though Zora now knew some of these truths by the end of the night, she had to walk in, smile, be herself, and hope that Juan's mother and sister liked her.

Back in Los Angeles, the two men had been holed up in Adolf's suite for a couple of days, working out every detail for their master plan—at least every detail Pie could think of. It's not easy building a business, illegal or legal. Pie had missed reaching out to Ivan for some info regarding the band, so Ivan did the only logical thing he could do. He decided to swing by Adolf's room to see what these guys were doing.

Most days in rehearsal were boring for Ivan. The band spent hours talking songs over and trying to find the best way to play them for the millionth time or so it felt that way to Ivan. This afternoon, Ivan had this free time to talk money for the tour. An issue above Ivan's expertise arose, so he turned to Pie for help: how does the band get more money from the label? These guys blew all their borrowed cash on drugs, women, and parties at the mansion, so now that it was time to pay for things like the rental house and food and the tour, well . . . everyone was kind of up shit's creek! So, Ivan went to find money from the only two people he knew had any in LA. Just like introducing Pie to Adolf, he knew it would come with a price the band might not be ready to pay but they did need cash in hand now.

When Ivan reached the hotel suite's door, the smell of cigarettes was so strong that he was sure they would be dead in there from smoke inhalation. Ivan braced himself for death by taking his hand-kerchief out of his back pocket and held it firm to his mouth and nose. Making his way through the haze, he passed empty bottles of tequila, room service trays lining the entrance hall and cocaine residue spread all over the tables. It looked as if they were running a powder donut business inside the suite. He found Adolf first, drunk and laughing to himself on the floor, and from the corner of his eye, he could see Pie sprawled out on the couch in the main room which looked to be turned into a war room. There were scribblings on pa-per pinned to the walls, the windows had marker drawings of huge buildings and the floor was covered in more crazy cryptic writings. Adolf was too drunk and high to have a coherent conversation, but Ivan was here to speak with Pie anyway. Leaving his drunk brother to laugh at the ceiling, Ivan picked up a bottle when entering the main room, made a few loud bangs with the empty tequila bottle on the TV stand, and woke Pie up. He rolled right off the couch and onto the floor. After incoherent slurring on the floor, Pie rose to his feet . . . slowly. The still-drunk roadie started to ramble on about french fries, dusted a couple cigarette butts off that had stuck to his chest and smiled, but those half-drunk slurs didn't last long once he realized it was Ivan.

"I thought you were room service bringing the burger I ordered a half hour ago. Wait. Who is watching the band?" Pie asked in a drunken haze. After pointing to a room service cart with ten burgers on it, Ivan posed the question from the band about the money. Pie thought for a long hard second, rubbed his face, looked at the burgers, looked back at Ivan, and then ran his hand down Ivan's face. Ivan stood there in shock, turned off by his friend's drunkenness, as Pie turned and walked past him and over to Adolf. Pie started shaking the drunk asshole plastered to the floor, who babbled with confusion, he asked Adolf how much money he could get from Juan and how fast.

The two went back and forth about how to handle this situation. Do they get a contract? How much cash do they advance? What are the consequences for no repayment? Instead of over-thinking the whole thing, Pie simply told Ivan that they would have their money for the tour and a lawyer would be over this week with cash and a few things to sign. Adolf was a little put off at how fast Pie just gave away some of Juan's money but what was he going to really say? Absolutely nothing, if he wanted this to work out, he was going to have to spend some money to make it, period. Even though Pie was new to this whole drug/cartel thing, the principals behind running an organization are the same. Pie was good at making split-second high-pressure decisions and that was only going to benefit the cartel and everyone involved at the end.

After handing out money like a rapper in a strip club, Adolf worried about the drugs in transit and the buildings. So, he asked about security for the coke. Who would keep an eye on the stuff once it left the trucks and started rolling around in these big arenas? Pie thought on this for a while. Tours back then didn't have security teams as you see on the road today. They usually hired biker gangs or local law enforcement depending on the show to help handle mainly crowd control. Quick on his feet and on fire with some other big choices, Pie blurted out the idea of a tour security position, a director of security. Again, this was a job that made the band think they are getting protection, and the venue thought the team looked more professional by having a crowd control expert on tour. In reality, it was the coke and cartel reaping the benefits. Sure, the security director would have to interact with the venue and others, but if we were using the venue the cartel owned, then that workday would be an easier tour day. Tour security would become the new standard for touring with the roadie cartel team, and many other tours would adopt such a practice—and Pie wrote this law into place way before I was born. By the end of the day, the coke would be secure, and the band would feel safer, and everybody won.

Adolf was still a few steps behind the visionary roadie. Pie had been in the game long enough to know where things could be hidden and where things could use improving. Combining the two would lead to a new and more efficient style of touring. One of those areas was in the merchandise business. First off, merch back then was nothing like it is today—a couple shirts if you were lucky and maybe a record. There just wasn't a mass producer of band tees yet. But seeing the demand going up for those items, Pie explained to Adolf that if they could find someone in the clothing business, they could have a place to hide the cut coke for transport as it rolled in and out of venues. After more head scratching from Adolf, Pie explained that even if he didn't see that logic yet, he should see the value in the merch guy, who—let's face it—had nothing to do all day. So, he could babysit the coke. The merch guy could take it to and from the truck and down into the lab. There were a few details still to be worked out, but Pie was a natural drug runner; now that he had the money and the drugs, he could finally execute his master plan he thought up after a vacation once, all thanks to Adolf.

Adolf had never been to a concert, mind you, so Pie had to keep his cool with every question that came along with every new idea that shot from his mouth. It was part of the role he took on by join-ing the cartel and basically establishing and reworking almost every aspect of Adolf's ridiculous plan. But, on the plus side, the plan was coming to life. On top of the extra cartel member now on tour, you had a place to hide the drugs. This was the key. Instead of having the cocaine hidden in the band's gear that rolls right out onto the arena floor, they would hide it in the merch boxes. Pie knew that the merchandise usually rolled to a concourse somewhere to be sifted through later. So instead of going to the concourse right away, the road case or boxes would roll down to the labs for processing first and would avoid the arena floor and exposing the cocaine to anyone who shouldn't know about it.

Nowadays, it's easy to spot a drug front, right? Maybe and maybe not . . . but when these guys were thinking of the best way to hide in plain sight, no one in the world would be thinking sports arena or music venue, especially the government. The drug fronts of their time were typical, from anything like a laundry fluff and fold open 24/7 to the Italian sub shop with only two subs on the menu.

We could go on for a while with places that looked more like a drug front than your local sporting arena, but I digress. Thinking logistically and practically, Pie thought the arena would be the best when it came to not calling attention to the roadie cartel. Getting it into the country was not their issue, yet, but making it more efficient and less of a headache, an arena could take some heat off of shipments coming north. Plus, who really believes the water bong smoke shop is not pushing a little something out the back door? Who has ever heard of a cocaine lab underneath arena bleachers, cutting and packaging blow by Mexican cartel members, all while there is a sold-out show going on above.

Take a couple seconds and work these questions out. Would you find it strange if a semi-truck showed up to an arena in the early morning hours to make a delivery? Would you question if that truck had drugs in it? At night after the show and you see the trucks leave, are you curious if they are about to transport large amounts of coke across state lines? Okay, so what was your answer? Look, you can even ask one of those Magic 8 balls and it will say, "Very doubtful." And this is what Pie was seeing when he first thought up the wild idea. No one was going to question a truck or two going in or leaving out of any venue, big or small. To make this work, they would need more than one mindset and a mind willing to dream, because they would need a network of arenas and music venues to pull this all off. The other gold deposit buried deep inside this thought was that this becomes a money-laundering paradise for the cartel. First off, they would need to find a way to make the sale and purchases of these arenas look legit. Second, the arenas and other venues would need to operate like a . . . well, like a legal business in the USA. Sounds a little illegal. It is. Pie was still working out all the details in his head, but he had a lawyer friend who was into a lot of shady deals around the world, and one of the types of deals he specialized in was hiding money; the other was buying commercial properties. Pie told Adolf he would reach out to this lawyer immediately. This guy, Pie, is why businessmen and women win when they take chances. Juan had millions to lose but tens of billions to gain if this all pulled together like the planning described.

Back on the open water, the two new love birds were getting ready to enjoy Juan's home, breathtaking land tucked in between two beautiful and lush green mountains. Robin Hood was a hero that most could and would associate with good. A man who stole from the rich and gave to the poor. Juan was that man in real life in the small coastal town in Mexico that he came from. His horrific crimes and stories of torture were only done to those who were out to steal from his wealth that he planned to give back to the communities and citizens in this small town and in the greater parts of Mexico. It is weird to say the man has done good things, but in some people's eyes, he was their savior, and it showed by how they worshipped the man.

Juan was loved by the young all the way to the elderly. The women adored him, and the men dreamed of what it would be like to live one day in his shoes. So, coming home was always an extravagant king's welcome for Juan. The people treated Juan and his family like royalty mainly because he treated them to the spoils of life from beautiful renovations to this small town all the way to gifts of gold.

Although his area of Mexico was one of the wealthiest due to his generosity, Juan continued to take the neediest in the community and ship them north to have them work for the cartel in America. He did like to help, but also knew he truly owned their souls for helping them out of the depths of poverty. Riding in on the beautiful Athena, Juan told Zora that his privacy in the town was better than any security detail he could search for. No one in the city spoke of him. Even if you had just shaken his hand, moments afterward, it was like the man had vanished into the mountains and had never been there. It was impossible to locate him, and looking for him became a deadly affair for the few law enforcement agents who dared to try. There were always the few in and around the area who hated seeing someone have more than them, but Juan's sister was notorious for making sure they never spoke again. Juan did have a few other things on his side that allowed for his world travel. His father had placed men into specific and strategic roles deep in the Mexican government and military years before he was murdered. So, even if there was a snitch, they usually didn't get very far. This also came in handy when the United States government would call the Mexican government looking for intel on this mysterious Juan fella.

Standing at the bow of the beautiful Athena, Zora's eyes were filled with the rich colors of the town as it came into view. The pinks and yellows on the buildings were in such contrast with the deep blue ocean below her feet and the vivid jungle green carpeting the mountains behind the city. In her wildest dreams, she had never pictured a town that looked as magnificent as this one. Juan came up from behind her, and as his arms wrapped around her midsection, he extended one arm and started to point out his favorite spots in the city. As they passed by each building, the small colorful town brought a tear to Zora's eyes as she flashed back to her childhood home and the small butcher shop where her father used to cut cheese for her after school before they would head home.

Before she could get too emotional, Juan finished pointing out his favorite delights. He stopped his finger at the small city's skyline on a majestic steeple atop a beautiful white church standing in the middle of the small town. He told her that he rebuilt it for his mother and her friends to enjoy on Sundays. As the church bells started to ring, they also started to hear music playing in the little town as the shore came closer. With the yacht dropping anchor and the crew getting the tender ready to take them to land, Zora stood in amazement, staring at the lush greens on the mountain contrasting the town's bright-colored buildings. This gem of a town was happy to know their Robin Hood was home.

Hitting land really brought the lively culture into perspective for Zora. Now she could feel the music and hear the people singing the songs of Mexico. Up the road from the dock, she spotted women dancing in native dresses with deep ruby reds and vibrant canary yellows to the grand music played on guitars, basses, and belting out trumpets. Zora was amazed and in a state of astonishment. Sure, she had seen some of this in Cabo, but these sights were nothing on the scale of how Juan's town welcomed him. For a man so ruthless in many other aspects of life, he was godlike to the people. The children gazed from the windows and doorways as Juan and Zora passed through the crowd toward the farm. The town was in a full-on Mexican party as the firstborn was coming home. Zora wanted to stay and celebrate with them, but they had to get to the house to see the women this trip was really about. Juan's biggest cheerleader was waiting, and, like I stated before, the last thing you ever want to do was piss off a Mexican mother. As they made their way through town, past the stone fences and colorful buildings, Zora stared out the window, smiling and reminiscing. The zigzagging dirt roads through the mountains and farmland made Zora even more homesick.

Much like the drive to the house in Juarez, this mansion was difficult to reach, if not harder. It was that way for many reasons. Even though the locals, for the most part, loved Juan's family, many outsiders wanted to see them all burn for the crimes and drugs they pushed in the community and world. The drive consisted of a few tunnels, bridges, and a handful of checkpoints along the way. Obviously, this part of the world didn't have many sightseers and honeymooners. This farm was way more valuable and way more secretive than the other houses Juan stayed at. This might have been Mexico's Area 51. Zora knew this and was trying her hardest to fit in; if you had seen the two together, you would assume they had been a couple for many years, they just fit like you would picture a strong couple would. When pulling into the main house, trees hid a large metal wall, and a long driveway led to a space-aged metal and concrete palace fit for a king or even an army.

A scream of excitement as loud as a train horn came out from the main house as the car came to a stop. It was Juan's mother. She had gotten word her baby boy had finally arrived home. She rarely got to see Juan, let alone leave the house in recent months. This was obviously for her protection and ensured the cartel never got blackmailed. Juan's mother came running, a short little Mexican lady with jet black hair, big grandmother glasses, and a million hugs and kisses for her son. Not even the head of a cartel can get away from a mother's love. The two hugged it out for what seemed like forever, but Zora stayed patient and full of smiles. She did not need to upset the balance in the house. Finally, it was Zora's turn. The little Mexican lady stopped and with a straight face gave her a look up and then a long look down. Juan stood still in complete silence as if his mother's anger worked similarly to a T-rex's vision. Waiting for any sign of joy–hell, even disappointment, Juan stood frozen, watching their interaction. Then without any warning, this little old lady's smile went ear to ear as she picked Zora up in an embrace and said many things in Spanish that not even Juan could put together in his mind fast enough. That was a big win for the two.

Now, it was time to introduce Zora to La Reina, the woman that Juan feared most to upset. Much like a bad horror movie scene, the shadow of Juan's sister appeared by the main house's front door not long after their mother let go of Zora. She stood staring down at the three gathered by the truck. Standing there with arms crossed, Juan yelled up at her to stay there; they would be right up. Zora had passed the mom test, but it did not appear that she would pass the sister test. Zora was hesitant to follow Juan; it was like watching a mailman approach a pit bull. Was the angry pooch going to sit on the porch like a good dog should, or would it stare at you like a bloody steak and, at any moment, jump off that porch, latch onto your throat, and have you for lunch?

Once they got to Juan's sister, she gave Juan a half-hearted hug. She pulled away as if hugging a stranger. "Nice of you to swing by from your rich world-traveling lifestyle to check in on us, considering you leave me here in Mexico with our crazy mother." Juan's sister paused and stared at Zora with deep brown eyes of hate and, without a word, turned and headed back into the house. Juan smiled at Zora, put one arm around her as he whispered to her, "Welcome to the family."

>>>STOP RECORDING<<<

CHAPTER 10

The Founding Fathers Head South

A day off, again. . .

I love a good day off, but today is not typical. Instead, I am sitting in the living-kitchen area of my hotel room by the sliding glass doors that overlook the backside of the strip mall. I laugh to myself, because normally I would be plastered off cheap booze at some hole-in-the-wall bar and blasting key bumps of blow off my hotel room card—but not this time in Bakersfield. I no longer have the energy to waste leaving my room, it is all going toward this new social media app. As I start to pull items from my backpack that I will need to record the video diary and my day stuck in the hotel room, I laugh to myself once again. The bag of goldfish I took from the bus had exploded and lucky for me I had already made my day off fortress and moved my bedding to the floor in preparation from any surprised attacks on my room. It sucks to live out the remaining days of my life in a bit of fear, but it has given me purpose each day that I do wake up alive. I am not trying to push my luck here but The Butcher nor his sicarios have come for me yet . . . so I will continue to build my makeshift fort and not sleep on the hotel beds.

I had a long night and my head was still a little cloudy from the drive in so as I gathered my phone and ear-buds for the recording I started to think about this specific run of events. This video I wanted to showcase these pioneers of the drug and music industries. I think what they have done is outrageous and even mental but next to the government, these four men wrote the book on how to launder money like a pro. If someone was telling me this story about a couple roadies who created the world's largest front, I would laugh in their face, but each second some kid used their services to enjoy entertainment and for that reason alone I must continue to elaborate on what exactly these men did to take over the music scene.

>>>START RECORDING<<<

This is video Diary #9 October 25, 2009. Bakersfield, California

The dawn of each new day brought the men closer to the deadline of the roadie cartel's first tour leaving. It was time for moves to happen, or they would all find themselves hanging from an over-pass on I-10 if they didn't please Juan. It was time to bring in the big guns—someone who truly took these men to the top. Juan was good and had the cash, but Pie's lawyer friend knew the right people around the world and he was great at manipulating any situation for his clients' benefits. He was not your typical criminal. This college graduate was a very intelligent one who first and foremost knew the laws like the back of his hand; he had a few talents, none of which really did society any good. One amazing talent, the man special-ized on how to write up contracts to make shit happen and keep people out of trouble. Don't get me wrong—I'm sure there are plenty of law-abiding, honest, never-hurt-a-soul, sweet-as-can-be lawyers you could take home to meet your mother. This guy was not that, for sure. This guy was ruthless when it came to getting his way and the true definition of a crook, but they would need a guy like him. There are people who take the high road and do business deals the honest way, but these men didn't have that kind of time for that. Pie's "buddy" had to be the next man added to The Roadie Cartel before anyone else, especially when buying arenas. The next big piece in the history in this cartel was about to happen once the band signed their lives away to them for more advance money. Hell, now that Pie and Adolf were talking about it, for all they knew, this guy might have already been on Juan's payroll; he did deal with some of the biggest criminals in the world.

Pie had reached out to Dick via a simple phone call about a guy who needed some contracts made for a new up-and coming band—if it worked out there would be more and a big percentage. Pie also added the new band came with a nice house in Mexico he could use from time to time. That part was kind of a lie but he knew it would attract the south of the border loving American. He told Dick to come by and discuss payments over some booze and a big white lady—big bag of cocaine if you are new to my videos—the lawyer was on his way before Pie could hang up the phone.

Still holed up in their luxurious suite at their Beverly Hills hotel, Pie and Adolf waited for the man of the hour to join in on the last brainstorming sessions before meeting with Juan down in Mexico. Shortly after Ivan had asked for the money for the band, Adolf received a call stating that a jet would be waiting for the men in a week. Pie was just about to warn Adolf that his lawyer friend was a little "out there," but as the words were about to exit his mouth, Dick joined the party in the only way he would, by pushing his way through the two security guys and right through the hotel door as if he owned the place. I think you all can picture a lawyer walking into a room, a sharp-looking fella in a three-piece suit, carrying a briefcase, maybe back then smoking a cigar. Dick was a lot different. Imagine a short, chubby, sweaty, pale, red-cheeked man, who looks like he just left a whorehouse, coming through the door and making a beeline for the cocaine on the table as if he could smell it once the elevator doors opened.

Webster's dictionary would define Dick with a few words; foul, immoral, vile, and malevolent. He had a confident saunter and smirked in a way that, when he entered the room, even the criminals shivered with chills down their backs and goose pimples down their arms from his aura. Holding a brown leather briefcase and wearing an untucked shirt with red lipstick on the collar and a pre-cut-cocaine-straw (probably from the last hotel bar he was at) hanging out of his chest pocket, Dick did not impress Adolf. Looking at Dick, you would never take him for much more than a dirty old regular at Hooters who wore too much gold jewelry. He also had a horrible comb-over that would fly to the other side of his head with a leisurely breeze. He could peel paint off a wall with his perpetual beer and cocaine halitosis. The man was a mess, but a "brilliant lawyer" who knew how to swindle a swindler; he was the ugly mess they needed.

Dick might not have brought charm or class to this bunch, but with his bad breath also came years of experience in real estate. The man had bought, sold, and rented commercial buildings to everyone. He even spent a few years selling mansions to the rich and famous out in California. At the time, Richard Tuff was also one of the greatest attorneys at law in Los Angeles . . . well, actually, in the United States. He knew the ins and outs of every possible loophole when getting you to sign a contract and could flip around and get you off a first-degree murder charge the same day. The man just knew his way around legal documents.

The music industry at this time was full of snakes taking advantage of people (a fact that wouldn't be exposed till years later), hence why Richard was in the business. But the touring industry was fresh and wide open for these men to write new rules daily. Much like life, it was an unfair business at times, and Adolf and company wanted to eat the weak ones alive. They also had a very rich money man who was willing to pay a price to win. Richard was going to be the snake in the grass waiting to strike. Pie knew that Dick was a magician at the fine print or sometimes being a little wordy and back then no one read the small print and the cartel was going to show zero mercy.

In shock at this man, Adolf looked at Pie as if a mud-covered pig was rolling around on the rug. Pie's eyes opened so wide, it was as if he was trying to pop them out of their sockets, like he was saying to Adolf, "Trust me, he's here for a reason." Dick was on the payroll at some fancy management company where he would read artists' contracts, so while artists were off trying to fuck everything that walked, he was looking at the fine print. He knew how to play both sides of the deal, if he liked the artist then he would make sure to help; if not he would contact the other party and workout a payout to keep his mouth shut on the deals. Pie wanted him to use that lump two-feet above his ass to squeeze these artists into shitty payouts so the cartel would take home way more than deserved. This was still just a thought and second to the main goal, transport more coke across the United States, but Dick loved where the future was aiming.

After all the big picture talk was finished the men were sitting around when suddenly Dick stood up. "I'm really glad we're getting into the drug game because my monthly cocaine bill is getting a bit out of control." The lawyer chuckled and twitched his head as he swallowed the cocaine drip that lingered in the back of his throat from his car ride over.

The founding fathers were set. They knew Juan would be calling soon to give details about a meeting but until then they started to work on a number that would give them a little purchasing freedom. They were going to need funds for trucks, buses and a venue.

For a man who wanted nothing to do with Adolf and his flashy lifestyle days prior, the money had seeped into Pie's veins. The man never stopped talking about "what else" they could do internally once they owned the venues. The list went on: ticket sales, parking, suites, and *blah blah blah*. Adolf and Dick didn't care; their little bromance was being fueled by coke, booze, and visions of grandeur. But like all good times, this party had to pack up and do some work if they were going to stay alive and in Juan's good graces.

Concerts existed before these guys took over, obviously. But how you, a fan, interact with the venue and the artist, these men created that new normal. Well, the present-day concert principals were created this weekend, it just took many years of implementing the bigger picture Pie and Adolf were constantly dreaming up. Just think from online purchasing—tickets, T-shirts made in Mexico, and purchasing a beer from the concessions while you're in your seat—are all The Roadie Cartel. Pie thought of this process with a joking statement after the first computer hit the market. "In the future, concertgoers won't have to wait in lines. With the crazy computer systems nowadays, we could charge customers everything with the click of a button!"

It sounded crazy back then, but watching the cartel's pockets grow more prominent with every beer order at their venues was proof these guys were on the right track the whole time. Dick was a good listener when he wanted to be, so he let the two ramble as he absorbed the vital process they were building while pickling himself with both tequila and beers. Adolf was still letting Pie take on all the logistics for the venue and transportation, but he liked all the money laundering talk. For a man who was never formally trained in anything, he was becoming an expert at hustling with other people's money.

The Beverly Hills hotel party was over. They headed to the private hangar with a baggy of coke in each of their pockets and a drink in each hand for the flight. Having the Mexican and American government on the payroll paid off for Juan, especially when flying internationally. Nowadays, we're lucky to have a cartel member or two on the inside to ease the process of crossing borders. We're spoiled when it comes to being at the top of the drug game. Though they had it pretty good back then, too, it was nothing like now. Those men laid down some solid gold roads in places around the world that make it almost impossible for the governments to touch us. Am I going to hate destroying them? Sure, a part of me misses that lifestyle already, even though I am technically still out here. But they fucked with the wrong roadie, and I hope to make everyone who ever had a part in this scheme pay.

Dick, being the man he was, was all in from the start. He was also the guy who was the first out of the car and into the jet. He grabbed the seat with the best view and the most leg room. But like a teen who just figured out the mini bar was left unlocked, he hopped right out of his chair and headed to the bar to raid it. Adolf watched on as this man-child started to inhale mini bottles of tequila, whiskey, and gin. Let's just say Adolf's relationship with Dick has always been an on-and-off again type where Dick's lack of manners chips away at Adolf's patience like a miner in a diamond mine. I say this because you have to know one thing about Adolf: he didn't play well with others. He was that kid on the playground that didn't take well to new people and change in his environments, especially environments where he demanded control. It was too late to change the game now as the plane started to taxi out to the runway. The jet departed Los Angeles, heading south for Juan's hometown in Mexico. If everything went as planned, Pie, Adolf, and Richard would be heading back with more cash than they had ever seen in person.

During an intense conversation about transporting coke, Dick asked, "So how do we get the artists to buy into this, exactly?"

Pie quickly responded with the enthusiasm of a used car salesman who just got his first client. "Well, let me tell you, Dick. It's an all-inclusive touring package deal for the artist. They would sign a contract to use our services, crews, and equipment exclusively for better rates and payouts—so they think. That way, we can use the same buses and trucks we rented them to transport the cocaine. They'll eventually play at selectively promoted routes and venues— we would also control. This is done specifically so we can transport our drugs where we need them to go. To create more control, we'll own those venues . . . and pocket more money since we won't have too much overhead when it comes to staff because those employees would be coming from down south from Juan's Mexican cartel. And Ivan—this guy's brother—" Pie jolted his head toward Adolf, "is going to start this off with the band he's production managing right now. It'll be a test run for trucking, merchandising, and getting this band used to a new team of roadies and road managers."

Without the slightest hint of worry, Dick nodded his head, snorted a big gagger off the jet's table, and said leisurely, "I already know who to call when we land back in LA, we had lunch last week, he is a heavy hitter in the music management department. He has been looking for something along this line with some of his bigger acts, he knows of you so, he will trust your new deals."

The cartel would also turn into a bank for these artists and later shift into a management company of sorts, hence the all-inclusive package Pie was dreaming up . . . a band's one-stop shop. No more going to mom and dad, the label, or friends and asking for money. They could borrow—and here was the kicker—as much money from the cartel as they wanted and whenever for a small fee. You don't need to be some psychologist to know that when an addict wants more, they'll do dumb shit and usually get screwed owing money. Ironically, and it's sad to say, the artists who have signed a deal with us likely make more money—and with better contracts—than had they worked with some of the other crooks running the music industry before us. There have also been a few bands over the years, who, well . . . fell through the cracks, never to be seen again due to a lack of paying debts off. That's another story.

Dick lifted his head from the table, and he squinted his eyes and nose in a valiant effort to squeeze another line of coke up his already clogged nasal passage. "To get more bands to sign deals, we could give them their full payment in cash up front instead of quarterly or monthly installments like the rest of the music industry."

Adolf and Pie looked at each other and nodded in agreement. The cartel couldn't give a rat's ass how money's spent as long as it worked out in the long run. We only care when it's time for them to pay us back. With Pie's long list of clients in his back pocket and his fancy new management title provided by the roadie cartel, he could schmooze these bands and turn this kind of deal into a new trend. The kind of deal where a nonrepayment forfeited the band's music and rights in perpetuity to the cartel instantly with tight NDAs. The vast southwest desert can hide a body, so not many bands mouth off at Dick when payments are due.

In Adolf's eyes, Juan had plenty of money, so he was confident, figuring they could produce results. I think Adolf was crazy enough not to care if he died if it all backfired—Dick, too—but Pie was starting to get nervous suddenly, which was strange to the other guys because Pie had been the most composed up until now. I do not know what spooked him—maybe it was the idea of not living up to his potential in life—the thought of being known as a dead-drug-smuggler, who never actually got the chance to smuggle a single baggie; that shit wouldn't read well for his eulogy. His eyes darted around the jet as if he were about to bail. But thankfully for Pie, Adolf turned towards him, pulled back his arm, and slapped him, leaving Pie's jaw open in shock. Dick grabbed his drink and then pushed back into his seat, unsure what Pie—who was not a small man—would do to the small Adolf.

The physical altercation brought Pie back to his old self. He rubbed the pained cheek gently and exhaled. "Thanks."

Dick, who was so high he could have been running next to the jet, calmly slid back into a relaxed position in his seat, glanced at Adolf and then at Pie. He shrugged his shoulders, finished his drink, and went back to drawing lines in his pile of coke with a straw.

The jet had been running higher than normal in altitude as it made its way south through a stormy night in radio silence and down the cloud-covered coast for most of the flight. It veered east and headed over the mountains that surrounded Juan's hometown. Most crews on Juan's private jets are pretty friendly, but this one was a little different. The men were so amped up about the trip to see Juan they never paid attention, but there were no flight attendants. The trip went from a fairly smooth ride, to a good amount of turbulence and then a very sudden drop in altitude. The men looked around and finally realized they were alone, no attendants and no pilots coming back to let them know what was happening. Pie had been on enough flights now to know they were descending very rapidly, but not as if the jet was falling—but more like a rollercoaster on the first big drop. They all braced for the worst-case scenario while also holding on to hope that this was just how they had to come in for a landing here. Adolf had only been on two flights up till now so he was most freaked out.

"When I experienced an emergency landing a few years ago, the pilots had the decency to communicate with everyone on board," Pie murmured as he clenched his seat's armrests. "Only our pride was hurt that day; seats and underwear had to be cleaned up after we touched down." He added a feeble chuckle and looked a tad worried as he kept a close eye out the window for land.

Dick, high out of his mind finally snapped the longer the fast decent went on. Clenching his heart and praying to something, he was now just hoping that death came fast once they hit the ground. With his sweat covered face glued to the window waiting for a sign that he might survive this one, the plane leveled out and started to slow itself down for a landing. All that heavy breathing left Dicks window fogged up, so even if there was something to be seen he was going to miss it.

The clouds started to thin. The trio could make out blinking lights below them. Then, more lights appeared, but they weren't the standard orange-red color of the runway. These were blue and red. As the ground quickly approached, Pie muttered, "That looks like Mexican Federal *Policia* . . . not the runway lights."

If you're driving your own vehicle, and the cops flip on their lights behind you, you have a few options for escape if that's what you want to do. In this case, the men were helpless. The pilots were not responding, so pulling the plane up and out of Mexican air space was an impossible thing to ask for. But, Adolf ran toward the cockpit and started banging on the door. "Open up, you assholes! What are you doing? Are you fucking us over?" Adolf also added a few more choice words but you get the point, he was pissed, and that wasn't going to get the pilots to answer either.

Mexican jail is no place for a young man, a long-haired roadie, or a chubby drunk lawyer. Adolf thought about blowing out the back door once on the ground and beeline toward the surrounding darkness, but that wouldn't end well in that jungle . . . you are either going to have to fight an armed cartel guard, who is wondering why the fuck you are on the land or Chupacabra in that part of Mexico.

>>>PAUSE RECORDING<<<

I stopped and took a swig from a Red Bull and had to laugh a little at the thought of a vampire rabbit with antlers.

>>>RESUME RECORDING<<<

But let's be real in this situation, the luckiest thing that could happen was the cops found you; but it's not like you can tell the cops you were just cruising down the coast to pick up some cash and drugs for a fun night with boys—oh and the local drug lord. Dick, who was the most petrified, decided he should hide. He tried to squeeze his avocado-shaped body into the tiny shoebox of a closet to hide. Pie was now banging on the cockpit door, yelling, trying to bribe the pilots to keep going while Adolf slumped to the floor and lit a cigarette. With a measly couple of guns and a few rounds of ammunition on board, there was no way the men were going to be able to fight it out with what looked like twenty or more vehicles on the tarmac.

The only thing they could do was talk to the Mexican authorities and hope for a light sentence and be back in the states in twenty years if they were lucky. Mexican cops like to chit-chat, right? Come on now. Those cops were going to want one thing from these men. Like, lots of cash! Cold, hard American cash and nothing else. I don't how much they had on board, but looking at the jet they flew in on, I am sure those officers of the law were not going to settle for a few twenties, a fifty and a watch.

There was also no time to think up a whole story they could all remember. No matter the cost, the last thing they wanted to do was be honest about who they were meeting. "Snitches get stitches" is something to live by, well in my world it is. You don't have to lie, but you don't have to say anything either. They were smart enough to know that talking would never end well for the trio. Not one thing in this moment was a positive for them. They would have a better shot at fighting off the other inmates in a Mexican jail cell than face the wrath of Juan if he found out they said his name around the cops. Even if he did have many of them on the payroll.

Time was up as the trio taxied toward the inevitable end of the roadie cartel, unless this was a genius plan and Juan was going to move forward without them . . .

Inching slowly to the edge of the runway, the jet approached a line of what appeared to be SWAT-style trucks, equipped with off-road style lighting on the top rails and each light set on stun that focused directly on the windows of the jet. The vehicles had executed a flanking maneuver by the time the pilots had cut power to the engines, and the men could hear sirens as the jet grew quiet. With all the resources and money Juan and his late father had pumped into the government and military over the years, it still wasn't enough to have every movement go unseen or overlooked. There were still many law enforcement agents that wanted to take drug smugglers down. Cartels often snitched on their rivals to free up space too.

In a blink of an eye, Pie, Dick, and Adolf's dream came to an abrupt stop as the pilots hit the brakes and killed power. The men sat defeated in light from the trucks that that surrounded them.

A deep, raspy Mexican voice, one of distinct leadership, echoed through a megaphone. The voice barked orders. "¡*Salgan del avión, cerdos americanos!*"

The passengers were frozen. They had no idea what the hell this guy was saying.

"¡*Apresúrate! ¡Tengo una mujer a la que joder, feos pedazos de mierda!*"

The three knew nothing except that their future would switch from unlimited cash to an all-inclusive-stay in a Mexican prison cell.

The cockpit door squeaked open. Adolf and Pie sat closely together as they slowly eyed the pilots, disgusted. They stepped out of their fortress and pulled the handle to extend the jet door and stairs. They quietly exited the plane and disappeared into the blinding lights.

The dust from all the vehicles shifting spots created clouds that rolled through the lights, adding more mystery to what lay beyond the edge of light. What fate would they face? Dick had enough of the man yelling at them and finally exited his little hiding place at the plane's rear. As the fat lawyer inched closer to the exit, Pie's glare turned to Adolf. And like that, Dick was lost in the bright lights shining into the jet. Once swept up in the money and lifestyle, he now watched his dreams of new cars, houses, and helping his mother fly out the window; hatred filled the roadie's eyes, mind, and heart. He had given his life to Adolf in hopes of paradise, only to end up in a Mexican hellhole with these assholes.

Begrudgingly, the hopeless figure of Pie followed Dick off the plane and was gone.

Now alone, Adolf found himself in a dark place in his mind. He didn't want to see it end here, especially considering he had never moved a single bag of coke for Juan yet.

"Maybe this is what my whole life has always been—just a big tease. A big lie. My life has meant nothing." Adolf thought to himself, as he picked himself up off the floor and sat in a nearby chair. He lit his last cigarette and pulled his gun from the waistline of his jeans. Adolf questioned whether to exit and if so, how was it going to end? Or let those Mexican pigs come and rip his dead body out of that jet?

The Mexican police were at the end of their rope too. The voice shouting through the megaphone was angrier and darker than before. "¡Apuntar alto! ¡Asustarlo!"

A round of bullets, starting up close to the cockpit, met the side of the plane.

"¡Otra vez!"

Another round barreled through the cabin, blowing out numerous bottles on the bar and shattering a mirror behind them.

Sitting there with his eyes closed, Adolf imagined his options. He exhaled forcibly and placed the gun on the table next to him. He stood up to exit the plane. Adolf was a scam-artist so whatever he had planned was going to have to work or it would be the last hustle he ever was going to pull. Stepping out from the dark cavern that was the jet and onto the stairs of the plane, going from the darkish cabin to what the eyes could only describe as day. As the disorienting lights beamed directly on Adolf, temporary blindness prevailed until his eyes could open slowly and adjust.

With both feet planted on the tarmac, Adolf could barely determine where they wanted him to go but he headed toward two shadows laid out on the runway. He wasn't sure if the shots fired had gone through his two partners to only end up hitting the plane next, but he hoped this shit show would end with them alive. The selfish Adolf also knew the dead can't tell a story, so maybe it was for the better if they only heard his side of a tale he was now procuring in his head.

With Adolf's hands high in the air and a look of utter defeat slowly spreading across his face, reality forced Adolf to take hold of his situation. His dreams of being an international criminal were short-lived at best, and he had only just started to get a taste of the riches in life. Would Juan's name be his saving grace? Or would connections with a drug lord backfire? Should he choose a brutal life in a Mexican jail cell or a one-way trip to hell through a gunshot to the head? For Adolf, that was a hard choice. He kept looking down at his right side . . .

Out of the dark and from beyond the lights, an unknown figure pushed Adolf forcibly to the ground. On his hands and knees, he heard a set of footsteps approaching. Adolf's mind was racing to places that no man likes to go. Dark places. Adolf closed his eyes and waited.

With each step, the air grew thicker with anticipation. Death has a weird heavy feeling; it is like gravity starts to pull you through the surface. Gravity tugged on Adolf, it started to pull him closer to fire and hell as sweat poured down his face. It was agony listening to the sounds of boots slowly walk on gravel toward him. The footsteps stopped just shy of his soon to be lifeless body. The smell of a cigar wafted toward the defeated man.

"Get that shit out of my face," a voice muttered nearby.

Adolf whipped his head to the left where the two shadowed figures lay on the ground nearby. No telling how he really felt but Adolf smirked as he realized Pie and Dick were alive.

Pie continued. "I've heard the grim reaper smokes, but I'll be damned if that's the last thing I have to smell before I meet my maker." He said in a way that sounded like he wanted this man to kill him.

I guess the thought of jail for some is just too much. I know I personally wouldn't want to be in a prison south of the border for the rest of my life.

With a loud whistle from the cigar smoking grim reaper, the sirens and yelling stopped and then the whole country seemed to have gone still. The paper and its tobacco contents sizzled lazily above. The sound became so crisp and clear—it was like the men were in an anechoic chamber. Then the three men heard something not one of them truly wanted to hear. It was the distinct sound of someone spinning the cylinder of a revolver and then slowly pulling the hammer back, ready to be fired; they waited for the cold hand of death to make its appearance. Everything around the men paused. Even the stars in the sky looking over the tropical forest stopped twinkling as if they were waiting in anticipation for an execution . . .

CLICK.

Silence . . .

Still alive. The captives lie there with their eyes tightly clinched shut, waiting for something to happen now that it appears the first shot was a misfire.

Still, nothing moved except the sound of the cigar paper still burning.

Then . . . slowly, a soft chuckle built from the belly of the shooter. Adolf opened his eyes slowly, one at a time. With some hesitation, he decided to roll his head to face the standing silhouette.

The chuckle grew into laughter. And there he stood. Juan! Who was full on laughing now, as tears were streaming down his face, a cigar hanging from one side of his mouth, and a giant revolver in his hand.

I had always questioned what turned Adolf into the man that he was. Maybe this situation is what drove him to stand up for himself more. He never seemed right after this moment. Not many people can say their boss toyed with their life and then laughed at you. He saw what psychological warfare could do to a man, and I think he got a sick pleasure from making his victims suffer like he did that night on the runway.

Rising to their feet and dusting off the runway dirt, their audience of men laughed in unison. As the Mexican police started to shut down the halogen lights, the victims of Juan's practical joke could see again. About fifty or so Mexican police and military men stood around, along with two people Pie and Richard would become very close with.

Adolf introduced his companions to the new boss and his sister.

"It's good to see you all aren't a bunch of snitches. I had this gun ready for anyone who said my name." Pulling a gun from a side holster, Juan pointed it at the jet and opened fire, blowing out a few windows and the light blinking on the top of the craft. He was having a blast. Hell, Juan shot his jet a few times now, all to put on a show for friends. Pie and Dick quickly learned Juan loved to spend money and had a zero-tolerance policy when testing his employees.

Juan was constantly breaking down and testing loyalty; he wanted to see where people were mentally and sometimes physically. He believed true colors would shine under heavy pressure, and in that last moment before breaking, if you held on and kept your shit together, that would separate the wheat from the chaff. He ordered Dick to wait in a car alone with a couple of hitmen who didn't speak English—a test to see if the walking avocado could hang with the big boys. Then, the parched Juan who was ready to tie one on with the other men, whistled at two police officers standing by a truck who brought over beers and tequila to help quench his thirst, calm their nerves and get them ready for the wild ride back to the main farm.

Juan, Adolf, Pie, and Zora piled into an armored military truck that had been transformed inside, much like a limousine, complete with a mini fridge, ice, and leather seats. Pie looked out his passenger window and caught a glimpse of Dick's face, pale and terrified, while Adolf filled in some details with his old/new friend about the lawyer.

Juan replied, carefully enunciating every word. "'Faithless is he that says farewell when the road darkens.'" He added, *"No me jodas. ¡Salud!"*

The kicker with Juan was you never knew how many of his tests you had to pass, but he'd forever have your back if you succeeded. Although Adolf had passed his first test when he had killed the cartel member for Juan, tonight's assessment was probably because he was about to spend a lot of Juan's money. He provides the wealth everyone dreams of having that the majority are not willing to go after. That was the point, though. Were you ready to be brutally loyal so that Juan never had to question you? Was that worth going through hell on earth even if he would give you all the money you would ever need? He needed to find that out about the lawyer. For some reason, Juan took to Pie fairly quickly.

"I hear you are some kind of . . . touring logistical genius or expert?" Juan asked Pie in a seriocomic manner.

"Yeah, I am pretty good at moving gear and other shit around the world," Pie said with a humble smirk.

"And the chubby drunk one in the other truck understands how to manipulate contracts and hide money very well, yes? But I would have imagined you to be the drunk one," Juan joked to Pie.

"Dick knows what we need to do to buy and build a bigger than normal legal business on paper to launder money back down here to you," Pie pushed back with a little fire.

With a loud snort, Zora spit out her tequila. She had never heard "dick" used in any other way than describing the male anatomy. Adolf—who doesn't do this often—chuckled, shook his head in a playful manner, and reached for the bottle of tequila in the center console; he poured her another shot and took a big pull right from the bottle. His nerves were still going a mile a minute.

Juan's cartel was always heavily armed when they traveled—anywhere—and although Juan and his guests were partying, his security details had their safety off and finger on the trigger, ready for anyone who cared to break up the fun. They all had to be loyal and willing to do whatever Juan demanded, mainly for the security and exclusivity of being welcomed into his cartel. So, as the caravan of trucks made their speedy exit from the runway heading to the hills and back mountain roads to Juan's compound, he handed Pie and Adolf each a gun too.

"Although most people in this area love me, there are enemies who try to pick a fight from time to time. So, if anyone tries anything," Juan's smile broadened, "just shoot—and don't worry about asking questions. Anyone with an ounce of smarts in the town will not ask."

A roadie, a cartel boss, a lawyer, and two Czech immigrants leave an airport . . .

Now that sounds like the start to a bad joke. In seriousness, none of them could have ever dreamt the punchline in a million years. They did all have similar qualities—and different ones too. All (except for perhaps one) didn't want to live by the traditional rules of society. Hell, none of them ever wanted to get a normal nine-to-five "job." Roadies found sanctuary in groups when—you guessed it—on the road together, much like a gang or cartel members. Touring and cartels are businesses that had no rules, regulations, or "big brother" looking down, telling them how to do their gig. Roadies just sucked it up, good or bad, rain or shine, sober or drunk. No matter your job.

And on tour, there was only one goal: the show, well, until now.

The road was not just a home to Ivan; it was also the only family he had now, so he took the roadie life very seriously. He loved the hard work and accomplished feeling after the show. Of course, he was pissed that his brother was tainting something he found pleasure in, again. Sure, those guys were "working and building an idea," but Ivan was stuck back in La La Land. He was there learning to be a production manager via trial by fire—one of the greatest tests a man can go through but still he missed his friend Pie teaching him. Yeah, he had seen Pie in action, but that is nothing compared to doing it yourself. He had never managed anything aside from a few sheep back on the farm, and he was learning firsthand that dealing with artists and band members was like herding cats, not sheep. And Ivan had to wear a lot of hats up at rehearsals in the mansion: pot buyer, pot finder, cocaine buyer, cocaine finder, LSD buyer, LSD finder, chef, maid, door greeter, groupie bouncer, and many other hats that he didn't sign up for. But this was the mess Pie left for him to work on. And Ivan was not someone to let down on a job when told to do it.

This would shift once the roadie cartel started touring. They flipped the game to be about the money and cocaine, sure there was a show, but not for the right reasons. Ivan was in a good spot, though. He had a new gig that was way better in many aspects than what Pie was going through down in Mexico. Was Pie going to make more money? Sure, but Ivan only had to answer to Pie and make sure the drugs would get around the states. He obviously didn't know what his job would be yet, but in the end, he would be relieved to find out he wouldn't have to answer to Adolf or Juan directly. This was a big deal because, even though Ivan was soon going to be a "drug trafficker," he was not like the rest. There was a big difference between Ivan and the rest of the roadie cartel members: his conscience. He would let the good in him fight temptations of evil unlike the rest of them. Over the years, I saw Ivan do things that would have gotten him killed if the cartel saw him putting them in jeopardy. On numerous occasions, he donated his entire salary and bonus from a tour to charities for children (and in person nonetheless), but that was Ivan. He was better off far away from the craziness happening in Mexico and lucky to be a green production manager finding weed than what the others were doing.

Sadly, over time, Ivan would become the underappreciated workhorse for the cartel, just another number in a giant conglomerate that used to call him family. Some people may see these videos and think being a rich roadie cartel member sounds amazing, but they don't understand the struggle and sacrifice. They only hear me talking about the travel and money. People view the music industry similarly, hence why this front was so seamless. Everyone thinks they would love to work for their favorite artist, but truth be told, you would be surprised by how many little crybaby divas there are. Ivan has been lucky, for the most part, with his artists. Not all of them were complete jerks over the years, but a special few could have used a punch to the jaw. Artists weren't the only self-important and temperamental people on tour either, Ivan dealt with many personalities over the years. There are plenty of crew and band members who would make Ivan's life hell some days as he rose to be a great production manager. Needless to say, running a tour is challenging on its own. The Roadie Cartel only added stress by moving millions of dollars of coke around the country on top of all the band equipment and show pressure already going on. I don't think anyone saw it growing the way it did, except Pie.

Luckily for Ivan, his first gig was a simple rock band that just wanted to party. He got to learn the ins and outs of being a production manager before he was really under intense pressure from the roadie cartel. Ivan was in this game whether he liked it or not. So, while the guys were down south slugging shots of fine tequila and carrying on, he was the responsible one learning a new craft and keeping the ship floating till they got back with money, trucks, and supplies. Although the band was pretty laid back, Ivan was in a tough spot because Pie had skipped town and left him without answers to many production questions. The only thing he could do to keep his artists from asking more of the same questions was to get them high again or to use words that were above their knowledge of the touring world.

Remember, there wasn't email or text messaging back then; instead, it was letters and phone calls. In the band's defense, Ivan was waiting for Pie to call, write, show up . . . anything at this point with money or some final venue routing. With just under a few weeks to go, the countdown had started for the roadie cartel's first client to leave on tour. Pie and Dick had to make sure they were back with cash in hand to purchase trucks and buses, followed by distribution planning.

There was no real magic to this business except the idea that they would make touring easier for the bands if they used their all-in-one services of buses, trucks, security, promoter, management, and production crew. Ivan was trying to get the band to understand that their situation was under control and that, even though Pie was no longer their production manager, he still had their back and best interests. Ivan was handling the situation like a pro but like any new face in an organization it can be difficult.

Sometimes a little tough love goes a long way. He won the band over one night during a rehearsal when he flipped his production table over and told them, "Play your fucking music, and leave the bus, merchandise and routing for your fucking show to me to figure out." This attitude of a hard-love father figure made Ivan indispensable to artists over the years.

Whatever Ivan was doing, he knew that making this roadie cartel thing work, even though it went against what he really wanted to do in the industry, would make his situation better. At least he kept telling himself that because being stuck in Los Angeles sucked for him. He was alone, beat up from working with the band twenty hours a day and homesick for Czechoslovakia; regardless, he kept working on the project, hoping those four were not just down south partying the nights away. And like that, Ivan stopped thinking about his brother's stupid choices and just did what he could to be ready for their arrival back in LA. He knew they would not give him the heads up when it would be go-time, so he was prepped for anything thrown his way. That prep started with the band trusting him to get all the logistics and travel arranged so they could have their morning LSD drops as they practiced the same song repeatedly.

Ivan had his lonely hotel room in Beverly Hills each night. Even the nicest rooms, all the women in the world, and the finest booze can leave the hardest of men homesick. Sitting on a bed next to a phone that doesn't ring is a hard pill to swallow. It's a funny trade-off: the longer you tour, the more you want out, even though everyone you meet would die to live two seconds in your shoes. Sadly, Ivan no longer had contact with his mother and father, his sister and brother were always away, and the one guy he'd hang with on occasion was now best buddies with his deranged older brother and a drug lord. Life was shitting on him once again. On nights like these where a headfirst dive into the warm city concrete below sounds like a nice option, Ivan never went there. He loved life way too much, even on the shittiest of days.

Looking back, maybe that's why Ivan became so close to me when I came around. He treated me like the family he had lost and showed me the world I would never have expected. I didn't understand why Ivan never returned home, leaving his brother and sister—who obviously had more important things on their minds. But he would tell me he'd cause too much pain if he went back. Adolf had told him that the town would have run him off along with their mother and father for what he had done that night before they ran away. Usually, if we were on this subject, it was late and we were very drunk, so Ivan tended to trail off soon after that, and we never soberly talked about him leaving Czechoslovakia or even the potential of a surprise return one day.

The silver lining is that his loneliness and having to grow up so fast turned him into one hell of a detailed production manager. They say he is the best in the business. I'm sure he was corrupt with certain parts of the touring industry, but one thing was certain: the crew came first to him, always. Not just the roadie cartel crew either. Even though we got some extra perks, he cared for the crew more than the rock stars. This was for obvious reasons. The bands and the cocaine wouldn't get anywhere without the crew, and, seeing that most bands and the cartel never realized that, he went above and beyond and made it a point to make the crew feel like the real rock stars.

Back in Mexico, the police escort made it to the farm, and everyone was ready to continue the fun night. Adolf, Pie, and Dick had all but forgotten the joke pulled on them back at the private runway. By the time they reached the front door, the four horsemen were lit up like the fourth of July sky, so Zora decided it was guys' night and left them to do what boys do best—get into trouble. And trouble for Juan and the men was nothing like the average person's shenanigans. Who the hell was going to tell Juan to turn the music down? Or stop firing your guns into the night sky?

Dick was the drunkest out of them all and, in no way, shape, or form, ready for business talks. He had the most fun on his ride with his new sicario friends. They tried to intimidate him at first, but after they saw the fat gringo could drink some mezcal and take a joke, the party turned up. Dick never shot a gun until that point in life; with a few rails of coke and a liter of booze, they let him up through the sunroof for his own rumble in the jungle rampage. I don't think he hit anything except a few trees and maybe the truck's tailgate a time or two, but his adrenalin was at an all-time high, along with his testosterone. Dick wanted to party—and party with all the women of Juan's small town; the money laundering and contract talk could wait.

As the men retreated to the billiard room to rage, Zora strolled the house back to her guest room. It was gaudy like all the mansions. Juan's family had a thing for bullfighters, so beautiful paintings of Mexican bullfighters and conquistadors lined the hallway. Every painting stretched nearly from floor to ceiling, and a handful showcased a half-naked woman in the arms of the bullfighter, rescued from the evil bull that was now lying dead under the bullfighter's foot—very epic. A common embellishment was the family's favorite precious metal: gold. I mean, I guess if I had millions in cash under each bed, I would have toothbrushes, threaded rugs, and handrails made from gold too.

Exhausted and a little drunk from the tequila she slugged on the ride back to the mansion, Zora wanted to find her bed, close her eyes, and get a good night's rest. When she finally got into her room, she soon realized she wasn't alone in the room. . .

>>>STOP RECORDING<<<

CHAPTER 11

North on Interstate 5

I have always hated coming to this old arena. Mainly because after all the years it is still the same as it was when Ivan and Pie brought the first big show through the doors. It boils down to this, more work for the crew and me. Looking at the time, we did finally get all the gear in and the product to the lab faster than expected, which means we earned a small victory today. Okay, so the people are pretty solid, the food around here rocks and the place is kind of iconic; they did shoot a movie here. But it is one of the cartel's older arenas and in my opinion, still a shit hole.

Looking at an empty wall with my feet up on my desk, I think about the tiny wins that got the cartel this far. There is no coincidence that we are at the top of the food chain not only with all the illegal cartel stuff but also the whole music side to the hustle. I think back to the stories I have heard about the first tour and think of where the cartel is now. Holy shit, The Roadie Cartel has come a long way.

I feel like I have come a long way since starting these video diary/vlog things. I know my life might not be exactly where I want it to be this second, but each day that I stay above ground is a good day, I guess.

I took a second to ponder before I hit the red dot on my screen. I think . . . I had left off with everyone except Ivan down in Mexico . . . and . . . *hmmmmm* . . . raising an eyebrow and looking around the room . . .

"Oh yeah, Zora!" I said aloud as I pressed the red button with my thumb.

>>>START RECORDING<<<

This is Video Diary #10 and it is October 27, 2009,
San Diego, California

Life is a giant gamble. A winner—take all kind of sport—the biggest one-time, all-in roll of the dice you can ever play. The sad part is most end up like me: in a job you get sucked into, that eventually makes you question your morals after something traumatic happens, and then—bam it's over. In a second you are six feet under, left to rot in a metal drum in the middle of some desert and before the sun goes down on your new plot of land, you are replaced. If I would have known better, I would have bet on myself in a different way. I don't know what I would have done, but I'm sure my younger self, holding my stuffed tiger and standing at the first step of that tour bus, saw this touring life a little different back then.

The three men down in Mexico, Pie, Dick and Adolf, gambled with their lives in the biggest way possible in those early days. Most never take full advantage of their momentary time here on this sphere we call Earth. These men had one shot at making this roadie cartel work and creating a payout for Juan that no other cartel or person in history could fathom. The roadie cartel is exactly what it says: a cartel. But it was so much more too; we were misfits with multiple businesses coming together to manipulate a service for a very big monetary gain, and there were no second chances. Juan was not in a—what I have coined "friend-ness" no, he was in business with these men. So, they better fucking produce results or their time on this planet would end quicker than this little faction started. At this point, well, once the trucks start running, he was expecting that the money he was fronting these three would start to yield a very high return. He was a businessman, and he knew it was a gamble. Juan was versatile, so he could facilitate certain equipment and textiles for making merchandise to help the men on their journey. But there was no guarantee on any of this. The only assurance Juan had in the deal was that their three lives were on the line, and I imagine that was plenty of inspiration for the trio to get back to the states and make this operation successful.

Pie continued to push when anxiety ran high; he insisted that the touring industry needed something to catapult it further into the mainstream market. Sure, they were building the industry up for selfish reasons. No matter the reasoning, the artists and managers who would buy into this idea and help turn it into a billion-dollar industry needed better promoting options, transportation, and new music venues. Pie also added that once the fans were able to consume their favorite music live in more cities, more often and in venues with better equipment, well, then the cartel would win the game. Much like Juan's cartel, the music industry, especially the venues these artists were playing were in dire need of some serious work—a makeover of epic proportions! For one, most were made for sporting events, not concerts, hence why we developed places made just for concerts . . . amphitheaters.

Coming into an already booming industry as a kid, I knew millions of fans worldwide would pay billions of dollars over and over to see these artists. So, when I was finally privileged enough to see the money that we took in from taxing the artists and owning the venues, I was in shock. The amount of money the roadie cartel makes from their splits post-ticket sales, merchandise splits, venue splits and management fees . . . well, let's just put it this way. The cartel makes more per minute than most middle-class American families do in a year, and the cartel makes this all day, every day and each year that number grows. No wonder artists tour nonstop year after year the way they do; we own them, and we will get our money back from them one way or another. If they tried to slow their touring down, they would be dead broke, washed up, and back on Beale Street playing covers of "Jessie's Girl."

While the men were down south trying to build up this new faction to the Mexican cartel, they had to also remember, Juan's mother and sister were pioneers in the game too. The resources they needed were endless and part of their team. This was good and bad but more on that later. La Reina was a ruthless queen in a sea of men who wanted to be kings, but never in a thousand lifetimes would they have the guts to go against her. She and Juan ran the show down in Mexico and—up until recently—what she said was law. She played ruler while her brother was off spending money and having fun. To La Reina's surprise, when he showed up with this new love interest and three men ready to be partners in the family business, she was livid. The last thing she wanted was to be taken down a peg or two to answer to her big brother and be second fiddle to his new play dates.

From the second Zora walked in, La Reina hated her. She wouldn't even acknowledge her presence in a room. There were already two women in the cartel, which was one too many in her opinion. But La Reina was not ready to kill her mom for total dominance, at least from how the story was told to me. Plus, Juan's mother, after Juan Sr.'s death, mainly cooked and played dress up on weekends for one outing to church, so there was no real threat. Zora now made three, and from what La Reina could see, she already had Juan's ear. Now, I don't think Zora had ever said where to spend any money, but just the idea that he was spending money on her and Adolf was driving Juan's sister crazy. I assume most spoiled children from rich families feel that way when they watch an outsider come in. For all they know, the outsider might actually make the situation better. Regardless, bratty family members can make the outsider's life hell. Zora was tough, though. Even if she did appear to be a skinny model type from Europe, she had been through a lot. From growing up on a farm to hustling the streets of New York at night, she wouldn't go down without a fight.

The night had already been highly intense with the prank on the men as they landed. Let's also include the wild and reckless ride back to the compound. And then there was the awkward meeting of family. This was Juan though, he loved that wild and crazy party lifestyle that a bachelor with his money totally would gravitate to. Although he had access to the money, Juan was not the one who kept an eye on the books. Yes, cartels have books, how do you think we remember who owes us debts? La Reina was the overseer of these books and with each new business venture, she watched her inheritance slowly dwindle. Juan assured her this was different, but after Juan blasted a few holes in the side of his multi-million-dollar jet with his gun like it was a coffee can on a fence post, she wasn't sure just yet. She was interested in the idea; it was just going to take her time to come around or at least she would believe once money rolled in. That is what makes the sibling rivalry so deep, especially in this household, they aren't playing for a hundred-dollar bill, no, they are playing for a few hundred million if Juan fucks this deal up.

So, knowing that info the four horsemen of the cartel had to focus. The men had one logical thing left for them to do before the deal was set in stone—and it was not heading to one of Juan's nightclubs to drink all the booze. Close, and there was tequila but this night the men needed to light up a few cigars, sit around and have a male bonding session. They were about to work together and Juan was all about "family." It was time to seal this deal in history and walk into battle, first in North America, then they were going to cash in a few European favors people owed to the Mexican Cartel.

While the misfits sipped fine tequila, Zora made her way up to her bedroom. There was no place for her in their little male bonding session, so sleep was the main priority. So as the sheep got ready for the counting, Zora decided to take a leisurely walk past some stunning views inside the mansion walls, of paintings, statues, and imported marble that lined the walkways and pillars. Her room was located adjacent to Juan's master quarters. She had one of the more spacious rooms in the house. After a long couple of weeks —maybe even a long couple of months since leaving Czechoslovakia—Zora was ready to sleep like a bear even if only for a night. Unfortunately, there were other plans for her that she soon would find out about.

Before I get to the details about what I know from this night, I want to share a thought. There is something fun about a good old-fashioned fist fight. I have been in a few. I know it sounds weird coming from a tattooed roadie, but I do believe getting your bell rung will change the way words come out of your mouth toward another human. Maybe I am just rowdier than most, but I will forever at least know if I am about to tell you my thoughts, then I am also ready for the consequences of maybe having to take one on the chin. Now, I will say fuck anyone who sucker punches another person, only chicken shits do that shit. I have never killed anyone for this cartel, but Adolf and La Reina are a different breed, even inside this criminal empire where we have a few hired guns to handle business. I don't know which one was worse, La Reina or The Butcher. . . each had Machiavellian, narcissistic and psychopathic traits. Zora was obviously taking up lots of real-estate in La Reina's mind and the storm boiling inside her was not going to produce a beautiful rainbow after the dark clouds released her wrath.

Although she had been there for a few days now, Zora leisurely strolled down the half-dark hallway toward her room, stopping long enough to analyze each picture a little more than the time before, which were lit from above by old, golden fixtures. There was one eerie thing that she overlooked during her momentary pauses in the dim lights that only seemed to illuminate the paintings. There was not a single other soul in the halls. It was as if the help had been told to retire early from their duties on that side of the mansion this night; the only movement came from a lonely house cat wanting attention. Zora paused once again and bent over to stroke the tail of her new furry friend. After a little biscuit making and a few soft mews, the cat suddenly startled. It looked down the hall, but as Zora turned to look in that direction, the not-so-brave feline scurried off. Okay, so there is no one around, and a cat ran off. There's nothing wrong with this picture, at least in Zora's mind. In her young life, she has dealt with scarier situations, plus all she was worried about at this point was how long Juan was going to let her sleep in tomorrow. So, she moved on toward her room. This last detail is one that would have even put me on edge a little, but if you don't think you have an enemy or something out to harm you . . . then why would you have a concern to not move forward? And Zora wanted that bed, badly. She opened the door, and as she flipped the switch, nothing. Standing in the doorway looking into the dark room, her hand pushed the switch down. Then up again. One more time she tried the old small light switch,

down . . .

up . . .

Darkness still.

In Zora's room was a small crack in the blinds that let the moonlight illuminate a small strip of floor, which helped guide her to the bathroom, where she hoped that light worked. She navigated the dark walk past the bed located on her left and narrowly missed the large oversize bench that sat in front of it. She shuffled her feet slowly across the floor on the way to the far right-hand corner of the room. With fifteen feet or so left in her journey, she encountered the reading chairs in front of the fireplace to her right. After a couple close missteps, she made it to a familiar feeling, the mink rug. This thing was so plush that each step felt like what one would think walking across the clouds to feel like. She knew once that pillow-like sensation was over, there would only be about ten more steps to the bathroom door which was closed, aiding in the extra darkness in the room.

It reminds me of a few drunk nights in dark hotel rooms. You kind of remember where things are when you get up in the middle of the night to pee, and with the little bit of light from the alarm clock guiding your way to the bathroom, you feel like a world-class hurdler that has made the last jump on your way to gold when you finally reach the toilet. But I have peed in a few chairs and a closet over the years.

The house was by no means silent, but a subtle sound—one that didn't blend in with the creaks of an old mansion—behind Zora brought her to a dead stop. In darkness, it's amazing how much the human hearing elevates to compensate for lack of sight. She stopped dead in her tracks just a few paces shy of the bathroom door. As she turned, she gave it a long, silent three-count to see if it happened again . . . all stayed still in the room.

She whispered reassurance to herself in her native tongue, trying to calm herself down. She advanced toward the bathroom door, which was sitting no more than a few feet from her now. When she glanced back to start the last of her journey, she saw a figure that wasn't there before.

Seeing a shadow move in an empty room can cause the toughest of people let out a noise. Zora's noise was similar to a dog who just found the electric fence for the first time. The yelp she let out, although loud, wasn't loud enough to make it through the thick solid wood bedroom door, then down the halls, through the music playing on the jukebox, and out to the men carrying on with bevvies and cigars. Her eyes, in a constant refocusing state, could only make out the long hair and silhouette of a woman. Everything made her think she was staring at a ghost. The shadow let out its own cry, one of a banshee. The lioness, La Reina, lunged at Zora as if attacking a baby water buffalo who wandered too far from her mother. Her cold hands closed tightly around Zora's neck. With each new clench of her hands, her fingers acted like ten pythons slowly working each molecule of air out of Zora's windpipe.

But like I said, Zora is one tough woman. Even with this death grip on her neck, the young Zora wrapped her arms and a leg around Juan's sister in some farm-hog wrestling move. Then with the other free leg, Zora took one quick step to the side, and they both went to the ground like a sack of potatoes. Remember, this was a watered-down version told to me over beers one night, so for all I know it was way more violent. Soon, the seemingly uneven fight turned, and it was like watching two alligators' death rolling each other on a *National Geographic* special.

Fighting requires two things: skill and the desire to win. The problem is that when both parties want to live and are equally aggressive, the fight gets ugly quickly, which Juan's sister didn't expect in the slightest. Zora may not have trained in mixed martial arts, but she grew up on a farm with two brothers and stubborn ass animals. She had that farm-girl strength from years of wrestling cows into their stalls and fighting her younger brother, who loved trying his new wrestling moves on her. No one knows how long this fight truly lasted; I feel like a minute in some fights is too long. Zora was fighting for her life and was shocked and impressed with just how feisty and ruthless this little Latina was. I do not see this being a cat fight with hair pulling between hormonal pre-teen girls. I picture it more like Mike Tyson is fighting a grizzly bear with the fight in the middle of a cage, and that cage is lined with knives and guns, but they ignore all the weapons and just keep swinging for the knockout punch.

Okay, so there are so many unknowns. But hell, that's life. For instance, does a tree make a sound when it falls in a forest if no one is around? Does a bear shit in the woods? What is the proper etiquette with toilet paper, over or under when on the roll? But my quandary: just how did the fight end? No one really knows. Between our small circle, we think in the midnight hour, Zora got the upper hand and forced La Reina to call a truce. It is the only logical answer. Both women are still alive. One thing for sure is you'll never see them in a room together. I don't think they even like to be in the same country at the same time. But whatever went down that night, they have left each other alone ever since. There isn't one person in the cartel that will mess with Zora to this day either. We all know La Reina is a ruthless, feed-your-teeth-to-you-from-a-curb-style Latina, but what Zora did that night was something the cartel never expected to see from that little European girl. She came out of the room alive.

On the other side of the house, the male-bonding tequila retreat was going just as everyone thought it would. Everyone was lit. Very little work was getting done, but they did talk about how great they'll all be once they pull off this scheme. They were finishing some things, technically: shot after shot of some of the best tequila in all of Mexico and plenty of blow was slowly diminishing. I mean, what did they really have to do at this point? Ivan was picking up the slack in Los Angeles, Pie had his team of promoters working on new artist deals that he would go after when he got back, and Dick was ready to draw up contracts at a moment's notice. So, in reality, the main point of the trip was to get everyone on the same page and to make sure Juan also liked Richard and Pie. Oh, and they had to get Juan up to speed on the roadie cartel's business ventures like buying arenas, merchandising, and offshore accounts for laundering the money. Okay, there was still plenty on the table to do, but those loose ends would be solidified once back in California. Dick just needed a giant lump of cash to go back with him, shortly followed by another and even bigger lump of cash so he could start the buying of arenas.

The guys lived at a different tempo when they were with Juan. It was not island time, but it was similar. Could you blame the man? Juan was great at delegating work, and if you happened to be in the room when he wanted to party, then chances were good that you were joining the celebration. The early hours of a new day found the men still swigging tequila on one of the many balconies overlooking the mountain terrain. That was where most of their conversations happened that night. Juan told the guys repeatedly that his main concern was doubling—then tripling—the cocaine he was currently moving into the United States. That was it! "I do not care what it costs or how it was done," he tended to say that with a laugh and a smirk and would sometimes follow that statement with, "I like you guys and would hate to kill you if you fuck this up." Maybe there was a small amount of urgency in the conversations, but they all knew there was not much they could do until Juan was ready to stop playing host, give them money and get back to the grind.

Juan is a hangover champion. He is the last to go down and the first to be up. I think he might have even gotten a swim in before the others rose from their mini-comas midday, but it was go time. He had his fun, and so did the men, and now certain items needed tending to. Dick was there to start drawing up all the legal documents. He would also follow along with Adolf and Pie as they described more of the plans to Juan. Dick was there to make sure he and his team could take this illegal idea and bend the rules regarding the laws and Uncle Sam. To ensure the arena's success, they had to make this look like legit businesses with "real" investors and partners. Even down to the city code inspectors coming in to make sure the bleach was kept in the proper closet for the cleaning crew. They wouldn't be able to bounce back if they blew their cover mainly because they would all be dead. So, Richard's team had a lot on their plate, but that's why they brought in the best legal criminal money could buy.

Buying buildings, setting up a merchandise company, and an off-shore account that funds it all, was going to be an intense game of chess with customs and the United States government. Especially the tax man; he's the one you never want to mess with . . . because he will find you. Luckily, Dick had already set up a fake identity (years before meeting Pie) with the belief that he would need an escape plan for the shady shit he'd get into. Although he had not lived his second identity yet, ole "Duke Vaughn Johnson" from Massachusetts is now residing in the Cayman Islands with his beautiful third wife and their two golden retrievers. "Duke" still had a house, a boat, and a bar tab out on Cape Cod. But the business, that was in the Caymans; he didn't like working in that cold New England weather . . . *wink, wink.*

Okay, the scam goes a little like this:

The Roadie Cartel/Mexican cartel would operate with Duke Vaughn Johnson as the main investor of all the properties/businesses. For all tax purposes, he lives in the Cayman Islands. Now DVJ, we will call him, can be exempted from all his taxes, but what he lends out has to come back clean as a whistle. The nice part is that Dick's team can fudge the books to look like whatever the cartel sends back is exactly what they borrowed; they make zero profit. So, this happens to be exactly what DVJ lent them in the first place. But here is the rub. The cartel is not able to be that borrower, so we have created one more person. We will call him the "fall guy." The fall guy is the one on all the documents and business cards and taxes. He's the one who took the loan from DVJ to buy all his new arenas. Now DVJ International, AKA The Roadie Cartel's trust can do what they want with this property as long as all cash goes back to Mr. Johnson's bank account outside the United States. So, whether The Roadie Cartel's Trust rents the arena for a daily rental by your favorite musical act or annually by the local hockey team, they don't technically own it. Mr. Johnson does and whatever money they take in first has to go back to pay off their debts to him. Well, once that debt is paid, wouldn't you know it . . . the arena needs some new renovations, which you guessed it, get done by Mexican cartel hired men for pennies on the dollar.

Dick was going to set up a second man as the fall guy; he was no dummy and The Roadie Cartel's trust is not named that, I wish I knew that info. Maybe, just maybe the key I have will lead me to this answer. So, he created an identity inside the states who was the taker of the money, who would then be able to borrow the money from DVJ. On top of funneling all earnings back to Mr. Johnson in the Caymans, the fall guy would pay back the amount originally borrowed, per the contract, resulting in no taxes needing to be paid. Then Duke, being the nice guy he was, would lend the fall guy a second loan since he made him a profit on the first one, thus continuing the feedback loop.

The money would be able to go across the states only to buy another venue and renovations. Then all borrowed money would be able to return to the Caymans via a money wire along with the profits per the contract written up by Dick's team. Then Mr. Johnson cashes out his bank account for cash, which could then leave via boat, plane, or whatever form Juan decided to get his cash back to his hometown in Mexico. The trick was to bypass the tax system and shuffle money out the back door of more banks on the island. It was only fair not to bring any more heat into Juan's life. He was just a hard-working drug tycoon trying to feed his small town in Mexico.

Now, Pie was there to make sure Juan's textile plants would get up to speed on making merchandise for the clients they would soon take on to help hide the drugs. Plus, they would make the products at a fraction of the cost they were paying in the states. The roadie cartel would then turn around and charge the client the same price, seeing that they are already comfortable paying that amount.

Then over the years, the roadie cartel could gradually increase the amount initially charged. At the time, most band shirts were being printed by friends of friends who could only handle making small batch quantities anyways. Their company would be the first merchandise manufacturer to cater specifically to the touring world's high-volume needs. The Roadie Cartel was planning on bringing mass quantities and multiple prints to the merch table. Of course, they would offer more items down the road, but the idea of having two, three, or even four tour T-shirts to choose from was unheard of. But, Juan had the factories to make this reality come to life.

Pie had to explain how the merch table operated at concerts, not because the principal was hard to grasp, but obviously drinking booze into the early morning tends to black some brain cells out. This merchandising venture would add a position to the road crew and be one more way to legally funnel cocaine cash money back to Juan, no one but the tour at this time needed to know how many T-shirts were being sold. Plus, the extra position would allow the roadie cartel to make a little extra money off the band while that merch tech can babysit the cocaine.

This job came with two responsibilities. First, they count in the shirts and other merch items and then obviously sell during the show. Secondly, they would pull the stashed bricks and bundles from the shipped-in boxes. Looking back at what they came up with, it's hard to believe they were the first to do it this way, especially with how cheap the shirts were to make in Mexico. Adolf never saw his plan getting to this level. It was pretty amazing for Juan to see this man, who just a few weeks earlier wanted nothing to do with this crazy Czech and his "transportation business," put together the world's greatest drug front.

For Juan to take hold of the tour clothing market, his knock-off denim jean company would have to switch priorities and focus on printing band T-shirts and sweatshirts. This would take a hot minute to get supplies ready and swap logistics in the factory, but it was doable. Getting this factory and others up and running was one of the most pivotal roles in how this operation would be moving merchandise and drugs north into the states the second they could start packaging and then shipping. But this was the main point Pie continued to speak on. They couldn't just transport these shirts anywhere; it had to be to a central location so they could start distributing to tours for movement across the states.

Pie and Dick had to join brains and focus on where they should purchase the cartel's first arena. For distribution purposes, they had to have a building on a major highway system that could receive these merchandise packages 24/7 and then also have the ability to move the product back out the door with as little interruption and minimum visibility from the outside world as possible. Supply and demand for cocaine was climbing in the states too, so the last thing the cartel wanted was to have a third party move in on their territories. The roadie cartel would play the biggest role in keeping Juan's cartel at the forefront of the cocaine distribution and trafficking game in the states and then the world.

With all this talk of transportation and geographic locations, Pie was happy to see Juan had a giant globe of the earth in one of his many libraries at the house. He walked the three men into the room and described the star topology of the road systems in the United States. Roads, byways, and backwoods dirt farm roads were essential to running the blow and moonshine around the states in the past. Now there were superhighways, freeways and airports that were passing through every town, city, and township. The future of transporting coke was here and the men had literally an open road and clear skies to do with it as they pleased.

Pie, without hesitation, pointed to Nebraska on the giant globe. This is where they would buy the first arena. This is where they would build a state-of-the-art-lab in the basement to house, cut, and package the blow. This fucking arena was going to be the first of its kind and the game changer in drug manufacturing and distribution of cocaine. Then, they were going to start peppering the country with more roadie cartel owned arenas and venues, Pie went on to explain. One city at a time. Top to bottom, left to right, and everything in between. Dick sat up and in what sounded like a form of English but was just his hungover tone asked one of those questions that stopped everyone dead in their thoughts. "What if one of the owners of an arena doesn't want to sell? What is our move then?"

This was a great point. Although it was hard for everyone to look at him seriously seeing that his nostrils were stained white from all the blow, it needed to be addressed. Sure, Pie had said eventually with profits they could build new venues but what if they couldn't buy their way into something for once? Then what was the plan?

Juan stood up, and in total boss mode said, "They will sell! And if not, then we will kill 'em! We will burn their fucking arena to the ground with them and their families in it and build ours right on top, understand? We will quadruple this cartels value, at all costs, *amigos*!"

Everyone but Adolf nervously laughed, but Juan was as serious as a heart attack. There is something very dark and true about what Juan said. He was not here to appease or play games with a person who stood in his way. He was going to win at all costs, across all games, even if it meant death to those in his way. Juan was a fun guy when he wanted to be, but when it was time for business, he turned into the boss. Though the men laughed and half smiled at his statement, he was serious, and over time, I watched The Roadie Cartel's "fall-guy" acquire arena after arena. You used to be able to know which city you were in by the name of the arena. Not anymore. They are all the same, and the names change almost yearly thanks to Dick having sponsors on his hook now and bringing in even more money into the hands of the cartel. But like Juan said, they would quadruple this cartel's value. They did that and more by the time I went on my first tour for them.

Dick would have his eyes set on their first arena purchase in Nebraska as soon as the wheels touched down in Los Angeles in a few days. The biggest perk about having an arena as your distribution center is its fairly large size, with corridors and basements for hiding and cutting coke down in a far-away location. Sure, they would modify the arena once purchased to accommodate chemists and the hundreds of bricks shuffling in and out weekly.

The other brilliant part of the plan was that the roadie cartel could operate out of any sized arena. The cartel's arena in Dallas might be bigger than the one in Kalamazoo, but both could cut and house the product with no problem. Once the cartel purchased a venue, they could staff security with all cartel members who would keep an eye out if someone started to snoop around too much. Pie made a good point too—that no one in a million years would question a semi-truck pulling up to a venue at three in the morning or even two in the afternoon. That was a great point, but over the years Pie took it one step further. His agents (yes, we run an agency which books acts—some we also manage) can make sure our tours carry our product exactly to where we want it to go. Pie figured out this equation early on, but also made sure each tour carried the same amount of roadie cartel members or more to facilitate the work needed to go into any size venue.

Juan had always wanted a place to let the product sit if there was too much heat from local or government law enforcement at the borders. This one was a big one. Most dealers sit on a small amount, and once they are out, it's not like there's a super—Costco style—warehouse of coke. Most guys have to wait till their connection re-ups, and if the big boss's dope is held up—well—then no one gets their fix. Juan had the idea long ago but never thought he would have a big building that could hide his product in plain sight of the law. Pie's idea of multi-infrastructure added layers to allow for unlimited distribution and cutting . . . something Juan had always dreamed of.

Close your eyes and think of the times you've seen a semitruck on the road. Now picture what is inside. Now picture a trailer with your favorite band's name across the side. Then picture that semitruck pulling in for a show at your local arena. No one would ever expect a team of criminals to be running a cocaine enterprise out of the arena or using that sweet boy band as a front. No, all you see are the events in and around the arena or amphitheater. You're at a concert with your ice-cold beer, which was over-priced, just like the fees you paid when buying the ticket, for a very specific reason. You pull your ticket out, find your seat—thanks to a nice old lady usher who works for the cartel—you sit down, and the show starts. Do you suddenly say to yourself, "Wow, they must cut a lot of cocaine underneath that stage down there?" Hell no, you don't! You are so tuned into the concert that all you can think about is how cool it is to be there and how you can't wait to leave and tell everyone you know.

Juan enjoyed Pie's go-getter attitude when it came to the ideas of how to make him money, but he also loved the idea that he would finally be able to place more people from Mexico into the labor pool around America. Pie described to Juan what a day is like for a tour coming into a town. He also told the guys about the stagehands that help the crew bring gear in and out. This info was crucial, seeing that Juan had been slowly filling communities with men, women, and children who, up until now, had been working odd jobs for the cartel. These arena purchases would ensure that there was work, and Juan could relocate more families to the states. The roadie cartel would also start looking into loading the stagehand unions with workers for the event fields and the teamsters who help load trucks in certain cities. These chess moves would benefit the roadie cartel many years down the road when it was time to move product around the arenas and other venues. But nothing was going to happen until they got done talking and got the ball rolling on these projects asap. Pie pointed out to Juan the importance of having competent multi-lingual men and women to help assist in these arenas. Juan agreed with the non-Spanish-speaking gringo. The Mexican cartel side should not only learn more English, but every roadie cartel member would need to speak some amount of Spanish—and not just the dirty words.

From a big corporation down to your mom-and-pop ice cream parlor, everyone starts to know their role in the hierarchy. This was naturally happening as the men unknowingly shifted from having a friendly hangout to a mastermind class. Juan was focused on cartel dealings from the top while the others fell into their positions seamlessly. Dick was busy snorting coke and building outlines of contracts so his team could type them up ASAP once he landed. Pie was getting prepped to have a meeting with Juan and factory bosses about the merchandise deals he had thought up. Like I stated earlier in this video, this was not an idea that can fail, so the play was over for the moment. I would love to say these four misfits got lucky, but there was no lotto drawing or big Las Vegas jackpot. Sweat, blood, and tears (whether from the founding fathers or people in their way) were put in daily from this day forward. The hard work paid off so much that a photo of the first truck they ever sent on tour with Pie standing next to it, is hanging in the Rock Hall of Fame commemorating their achievements in shaping the transportation and over all innovation in the concert touring world. Adolf he was left out of his own idea because Juan had other plans for him that pushed him into an even darker human than he already was.

If you could picture some super cheesy 1970s movie montage where everyone was working hard on building the roadie cartel—you know, people on phones, Pie driving in cars to factories, Dick snorting coke while scribbling notes on paper and then lots of money, cars, and even a tiger cut together in some off-color video footage—and then one person is off taking care of some dirty deeds for the big man, Juan. And this meeting was the last where Adolf had a part in growing his own idea . . . bitter might be one way to describe him.

I don't know Adolf well, but I have never wanted to. I also have never met a person, young or old, who grew up intending to become a professional killer. I don't think Adolf grew up that way. But he turned into one at a young age and never stopped, hence why I tend to give him a wide berth. Sure, some kids grow up playing military heroes, or cops and robbers. Hell, some play house, but never do any play a cash-in-hand-cartel-hitman. That job isn't usually the one kids on a playground want to play. Money can bring out the devil, and Juan knew how to use money to manipulate young men, much like women who prey on sugar daddies. While everyone else was working diligently, Juan leaned in toward Adolf and whispered something into his ear and Adolf smiled much like that green man in that Christmas movie. I am certain whatever was actually said also contained a monetary value for his new role. Juan was confident that Adolf would best fit as a stealth enforcer for the cartel. He had smarts, but it was not in business. With his ruthless attitude and sleight-of-hand knowledge, Adolf would get his hands dirty while also keeping the trail of murders and "suicides" clean. He was about to become the cartel's premier hitman, one without a real identity. Only his dark shadow would be known. His new persona would slowly shift from Adolf to the moniker he is known by now: "Reznik, The Butcher."

As Juan was finishing his conversation with Adolf, Dick gathered his new cartel luggage of cash and coke for the private flight home. Since credit cards and loans were not as big of a thing back then, making large purchases with cash was not unheard of. But some of that cash would be placed in the newly opened bank account in the Caymans. With a couple manly handshakes and a few words of encouragement, Dick was the first to leave. The lawyer's life would never be the same as he took those first steps with his new cartel guards by his side. You didn't think Juan was going to leave him alone with a hundred million his first go around, did you? It was Dick, a man who loved hookers and blow.

Pie was next to depart the mansion. He was on his way to Mexico City. There he would make a pit stop at one of Juan's factories to jumpstart band T-shirts packaged alongside the coke to keep hidden throughout transportation. In the early stages, they just packaged the coke in bundles hidden under the shirts and flew it in nightly. As technology improved, Pie had some bands sign up for exclusive deals, including printing and selling customized merchandise for them during upcoming tours. The newly formed position of merchandise tech, then, needed to be someone Juan truly trusted. After Pie shook Juan's hand to leave the mansion, he was off for a ride of a lifetime, writing **THE** handbook for all the future roadie cartel merch techs to follow. Shit, more like he wrote the handbook everyone in the industry follows to this day.

The original two men of The Roadie Cartel remained. Once they got back into Juan's office, he and Adolf pulled up a chair, lit a couple cigars, and as they sipped on tequila, they examined the photos and info of the man Juan wanted dead. This man had spread rumors about Juan throughout the town, trying to paint him as a user and a killer. And even though the gossip was true, anyone who messed with Juan's reputation and the money going into his pockets was his mortal enemy. Juan told Adolf he wanted him dead within a couple weeks at the latest.

The office door that led out to the pool in the back of the house opened. Juan was ready to kill the fucker who dared to interrupt his meeting with Adolf; he had given instructions not to be bothered and would not tolerate the disrespect. But, surprisingly, in walked Zora.

"Your face!" the men exclaimed. They had been in their little world for so long that they had no idea Zora had been attacked. Once Juan and Adolf learned it was not the staff, there were only so many more options as to who was on the other end of her bruised and cut knuckles.

As they all stood there silent, waiting for the other to say . . . anything, Zora spoke up. "One of the feral pussy-cats snuck into my room, and I had to teach it a lesson when it jumped on me . . ." She paused. "But I think it learned that next time I will make a scarf out of it."

"Do you need me to have a conversation with this cat?" Juan said while holding back a tiny smile, knowing damn well that she just battled a beast and came out alive.

"Nope, I just need you to have someone come clean my room. It has been a mess, and I don't speak Spanish." Zora calmly turned and headed back outside for some fresh air.

Juan never had to take sides, but I think that was because La Reina knew she was not messing with just some gold-digging princess from Europe. Zora held her own, and I think that also earned her more respect from the drug lord she called her boyfriend. He had never had a strong woman in his life outside his own blood. So, this was big for them both. A new power-couple who were ready to take on the world together. As she made her way out of the door leading to his office, Juan leaped from his chair, ran to her. With both hands, he grabbed her bruised face and kissed her. He kissed her passionately and at length. The kiss lasted so long, in fact, that Adolf excused himself from their little meeting. He knew his task and was ready to start his new life inside the two cartels as the killer he never knew he could become.

The next morning when Adolf awoke from his slumber, he was alone in the big house. Outside his door, on a catering platter, he found a note that read, "Slaughter the pig. Enjoy the house. The jet will fly you to me once the job is complete." Juan was a funny man. He didn't waste any time with his relationship with Zora. The new Bonnie and Clyde were gone. They had set off to enjoy life and let the other people in the cartel make them more money than either could ever dream of.

Adolf made his way to an outside table on the bedroom patio and pulled the cigar from his robe pocket when a voice from behind said in a sultry tone, "Need a light and a stiff drink?" With two glasses of tequila in her hand, this woman whom Adolf had never met, slid one across the outdoor table. With a nudge of her hip, she moved the chair to sit with him. Adolf needed a little company at that moment, feeling left out from his own hustle. He smirked and clinked his glass against hers.

>>>STOP RECORDING<<<

CHAPTER 12

The Star-Spangled . . . Powder

>>>START RECORDING<<<
This is video Diary #11 October 28, 2009. Anaheim, California.

Today is another Show Day, and lucky for me, I am stuck in another concrete box (followed with a long eye roll).

Over the years, I have come to realize some people become roadies because of their love for music, while others never made it as a musician and some . . . well, some loved electronics. None of the above were the appeal for me. Rather than the music as inspiration, I got into the business for the drugs, sex, money, and the bigger more obvious reason, my family. I am telling you this because when I look back at why I am here, stuck and fatherless, it's because I chose to be part of something built on greed. And the one thing music should never only be about is the money, but for me and the cartel members, it was the only thing pushing The Roadie Cartel further into the industry.

Reminiscing on all the shows I have been a part of around the world, I am left a little sad I didn't enjoy the moments more. Music is meant to inspire people . . .to dance, to make love, to cry, to smile, to fight, to make up, to lift you higher. For sure, I missed out. In our case, as The Roadie Cartel, we hoped it inspired fans to spend money—all their money—on their favorite artist, band or sports team. And while coke is a powerful drug and our main source of success, so is music and we exploited that obsession. As someone who has seen Dick and Pie bring up an artist strictly for The Roadie Cartel to profit, well, it is something out of a fiction novel. From conception to the new trends that they can get fans to spend money on, it is sad that it was all done for money. We have created a machine and it is learning and growing more powerful. I will come back to actual music in one second but think about this little fun insider secret and it might make more sense as to the full scope of the cartel and its influence on the music scene. The Internet changed lots of things for lots of companies over the years, so when some nerd started to give music away for free on there, the cartel started to lose big bucks on sales of records and even radio ad money—yes, they have their hands deep in the media, TV, Radio and a new trend, internet music. I do not know much about it but overheard my father talking about it one day. Let's just say that Juan's cartels will find a way to get your money into their pockets.

I digress. Back to music and why Pie was so good at getting this business started. Yes, I am going somewhere with this just let me get back on track. . .

What is music? My crude understanding of it is the combination of vocal and manmade instruments combining to create beauty in the form of harmony and the expression of emotion. It's also a living entity in the ears of the listener. It's ever-changing and growing, a very nonlinear item. Music and musicians drive trends and put butts in seats. Nowadays, trends start with many of the productions Pie and Dick executive produce: the proper stylist on a hot TV show, the newest car in a music video, and magazine covers depicting your favorite junkie musician with those dark, smokey, been-up-all-night-snorting-cocaine eyes. The Roadie Cartel was established around the time when cocaine-loving musicians and the disco club scene were the hottest trends. Now, The Roadie Cartel *IS* the music industry, just hidden behind a cornucopia of other aliases. These artists back then stuffed more money unknowingly into Juan's pockets by driving the coke frenzy that everyone thought would eventually die off. Instead, it only continued to skyrocket into my generation.

The decade that followed the hippie summer of love drove excess to the forefront of society. From parties to clothing, over-the-top lifestyles in the media showcased the newest styles and music. Much like the state of Texas, everything was bigger, including drug habits, hair, and the cartel. By the decade's end, so many people were doing cocaine around the United States that our weekly shipments weren't enough. Our arena chemist couldn't keep up with demand. From members of Congress to washed up models on Skid Row, we moved the product according to supply and demand. In our line of business, we lived for bribing government officials, local police, and politicians who didn't have a backbone, but loved sex and money.

Word spread that the bands working with Pie received huge

chunks of cash upfront with overall cheaper touring costs, quicker show payouts, more radio play and big merchandise sales. This not only boosted bands egos and fan base, but it helped in boosting The Roadie Cartel brand name exponentially around the industry. Better known as "TRC Productions and Entertainment"—at least that's what it said in our business documents—we were becoming a name brand for how bands made music, sold merch, where they played shows and toured the world.

I was a child when Ivan, Adolf, Pie, Juan and anyone in the cartel's core group were deep into the Great White Gold Rush of the early '80s, if you had to give it a name. Next to the large tobacco cartels of America, cocaine was so popular that if there was a way to have it in vending machines, they would have done it. The world, especially North America, wanted to feel the highest highs of this powerful drug, and hourly. Marketing coke was the easiest for the men and cost the cartel zero dollars. The glamorization of the substance did all the marketing the cartel could dream of. Even the government's anti-drug campaigns were having the opposite effect on the youth than they intended. The more they told you it was bad and to stay away from the drug, the more mirrors, razor blades, and straws flew off the shelves of your local pharmacy. I could only imagine hearing a politician telling you not to do cocaine in those days. Then a week later, they are busted with their pants down in a downtown hotel room with a hooker and enough coke to kill an elephant. In those kind of moments, the cartel coined golden opportunities. The high-end busts allowed Richard and his team of lawyers to lend a helping hand, with the unspoken agreement that when the cartel would come asking for favors, they would make sure to pay back the favor. During this time period, Pie and Dick also dug up dirt on music managers, Hollywood executives and anyone who had anything to do with an artist out touring. This was how some of the biggest names of the day started to use the services The Roadie Cartel provided.

This demand was a great thing. So great that Juan, Pie, and Dick had to sometimes shuffle hundreds of millions of dollars weekly, even daily, into accounts to maintain the new infrastructure. Remember, it was nice to have friends in high places, like, banks and such that owed these men a few favors. Everything the men touched

220 • PHILLIP J KRIZ

grew at an astounding pace. As a bonus to it all, arenas were purchased, and cities were filled with Juan's cartel armies of men, women, and children to run it all.

Pie had one other job, finding roadies who wanted to be criminals. He had his fair share of disappointments but also a great deal of luck finding roadie cartel members. The biggest numbers of new members were from the club scenes rolling through towns with up-and-coming younger acts. He even hired some of his old friends who were biding their time, waiting for their break to get into the big leagues of tours. There were a lot of hungry, underpaid, and underappreciated roadies who worked in hole-in-the-wall clubs and smaller venues, looking to get out. Nice part for Pie was that all of them had one thing in common. They were itching for a chance to tour the world and were willing to take orders from Pie for a new salary that no club gig would ever come close to paying. There has always been a screening process to getting the gig, though, involving the hunger for making money and willingness to take risks for The Roadie Cartel's success through its riches.

By the time I came along, gigging was pretty simple because all of The Roadie Cartel members before me had laid a solid gold path for success. You would think putting a show on would be harder at times, but maybe I'm biased because the most challenging part of my day is making sure the coke and money get appropriately distributed to the right trucks. The system ran itself as long as each person stayed in their lane. It's not rocket science that the main production teams and building managers did most of the work. The rest played defense keeping wondering eyes at bay. Pretty simple.

The production manager was the leader of The Roadie Cartel team on tours. Without a good one, there would be no hope for success. His main job was managing the crucial logistics role regarding an artist's touring gear and Juan's coke. He or she would ensure the show got from city to city and the proper working necessities were ready in each town. The production manager looks after the teams on tour, regardless of their affiliation with the cartel. That sounds simple, but this was a very fine line. When roadies from various departments operate like one body, the production manager can do his job the best. And this was best showcased through fair play, everyone had a job, so go do it. Sure, cartel members made more money and might get a bigger room somedays, but in the end, everyone had to work hard. We lead by example, which I know sounds funny to say, but we did. The production manager would eventually let the tour run on autopilot so that he can attend to the building manager—more on this role later—and whatever Pie may need.

Therefore, Pie hires great stage managers to assist, yep, the production manager. They do the dirty work when the production manager is off holding babies and kissing hands with the cartel building managers and union bosses. Ivan is the best production manager in TRC's eyes. The best production managers know the road like the back of their hand, and the great ones live by the "first off the bus in the morning and last in at night" motto. Because it fell on their shoulders if a bundle of cocaine or money didn't make it on a truck or the show didn't make it on time. The other part to a great stage manager freed up the cartel production and building managers to run the final checks. We called this little check the "dummy" or "stupid" check because, let's face it, you're a dummy if you're leaving a big bundle of coke behind. That shit will get you killed. So, it was the production and building manager's responsibility to check to make sure all the blow had left the building. It also looked good in the eyes of the non-roadie cartel members that the heads of the tours looked like they cared about the tour and equipment leaving for the next venue. But without a great stage manager, the team could fall apart really quick.

The building's production manager played the role of coke liaison for incoming tours. They communicated between Mexico and the tour's production manager to make sure they knew what was coming and going and how much coke needed to be cut. That job might be the most stressful out of them all. Trying to have one or two kilos cut and shipped within twenty-four hours is no walk in the park; now talk about twenty or more, that shit is stressful. Between the building and production managers, it was an elegant waltz of trucks, cases, coke, cash, and people. Once the truck doors opened and it hit the loading docks, this dance between TRC and the building cartel members was something of sheer genius on Pie's part. He did design this process, from top to bottom. From the cases rolling to special elevators, down to custom-built labs for cutting coke, to the merch tech counting and packaging bundles of coke, it was a very refined symphony in the drug world. All of these steps and finely detailed moves did not happen overnight either, but it was down pat by my era in TRC.

The next most important position was the merchandise tech. This position was looked at as second-in-line to the shot caller. Most would never know this or suspect them to be this high up, but that was the point; we, the roadie cartel members, are always hiding in plain sight, not only on show days, but every day. In our touring world, the merch tech is the only other person on the road crew who knows how much coke and money goes in and out of the buildings daily. This was mainly because he unloaded and loaded the cocaine and cash into trucks at the end of the night. Plus, the fewer who knew, the better. All our merch techs also had one other thing in common: they were all from Mexico. So, they could speak to the uncut coke farms and factories down south if a problem arose. As the decades roll forward and new tours pop up that are not affiliated with us, the merch tech role is getting filled by more friends of the band. Still, we at TRC keep the tradition of ensuring **ALL OUR** tours are staffed with the men and women we choose, regardless of what the artist might suggest. With newer acts that came on with the cartel management side, we have to discuss the reality and why we come equipped with our own guys and gals for these bands, we are just better at our jobs than others. Another cool fact about our merchandise techs was that they were not only multi-lingual but also trained chemists from universities. This became very handy when the merch techs were on the road and started to help Juan develop new and more efficient ways to manufacture, cut, package, and transport the cocaine to stay ahead of the game from law enforcement and other rival cartels. Juan hated other dope dealers and sharing the spotlight even more than he hated cops, so he wanted to keep the cocaine business operating at levels that only the most elite and criminal minds could think up.

Next, the "magicians"—all the other roadies on tour. The backstage smoke and mirror guys kept the tour moving and running while the main cartel roles went to work on the gear that Juan cared most about, the coke. Unfortunately, this is where Adolf had always wanted to shine in The Roadie Cartel. He was great with the sleight of hand, the illusion of making the audience look at one thing while the main action was happening just out of sight. Sadly, his childhood passion for hustling and conning people was put on hold, for he was busy doing the extra dirty work for Juan. The business of touring is already mysterious. Here are men and women who roll into a town on buses in the dead of night, set up a big rock show, live in the darkness during the show, and then leave. Our teams had their hands full, hiding TRC's secret in plain sight of the other roadies that toured next to us. Every card and every detail had to be played just right so they would never raise attention to the trick. Roadies are not dumb, so to keep a multi-billion-dollar drug front hidden was a whole other job sometimes. Every aspect of how the product was handled was important. How the dock workers took the road cases and merchandise boxes out of trucks needed to be the same for every case, whether there was blow in it or not. This was so that no one could ever think there was something more important in one case than another. Pie also made it clear to the teams of roadies that only the production manager and merch tech were to ever interact with the building cartel managers. This was to keep all chatter and deals down to a bare minimum.

One position that might not have been the most physically demanding, but came with the most headaches, mainly due to the long list of daily needs and wants asked of them, was the production assistant. It usually was a tough-as-nails woman, but we had a dude every once in a while. The production assistant had it rough most days because they had to deal with direct needs for all the touring crew, first and foremost. The PA was also in charge of the greater touring staff regarding hotel rooms, catering demands, bus stock lists, laundry, and a lot more that no one wanted to deal with other than these gluttons for punishment. Our production assistants did that job and had to play defense against people trying to come into the production office and chat up the production manager. Some days, that just wasn't an option. It is always amazing to me when I'm in my production office working diligently on a task, and in comes a roadie from a department outside the cartel to waste my assistant's time by asking questions any responsible human could handle on their own.

Then there were the dock managers who worked right alongside the stage manager. Some tours had both; most only had stage managers. These ruthless characters came with more energy than a superhero. They quite possibly made or broke the day. They had the daily logistics of the show down to an inch some days. Literally, they had to squeeze cases in and out of the labs underneath the venues for cutting dope. Figuratively, they were the key to bringing in the show through these backdoor loading docks and endless miles of hallways and corridors. They, my friend, are who made the production managers and The Roadie Cartel look great. Sure, they were heartless and arrogant some days, but it takes that kind of confidence in a person to guarantee a successful show and coke run. We paid them well to ensure the band gear and Juan's gear made it city to city with no questions asked. Juan loved them because they shared a very similar business motto; the tour should be all about business and not "friend-ness." Everyone has to be equal in their eyes. If you are on their floor or loading the dock, it's because you chose to be there, so shut up and work or go home.

Another prominent position on tour was one The Roadie Cartel helped develop over the years, mainly out of necessity—our specialized security teams. This grew, as did anything in this business, mainly from word of mouth and artists trying to outdo each other when it came to who had what. For a lack of better words, tour size became a pissing contest. As artists got more popular with fans—and after a few high-profile deaths that we had nothing to do with (*wink, wink*), artists needed security, and so did we. A typical person would assume our security team dealt mainly with crowd control, but their biggest daily task was keeping an eye on the dope moving around the buildings; we had cops on-site for an event's crowd control. And tour security started with one guy doing it all. But over the years, some tours have had teams of six or more for the artists, their rowdy friends, and annoying overpriced girlfriends they would bring on tour with them. During the morning, we used the security team to play lookout over the arena. They would monitor who was where and would make sure when the drugs moved to the lab that no one, besides the merch tech and production manager, was following.

We still use a "telephone system" of sorts when moving the drugs. What is that, you ask? It is a series of whistles to send warnings inside these arenas if we suspect danger. This came from the cartels showing us in Mexico how they kept an eye out for Juan on the outskirts of his farm and in the cities. These whistles were mainly to alert to snoops in law enforcement and other cartels looking to make moves they would ultimately regret. Overall, our security teams knew their second job was to keep the tour and artists safe, but their main objective was to keep an eye on TRC members and to make sure the drugs were safe moving from city to city.

We always kept a few swing positions open, depending on the tour. Sometimes we needed a second stage manager or two merchandise techs due to the high volumes of cutting and shipping on that tour. We had to stay versatile so that The Roadie Cartel was evolving with new technologies concerning the government and daily life in general. TRC utilizes the World Wide Web for interactions that we can code and encrypt. Our cyber defense team has hacked into so many government computers for info that we could teach them a thing or two about passwords. Not only does the Internet help us stay ahead, but we have also pumped millions and millions of dollars and cartel members into a cell phone company. Talk about a system that keeps us one step ahead. We love to flip the script on Big Brother and keep watchful eyes on them. We also loved to stir the pot when it came to foreign relationships. The more the government looked to the east and kept its eyes off the south, the better. For the four horsemen who founded The Roadie Cartel, it was a brilliant time to be alive and re-energizing the drug game. They were the front runners in the world of drug trafficking technology. They were hands down changing the touring industry forever. Juan knew that if the people at the bottom were happy and getting paid, no one would care what the top was asking of them. Artists will throw around the term "family" very quickly, but Juan's Mexican cartel and TRC truly lived that family life, until you crossed them, no second chances.

Over the years, the other women we have brought on as young cartel members have outshined the men many times over. Most are now running tours and making high-dollar moves for the cartel daily. This job was never for the white-gloved sound engineers who could barely mix a margarita or a show. Although they're fun to chat and enjoy a pint with, The Roadie Cartel was a different bunch of misfit leaders who would cut your throat in a bar fight for Juan.

Tours involve many people, but Pie had decided to keep the arenas more staffed with cartel members while the tours would have less. The fewer people on a need-to-know basis, the better. Your standard roadie cartel teams had more than six or seven guys or girls on tour. After Pie deemed you worthy of the cut into the money and trusted that you would never talk about the operation, the next step was to disappear into the shadows and fit in on tour and in daily life. No one, especially Juan or Pie, had time to care that your French press was broken or that you had a middle seat on a long flight, though that rarely happened. No, our goal was to move drugs and make money. If you wanted to be pampered, go to a spa on your day off, but on Juan's time, he paid you too well to worry about your special soy latte.

But most days, Pie and The Roadie Cartel spoiled us on the road. They made sure that if we didn't talk, did our jobs for the show, and then moved the coke, we all got a hefty end-of-tour cash bonus paid straight out of cocaine profits; if the amount didn't have at least three zeros, it was a slow or short tour. Even the non-cartel members got a smaller bonus, we all did the tour so we all reaped the rewards. Ten thousand always seemed to be the reward for a four-to-six-month tour for us cartel members. The bonus was great and paid in my favorite way, **CASH IN HAND**. They did the bonuses that way to keep the books looking legit when it came to roadie pay and the books for the Cayman Island investors (I said with a grin).

Soon after the four horsemen broke from their meeting at Juan's years prior, Adolf went on his own and only spoke to three people: La Reina, Juan, and Pie. He mainly spent his time between the Juarez mansion, the Mexican coastal farm, and Juan's yacht wherever that may be docked that day. He only steps foot in the states when someone is getting "fired." The reality was that if they were close enough to the border, they just had that person taken south to The Butcher. He was soon known to everyone as the scariest of all the sicarios in the world. He was the judge, jury, and executioner for the cartel. He was not as busy in the beginning, but like with every business, you start with loyal motivated people, but eventually, some lazy and stupid ones work their greasy paws into the mix. The stories of his kills were well known in the cartel and some of the aftermath of those kills had been seen by the public, but there was one tale that seemed like a tall tale to scare people from fucking with the cartel. This is all hearsay and there has never been a human to have ever made it out from this place, but he supposedly has a kill shack. Yes, a slaughterhouse for humans out in the middle of the desert. The stories say this is where he takes the special few that he feels need a worse death than just a bullet to the skull.

Ivan was always busy with tours. Between Pie and Adolf, they took advantage of him constantly, even from a distance. One week, he would be on a plane to get a new production manager started on a new tour that would start in a building with one of the more ruthless building managers the cartel had, and that isn't a good combo when you have to count out millions of dollars with someone who had been doing it for years. The next week, he would be bouncing coast to coast, meeting new merchandise techs for the cartel and making sure they got to know the production manager's wants and needs. To top it off, he was "blessed" with checking in on other tours to keep an eye on their operations. Ivan was the king of multi-tasking and delegating. He could run a tour from hundreds of miles away if Pie demanded he fly to the other end of the globe to put out a fire. He had become a household name in TRC's crews and the world of touring across all other crews and vendors. They do pay the man very handsomely, but he is one of the rare ones that truly does this job for the sake of the crew to make sure he never loses someone close to him again.

Before I get too far into the future, I have to say Pie was doing his job better than anyone could have imagined. If we were to look back on that night in the hotel with his mom and Adolf, I would have guessed he would have folded and ratted out the cartel. But he didn't, and thanks to his new ideas and game-changing procedures, he was reaping the benefits of being one of the richest men in the cartel. He always said the roadie in him was the problem solver to Juan's conundrum (how to make his father's cartel successful again). There was even a moment when the cartel couldn't clear the borders for our merchandise trucks to cross over, so Pie took a few of Juan's jets from Mexico. He stuffed them full of band T-shirts, and when the officers at the little airport in middle America saw them, they just smiled, waved, and said have a nice show. Eventually, Juan got a couple of 737s to move the cocaine-filled T-shirt boxes up from Mexico. They even named one of the planes "Pie in the Sky," rightfully so. Richard and Pie partnered with a big-time airline company to start a daily flight from Mexico to Kansas City for the sole purpose of loading the plane with uncut blow for a drop. That might sound a little far-fetched, but the owner of the airline loved concerts, so they hooked him up with unlimited shows . . . until he went missing on a fishing trip down in Mexico. Strange.

By the mid-'80s, Juan had become the most wanted drug trafficker in the world. His face was plastered on every wanted poster across the states, but law enforcement never investigated TRC. They only saw Juan as the importer of cocaine into the states—never the distributor in the states. I will say it one more time for the people in the back . . .

"They only saw Juan as the importer of cocaine into the states— never the distributor in the states!"

The hard work of putting men on the inside was paying off. Juan and Zora couldn't travel into the states much anymore, but why leave a private life in the middle of an island paradise to deal with something like a New York subway system full of rats? Pie, Dick, and Adolf would be the only ones to have contact with him at this point, and it was more like he would reach out to them if he had an emergency. Everything else was done through the Mexican farm and Juan's sister. And with the "businessman" in the Caymans feeding the funds. And lots of funds at that! Juan and Zora lived a billionaire's dream life. He rotated jets and yachts like you would rotate pants. Eventually, he would start renting his planes and boats to celebrities and rock stars for travel and music videos. When hip hop hit the streets, Juan became somewhat of an icon to these rappers who wanted to live that lifestyle full of glam, glitz, Ferraris, blow, tigers, jets and exotic women.

These men were living the American dream. They were on top of cocaine mountain singing their own version of the national anthem: the star-spangled powdered version.

There was one thing the cartel never saw coming, though . . . me.

>>>STOP RECORDING<<<

Until I say it out loud and into this camera, I forget how big this thing got. It actually makes me very uneasy thinking about it. I don't know if I will ever have an impact on this monster. . . but as I slid my phone into my pocket, I could hear my father's voice in my head. He was never happy that I wanted to follow in his footsteps as a roadie but he told me this once and it always stuck with me. "Wyatt, this beast is not kind, so when it is time to fight back, take the shot and don't hesitate. It can smell your fear and it will get you if you don't believe in yourself." I always thought he meant—touring—was a beast but he meant the cartel was the one I needed to be ready to fight. I still have my doubts, but his voice of hope is helping me keep my head above water.

CHAPTER 13

When The Road is Your Playground

Standing next to my production road case and thinking about my father again, I am catapulted back to my childhood. I can remember watching him come home off the road, and after emptying his pockets, he would set his work keys on his night stand next to the bed. Now, I have them and here they sit in front of me on my production road case, that was once his too. These keys have seen it all out here on the road and if they could talk, oh the secrets they would tell. But there they sit, stuck in time, like an old storyteller sitting in front of his tribe, waiting to tell old tales of great men before him. I wonder what these keys are trying to tell me. I know they continue to remind me of the one great man in my life. My father, he was the greatest. No matter what I know, he did his best inside this cartel to live a somewhat stand-up life . . . I mean he did save my life in my first few hours on this planet. I don't think he saved me so I could be here now fighting for him now that he is gone but that is what I must do to honor him.

Gazing deeper at the keys I noticed something interesting about one item in particular on the key ring. Ivan drilled a hole in a coin that lives on a secondary key ring, it was his good luck memento, that is how I viewed it always. I rub the coin softly—kind of like he used to—and as I turned it over, I notice his favorite number, 713, on the coin. I ponder on this number and the coin for a few minutes, then in a quick recollection to when I was around ten or eleven, I remember him showing me why this one was special. Ivan explained to me that the coin was a misprint from a Czechoslovakian commemorative token made for a folklore, an old Robin Hood legend, in eastern Europe. This specific Jánosík token had a double-stamped head on one side, but both sides were missing the number one in the year 1713, hence why it only read 713. At that young age, I had no realization of what it was like to have superstitions or even a lucky number, but that number was something that came up time and time again for him. I even see it now, more than I ever had in recent years. One story about the number and his obsession with it always made me laugh because it really wasn't that lucky of a number in my eyes. For one, the man had plenty of money, but he loved to play the pick-three lottery tickets and used that number every time. He never won.

When he handed me the keys one day as he was passing down his production case to me, I finally asked what made this coin so special to him? And who gave it to him? He told me his father had given it to him at a young age as a thank you for cleaning the butcher shop before school one day. He told Ivan a story about a man who had come into the shop hungry but with no money except that coin. The coin was worth nothing, but he explained how this Jánosík guy on the coin took from the rich and gave to the poor. He asked if Ivan's father would be so kind to be his Robin Hood that day and take from himself. Ivan's father was no millionaire like his son is today, but he was rich in family and love. So, when Ivan's father, my grandfather, gave him the tarnished coin, it came with a special meaning of self-worth. Ivan shined that coin till he found that it held an even deeper treasure, it was a misprint and was one of a kind. His father reminded him to always give back, no matter who you become in life.

Looking at this coin, it all makes sense. Ivan was a huge giver of all things, especially his time. He was the only one willing to show me this road life and teach me his ways. And sadly, now the only man who has given his everything to make sure I was taken care of is gone.

The dialog continued to run in my mind as I waited to hit the record button on the phone's screen. Today's video diary was going to be a rough one for a few reasons. Biggest reasons that really made today tough were that I hated that I was here; here in this arena, here working for this fucking cartel and that I was here without my father. I closed my eyes, shook my head and remembered, that he wouldn't want me to stop now. Ivan wouldn't want me to play the victim. He would only expect me to be great and truthful. His words echoed in my head like they had so many times before, "Wyatt, you are the bravest girl any father could ever ask for."

Wiping a tear from my cheek, I knew what I had to do . . .

>>START RECORDING<<<

This is video Diary #12

October 30, 2009, Las Vegas, Nevada: Night 1 of 2

I guess it is time to tell you how I ended up here . . . it might not be as far of a journey as my father's but I think it is pertinent to know all the details.

There are a few things in life that everyone has to go through; birth, death and most everyone pays taxes. None of them are usually fair and not every birth is a beautiful experience. I think most people could imagine a "smooth" birth is at times stressful but magical, a moment when the mother is in her hospital bed, feet up, her face is beet red, and sweat running down her cheeks. There are probably nurses and a doctor encouraging her efforts. A loving father in blue scrubs videotapes from over the doctor's shoulder with a huge smile as his child slides out, head first as if it was stealing second base. Realistically, my mind sees chaos, doctors demanding birthing tools, nurses covered in blood and shit and screaming for towels. Everyone's running in circles, and dad is nowhere to be found.

I've been told my birth was like a wild night out on tour where you end up on the wrong side of the railroad tracks at an all-nude club called—Tig Ol' Bitties—at 3 a.m. You get so stinkin' drunk during Amateur-KY-Jelly-Wrestling-Night that they kick you out naked, soaked, confused, and penniless. Now you're alone, wet and afraid, wondering what the hell happened. My father said he found me lying on my back, covered in blood, left to die. I obviously don't remember a thing from that night, but I will say I don't think I had as much fun that night as I did getting kicked out of that strip club that wild night on tour.

I mainly grew up with roadies who were amazing, but let's be real. Roadies in the '80s & '90s weren't setting up a backstage toddler room for me, especially the misfits on The Roadie Cartel crews. They were more likely setting up stripper poles and pre-railed lines of cocaine for the bands between still trying to ship out another hundred pounds of blow from downstairs in the lab. Roadies didn't have time for ponies and dollhouses. So, I grew up like a tomboy and I wouldn't change a thing. Now, don't get me wrong either, the bands in the '80s they didn't mind dress up parties and nail painting with me but the cartel crews, they made me tough as nails.

Before I go too far, I don't know who my birth father is, and my mom . . . well, the closest I ever came to a real one was Ivan's long-time girlfriend—wife now—but in the beginning, she was just a booty call to Ivan. Now, I'm not looking for justifications for some of the horrible things done at my relatively young age. I'm merely painting the contrast between a seemingly healthy upbringing and my wild childhood. We all have a family, some better than others . . . and some just outright fucking suck. My family consisted of angels and assholes who I downright hated at times, but I loved the wild, adventurous life I was given. Who could say they hate growing up on high-dollar tour buses, flying around on private jets, and staying in some of the finest hotels around the world—and doing it all before I was ten. It was an indescribable feeling to live in such a way, but it did come with a very heavy price that I am now having to pay.

I know I'll trigger some haters for saying this, but money wasn't an issue in my life. Not now, and not then. But, even with all the money and cartel clout in the world, I wasn't allowed to be a spoiled brat who lived in the hills, sucking down pain pills with my morning champagne and complaining to the local vegan shop about where they sourced their bacon-flavored tofu dog treats for my Doxiepoo. No, Ivan primed me at a young age to work hard for the money I would come into and that I had to earn the respect of my fellow roadie cartel members—he wasn't going to just pull strings because I was his daughter.

The roadies who I was around growing up gave me my first taste of falling and picking myself back up. Sure, they could have babied me, but instead, they gave me hell and pushed me from a young age to one day become a great roadie cartel member, even though my father fought it for a long time. I missed out on things "normal" girls go through, like being on the cheer team or dance or even attending senior prom, but some of those I wouldn't have done anyway. We all have choices in life and I chose to walk a path I knew was leading me directly into the fire, but I knew I would always be close to Ivan. I had to live with the good, the bad, and the ugly that came with the role I knew I would one day live. Now, it was many years before I figured out, I was raised around a bunch of criminals but more on that later. Ivan gave me a chance at life; without him, I would have never gotten to live the super-deluxe life I have lived. And for all of that I will give credit to the roadies of the cartel and of course the one man who saved my life.

Ivan. Where do I even start with this man? Like I said, growing up I never knew who my real father was. I assumed it was Ivan, but every time I asked him about my mom and him, he would smile and say, "It's better that you don't know," and then go back to whatever it was he was doing. So, I quit asking, until I was old enough to understand that bad people are everywhere and to be bad or mean is a choice. But once I knew about my birth, Ivan loved to recount the story to me and to others when I was around him. I'm pretty sure it was his way of getting me to do something for him—you know, in return for what he did that wild night. He tells it best when he is drunk because that night was one of the most drunken nights of his life next to his drunken New York City adventure. The night I was born, there were laughs, tears, booze, and a baby. Most people in his situation—you know, a drug-running criminal, not some nice guy walking his dog at night—would have just left me, but Ivan was built different . . .

I stop speaking for a second to gather my emotions. This story always chokes me up.

Night had fallen on the twin cities of El Paso and Juarez where tragedy turned into a stroke of luck. Maybe the big man upstairs had a hand in this when Ivan and Pie decided to hit their last bar for the evening. They went to downtown Juarez with a small entourage mainly consisting of security who could drive them around. Pie showed up in a Suburban with a few armed cartel gunners, and Ivan was in his beautiful 1966 Lincoln Continental with his one gunner that followed him around town for his personal security.

As they were closing their tab to head to the next bar a little closer out toward the Juarez ranch, Pie decided it was time for a joy ride. Now, I would never say drinking and driving is a good thing. Pie, on a normal night, would have agreed it'd probably better to be driven, but he had his eyes set on the big gal Ivan had. Yes, that was the cars name and Ivan let me name it many years later while we were cruising around town. The song "Big Girls Don't Cry" was on the radio and it was making me laugh, so I started to say, "this big gal don't cry" referring to myself but Ivan heard it as the car didn't cry . . . silly story but I loved that he eventually got a license plate that read "BigGal." Anyways, Pie wanted to stomp his foot on her pedal and feel that American-made, 462 cubic-inch V8 engine that produced a massive 340 horsepower. He was ready to move that big gal down the road. It was a beast of a car in a time when cars were getting more compact.

With this sexy black "yacht" of a car hogging up the road and her wide body hugging the white lines, it didn't give Pie a fighting chance to get her home in one piece after all the booze he had consumed. Pie's blurred vision, plus the sporadic rain showers that had been rolling through the desert towns all day, caused him to ping-pong off parked cars; it looked like a child's first time bowling with the bumpers up. Pie was next-level drunk and having the time of his life with his old friend.

Ivan was drunk too, but he must have really missed Pie to let him mangle his car. After all, it was just a car and Pie, he was the only person who Ivan trusted as family since leaving his little farm in Europe. With the Suburban not far behind, the security team was watching them swerve in and out of lanes of traffic while side-swiping cars parked on the side of the road as they approached the new bar. Ivan and Pie, took one look at each other, smiled, and proceeded to pass the next bar and headed out to the desert road that led out toward Juan's ranch to finish the night. Even the drunkest of friends realize at one point that the best bar is the home bar. It never closes and the ability to do whatever you want within the walls of your home is way more fun than any establishment I have been to, especially when it's a bar at Juan's home.

The pals arrived in one piece, surprisingly (the car, not so much). Once Pie and Ivan planted their feet solidly into the ground, they stumbled in opposite directions on their way to the mansion. Pie, well he went straight for the liquor cabinet, and Ivan headed for the side yard for a moment to himself. The house was eerily empty considering the meeting that took place earlier in the day. Some of the heavy hitters in the cartel had come to speak directly with Pie, maybe even Juan and Adolf—but for sure Pie, concerning changes that couldn't be shared over the most secure lines. But maybe the others had headed into town or were at one of the smaller houses on the property. In any case, Pie and Ivan were not heading back to drink with any of the cartel members anyway. They were having a good old fashioned bro session, craving the bond from years before. I think that's one reason why I'm holding on to hope with my two friends as I make these video entries. If Pie and Ivan can go years apart and then pick back up, then I know my friends can have a fight with me and end up right back to the days of running around as best friends in El Paso. I don't want us to be fighting and then . . . (long pause) they die because of my feud with my family. Sadly, I think we're all sitting ducks because of what we know, but we will cross that bridge soon enough.

Ivan found himself on the side of the house; he stumbled forward, then in some crazy maneuver outside of physics, simultaneously started walking and falling all while puking his brains out. The average person would have faceplanted onto the cemented path and called it a night. But not Ivan; his upper body was practically parallel to the ground in a magnificent tippy-toe walk. This propelled him headfirst into the side of the metal, industrial-style dumpster on Juan's property. Ivan said he hit it so hard that he swore he saw little birds floating around his head.

He has told me many times that he never blacked out, but his head was ringing pretty, pretty, pretty good, while lying on the floor. Both hands held Ivan's face as he lay on the ground holding back tears; he told himself to wake up when he heard faint cries from within the bin. In a daze of alcohol and a good old-fashioned hit to the skull, Ivan was in disbelief that there was a baby now crying from inside this big trash receptacle. Slowly sitting up with his back pressed against the dumpster, he winced as he slid up the metal wall and managed to get on his feet. Inching closer to the nearby infant screams, Ivan rounded the trash bin to reach a ladder built into one side.

He took a deep breath as his hands clenched the top rung. He paused. The crying went away. Taking one hand off the ladder to rub his head, Ivan heard the tiny infant in distress again. He was hoping this to be a dream—or one of those weird tales about a man who hit his head and hears imaginary noises. He closed his eyes tight, shook his head in disbelief, and placed his hand back on to the ladder rung. There was no going back on something like this. Pulling a baby from the trash was obviously the right thing to do, but that commitment would clearly lead to consequences he would have to deal with down the road. Still, he knew that no matter what happened, he was willing to save whatever life was on the other side. As he pulled himself up, his legs leaped up and over, landing on construction material and bags of old insulation fiber. On a cold night in November and with an umbilical cord wrapped around my neck, Ivan pulled me from my death bed.

I have tried to thank Ivan, the man who became a father figure to me, many times for saving me. But he says, "It was meant to be like that. God clearly had bigger things for me that night, and it had nothing to do with the cartel." He has told me that line verbatim fifty times and each time I giggle a little inside. This strikes me as funny since growing up he's never been the religious type, and honestly no matter what the man said, all I could do ever was hug him and say, "Thank you."

Meanwhile, Pie finished his drink in the party room toward the back of the mansion, which overlooked the pool and outside lounge area. Drunk and high, he wasn't keeping tabs on Ivan's time away. Instead, Pie air-drummed and sang off key while trying to remember the lyrics of "Lonely Is The Night" as it played on the stereo, using rolled-up hundred-dollar bills as drumsticks before snorting another line of coke. When he lifted his head after snorting a line the size of the Texas and Mexican border, Pie caught a glimpse of Ivan walking toward the two big bay windows out past the pool. He squinted and could barely make out that Ivan was in somewhat of a hurry from the looks of it. Pie's vision was as clear as the Mississippi River that night, so he thought Ivan was carrying a sack of trash in his arms. Very confused, Pie rubbed his eyes, blinked and rubbed them once again, when Ivan was closer and his vision focused, he saw the blood on his friend's clothes.

Ivan kicked open the French doors leading into the bar area and, with a look of horror, shouted to Pie to find a car. They had to get to a hospital immediately. Ivan described the drive as the scariest and most nerve-wracking in his life, not because he was drunk or because Pie was the one now throwing up out the window. Ivan still had no idea where I had come from. With every turn and new set of lights that pulled up behind the suburban, he wondered what the ramifications of pulling me from the dumpster would be. He knew one thing, someone did not want me in their life and whoever threw me in that dumpster, wanted me to stay in there.

I couldn't blame the man for being nervous when lights would speed up behind them. Life would never be the same for the two of us. And not because Ivan didn't like or want kids, but because his life was overwhelmingly busy with things he just wasn't ready to introduce a kid to.

Upon arrival to the hospital, a nurse approached Ivan at the main emergency entrance. With little warning, she rushed Ivan and me out of the main lobby and darted us down into a hall that led to our room. She instructed Ivan to stay put and said someone would be in to see us shortly. Still trying to process this madness, Ivan was left alone in a chair, staring at me while I lay wrapped in a sportscoat he had found in the the Continental. Pie, too out of it to drive home, joined Ivan in the hospital room; he climbed into the available bed and passed out. Maybe it was the hit to the head, or maybe all the adrenaline finally drained from his system, but Ivan nodded off with me tightly in his arms. It might have been for an hour or thirty seconds, but however long it was, Ivan got a little deep sleep.

The sound of a closing door woke the two men out of sleep. Ivan looked down to empty arms. They panned the room. No baby. In a slight panic, they tried to piece together what little memory they had of the night. Pie just as dazed was positive he brought Ivan to the hospital because he was dying and had no recollection of a third party. And the baby? "What baby?" Pie asked. A figment of imagination, thanks to a bump on the head and too much tequila.

"Good morning!"

The men jumped, and the woman directed her attention to Ivan. "I'm Virginia, the PA who is assisting today. Your daughter has a little bruising around her neck, but other than that, she is healthy. Her vitals are stable, and she can be released by the end of the week. We'll send you home with some antibiotics for precautionary reasons in case there's an infection that hasn't presented symptoms. Do you have any questions before we head to the PICU nursery?"

Ivan, in shock from the nurse's wording, paused. "Wait . . . My daughter?" Maybe it was the look Virginia gave him, or maybe images of the nearby orphanage that Ivan had passed by countless times and once popped his head in; he quickly added, "Of course," with a slight grin, continued with, "yes, my beautiful daughter."

Ivan stayed the next week with me in the hospital. I've been told we bonded pretty well for a man who had never held a baby before. He told me that looking into my deep brown eyes was like quicksand. He was stuck. He did, though, try thinking of all the reasons he should run for the road. He even got to the elevators one morning when I was crying, he told me, but he came back. I gained one rad dad, all thanks to too much liquor and a fucked-up situation.

Ivan was somewhat of a player with the ladies on the road, but in town, he had a long-time-on-and-off-again girlfriend he would seem to fall in love with every time he was home. The hard part was he had blown her off recently to hang out with a friend visiting for a few nights. She was really going to have some choice words for him when he called, to ask her to help babysit his new kid. But Ivan knew he was going to need help, and that help was not coming from anyone in The Roadie Cartel or his family.

The big day arrived; we were heading home. With a pair of scrubs that the doctor had given him, he held me in one arm and a bag of gifts from Virginia in the other: diapers, formula, a couple bottles, and some hospital baby clothes. Ivan said he was terrified walking out of the hospital to head to his bachelor pad on the mountain, knowing he'd probably have to deal with fatherhood alone. Mary, the girl he loved when he was home, hadn't answered any of his calls. Or rang him while at the hospital.

The Lincoln Continental was a "little" beat up from the night on the town, but Ivan strapped me in and we were gone. He was driving a bit more carefully now that he had precious cargo in the backseat. He made his way up the mountain and reached Juan's property. Pulling through the gates to the mansion, Ivan could see a figure by the front door. Not sure who it could be, and really hoping it wasn't someone looking for a baby he pulled into the driveway. A beautiful Mexican woman with olive skin and dark eyes that were glaring at the new father—like two missiles fired from a war ship—met Ivan with many emotions, anger being the first one, but he suddenly felt at ease seeing Mary.

Mary was born in Juarez and met Ivan when she was serving beers

and food at his favorite spot in town when he first moved to the
area. She wasn't hip to Ivan's real career, always gone and living
that roadie life, but she knew her part-time-man was something important since he was living in Juan's house. Looking back on the
situation, she kept him around and she had him wrapped around her
finger. Now, keep in mind, Juan had originally bought the house for
himself but passed it on to Zora and Adolf, technically. But since
Zora had become his official arm candy and Adolf was never around,
it made sense to let Ivan take it over. And as a bachelor pad for some
time, the house needed serious cleaning, picking up and now baby
proofing. Mary was truly an angel sent to help domesticate the place
and the new roadie father. When she heard Ivan's voicemail about
finding me, there was something in his voice that told her she needed to be there.

Ivan and Mary had to figure their shit out as a couple once I became part of the family. They had always been friends with benefits
and never actually lived together until I joined the party. As time
moved forward, the three of us made a perfect match. The odds
were stacked against us in every way, but over the years, we always
found ways to make each other feel loved. When Ivan wasn't on
the road being a criminal, he was Dad. He was the guardian of our
family. And Mary was the queen bee. She ran the house like a boss—
not that I always listened—and made sure our dysfunctional family
didn't fall apart. I was a bit of a handful, but Mary truly did show
us patience like no one I have ever met in my life. My shenanigans
in life added grey hairs to their heads and took years off their lives.

I call Mary "Mom." She took me gently from Dad's arms as I was
crying hysterically when I first arrived at the house. Once she cra-
dled me against her chest, I instantly stopped and felt comforted.
Ivan says Mary has a woman's touch that could pacify the most
disgruntled asshole . . . and I'm pretty sure he was referring to
himself. She would watch me when Ivan left for tours, and I loved
every minute of it. We enjoyed food, darts, desert off-roading, and
cruising down Mesa Street. (She would take me to my favorite BBQ
restaurant just down the street; I would always end each meal with
the peach cobbler.)

Then there was also gun shooting, hiking, and horseback riding when Ivan was in town. I was allowed to shine the rims of his '66 Continental once I was old enough to stand, and we'd take long dirt bike rides on Uncle Juan's land. Our favorite thing to do, though, was spread butter on fresh-made flour tortillas Mary—mom—would make on Sundays while Ivan and I lounged by the pool and talked. Those younger years sure do hold a special place in my memory bank, but the road life was the time I couldn't wait to experience with Ivan. The road was my true calling, and I would always tell him—one day I am going to be a big-time production manager like you dad. And over the years, I had some of the most fun childhood memories on the road with my big "duder."

As time progressed, I realized that when Ivan was packing his bags, I wouldn't see him for a while. As I got older, I wanted to go everywhere with Ivan instead of staying stuck at the house with Mary. I wanted to be a roadie like my father. He dressed in black and had tattoos. He looked like a rock star—well, at least in my eyes as a young kid. For all I knew, being a roadie was about hanging with bands and riding on cool-ass buses because that's all I saw growing up. I was young and naïve. How was I to know he was part of the world's largest drug trafficking cartel? And that his job was actually really fucking important. Ivan always tried to steer me clear of the road, I see why now. He told me I could do anything, much like any good parent would, but it just looked too cool not to be a mini him, but a girl version.

I was young the first time I was told that Ivan would bring me out on a short-tour run. This was going to be epic. I wasn't even ten years old yet, but I knew this would be more memorable than anything Ivan and I had ever done up till then. While most kids my age were heading off to summer camps to play with other kids or heading to grandma's house for their summer vacation, I was a full-on roadie for a summer of touring. Being the practical one, Mary tried many times to tell me I would not enjoy old men talking about women, flatulence and how much work sucks. "Oh, but I think I will. I love a good fart story," I would tell her. Ivan was on my side, although he never wanted me to live that cartel lifestyle. I think he just missed me and wanted me around him.

The first bag I ever packed was probably a mess, but I had seen

Ivan do it over the years and wanted to try my hand. So, I started with socks and underwear. Check. Next, all my black T-shirts. Check. Then, my two pairs of short black pants. Check. Next, my fake gum cigarettes that Mary had been so kind to find since I was too young to smoke. Check. Then off to the bathroom to grab the Gold Bond. (I didn't know what it was at the time, but my father packed it, so I should too.) Check. All that was left was soap on a rope and my toothbrush. Check and check. I was ready for the open road, or so I assumed.

"Wait." I ran to Mary. "Will I be able to take my favorite tiger stuffed animal or is that not what a roadie takes?"

"That is the most punk-rock-roadie thing you could take," she said with a smile. "If someone makes fun of you, then they will have to answer to Ivan and me—and that is their worst nightmare!" my mom replied with a teasing grin.

When Mom and I sat there in the car waiting for the tour bus, it felt like eternity for me. As the eagle swooped into the truck stop, the grand bus's headlight beams shone through the dusty parking lot and came to a halt in front of the Continental. The bus door opened, and there stood my duder with his hand out ready for my little backpack. The driver, Kevin, got off the bus to put my travel bag in the bay under the old bird. At the top of the stairs, I turned and waved at my mom. She blew Ivan and me a kiss as the bus door closed.

I was finally ready to . . . *uhm.* Well, I still had no idea what these guys do in here, but I was ready for anything. My dad gave me a tour of the front lounge where there was a very small TV, a little table, junk food drawer and a mini refrigerator. It looked like everything was made for tiny people like me, so that was nice. He showed me the bathroom. "Don't drop one of your gross shits in here," Ivan said with a smile. He told me to ask Kevin to pull over if I had to crap. Or, if I couldn't wait, I would need to drop a deuce in a plastic bag. This bus ride was sounding kind of fun so far . . . shitting in bags, junk food and TV. I was in!

Ivan gave me his bunk and told me he would be below in the "junk bunk." I instantly complained that it smelled like smoke—such a kid thing to do—but it was true because, back then, it wasn't frowned upon to light up a ciggy in your underwear just before bed. Ivan rolled his eyes. "Leave that complaining to the noise boys," he said with a chuckle. I hopped back down out of my bunk and with a very fatherly tone in his voice, he got down to eye level with me. "There's a good chance you're going to see adult things on and off the bus. Do not share your experiences with your friends, or else I can't bring you along anymore." With a threat like that, my lips were sealed. And I soon learned girls that came to these shows would reveal everything to the band to get a VIP backstage pass . . . and a chance at being more intimate too.

After the first run with Ivan, I was hooked. I think he hated himself for that, but he also knew he would be able to keep a close eye on me later in life. He was always terrified that pulling me from that dumpster would come back to haunt him when he wouldn't be close by to protect me. Every chance I could go out on the road, I took it. This was my dream coming true. It was a few years until I was briefed on the true business of the roadie cartel, but up until then I just dreamed of one day running the whole show just like my father, Ivan.

My name is Wyatt Rose Reznik, born in the late hours on the 6th of November in 1982, and I am the new generation in the ever-growing world of cocaine trafficking and The Roadie Cartel. Welcome to my life and thanks for helping me find myself and this lone cop.

>>>STOP RECORDING<<<

CHAPTER 14

Just How Big Can One Cartel Get...

Sitting on a curb outside a venue having a cigarette.

Looking at my cigarette, I am instantly lost watching the cherry burn the paper down slowly as smoke rises into the sunny day. My eyes lock on to one specific smoke curl and through the grey smoke; there sits one of many massive arenas the cartel owns. I ponder who pumps more money into the politicians' pockets to stay in business: The Roadie Cartel or the cigarette manufacturers? It doesn't really matter; it was just a thought as I look at this new hundreds-of-millions-of-dollars sports arena. Juan, Pie, and Dick had been tearing down their old arenas and building new even more state-of-the-art multi-purpose stadiums and arenas. I think one of the funniest things that sat on my mind was that these men got this city to pay half of the cost. It is just mind-boggling to think about all the things the cartel gets away with and no one, and I mean no one sees us, TRC productions, as anything other than the childhood hero—Robin Hood.

Pulling my headphones from my jeans, I think to myself about a short video I could do. Yes, a video about some of the things that don't necessarily follow the story I am sharing, but will give the viewers the reach of the cartel. Now, these cartel facts that I am about to let you know might or might not be deep, dark secrets, but it is time to really open up about some of the back of house details in the world I have been living in since a child.

>>>START RECORDING<<<

Video Diary #13 October 31st, 2009. Las Vegas, Nevada: Night 2

I know I have been sharing the story of how this cartel started and some of the dealings inside these cartel walls, but I think I need to really blow your mind. I get the feeling the few people who have watched these videos don't truly believe me. Viewers have left comments, thinking I'm some conspiracy theorist, or like bigDjimmy9696 said, "this sensitive clown shoe has watched too many Miami Vice episodes, stop breathing and leave the storytelling to the big kids."

I don't get this new social media stuff, probably like the rest of the people my age, but I get what bigDjimmy9696 said. This cartel seems unreal, almost out of this planet supervillain status at times. So, I figure before I get too far into the rest of the story—and seeing that we are caught up to my life—it is time that I share just how vast our reach is, what we actually own and what we have had a hand in creating.

First off, the myths or gossip and even some of the tall tales you have seen on the news or even read in the papers, seen in a movie, or watched on Miami Vice about Juan's Mexican cartel is all real but skewed a touch. Yes, there is always a bit of a twist to what is said or shown, sometimes in Juan's favor and sometimes not. But one thing to keep in mind is that everything you have heard about this cartel, is really only about Juan's Mexican cartel, no one realizes that The Roadie Cartel is the actual man behind the curtain, to put it in simple terms. The movie industry has painted him as a tiger owning, private jet flying, Gucci bag toting criminal with a hairy chest. That is all true too, but there is so much more. The reality is that Juan might have enough money to buy half of Europe, but he is also smart enough to stay under the radar, for the most part. He has the yachts and the houses, but a long time ago he stopped traveling into the states. He stopped docking his yacht in countries that didn't owe him in some way or another. The other thing to keep in mind is that Juan put very specific players in very specific roles in his cartels, so that he could sit on a beach with Zora.

But back to the cartel lifestyle we are all so familiar with from the media. We are all very rich, but because everyone under Juan, Pie and Adolf are so brainwashed, no one shows off. Doesn't mean guys or gals don't take trips or rip around town in a nice car. No, it just means we make it look like this touring life pays really well. Thanks to Dick and his teams, Uncle Sam thinks it is a nice paying job, but nothing to throw red flags at.

Like I said earlier, I am met with some backlash when talking about this cartel that is in the public eye. Mainly because Juan has the media in his pocket, but more on that later. But here I am, trying to spill the fucking beans on them, and all my videos fall on deaf ears. Why? Because it is so hard to believe something you love so much, like going to a live show or a famous music artist or a sporting team, could manipulate you so badly. Honestly, not one person on this social media app can picture Juan's cartel operating here in the states (and now the world), but they are.

Pie and Dick have figured out the formula to rake in billions of dollars monthly (illegal and legal) and move it in and out of the country like a convenience store moves cheap beer on payday. So, sitting here, staring at this arena, all I can think about are some details that I have been privy to over the years thanks to Ivan:

- In the early '70s, TRC owned one arena and it was in middle America.
- Over three decades later, TRC owns over 300 around the world.
- We deploy the same tactics the Italians did with protecting their neighborhood mom and pop shops. They called it running a tax/ protection fee.
- The Roadie Cartel calls it managing or consulting fees. We also like to use the term "operating." It sounds nicer than taking over your small club, amphitheater, bowling alley, theater or the giant sports venues. We like to help you operate it in a more efficient way for our pocketbook, is how Pie likes to say it.

Billions of dollars flood in monthly from venues alone when putting on shows, plays, sporting events, and more. And when I say more, our ticketing system is running 24/7; colleges use them for all their events. So do movie theaters, comedy clubs, conventions, and even churches. It's not like any of these people or companies know they're buying a system from a bunch of crooks. Nor do they know the system fees we charge are funding even bigger projects to keep money flowing in. Some of that money is also used to innovate old touring or broadcast technology.

The cartel hired nerds early in the game to do more than just cook, cut, and figure out ways to transport coke differently than their competitors. From hydro-cain-i-zation—that is one of the ways we transport cocaine—to our mega merchandise factories who supply anything from a coffee mug of your favorite team to the band shirt you just paid way too much for, we are in your everyday purchases.

The Roadie Cartel has clean money coming in too. So clean and so much that Juan could stop selling coke and still be one of the richest men in the world. But where is the fun in that, right? Nah, that asshole sells almost another billion in dope a month.

TRC and Juan's Mexican cartel in the United States run a legit business when it comes to employees. They have for years. All of it is for the cartel's continued success. Even the cleaning services they have started operate with one-hundred percent clean books. They did this because, it doesn't look good when high-up government officials are shaking hands with the bad guys south of the border. But when your local official is a representative for the local sporting team and the revenue they bring in, then he is shaking hands and making sure the criminals are a priority in high-up discussions.

The number of cartel employees Juan and his teams of smugglers have brought over to work in venues, schools, local government jobs, hospitals and so many other positions, is hovering close to 200,000. That makes for a fun Christmas party, right? (Ok, there isn't really a holiday gathering, but that would be funny if there was one). One thing is for sure: if you don't believe me when I say that the cartel is running the local arena that holds the big concerts, okay. Fine. But don't come crying to me when you cross the wrong fucking guy or girl in town and your life slowly starts to change. Little things start to happen to you in and around the community that just don't seem right, you get pulled over more, you may have problems at work and then one day you and your family are missing but no one cares. Juan always dreamed of his men and women running cities and being able to control their narrative through community life. He knew the herd mentality would kick in for most and the others, well they get a special visit. I have heard stories from Ivan about The Butcher and the killings he has done for the cartel. No one is spared. And don't think this cartel isn't planning to one day brainwash people via these new social media platforms once they find out more about it. This social media shit is just as addicting as the cocaine Juan first got Americans hooked on. Here are some more fun details about the cartel:

- Juan has deployed men and women to develop software to help his drug fronts make more money for decades, such as—

- Ticketing software,
- Security systems and software, and
- Cell phone tower technology (which is older now, but big at one time).
- Now the cartel only uses satellite phones.
- I am not sure which media company they are a part of, but radio, television and even print is being infiltrated and then manipulated. The more they can keep you focused on other, lesser issues but more emotional, then The Roadie Cartel can continue to distribute cocaine as if we were the soda-pop brand.

>>>PAUSE RECORDING<<<

My cigarette is almost done so I took a quick pause and lit another in between thoughts. I know I am trying to keep it short but there a few more things I have to speak about.

While sliding the pack of cigarettes back into my pocket, I felt my cartel phone go off. My mind very quickly went to the technology behind these phones. No one in The Roadie Cartel is allowed a normal consumer phone on them ever. Death is literally the penalty. I could suddenly picture the Japanese and European men who would show up on tour and even as a kid I would see them around Juan's ranch house. They must have been the ones who helped develop these very high-tech phones that keep us hidden.

Puzzled and perplexed by my epiphany, I shook my head to clear out a little room for more discussion . . .

>>>RESUME RECORDING<<<

Excuse my silence, I was just thinking about how detailed these men have been with their innovations in the world of drug trafficking. Sure, while you are left to believe these cartel members are just a bunch of hicks strapping bricks of coke to cars, they are actually sending shit into space to help them communicate better. For anyone watching and leaving comments on these videos, if you still think I am just making this up for entertainment, I wish you luck in the future because if I can't stop them soon, no one can.

Look, Juan and his cartels have their hands in more than you would like to believe, and that's because he has the money to do the craziest research and then develop items and systems that will only bring in more money. Nowadays, you can't go to an event without seeing our "TRC (The Roadie Cartel) Productions and Entertainment" signage. When a typical roadie or someone backstage asks what the TRC stands for, we are told to tell people that we are the industry's premier and most **TRUSTED, REPUTABLE,** and **CARING** company in the production, artist management, booking, and entertainment world. Ta-da! Simple, but Dick's brilliant company motto has brainwashed a whole industry to relying on us to transport, book, and deliver the most badass shows night after night, while stealing everyone's money right from under their noses. Our seamless and integrated business structure gives us a certain cohesion when presented to society. We look and operate at a very high level, so we must be good, and good humans too.

Before I end this video, I am going to share the scariest part of Juan's cartels and what I know is only the tip of the iceberg. I had gone to the Juarez mansion with Ivan one afternoon so he could meet Pie to pick up some money—or some shit he needed for the road. But when we got there, Juan, Dick, and Pie were standing in the driveway. I was told to stay in the car. Why? Who knows. As a young pre-teen, I didn't listen anyway. So, after the men left the driveway, I got bored and decided I needed to walk around. I knew my way around the house, so I decided I would let myself in the front since everyone else went around the back. I thought I would be sneaky and leave out the side door, but first I was going to grab a bottle of Juan's fine tequila from the back bar for me and my friends later. Big mistake. I walked right into Juan's conversation:

"Men, my papa always told me if I wanted true control of this world, there is only one way. And the only way to set the guilty free and lock up the honest man is to control the media. They set the rules, and they control the thoughts of a society. We are the devil in the details, and it is time we keep our legacy clean by owning the whole damn world! A toast! This drink is for Dick and Pie. Job well done on getting that deal signed."

Now, I never heard what deal he was talking about, and to be honest, only the few at the top—Juan, Adolf, Pie, and Dick—know how big this entity truly has become. But know this: Juan isn't just distributing cocaine and cleaning money these days. No, his cartel is slowly building a new civilization, where whoever was the 0.01% running the show were about to be handing the keys to mankind over to these four men sooner than later.

I think of TRC much like I think of the men who headed west to be part of the great American gold rush. They took the risk, and those who made it struck gold. Are we the only cartel in the world? Absolutely not, but we are the only one trafficking the way we do. We took advantage of a market that had never been tapped into before. We found a niche in the touring world that allowed us to have the upper hand in the drug game. Juan and Adolf's plan was about longevity from the start. We fought the war on drugs in the most unfair way over the years, and that was from the inside. It was the most punk rock thing ever. The machine is well oiled and I'm not sure just how I am going to stop it, but each day I get closer to the place where it all started. Maybe the answer sits dormant there.

As you go to bed tonight, just know the success of The Roadie Cartel is one hundred percent thanks to how much everyone loves cocaine and the effect it has at social events. If the seventies and eighties were us striking gold, then the years to follow were basically us printing our own money. The demand for the drug has never stopped. Once we pass it off to our smaller cartel factions on the city level, they flip the drug once again. Some of these off-shoots flip it to its even more popular stepbrother, crack. Between up-the-nose sales and the smokable stuff, we can barely keep up with demand.

Everyone wants some form of a drug, whether that be a new mixed alcohol with "New High Energy" built into each can or a new synthetic "snort-able" type of pick-me-up. People around the world are demanding drugs to be better, stronger, faster hitting, and longer lasting. Just like the shows we put on, it is all an addiction and we run the whole damn market. All we have to do is make one of our insiders in the press sprinkle in a great new article about a "new" form of coke seized off the gulf coast—and like any great piece of bad press, we are up in sales. Press is press, good or bad, and seeing that a good majority of our clients were celebrities, if they were caught with the booger sugar, it dramatically increased its popularity.

All I can say is pay attention . . . magicians use smoke and mirrors for a reason.

>>>STOP RECORDING<<<

As I flicked my cigarette toward an old coffee can that was overflowing with butts, I look up toward the arena. I am grateful in a weird way to be here because of this cartel, but I am also very sickened by the destruction I know we have caused over the decades. There is only one thing to do, find this guy Michael.

CHAPTER 15

We Are The "Tesla" of The Drug Game

>>>START RECORDING<<<

This is video diary #14, November 1, 2009. LA, California: Night 1 of 2.

The future. . .

>>>PAUSE RECORDING<<<

I stop to take a second to think and grab a sip of water. I am suddenly nervous about making this video. All the other stuff I have mentioned is in the past, I want to make this video to show where the cartel is heading. *Ugh*, I am certainly playing with fire now. Just the thought of how big the cartel has grown in the last 30 years is a big mindfuck but it stops me in my tracks every time I think about this organization's endless potential. Even before I wanted to see this organization crumble—there have been times where I couldn't wrap my head around the technology or ideas Ivan would tell me about. Maybe this cartel has that same forward motion that that one dude Newton was talking about. They, The Roadie Cartel, are going to keep growing and pushing the limits until some other, bigger force changes its trajectory.

>>>RESUME RECORDING<<<

The future, we each have our own unique ideas about the future. Your vision might include flying cars, time travel, artificial intelligence, cyborgs, digital currency—or maybe something simple like a sandwich-making-robot for the kitchen. But we all have some sort of belief that this is not it, there is more to this life than what we stand on today. Maybe, there are a few questions we should ask ourselves first about our vision of the future. What is the time dimension of your perceived future? Is it ten minutes from now? Ten years? Ten million years? Some believe our existence will end in a few years.

I can say my vision is very short, I know my time on this planet is winding down, so I better get to making the most out of these video diaries.

The Roadie Cartel's idea of the future is a little different than most. From its inception, Pie was looking fifty years ahead. Not many people like to do that, too many variables, but that is why Pie sits where he sits in the hierarchy of this organization. They also looked at crime and the criminals differently than most Americans. They wanted to build up normal humans, with semi-normal jobs, everyday people who walked amongst you, but who were unseen lawbreakers. But I think most importantly and what changed the game was the emphasis on street smarts with bigger importance on book smarts. They envisioned a more educated criminal, one who could not only build a high-speed tunnel system to transport drugs with their hands, but one who could **design it**. Or new ways to steal your money without ever holding a gun to your head—or without leaving the comfort of a production office chair.

Since The Roadie Cartel's conception, Pie mentioned that one day they would have the ability to manipulate something with the stroke of a keyboard from thousands of miles away. And that one futuristic thing the cartel has been working on is how they move data at higher speeds across the globe. Okay, okay, I know this one sounds totally not like what a cartel would do, but when you own a portion of the media around the globe, it is very important to move your messages and fast. This data shuffle was also important in many other ways, it helped with communication for the cartel internally and also with how money was transferred from account to account. Money was the leading factor in making the world better—for the cartel—and let's face it, Juan had a lot of money to make his machine the best. The key ingredient in most of the cartel's master plans that continued to allow them the freedom to run illegally, was finding safe working environments in countries with very lax laws. The equation was pretty simple, it had worked for Juan when he started to bring his Mexican people over the border to live and work in cities across America. So, the men copy and pasted what was done once and did the same with the technology side of the cartel. They found countries that needed money or protection and in return for those items they were able to operate the cartel out of those countries un-detected. Some countries the cartel works out of, are not poor and do not need protection, but their leaders didn't need to have their reputations ruined either, if you are catching what I am spitting out. It's amazing what a country's leader will allow you to hide in their kingdom when they need to save face.

What surprised me as I grew up in the cartel was how much tech-nology was a part of everyday life for typical men and women, no one in society batted an eye as more components were added to their daily lives. So, we just let ourselves in that back door to join the party. Think about how consumed people are nowadays by simple technology; then, add in the supercomputer in your pocket, digital maps that tell you when to turn and an application that lets you talk to friends across the world instantly . . . the list could go on for a while. My point is when you hear the term "cartel," you don't think we're in Silicon Valley and you sure as shit don't think about the concert you just attended. But you will now! Instead, you think of a dirt tunnel, with a simple rail system in it, that dead ends in a garage in Arizona somewhere with a bunch of Mexicans pulling bricks of blow out of the ground and throwing them into a minivan. And hell, some of Juan's Mexican "Cartel" members are exactly how you picture them to be too; snorting coke off big mirrors while taking lavish baths and driving expensive sports cars with the top down, chest hair blowing in the wind and money hidden in walls for days. And the word "roadie" comes with stereotypes too. All roadies must be long-haired drunks, sleeping our way across America and frequent-ing every strip club, bar, and Taco Bell ever opened. Some of that is truth too. Now combine the two words and you constructed in your mind a vision of a cartel roadie, basically a bean burrito-eating walking erection that builds tunnels while high on cocaine and trav-els the world drunk while tuning the artist's guitars. That would be the biggest understatement of the century.

Well, you're kind of wrong. The Roadie Cartel never built a tunnel into Arizona.

Okay, enough of my sarcasm! The Roadie Cartel has no stereo-types, to be honest. Mostly because no one knows we exist, they only know Juan's Mexican cartel. But our side of the cartel, we have been working undercover around the world for decades now thanks to trust and other legal loopholes. Pie has spent good money over the years on not only legal work arounds for all the companies, but also on our employees, the real criminals. We've had multiple cartel members walk across prestigious university stages, earning high degrees from these schools. The reality is the cartel has looked into the future since the day the four men came up with this wild idea to transport coke in new and inventive ways. In that meeting, they determined education needed to be their focus because they knew the future wasn't something that waited for you to catch up to it. They had to stay ahead of their competition and the government; luck doesn't pay the bills. To win, it was going to take a mentality that learned from past mistakes to grow. The Roadie Cartel knew way before our competitors that there were only going to be so many barbaric ways to bring drugs down a tunnel and into the United States. Oh, you're going to bring them in a car, on a plane, or in a boat? Then what? What the hell do you do once all those ways have been figured out? I'm not saying we don't use some of that old technology. We just didn't put all our eggs in one basket.

The cartel got crafty. We stopped stuffing coke into tires years ago. We went big once the cartel and the roadies merged into one, and we set our aim as high as a cartel could. So, when we move drugs on tours and over borders, we move hundreds—sometimes thousands—of kilos a day. We don't want to strap grandma with a lousy quarter ounce and hope to flip that for a new Ford Escort. No, we wanted major money payouts. To make money, you have to spend money in the right areas, not just on cars and mansions. Pie knew they would have to spend it on the crew, they would be the difference makers.

The Roadie Cartel is similar to any great investor or a great inventor. Not all the people at the top are book smart; instead, the majority learn the hard way. Ivan was Pie's apprentice—and Adolf started as Juan's, but he was slowly pushed to the side when Juan realized the real potential was in Pie. Rather than a degree hanging on a wall, Pie had a certificate from the school of hard knocks with a framed mug shot to prove it. We have a wide range of young cartel members, though, who are educated through the American university systems and others through some specialty trade schools. This is a different war Pie wanted to help Juan and the Roadie Cartel fight and win. Pie knew that Juan's Mexican cartel would never find its way back to the top if they didn't bring in a new style of fighting. The fight was not always going to be with guns and tunnels; the cartel needed men and women with new, sophisticated war techniques. If the cartel was only built with muscle, there would come a day when physical strength alone will not conquer. With strength, knowledge, and some pretty big balls, they might have a shot at greatness and so far, Pie's plan is paying off.

And here is one of the biggest reasons why Pie's plan is helping the cartel win. Juan decided to start a well-funded scholarship program while also upgrading schools with up-to-date technologies because he knew the cartel could never recruit children who came from money or had an average upbringing. Juan and Pie knew they would never be loyal if they already had the world given to them on a silver platter. Now, a kid in poverty trying to just feed his family or get to the next level was who they needed. It was a solid idea that no one saw working out perfectly, the poor were an untapped gold mine. You might say Juan was the Barcelona Football Club of the cartel world, signing a young Messi, but multiply that number by a thousand. The men had figured out they could scout these young minds at schools around Mexico, much like a manager would when looking for a new striker at some big football club in Europe. They developed a system in the schools for teachers who were loyal to Juan and the cartel to keep an eye out for kids who wanted more in life or were extremely gifted in science. Over the years, The Roadie Cartel would groom them to have the same mindset and value system as the cartel's; Pie got them to drink the Kool-Aid early in life. Pie knew the key is, one day, when an issue threatens the Roadie Cartel's values, a young star is more willing to handle it the way you trained them. We have found they don't stray from the herd, and these young minds feel comforted by the brotherhood we have built. Again, with all great businesses, you have the ones fighting for the cause with force, and then you have the game changers who are developing new technologies to crush the market and competition without lifting a finger. The Roadie Cartel bred them both.

We've had the ones who would straight-up kill you down to the ones who know how to move a mountain mathematically via a computer code they wrote while on the shitter. Yes, the Roadie Cartel hires roadies—and lots of them—but we've also had business masters, marketing geniuses, the best lawyers in the world, computer nerds, chemists, all sorts of engineers to run the buildings and factories, and even a couple of geologists. Those don't even begin to scratch the surface of the vast variety of careers the cartel members have held positions in. Doctors, accountants, lots of accountants and a few veterinarians . . . garbage men and a barista or two. We have infiltrated society on a mass scale.

The cartel hits all angles of cities, states, and governments to stay in the lead, so incentives are offered as part of the brother and sisterhood. Everything is paid for when in school; once out of school, we have a bonus structure that no Fortune 500 company could match. If you do a job for the roadie cartel and it's successful—like operating on a member who had been shot and leaving the cops out of it—you clearly get your paycheck, but the roadie cartel always drops off a hefty bonus or gift to go with that. Remember, not only are we taking in money from the cocaine, which on its own was a beautifully rich business; we have many other income sources. Money streams in from ticket sales, merchandise sales, and the concessions at our venues. Then add in our multiple transportation options like trucking and our charter planes . . . all of those plus the businesses Juan owned prior like the car dealerships. And now the cartels operate many technology companies that aid consumers daily life like; on-line ticket selling and buying and even a sports book. Money is everywhere and when Pie and Juan saw the opportunities, it was then up to Dick and his teams to create ways to use Juan's profits from cocaine to fund legal business ventures.

We take our chemists, engineers, and the advertising geniuses down to our merchandise and cocaine manufacturing plants to grow those in ways never seen before. The manufacturing of the pure cocaine paste is the easy part. Our guys take coco leaves, mix them with some chemicals, and bingo—you have the greatest money maker in the world, outside of the one thing we don't touch, porn. Even with the advantages we have, it's by no means a perfect system. We

have very few business limitations, but the cartel encourages in-
finite mentality, and that's what drives our production, technology,
and education inside the cartel.

One thing we constantly have to stay ahead of is border technology. And not just the southern border, all borders, so as we grow, so to
it also has to grow along with us. We make a few moves; they make a
move . . . it's a super calculated and juvenile game of cat and mouse
at times. The oldest was the test match of getting busted at one location with the goal of getting more dope across elsewhere. With the
help of inside info, we usually know when they're going to come
down on us at the border. So, we send a truck or two full of your
average coke—you know, the stuff that you would share with a party crowd and not close friends—to get busted purposefully. While
they're busy, we successfully cross five other semi-trucks with the
good stuff over. You have to let them win a time or two. Let them
relax. Hell, even if we lost all five trucks, the cartel is still collecting
billions of dollars each day on those digital ticket fees. Although we
still play this old game of cat and mouse by driving trucks over, the
technology we are using to hide the product is getting much more
difficult for their scanners and K-9 friends to detect. So, when I say
we still use old technology, we do, but with very modern twists on
how the coke gets packaged and shipped over.

With the invention of the Internet, wars and manipulations are
now something that can be done daily and with faceless men. Some
are childish and for fun; others are million-dollar takeovers from
well-established criminals like us. You have the ability online to be
anything you want, and The Roadie Cartel decided to dress up as
wolf in sheep's clothing. As a result, the cartel has built some serious Internet thugs. You know them as hackers, but these men and
women do more than just hack into bank files or shut down servers
to ruin a company's day. They are new-age spies for the cartel and
virtually unstoppable once they figured out how to access the government data and now your own personal data. Now sure, this might
seem a little cliché, but ask yourself why there hasn't been any end
to the war on drugs? Why is it that no politician has fixed the pill
epidemic? Why do some drug dealers spend forever behind bars
and others walk away scot-free? Well, the easy answer is, because

we pay our way in and out of situations when needed. The deeper answer is, because the government would rather deal with one snake in the cage than fifty all trying to get out at once.

The war on drugs will never end. There will always be some new to the drug task force hot shot cop who wants to try their hand at shutting down drugs, but the cartel will always win in the end. When the roadie cartel is confronted, they don't back down from any fight. With all the agencies trying to shut down the cocaine business, it has only made us stronger and harder to fight. The corruption inside the government's own system makes for a highly volatile situation requiring highly strategic tactics when moving the product. We never know which mayor, governor, congresswoman, or senator is on the chopping block and might be willing to take a shot at us. That's why we have hired bright minds to help hide the substances in plain sight. Even with all the government drama, we still move tons of cocaine through the air, land, and sea. Bottom line is this: while the U.S. government continues to pump money into other countries and neglects its own drug, crime, and social issues, Juan is going to keep capitalizing by pumping his own money into the border communities to gain more power, support, and soldiers to fight his fight . . . and win!

Juan did something that set him apart from many that had come before him in the drug game. He made a very special friend who just happened to be a very powerful man, who just happened to be in telecommunications. Oh, and he loved rare tequilas almost more than Juan did. So, they bonded instantly, and over time, he allowed some of our tech team access to some of his high-tech labs, so the cartel nerds had time playing and learning on the company's toys. The idea of the roadie cartel learning how to spy on the feds is a funny thought, but it was something we had to do if we wanted to be the mouse that always got away with the cheese. We were the pizza van spying on the carpet cleaning truck down the street who was trying to spy on us. But the sad part is that we already knew they were on the way. Not only do we use some high-tech items to spy on our spies, but we have also got some internal spies that hold very high offices in Washington D.C., AKA the mecca of criminal activity. Sure, our guys and gals have not made it to the top seat, but the ones they hold get some pretty amazing secrets down to us.

Okay, I know you're thinking satellites and spy planes, but so much of our intelligence uses people. People are their own worst enemies at times. We got pictures all day long from sources that hated that U.S. government and liked to trade info for our help smuggling their brother through the southern border. We love to wine and dine the secret holders. They are all suckers for a sexy woman, expensive drinks, and some after dinner coke in a hotel room. Hell, the number of A-list kids in our little black books would cripple generations of these prestigious families if we released the goods, it is plain and simple blackmail. It's usually pretty easy to get these horny old men back to a hotel room, with that little trio of seduction, where we could use a little narcoanalysis on them.

Some of the chemists came up with a super potent strain of coke mixed with a little secret chemical. This stuff can turn the tightest of lips into a walking high school gossip queen. Much like I'm doing now with these videos is what we want government officials to do with intelligence concerning the roadie cartel. Loose lips really do sink ships. Then of course, after we get the info extracted, we blackmail them until they give us exactly what we demand, even something as simple as a window of time for a jet to go unnoticed as it crosses into internal waters and then back.

Money rolls in like waves off the coast of Hawaii. So instead of wasting it **ALL** on Ferraris and champagne like I stated, the cartel invests a great portion of it in the science and scientist who gave the cartel a leg up. Pie made it his mission to find a way to make an almost all odorless, tasteless, and basically invisible cocaine concentrate that they could then ship to the states faster. Less hold up trying to hide the coke means the roadie teams get it to the arena chemist teams faster for the cutting and manufacturing of the product for distribution.

After many years and hundreds of failed attempts, one nerd figured out a cocaine concentrated extract that has changed the game for a while at least. We lost a few good men in the process (snorting it and trying it at check points), but the payout for Juan and the cartels was bigger than a few lost men in their eyes. They cheated the system and created chemical compounds that laced into fabric fibers and now, you guessed it, make shirts out of these fibers in all of Juan's merchandising factories in Mexico. The process is so advanced that no dog or X-ray could pick it up, and it only adds ounces to what a normal T-shirt weighs. This allows us to fly, drive, and cross borders in numbers that my mind has a hard time processing. It's a super crazy and a very technical chemical process when it comes to lacing the fibers, but on the other side when it is time to extract the coke for cutting and shipping, it goes like this:

The merch tech receives his daily shipment from the cartel or travels in with it, depending on the situation. Once the shirts get loaded off the trucks, the cartel hands move the cases down to the chemist's lab in the arena. There, they "hydrocainize" the merchandise. Yes, that's a term the roadies use, so you won't find it in a dictionary. This process uses a chemical reaction to extract the coke with a secondary element. Once the shirts have a nice little soak in a warm bath mixture, you pull the shirts out. The chemist then sprinkles in the last chemical product, and then they drain the vats. What's left in the vat is a highly potent paste-like residue. Before they can package the coke, it goes under a few industrial-sized heating lamps, and after a little bake, you have high octane coke, which has crossed the border as threads of fabric. Once that cutting and baking process is all done, the cartel chemists and merch techs dry the shirts, refold, and count them in for the merch man or woman to sell later that night at the show. So even on the days when a hot-shot cop comes looking for his next big bust and pulls over a semi-truck carrying a load of shirts, it looks, smells, and feels like a shirt, or shorts, or sweater.

Now, I'm no dummy, but I don't feel like I'm on the same planet as some of our chemists. I might hate what this cartel has done to my life, but the stuff they do and create is mindboggling cool. I have seen amazing things, but this one takes the cake on shockingly cool, almost up there with the guy who invented the wheel. This system of "hydrocainization" became our new go-to for moving product. We didn't waste any time getting Dick and his little team of minions to write up contracts mandating that any artist, sporting team, or events inside our buildings have to use our merchandise company. Sure, that sucks, especially if you're getting a deal from Joe Schmo down the street—but our house, our rules. If you're a touring client of the roadie cartel, you'll use our merch and our merch tech and like it. This system also keeps us moving drugs and money on days the artist plays non-Roadie Cartel venues or festivals. There are a few days that our haul into the festival is just so we can drop a couple pounds or more of coke for the all-night party goers in the deserts. When it comes to merchandise, we own the market. Most companies can't keep up with our prices for the quality of shirt and the profit ratio the bands still make.

Our biggest market to open since discovering the "hydrocainization" process is the Brits. Those red-cheeked, football-loving cousins of ours can't get enough of Juan's product. Ivan has been a production manager for many years and never filled more sea containers full of T-shirts for tours to be taken overseas than when this new coke hit the streets in the UK. Juan now runs the whole cocaine game in the states plus the UK and Ireland; he had his men destroy all competition and sometimes acquire, depending on what they bring to the table. Now, I am not saying there weren't other cartels still trying to sell coke; they just stopped trying to compete with Juan. If you're buying coke, it's from us or a dealer that we allow to sell our stuff because we take a cut from them too. Juan loves taxing these other dealers. He knows they have to eat, but they eat on his terms.

The whole trafficking game is fun, but like all the games, the Roadie Cartel only wants the "W." Juan's team plays with their own rules and with a winner-take-all mentality. They are only trying to breed the smartest minds in the world to help us take over the world one arena at a time. There are many moves made with developing new ways to traffic and move the product daily, but a pressing issue needed attention. Pie was starting to become a target in the cartel. He had been spotted with Juan and some of the Mexican cartel heads one too many times, so Juan decided to move him to a remote island off of Mexico for a while. The thing was, he still needed to communicate with the team from time to time.

So, it was time to put our engineers to a test of smarts once again. We had been pressing our chemist for a while to create new and interesting ways to push the boundaries with coke, but now we needed a communication system. One that was able to send and receive hidden messages using existing cell phone towers and satellites . . . much like an old James Bond style, "This message self-destructs after you read it," type of idea. After a little down time and a few written letters—yeah, we went old, old, old school for a minute—these engineers came up with a two-way pager before the Hilton sisters made them cool. They designed Pie, Adolf, Dick, and Juan a military-grade communications system that only the four of them could access. Once Pie sent info to Dick or Adolf, then the rest of the roadie cartel would get informed via older methods of phone technology like pay phones banks and hotel lobby phones and now satellite phones. Most of this was thanks (again) to our telecommunication friend that liked fine tequila. He came to the rescue and helped us in a major way with the infrastructure side of it. He had some friends that not only built computers, but also designed chips and mother boards for specific high-tech tasks. I think one of them controls the toilet flushes on either the Russian or Chinese space shuttles. They wanted a system that had self-erasing and encryption functions for all conversations. I am making it sound way simpler and as if this process happened over night, but this truly was a testament to these men who now were holding the key to the cartel's secrecy. The cartel sent over a few nerds to hang with Juan's tequila buddy's nerds for some intensive work with a special circuit board called the "PIEcODE." We are now able to access and piggyback our phones undetected across major cell carriers and their towers and satellites.

Who knows what lies in store for the next generation of cartel members? With no stop in sight and so much of our cocaine profit going toward bettering the cartel (with man and weapon power alongside of book smarts), this is kind of a terrifying thought. I'm sure with that kind of power and technology, whatever may come of the new-age Roadie Cartel members, they'll find a way to further capitalize off the people of the world. One thing we'll always have is people's love of material items, technology and drugs. None of which are going away soon. The more people look to write their life the way they want, we will be there to help them stay in their little make-believe worlds one **white line** at a time.

Now that I'm on the other side of the cartel, watching law enforcement agencies and governments try to keep up, I truly hope my story gets to the man who can help bring the roadie cartel to justice. In a weird way, they keep the world's money flowing by creating jobs, producing hit artists, putting on concerts around the world, and making coke that people demand, but it's my job to bring them to justice. The Roadie Cartel is pushing people to be more inventive, whether that be on their side or the law's side. These new-age roadies are educated and willing to fight to win, and that's what makes them stand at the levels of Nicola Tesla and other greats who pushed the boundaries in life. Juan and Pie didn't build an empire to have it fall tomorrow, so they'll continue to grow and mold the young, the nerdy, the outcast and the willing, into cartel men and women roadies to step up the hustle for generations to come. Most importantly, these brainwashed souls will die fighting for their cause. The roadie cartel isn't going anywhere, and the world should be ready for the next wave of members. I know the world wasn't ready for the four men who founded this cartel, but then again, no one was ready for my two best friends and me to join in on the action either.

>>>STOP RECORDING<<<

After putting my phone and ear buds away, I was in need of some cold water on my face. Lucky for me I was in a room with a nice sink and shower but as I start to make my way over, I am caught off guard by a mirror on the wall. I paused and took a good long look at myself; my God I am losing so much weight from all this stress. I don't feel bad, but I also don't feel well. Although I was speaking about technology, I was still thinking about my father the whole time. I missed everything about the giant man that he was in my eyes. All these years I was so caught up on how to make money and grow with the cartel, that I missed out on so much time with him. I heard people, non-cartel people, talk about how fragile life can be, but I never believed something could happen to me. Ha, it's funny, all this money and technology in life yet no one has figured out how to stay alive forever . . . not even this cartel. I guess this stupid mirror had more to say than go eat a fucking double cheeseburger!

CHAPTER 16

Welcome The Newest Roadie Cartel Hooliguns

Getting to the venue early, way before any of the other roadies arrived, I was able to sit in silence—well almost silence, sounds from the cleaning crew, sweeping and tossing empty cans into trash bags from last night's show were filling the giant room with a form of music. Sitting on an empty perch that overlooks the arena floor of this world-famous venue—yes, The Roadie Cartel owns this venue—I am left thinking about all the artists and sports greats who have housed their events here. Some of the greatest concerts and some of the great athletes have strutted in, believing they were going be crowned the next champ or superstar down on that floor. I would like to assume the ones that did take the crown or title, weren't afraid to stand up to the reigning champ. The more I am alone, the more I am enjoying these moments of silence and self-reflection. I am pretty fucking lucky to be here, alive and with a chance to become a legend in my own way. Okay, it is a very small chance but there is still a shot in hell that I can pull this mission off. Looking back on it all I am pretty—blessed—usually I don't use that word, but I am pretty darn lucky to have seen what I have seen and experienced what I have experienced. Most people couldn't even dream up some of the shit I have done. Anyway, those days are changing, and as for my luck, I think that is changing too. I really do hope that after all of this and before I go from this world, I can watch the cartel start to burn to the ground.

I begin to get ready for my video entry today and just before I open the social media app, I get chills and goosebumps cover my skin. This video was going to be about two people I miss dearly; I hate that they have sided with the cartel and pushed me away. As I wipe a tear from my cheek, I open the app, and without scrolling down to view others' pictures, I get right down to business. Because with this one, it's not about slamming them, no, no, this video is about thanking them for bringing light to my life. I hope they get to see this one day and though it may never change the way they view me, at least I spoke about them from my heart and in the end, was able to share our awesome story as best friends. . .

With my eyes shut tight so that no more tears fall from my face, I let out a forceful exhale and hit record . . .

>>>START RECORDING<<<

This is video diary #15 November 2, 2009.

Los Angeles, California: Night 2

I am almost home—

[My voice cracks]

Ahem. Ahem! Okay, that was not cute. Let me start this again, guys.

I am almost home, and I am not excited or ready for this homecoming, not even in the slightest. Even though I have zero faith that these videos are reaching anyone important or that anyone really gives a fuck about what I am saying . . . I do have that gut feeling that my luck and time has run its course. I do not know when, but the cartel is coming for me soon.

Lately, my luck has been at an all-time low. It is honestly like karma is cashing a big debt that I got away with for way too long. Ha, karma. My father would have said "God," and my two old best friends would have said "the universe." Either way, the luckiest thing to happen to me, outside Ivan finding me in a dumpster, was meeting my two best friends when I was too innocent to know what my father did for a living. Boy, what different times. Now, I can't even get those guys to listen to me, let alone look at me these days. Lucky me (as I rolled my eyes and gave a long blink).

I'd be ignorant to think that all kids have a bond that lasts a lifetime. I know I was one of the lucky ones who had buddies at least for most of my life. Growing up, I was always confused about who my real family was, so the connection with my best pals made them family to me. We might not have been blood, but we sure acted like we had the same fire running through our veins.

We were in it together. Good or bad, right or wrong, up or down, we rolled through life with the mentality that if one was going through hell, we all went through it . . . until recently. I'm not sure what bonds you to your friends. Our friendship was bonded by more than drunk wrestling matches and late night hangs out in the middle of the desert, watching the sun come up. More importantly, we were there for one another through those tough teenage moments. We loved . . . I loved those dudes, platonically, and even saying those four words brings tears to my eyes. But I guess that's my unique story and how we define our friendship. All the fuck in, all the fucking time.

Although I'm emotional about my best friends—and they would both call me a little bitch for crying on camera—we did have lots of fun and many wild moments. Maybe our crazy bond as friends came from not only love but our wild moments growing up. We did it all as adolescents. We loved to push limits as kids. All of us loved to hangout and party. We loved shots—lots of shots. Beer. Pizza. Wild bus parties. Drunken bus arguments about who knows what at 3 a.m. in the front lounge that turns into a fight. Icy hot wars. Lines of coke. Beerbongs. Bad acid trips. Weed. Strip club mishaps. Vegas pool parties. Trips to Mexico. Around-the-world adventures. More lines of coke. Dirt bikes. Skydiving. Boats. Private jets. Tattoos. Day drinking. Drinking before school. Drinking before work. Drinking at work. The good and the bad and everything in between.

The list could go on forever obviously, but you get my point.

As the child of a touring roadie, I didn't grow up in a typical *Leave It to Beaver* household. Summer was always my favorite time of the year; school was out, and I didn't have to stay home bored out of my mind. I never went to a summer camp a day in my life, but I did tour with bands each summer surrounded by men who smelled like cigarettes, whiskey, and Gold Bond. There were some perks at my summer camp that I don't think I ever heard another kid come back to school bragging about. I was that lucky kid that came back each year for the fall semester and rubbed in my classmates' faces about my experiences. I would tell other kids the stories of the drunken roadies out in front of buses chugging beers, wrestling like wild fat bears just out of hibernation. And, of course, front and back lounge wild adventures my virgin eyes would stumble upon. I soon became one of the bros at school especially when it came time for me to tell a boob story.

Living on a bus with my father Ivan and his rowdy drunk roadie cartel friends is cool and all, but there were times I just wanted to be a girl. Let's be real, I could only enjoy and interact with about ten percent of the stories they would tell, maybe even less. I understood the fart jokes . . . maybe a Simpsons reference here or there. But I was barely learning about my own body parts, so how in the world could I grasp the X-rated jokes and stories about women that I would accidently hear from time to time? I was out of my league and Ivan and the roadies were usually on their best behavior around me but face it, I was a woman on a tour bus. Shit was bound to slip especially after the tequila started to flow. I wanted to make my own stories and have my own bad tales for when I came back to the road to follow in Ivan's footsteps one day. Up until my last summer as a kid on tour with Ivan, I only thought of the number sixty-nine as exactly that—a number. Wow! When I found out what that was later in my teen years, I was mortified but if being a roadie meant I had to hear about boobs and vaginas from time to time, so be it . . . I am sure I grossed a few out with a few of my wild nights out in a town. But, I wanted to see what the world offered for myself and not listen to a bunch of drunk men's ideas of what the world was like.

As much as these roadie cartel guys allowed me to be a part of their lives, I would never be able to use their stories of travel and adventure as my own. That's lame. The time had come to make a hard choice as a kid, and I told Ivan it was time for me to stay home and be as much of a kid as I could be before it was too late. It was time to find my own crew of friends to go on wild adventures with. It was time to make my own memories that didn't involve the stage manager half-naked in the front lounge dancing on the empty pizza boxes while singing Billy Squire or Eddie Money.

Thankfully, I didn't have to wait long after I decided not to join Ivan so much on tour anymore to find some actual friends my age. I flew back to El Paso and Mary came to pick me up at the airport like she usually would. She wasn't just a familiar face. She was the mom I never had. Plus, we became best friends over the years. We loved to do the girl shit Ivan hated to do. She would always take me to my favorite barbeque restaurant in all the world on our way home when she would pick me up from the end of a tour. It was her way of buttering me up for having to come back to a semi-normal kid's life. I had gotten back in town just in time to prepare for the new school year, which I usually hated. Normally, I would make a couple of friends for the year, leave for the summer, and they would move on to new friends by the time I returned. This school year, something in the desert air was screaming to buckle up! Turns out, the storm rolling into my life was not going to be a simple summer squall. No, this was going to be a full-on-superstorm which would only bring mayhem, destruction, fun, and a few broken hearts along the way. We became the **HooliGuns** in TRC, a special cell of roadies that took on the hardest assignments Pie could dish out. But before all that, the neighborhoods in El Paso just hated our antics.

Growing up, Ivan, Mary, and I lived up on the mountain not far from the university here in El Paso. There weren't a lot of families with kids my age that lived around us. While stuffing my face with Texas-style beef ribs and crispy curly fries, Mary informed me that a nice family moved in down the street from us over the summer. Not many things will distract me from my ribs, but my chewing paused when she mentioned two kids had unloaded their bicycles from the moving truck. I looked up from my plate with one big BBQ covered grin.

"Get the fuck out of here!" I blurted.

Mary was less than pleased with my new vocabulary word. I paid dearly for that fucking word for the next few days with extra chores to do around the house, but I was excited! Ivan had just bought me a BMX bike for Christmas the year before, I wanted a skateboard, but he thought I was safe on a bike. I was getting pretty good at riding and even doing some tricks that impressed Mary usually, but maybe my new neighbors would enjoy seeing my sick street style.

There was no way I could sleep that night unless I went for a ride to snoop around the ritzy 'hood for them. Before the car was in park, I bolted for my bedroom and ran straight to the closet. I went to find my helmet, gloves, and knee pads . . . wait, wait. Let me rephrase that last part. I went into the closet to find my badass custom-painted helmet, the dopest gloves, and the newest and coolest and most rad checkerboard red, white, and blue Vans I owned. Wow, that was a close call on almost looking like a geek. I ran for the garage and saddled up my GT Vertigo for a ride. I was now mounted upon my great steed and ready to give one grand push on the pedal, but I stopped and, well . . . I had no idea how to be a kid. What do I do? How in the world do I kid? Do other kids say hell and shit? What the hell do we talk about?

"Ah, the hell with this shit!" I said aloud to myself.

Mary poked her head into the garage. "Tack on another week of chores! You're not going anywhere with a mouth like that."

"FUUU . . . DDDDGE . . . " I said in a playful, devilish manner.

I batted my puppy-dog eyes at this saint of a woman and promised I'd do any chores she assigned for an extra month. She knew my excitement was innocent, even if my language wasn't. She sighed and shook her head, trying to hide her grin. She shooed me away—but warned me to return within a couple of hours—and headed back into the house.

Dammit, I was strangely hoping she would make me come inside to start those chores, but I was on my own. I was lost as a kid, again. These kids would look at me so weirdly; I just knew it. I could tell them a story from the road or a joke I knew. Yeah, a joke. That would go over well. I had seen enough roadies over the years tell a thousand different jokes. Okay, so which joke? I had managed to roll out onto the driveway, but I sat frozen on the seat of that bike, going through every dirty joke I had ever heard to soon break the ice. "A hooker walks into a bar . . ." No, no, it was about a hooker with a runny nose. *Ugh*, how did Ivan tell that damn hooker joke?

It was getting late. I had sat in the driveway for well over a half-hour, the right pedal suspending my foot in mid-air with anticipation to be pushed on. I guess Mary had been checking on me from the window and finally decided to come out and share some solid advice with me.

"Stop overthinking it," she said. She smiled and then added, "There should be no analyzing how to make friends. Just go out, scrape your knees, and have fun. Don't worry and be the awesome, funny and strong little woman I know you are. Now get out there, little fighter." I heard, "stop being a little bitch." But however, it should be said, Mary was right, I was over analyzing this. And as Mary walked away laughing, I smiled back to her because she sounded like Ivan telling one of the roadies to step their game up.

I stomped down on the pedal and rode off into my unknown future.

Before long, I saw the two kids Mary told me about, a boy and a girl. They were doing circles on their bikes in the middle of the street in front of their house. My heart raced, a boy; *ugh* of course, the boy looked to be my age. No stopping now, I peddled faster toward the kids, I had a brilliant idea that wasn't a lousy hooker joke. I would skid-stop my bike sideways! With a quick shake of the head to make sure my dope helmet was on tight, I was committed. In my mind, I knew this was going to look super cool. I had seen kids do it in that one movie, "Rad," that Ivan loved so much. This is what the cool kids do, but I came in way too fast and over-skidded the rear tire. The handlebars rotated out of my hands. The tire hit a small crack in the street, and I went flying off the bike as if I was being ejected from an Airforce fighter jet. Flying like a bag of peanuts just thrown at a Red Sox game, my dreams of new friends went flying one way as I went sailing off in the opposite direction.

I thought for sure I was going to be eating lunch alone for a while come the fall semester. Clearly, I was going to be known as the dork girl who couldn't stay on a bike. I was mid-air bracing for laughter—and road rash to join the pain—as the ground inched closer. I thought I was going to slide or roll more, but nope—I landed thankfully on my side mostly, but my legs decided to angle themselves very unnaturally as I skidded to a stop. Rather than laughs and insults, I heard the boy say, "Whoa duder, that was rad! For a chick, you sent that shit hard!"

I didn't understand half of what he said, but the epic crash gained all the glory. Friend one was found that nervous day.

Axel and I rode the bus to school every day, had most of the same classes, and since we lived down the street from each other, it gave us more of a chance to bond. We were not the typical duo, but we didn't care and even though we came from different backgrounds, we quickly became brother and sister from other mothers. Axel was originally from a cold town up north but moved to the West Coast at a very young age, hence the new words he taught me, like "duder." Now, I'm not sure how he felt about the move to El Paso, but I was selfishly happy he did.

After about a month of figuring out each other's likes and dislikes, we discovered we had a lot in common. We both loved pizza, staying up late, movies and talking about our crushes. We were young kids. What do you expect from us? Talks on the most endangered species of butterflies in South America? Okay, but seriously, we got along great. Plus, I could finally relate to someone. There was no way I could tell some crotchety old roadie on a bus about how hair started to grow in all sorts of places and boys, *ha*, I would have rather died then tell a roadie about a boy I liked. Who knows the wild answers they would have given me but my point is this, Axel and I were closest of friends and I could share anything with him, I trusted him and he trusted me.

It wasn't long after the new middle-grade school year had started when Axel and I had become pretty popular in the eyes of the other kids. But to top it off, we met the final puzzle piece to our little hooligun gang. It was a typical day, messing around and ignoring our teachers when in walked the new kid. He came from a school on the east side of town, so you know he was a little scrappy and down for a good old-fashioned schoolyard fight. He stayed to himself for the better half of the day until we reached the always entertaining and carefree period of the day, physical education. Since it was raining, we went into the gym for a fun and somewhat violent game of dodgeball. This was where you started to separate the weak from the strong. It was a mix always, boy and girls, but our team always seemed to come out the victors.

Axel and I took it upon ourselves to start a small war with the new kid. We were always on the side with the rowdy Mexicans and skater kids. The new kid got lumped in with the jocks, preppy kids, and nerds. We wanted to see what this kid was made of from the get-go. Axel and I didn't think he'd get the upper hand, but folks, he did— and quick. He took out Axel almost instantly after he launched the dodgeball. I managed to stay in and brought my duder back in, and then Axel sent a ball sailing into this kid's face. Didn't faze him in the slightest. In response was a Nolan Ryan fastball—that, when the ball smacked Axel, it knocked him to the floor. This was where we should have just let it go, but we took offense to the act of aggression we instigated. So, like any great duo, we walked side by side, I was boosting Axel's confidence the whole time. I had seen him beat on a few kids bigger than him already so there was no way I saw what happened next coming. As Axel went in for a punch, a one-hitter quitter took him down to the ground. I froze and for one split second, and although I was a girl, I thought I was going to take a punch to the face for all the shit talking I was doing. But before I could blink and about as fast as it started, it was broken up by our female volley-ball coach. She towered over us by a few feet it felt like. Her meaty hands grabbed the neck of our shirts, her thick shoulders straining through her collared Polo shirt while we struggled to get our feet back to solid ground. Honestly, I am lucky that I was not a boy that day, I would have had my teeth kicked down my throat by this kid.

We soon found ourselves in the school's main office. The ticking of the wall clock was the only sound as Axel and I sat with the new kid in the principal's office, waiting for our punishment. My bestie turned his head to our nemesis. "Dude, I can't believe I didn't get one single punch landed, and you knocked the shit out of me with a fucking ball!"

"Yeah, I don't know why you thought you'd have a better chance against my fist, but it looks like your buddy had your back either way. You are lucky that Arnold Schwarzenegger's female look-alike came and broke us all up," the new kid said with a smile as he waved at the muscular gym teacher.

Axel smirked at the new kid, then at me. We busted out laughing. Over the years of dealing with fights, the punch to Axel's dome takes the cake in my book. That single moment changed the course. We went from a duo to a three-piece band. Friend number two was found.

Over the next few weeks, we became very close, like brothers. Axel and I would carpool or ride the bus to school on days Mary couldn't drive us. There, we would wait for Wes to arrive since he still lived on the other side of the mountain. Some days, he was dropped off by his drunk mom; on others, he took the city bus. And if it was a really bad day, his father brought him, but we hated those days and hated to see the burn marks on his arms from talking back on the ride to school. Our favorite day was always Friday because we would all stay at my house after school while Ivan was gone on tour, which was always, and Mary usually caved with any wild or fun request we had. We were the three stooges, the three musketeers, the three amigos—all wrapped up into one spicy burrito. We complemented the others' missing qualities and made each other feel like badasses. And the moment the guys got wind of Ivan's lifestyle, they wanted in as the next generations of roadies. As young teens, though, we didn't realize that Ivan's roadies equaled trafficking coke and laundering money. We wanted to travel, meet people from all over, get all the tattoos, and have wild nights of partying.

Growing into teens, we did what we thought would best represent that lifestyle until we could get on our own tour bus one day. We focused on living fast and loving fast too. With all great friendships, bonds happen to help heal the brokenness we all had. We all came from broken homes. Wes and Axel both had a revolving door of stepdads, and you know my biological parents were non-existent. In effect, we all became closer, protecting each other from the ups and downs and the constantly changing environment a single mom brings to a family. Unlike myself, Alex and Wes had blood siblings, and with our new bonded friendship, I gained a few brothers and sisters out of the deal.

Axel and his sister lived close to me, but Wes lived a bit away from us, so our bike rides to get him were quite cumbersome and usually involved a bus or two and lots of pedaling. Axel and I lived at the top of the mountain which was accessed by a steep hill that was bothersome to ride up, especially on those hot summer days in that west Texas heat. That was our life as kids. We wanted to be outside with each other as much as possible. Those first years flew by as we entered our early teen years. One day, we were chasing each other on our bikes, laughing about farts and then we were chasing women and boys in cars trying to live that wild roadie life, or so we thought.

The older we got, the more of a nightmare we became to the residents of central El Paso. Middle school was all about trial and error. What would they let us get away with this week? How far could I push that teacher before they threw a pencil at me? The most fun was pushing each other and our teenage bodies to the limit. We knew our parents wouldn't care what we were doing—except maybe Mary— so we policed each other to make sure we didn't die. Regardless, we tried it all, except we all stayed platonic. We pushed our bodies to the limit at a young age, and, by the time we hit high school, we had broken a few bones and it was time we moved on to breaking hearts.

By the time we hit our junior year in high school, there wasn't much our grubby hands hadn't gotten into. One of our favorite passions was skipping school and heading over the border for tortas—Mexican sandwiches, cheap beers, and even cheaper strip clubs. Not every kid has a cartel keeping an eye on them for safety reasons, but we did, even when we didn't realize it, Ivan made sure of this.

Ivan told me I had a very rich aunt and uncle in Mexico; though I didn't see them much at all, they still were family. This came in handy when we would cross the border; it was like a whole new world opened up for us, and we never paid for anything—even when we tried—and we never got in trouble once across that border. I always thought we were popular, but nope; we just had Juan's Mexican cartel making sure we were good, just out of view from us.

As a kid, I met Juan a couple of times, but I did hang with Zora a few times, so when I was old enough to drive, they allowed us to go to the ranch on the outskirts of Juarez. Those were the best days as teens. We would pile into my little single-cab Toyota pickup and head west to the border. Pie or Ivan would pull some strings, so we were always met by Juan's armed guards to take us into the compound. We felt like rock stars. It wasn't until years later that we understood why only the three of us were ever allowed to play at the ranch. The property was massive, so we could have fun out on the land and around the house, but we could never leave without our security detail. As fun as it was, it was also something we only did occasionally—like when we wanted to shoot guns, drink beer, ride dirt bikes, and chill by Juan's beautiful desert oasis of a backyard. If we were extra lucky, my Uncle Pie would be in town and take us out in the helicopter for some high-speed hog shooting, but he was a busy man, so that was rare.

There comes a time when curiosity can get you into trouble. When riding dirt bikes on the ranch, we decided to rebel. We left the compound without our security guys. Within an hour, a few men rolled up on us with guns and demanded we get in the bed of their trucks. I was terrified and had no idea what was about to happen to us, but a string of shots rang out from the sky, shredding the bodies of our captors apart. As survivors, we looked up to watch our savior—a helicopter—blaze by.

Once Ivan filled us in on the truth—why those men died that day the way they did—well, we wanted in on the action. We weren't in it for anything sick or twisted; it's because we knew riches lay waiting for people who were in the drug game, and hell, we had a direct path in now. I think Ivan felt by letting us in on the cartel it was going to scare us away from that lifestyle. He was very wrong. We wanted in for all the wrong reasons but in reality, my father knew there needed to be a new generation to come up one day and they would need to be trustworthy. Plus, after that little mishap, if I was in then he could help protect me, or that at least is how I have always seen it. We would be the new generation of roadie cartel members, the hooliguns.

Toward the end of high school, our grades were starting to look like really good golf scores. A shift happened in our mentality because of how popular we had become. Once we determined we were joining the roadie cartel one day, our young arrogance took over. We walked a little taller, cared a little less, and all-around started to live a lifestyle we knew very little about, but wanted so badly. We were seen as rebel outcasts, and the student body loved it. Mary started to visit Ivan more on the road, so we did the only logical thing. We had the sickest parties at my house that overlooked the whole city. We had access to coke and drugs through a couple of security guys on the compound. Ivan probably would have killed them if he knew they were helping us score at such a young age. High school was a blast now, and no one else could keep up. No one else in the school could touch our swagger. Everyone wanted to be us, and we loved every second of the young power game. It was addicting.

Our morning routine had shifted now that I could drive. Axel lived down the street, but he basically lived at my house, so we would get in the Toyota and head off to Wes'. But Wes' mom hated us; she kicked my truck after dropping him off too drunk one night, so we started picking him up at the 7-11 down the street. Axel would grab donuts, Red Bulls, and smokes for the day. Usually, by the time he came out with the morning grub fest, Wes was in his seat with the door locked screaming, "I called shotgun yesterday, bitch!"

Normally, there would be a fight of some sort for the power to regain shotgun, but not today. By the time Axel came out from the 7-11 that morning, Wes hadn't shown up yet. We had a few smokes, and Axel hit his phone up a few times, but it went straight to voicemail.

Even though everything about life was working out for us, many things run through your mind when something messes with the daily ritual. Was he in trouble with the cops? Nah—we knew better, especially after Dick warned us after our first run-in with the law: "You think I am a jerk off? Don't make me call The Butcher next time." So even though we were wild, we learned our limitations. I had dropped Wes off at the 7-11 the night before, and he was pretty messed up on booze, but I didn't think it was enough to fuck him up where he didn't make it home.

Axel started compiling a list of haters he might need to pay a visit, but even then, Wes would still have his cell on—unless they beat him up that badly. After an hour, it was time to move. We decided to head over to his house and look at the last place he should have been.

As we pulled around the corner, we could see a small trailer attached to the back of a van parked in Wes' driveway, which we didn't recognize. It was like out of a nightmare when Wes appeared, carrying a dresser with a man we had never seen before. We screeched to a halt alongside the curb and bolted toward our brother Wes for immediate answers. His mom had lost her mind and was sending him to live with his grandparents out of state. She gave no warning, and when he woke up and walked out of his room, his grandparents—who he had never seen before—were sitting in the living room.

We knew that crazy bitch would come out swinging at Axel and me, so we tugged on his arms as we hotfooted it back to the Toyota. He stopped and stared blankly at us. Looking back at the trailer, it was as if he was giving up on life, like going with them was the only option. We begged him to join us and make The Roadie Cartel his new future family. With a couple good shakes and a slap to the face, his eyes went from a sad glaze to an alert determination. Wes turned and ran for the house. We stood there like a couple of idiots, wondering if he was done with us. But like a bat out of hell, he blew out of the front door, bag in hand, with his mother in full sprint behind him.

Axel and I had made it to the running truck. I flew into the driver's seat, threw it into gear, and with the tires spinning, Wes hopped and rolled into the truck bed, and we were gone. We saw his mom waving her arms frantically and screaming in the dust. School could wait. We had lots of beer to drink out in the desert to celebrate not losing a brother.

That was one of the more defining moments in our friendship (outside of that one time we delivered some coke to our English teacher's house party). In our eyes, that moment was another reason to flip the middle finger to high school and hit the road. After we made it back to the house and our adrenaline subsided, I got a hold of Ivan. I explained the situation to him and told him we were ready to leave the next day for a tour. He laughed at me over the phone. Looking back on that moment, I clearly had no idea how touring worked. He explained there was a little more to it than just getting us on a tour. Ivan seemed more concerned about the other two guys. He was never happy that he had to tell them about The Roadie Cartel. Still, after he threatened their lives and basically made them cry as they swore to never speak of the cartel, he slowly became agreeable with them wanting in.

"Do I really have to find tours for your tall, weird-looking friend with the big forehead? And does that ginger ever stop checking to see if his dick is still in his pants?"

I mean, Ivan wasn't wrong. Wes has a pretty large forehead, and Axel, for some reason, couldn't keep his hands out of his pants or look adults in the eye.

Overall, I'd say the conversation went well, and Ivan said he'd talk to Pie, who gave the go-ahead. I was worried how much Wes' family would put up a fight, trying to get him back, so we laid low. Mary hated that idea because now we were at my house all the time. Axel returned to school a few more times, mainly to appease his mother, but that soon ended. And I came to find out Wes' family were all meth trash that didn't even try to look for him. Sometimes it's better that way for kids when they lose their family. Doesn't make it right, but he was with his true family now.

The call came through on an early Tuesday morning, which for us, was around noon. Ivan told us to have our bags packed and ready by the end of the day because he had three tours to put each of us on. We wanted to be on the same tour, but I don't think we were in a position to be picky.

I hopped out of bed and ran for the spare room we gave Wes; Ivan had a few extra places to crash in that big mansion. I ripped off his sheets, and with old tequila and cigarettes on my breath, I screamed into his face, "We are going on tour, duder!"

He jumped up and almost hugged me, but he stopped short. We figured we could high-five for now, and once we put more clothes on, have a big hug. We laughed and rushed to find Axel. Finding him was always an adventure, he never seemed to make it to a real bed or even couch when he crashed at my house. Somehow, he would find a corner, closet, or pool float to pass out on. Running through the house, I spotted his sunburned red ass passed out next to the pool. There we all stood; me in my bra and panties, Wes in his boxers and Axel in a speedo, we were all high-fiving and fist-punching the air, too excited for clothes. One more reason why my neighbors don't talk to us.

Traveling for the cartel was like no other style of production touring. Once you started, there was no downtime. They rotated tours like some people do socks and underwear. So, the chance of us meeting on tour wasn't impossible, but the planets would need to be aligned. I filled Wes and Axel in with more stories as a kid out on the road with Ivan, which was like a Fantasy Factory summer camp. I didn't have work or responsibilities back then—well, that's kind of a lie. On one tour, I had to bring a stout whiskey and Coke on ice to this one sound engineer named Johnson each night during the show. I was young and got away with murder out on tour back then, things were about to be a lot different.

This go around was going to be a different beast for me getting on and off that bus for life on the road; I wasn't a little kid out to have fun. The most important part and the main focus was that we got a tour. We had to keep our A-game strong because these other roadies were going to try and break us nightly. So, we just had to keep our heads down, work hard and treat The Roadie Cartel like the movie Fight Club. Never talk about it. The three of us touring together would happen, just later, and that was fine with us. It felt wrong knowing that we were getting into something so highly illegal that only hard time in jail or death would be the only options for getting out. Death was the real way out because jail just meant death too. Those prison walls couldn't keep out La Reina or The Butcher. As we all signed by the X in blood, you could feel the cold chill sweep over the room—or maybe it was the open window—but we knew we belonged to Juan, Pie and La Reina now.

Axel was the first to leave the mansion on the mountain for the road. It was bittersweet watching a third of my gang leave, but Pie and Ivan had hooked him up with the biggest rock tour of the summer. With his little suitcase packed and a backpack full of his favorite Copenhagen long-cut dip, he waved goodbye out the window of his black sedan. The tour had one of those old-school, military-style production managers running the immaculate, well-oiled ship. This "ship" ran hundreds of pounds of cocaine each night. Axel was not prepared, to say the least. Pie made surprise visits from time to time to keep this client very happy, seeing that he was also the band's manager. They wanted to start moving more but were in desperate need of help on the loading dock. The production manager was looking for someone to help the stage manager when he was busy. It was all the top-tier roadies out there, but the designers of the show had found a way to shove thirty pounds of shit into a five-pound sack. In layman's terms, a person who doesn't have to do the daily work decided that more is better: more lights, more stage FX, more video elements, and more shit for the roadies to deal with inside arenas. Sorry, kind of went on a tangent. But while I'm slamming the cartel, I might as well take a punch at a few people who made my life hell over the years too.

Since the stage manager found himself getting pulled in too many directions trying to get the show in and out of arenas, this is where Axel would be the best help. Axel would take on dock duties; he'd direct the flow of gear daily while also assisting the merch tech in getting the coke either to the lab or back up after the coke was cut. Out of all of us, Axel played the dumbass well and looked like a window licker most of the time, but the kid would outwork us all. He could see paths for gear none of the other roadies could and was the only one with the guts to take chances on load ins and load outs. His take-no-prisoners mentality shined in that position because there was only one goal: get the coke in and out of the building without the stage or production manager yelling at him.

Wes hung with me for a couple more weeks while his tour was getting ready to ramp up. Between the three of us, we had guessed Axel would do stage management stuff, mainly because he was full of piss and vinegar. Me, well—we all knew that when the road called, I would end up with Ivan as his assistant on the production manager side of things. We had no idea where they would put Wes. He isn't someone you want running the dock or dealing with tour coordinating. He, for sure, wasn't going to be the PM or accountant, and he knew nothing about Spanish or chemistry, so merch tech was a definite no. All that was left was security. He didn't know anything about that, but he wasn't scared of anyone, and he had that killer right hook if ever needed.

Hip-hop and gangster rap were the two most popular new genres of music when Wes joined. There'd be forty-plus people on stage who had no reason to be there. The entourage could range from managers, friends, friends of friends, girlfriends . . . all the way down to enemies. Because of these "mobs," the head security guy demanded a heavy hitter for help on a new tour full of the most notorious West Coast rappers. They needed someone who would not only bring big balls but a solid punch, and most important of all, they also needed someone who could protect the dope and the artist.

It was a full-time job for the security team on some tours. The tamer shows didn't need an ex-linebacker who could bench press their weight multiplied by three. No, they just needed a guy who could pull a gun if a wise guy tried something with the blow. It was going to be a hard gig for Wes, but he was soon after nicknamed "The Sleeper" thanks to his fists. Once we found this out, Axel and I did a pretty good job of starting a rumor that his nickname deals with his moves in bed with the ladies. Wes didn't appreciate that much.

When it was my turn to work, Ivan decided it was payback time. He wanted me to feel the wrath of teenage drama I put him and Mary through. I also knew Ivan had started to show me years ago how to be a great production manager, but my head was still lost in all the glamour of the road back then, so I didn't learn. He bounced around some tours—from production manager to tour manager—but that was to help Pie with stubborn bands who needed Ivan's cool demeanor. This tour was not one of those, in fact this was with the band Ivan got his big break as a production manager way back in the day. So, I was going in as his—well and for lack of better words, as his bitch, and I was going to learn very quickly how to listen and do what he asked me to do. Time to be a sponge. He was looking for a kid he could trust, and I did owe him. Besides, my buddies creeped him out.

I waited at home for Ivan and the artist to finish the daily flights on the private jet, jumping from promo spot to promo spot on the big morning shows, and other late-night events promoting the big reunion tour, before he flew me out. And they obviously couldn't walk into a TV show or venue without Ivan. The tour was the biggest on the planet at this time, and it was going to be one hell of a banger with stadiums, arenas, and one-night specials at famous clubs. Why not try to cram all that and a bag of chips into every corner of the earth—twice? Over the years of being part of Ivan's touring career, these guys were always the wild ones. The buildings would be full of screaming women and rocker men, all trying to get a piece of the action. For me, this was going to beat any summer run that I had ever done with Ivan in the past. This was going to be the one that made me into one badass woman in an industry full of men (or at least a badass teen with a little extra respect from the veteran roadie cartel members).

The three of us stayed in touch as best as we could over the next few months. Then one day, Axel and Wes actually ended up close to the arena where Ivan and I were doing rehearsals at in the New York area. Those two knuckleheads took the train on their day off to visit and swap horror stories from their time on the road so far. I might have had it the easiest seeing that I had been sitting in the same city for rehearsals with our big rock show. It made our shipments of coke going in and out very easy. We weren't making any extra money since we hadn't played any shows yet, but we were charging an arm and a leg to the artist to rent the building for the rehearsals. The music business makes me laugh some days, mainly because of all the things they get away with making the artists pay for. Ivan had come full circle in this moment as we all sat in the production office catching up. He told us this building was one of the first of ten Juan had built and the first in the New York/New Jersey area. Now it is only used for rehearsals, so the lab is outdated, but still works. It was cool to sit in this place with one of the original members hearing tales from the early days of The Roadie Cartel.

Axel shared his stories of working with one of the rowdiest bunches of roadie cartel members. Just when he thought he was earning an inch of respect with them, they would knock him back a few inches. I think they just wanted to see this skinny skater kid break, but even through all the hellish days, he stayed calm and collected. He didn't need to call attention to himself. The all-night drinking sessions full of coke and tequila followed by a load-in with little more than a few minutes of sleep is not easy for anyone, but he pushed through. He appreciated all the boobs that got flashed at the big rock show, though. He said most of the women had boobs that looked like sad basset-hound ears, but the boys were still teens, and they couldn't hate on any boobs.

Wes was sweating it the most. He was seeing and doing things he never thought a kid from El Paso would. Each day, Wes strapped on his bulletproof vest, slid his loaded 9mm into his waistline, and transformed into The Sleeper. Now, he said that he never wanted to use it, but one night, he was forced to make the split-second decision to put someone down who was coming after the artist and manager. Dick and his team of cocky lawyers cleared the air before Music News got wind that a TRC Productions and Entertainment venue and employee were involved. Even though we might not have enjoyed every aspect of the job, it prepared us for the hard life ahead. Sure, there were easy days on the horizon, but the road was hard. It was the only way to get new roadie cartel members ready to transport hundreds of tons of coke yearly around the world.

Once my tour rehearsals ended, we hit the road, and Ivan turned me into his full-time production assistant, mainly because he was swamped with the artist and tour manager's daily needs; I had to pick up his production manager duties and not miss a beat. It was the whole trial by fire, I probably should have paid a little closer attention to how he was advancing shows in rehearsals. I was green as green could be when it came to the job, luckily for me Ivan was double checking me, or so he said. But I had zero complaints because I was on tour and learning the ropes. Our shows were busy, but even on the long days the crew let loose out by the buses post-show or even on days off. Sadly, I was not involved in the nightly fun, I was busy doing my last cartel coke and money checks with Ivan and the building manager.

In my eyes, the hardest part of touring wasn't the long hot days in stadiums. Or the cold winters of transporting blow through the great white north. Or even being stuck on a long bus ride with a toilet that was not functioning properly. Nope. The hardest part to any tour was sitting through an awful show the audience thought was entertaining. On the extra painful off-pitch days, I would have to remind myself I didn't get into this business for the music but to make a ton of money off people's love of coke and the world's love for paying outrageous prices for tickets to see their favorite artist. At the end of the day, the designers and artists could find a way to make pigs fly, and I would only care about getting the coke cut and moved to the next city. Ivan taught me how to play like I cared in front of the artist, their friends, and management when it was not just us. We needed them and we could be friendly, but we didn't need to be their best friends. Getting and keeping clients and moving drugs for Juan were the roadie cartel's responsibility, not being a friend to an underage pop star or washed-up rock guitar guru. To fill Ivan's shoes as a production manager and somehow work my way into becoming a go-to PM would take a lot, but Ivan was patient and showed me the ropes. Knowing I had a long career ahead of me kept my focus; sadly, many newbies have messed up and had to meet The Butcher or visit his little kill shack.

The most common question I'm asked is whether I get to meet the band. Yes, we do. Some are quite nice . . . others not so much. In fact, some artists, I would rather step on a nail repeatedly as I crossed a hot desert with a Muppets Christmas album stuck in my head than be in a room with them again. Until I became a roadie, I thought Ivan partied all night with bands and that I grew up with the king of all roadie gods. As a kid going out with him on tour, I didn't realize how hard this job was. So, I get that it's easy to think of the word roadie in association with parties, sex, drugs, and rock stars, but there is more work than play.

Gazing at my own production office, I am taken back to the years of sitting in Ivan's production office. I can see him rubbing his head and eyes with the palms of his hands as the radio incessantly shouts at him. With each question, a grey hair sprouted, and another cigarette was lit. As a kid, I never saw the constant running around to the dock, then back to the arena floor, then back to the office. The constant fixing of tour problems resting on your shoulders. Getting coke city to city. Even the best in the business still dealt with the daily struggle of traffic when rolling into town, the missing shipment of merch T-shirts that needed to get down to the lab two hours ago, and drama between crew members.

I laugh when people think it is a glamorous job. They don't see the roadies rolling into an arena at four in the morning only to find out one of our drivers is pulled over a hundred miles outside of town with the rigging hardware to hang the speakers and lights. They only see the effects of a long day's work filled with sweat—and some laughs—mixed with adrenaline to get the show up in a few hours. Never mind the fact that we also had to get all the coke cut and ready to meet the gear back at the dock post show. Time was never on our side!

The years fly by for roadies. There is no time to care what day or holiday it is, for that matter. We three—Wes, Axel and I—learned that all too quickly. We blinked, and like that, some of us got put on new tours while others stayed on the same ones for years. It felt like eons before we ended up in the same city together again.

We were all learning and growing in the industry we wanted to be a part of. Our bank accounts were growing along with the clout of having a few tours under the belt. It is awesome to finish a leg of a tour–when suddenly, all the old roadie cartel members look at you with those eyes like, "Well we didn't have to take him out back and shoot him. Maybe the kid's alright after all." That's a fact, though. If you make it through the first one, chances are you'll be just fine as a full-blown roadie cartel crew member if you keep your trap shut. We learned to drink more and work with hangovers the size of Texas. And we never learned our lesson after swearing we would never drink again.

We may be high school dropouts, but we've been doing what we love and getting paid for it. Up until my father's death, I looked past the drug trafficking and saw that it's an amazing life. We don't have to wear a suit and tie to work. We also don't have to sit at a desk all day crunching numbers. Now, I would never knock anyone with any job—and good on them to have the marbles to stick out a lackluster career—but I was a wild stallion born to run who just didn't know any better. And boy, have we run. We've run from west Texas and around the world many times over. We are the generation of mega tours and in-the-round arena and stadium concerts. From the tips of South America all the way to the cold tundra of Russia, we've brought you music that rocks your face off, and we've also brought the party where everyone wants to be seen. I have no regrets and I am here making this video because of these choices. Am I sad at my father's passing? Fuck yes, but if I never joined the cartel, I wouldn't have some of the memories I do have with him.

By the time the cartel owned almost every venue in the major markets, Ivan handed me the reigns for an upcoming tour, and I was told to bring my team along for the ride. My tour and our rules. We had gotten so big that Dick was forced to sell off some of the businesses to ensure all eyes didn't land on us. So, we sold ones we could still control, sort of. We had already established loopholes in the touring system that—even after the sale of our ticketing system—we still found a way to hack into it and take a cut of the profits. The cartel was a powerhouse that had ways to adapt and shift. Unless you were one of the heads or on the road with us, you would never know you worked for the cartel. As a production manager, the hardest part was just making sure the normal roadies and The Roadie Cartel crews never crossed streams when working or playing. But with Axel and Wes on my team, we were untouchable and always able to keep our crews happy.

Until now, I never realized how great I had it working with Ivan. I have been a little jaded the last few years. Most people might not realize just how great it is to have your best friend since birth around daily. Hell, I didn't. I bounced around a few tours over the years, but anytime Ivan went out with his long-time rock band, he took me with him. Years later, Ivan finally moved up to the tour manager,

probably because he had been with them since the old days of rehearsing in the hills of LA, but also because he is one of the best
roadie cartel members to walk the planet. And wouldn't you know
it, that asshole made me their new production manager on their
third reunion tour. I am not completely convinced the band likes
that move, but they loved Ivan and did whatever he said.

I have to wrap this video up, but in my next one, I want to explain
and show a day in my life because I get asked why I drink the second
the cocaine is in the truck and smoke so many cigarettes throughout
the day. Well, that day in the life of a production manager trafficking cocaine for the world's largest cartel and putting on shows for
some of the biggest names in music . . . it's pretty fucking stressful.
Stepping off the tour bus in the morning and turning my radio on,
it's time for my most famous words on a show day, "Go for Wyatt!"

A day in the life of a roadie cartel production manager might help
you understand better what actually happens backstage and here is
a sneak peak, it is not glamorous at all. I don't have time to share
my entire day with you this second but in my next video entry I will
take you into one of my days, actually I will take you back to the
workday leading up to my father's death . . .

Now that I say that, I am about to drop the fucking hammer on
Juan and his little cartel minions, it's fucking on!

>>>STOP RECORDING<<<

If I would have been holding a microphone, I would have dropped
that bitch, but I didn't so I just set my phone on my desk put my face
into my hands and started to cry . . . I don't know if I was ready to
talk about my father's death on the Internet.

CHAPTER 17

A Day in The Life of a P.M.

It was quiet day so far but that can change in the blink of an eye. We had another walk-away show, so while everyone ran off to hang at a bar, I decided to stay late and get lost in some thoughts. I recently overheard that Pie has found my replacement; my days on this earth are numbered. How many, who knows but I do know The Roadie Cartel is not done with me this second; they still need my services for a few more days, mainly for the band. Pie will need me to get this new dude up to speed with the band, there is no way they would say I am just leaving. I want to say "fuck it, kill me now," but then the only ones who suffer are the band members. And they loved Ivan, which then in turn made them give me a chance. So, I will do good by them, because that is what Ivan taught me to be, a decent human on this earth. I laugh to myself because it is such a double standard, I work for an organization that kills millions with its drugs each year but yet each year here I stand trying to do good by a few dudes with guitars and long hair. Oh, they loved Ivan, oh could he get them to laugh. Hopefully after this tour the cartel doesn't kill these guys off too, for asking about Ivan but if they do, I hope they meet him at the big concert in the sky—as I look to the ceiling, as if I am some sort of believer now, *ha*.

I am in a pretty pissed off mood, I don't want to tell some dude what I do each day, and it is not because I don't know how but because the end will be coming shortly after that. Fuck it, maybe I tell him and the world what I do . . . I did say in my last post how it would be helpful for the world to know more. To know exactly what it is we do backstage and each step we take.

I pull my earbuds and phone from my pocket. It is time to educate the world what it actually takes to get a show done in one day, while also getting a couple hundred pounds of Mexican nose candy ready for delivery.

>>>START RECORDING<<<

This is video diary #16, November 4, 2009.

PHOENIX, AZ: NIGHT 1 OF 2

Hello, viewers! Getting right to the point—I don't have any better way to say this—before my time expires, and I only thought it was right to enter in more video evidence against these assholes running this cartel. I have decided it is only fitting if I give you a day in my life as a production manager. I don't tend to be emotional in these videos, but when you know you only have a few more rotations left on this planet, you start to think about the "what ifs" and the "I wishes." The few days that lead up to the killing of my father, I wish I could have been in a better mood at work, so I could have smiled that one extra time with him. Those workdays were some of the hardest, so I thought I would share just how we roadie cartel members do our thing, which might also help me to get some pain off my chest of those last moments with him.

Each show ends differently . . . but kind of the same. As the confetti trickles down out of the sky, the sound guy fires up the walk-out music and the band bows at the downstage edge. There is only one thing left: LOAD OUT! House lights turn on, and while the crowd exits the building, the crew retrieves band gear, loads it in boxes, then show equipment and cocaine is quickly slammed back into semi-trucks and shuffled out of the building. Then, it is off to the next city, to set it all up again and repeat the process day in and day out till the tour is over. This specific night—I am going to talk about—was full of little quirks, but it was Buffalo on a back-to-back into Boston, where there were always little hiccups coming into and leaving that venue. It didn't matter, though. After Boston, we had a day off in my favorite place, New York City, and Ivan and I had big plans before a crazy load-in followed by a show and then a busy load out before the gear and cocaine head out west on a three-day cross-country drive to Seattle. Thankfully, the crew flew while buses and trucks put in an overdrive. We had a massive tour and a lot of shit to put up and tear down. This tour was stressful because it was moving more merchandise, tickets, coke and money than any other in roadie cartel history, so we were being heavily watched by

Pie and Adolf. But that is what made Ivan great—the pressure to perform—but really, it was all me by this point. That's probably also why the cartel is taking so long to knock me off, the move has to be calculated and everyone has to be ready to pick up the slack.

If you couldn't tell by now, a lot of money is involved when getting the cocaine in and out of buildings on time and is helped by paying the right people. Sure, the roadie and Mexican cartel own most of the industry's buildings and infrastructures, but we still had to pay stagehands. And when you're acting like a legit business, you have to play that part with employees. Once the load-out starts, it's "go" mode for my guys and the rest of the tour crew. On this specific tour, we had thirty semi-trailers; some nights, we stuffed upwards of a few tons of cocaine into two specific trailers, yes that is over 6,000 pounds of powder.

I have gone on long enough. Welcome to the real show of touring the world, which starts in the early hours of one day and doesn't end until the early hours of the next day.

OCTOBER 6, 2009, 00:00:01. BUFFALO, NY - LOADING OUT

One hour into load out, thunderous sounds and voices of crew members blast over the radios. Forklift alerts beep and road cases bang into one another, filling the backstage hallways all the way out to the loading docks. This was our busiest part of the load-out. Stagehands were rolling the cases filled with the cables, band gear, and the cartels most valued product out to the semi-trucks, ready to leave immediately once they were loaded. As the stagehands arrived with full cases, they were met with teams of truck loaders whose sole purpose was to waste no time stacking and assisting our crew in the semitrucks. Fortunately, on the loading dock, all the gear was performing its typical and very harmonious dance thanks to Axel. That was his gig, though, making sure gear left the dock to the next venue on time and the all-important blow or money left to its prospective home early. The last part to his show-day gig responsibilities, was keeping that labor bill low; as a business, we have to operate like a legit touring show. If we wanted to fudge a number here or there, we could, but it wasn't something you did on the regular. There is no easy way to do any of this, but that is what a great stage manager does. They use the available labor, good or bad, to get shit in and out and onto trucks like pros.

Some load-outs and load-ins just suck! It's the name of the game, but we still have a show to put up no matter how bad it can be and there are no excuses, too much money at stake. It takes skill to load thirty trucks for any team of roadies. Fortunately, Axel was great about getting these semis loaded and out of the loading docks so we could back another in ASAP. Generally, by now and in a different venue, I was breaking off to make sure the coke was coming up from the lab's elevator and heading for its home in a truck, but I was still out helping direct road case to the dock. I knew my merch tech would call, but I kept helping Axel clear space for all the gear and cases coming off the stage and the arena floor. My merch tech each night got a specific team of cartel-building stagehands to help him. They were heavily armed and ready to take anyone out back if they got in the way of the cash or coke. Most people in the building, though, were clueless as to what we were moving.

I had to wait for Axel's call tonight; he would let me know when to take that specific team to the "cut lab." Once we got to the "main merch table," AKA cut lab, there would be a second call for Axel, signaling to back the truck into the loading docks: "The count is done." We loved using language that was universal in the touring world, but The Roadie Cartel crews knew how to decipher the calls over the radios.

Tonight took longer than usual. I've missed radio calls before, but if the merch tech couldn't reach me, he would call Axel. Tonight, neither of us heard from our guy. As I was about to leave my post by the loading dock hallway and walk down to the lab, my radio went off.

"Merch for Wyatt."

"Go for Wyatt."

"*Ummm*, can you come to the main merch table NOW; the count is OFF!"

"10-4."

There isn't a quick route from one side of a large arena to the other and then down a few floors to the hydrocainization (cocaine-cutting) lab. We had zero time to spare, so I moved faster than a stagehand heading toward the donut station on break. The second I walked into the lab, the merch tech and chemist looked up at me and both of them with eyes the size of the moon, threw their hands up.

I glared at the merch guy and the chemist in the room. Before either one could give me an excuse as to why the blow wasn't ready to head to the trucks, I shouted, "Whatever excuse you two fucks are about to tell me, don't, because you know all I'm going to tell ya is to get that blow wrapped up and headed to the truck . . . NOW! That is your fucking job!"

But it was true, that was their jobs and if they didn't make it happen, well then . . . The Butcher will be coming for us all!

I closed my eyes in frustration, praying to the cocaine gods as I walked out of the lab. The decoy merch truck which held the coke had to reach Milwaukee before sunrise to hit an open space in time before the next tour rolled through those arena doors. Distribution was a big part of The Roadie Cartel, and Pie had been on edge lately over a few busts and a couple trucks that went missing. And when I say missing, they haven't found a trace of the drivers or trailers. We think it was a rival cartel or gang trying to play ball, but right now, it was in all The Roadie Cartel members' best interest to hit our windows with no delays.

As I returned to the backstage loading dock, I decided it was time for some quick deep breathing exercises to calm the nerves, so I lit a cigarette. Normally, I would be in a different mindset, thinking solely about the drugs leaving the building. But I had been worried about Ivan for the last couple of weeks. He seemed off lately. Thankfully, we had a day off in New York City, which would hopefully lift his spirits after a few cold ones and a slice or two. Even though it was a "school" night—you know, the night before a workday—I would need a few dozen beers once I got on the bus to calm my nerves after this shitshow of a load out.

00:24:44 Same Arena, Different View of the Load-Out

I stood off to the side of the loading docks, watching as another semi-truck closed its doors and slid out of the dock heading toward Boston. But the decoy truck was still parked and still empty. My merch truck should have been on the road ten minutes ago. I know it will eventually show up, but it is the anticipation that is killing me now. I don't like to be late and I definitely hate knowing that a shipment of blow is leaving the dock late. That leaves a very tight margin for errors on the drive.

I walked over to Axel. "Fuck! We're in deep shit. If this fucker doesn't show up by the time I finish in the ladies' room, I might have to kill him before they send you know who."

"If the driver misses his window to the arena in Milwaukee," Axel started to add in as he checked his watch, "we should head out of the country."

When I rolled my eyes at him, Axel added, "Why not? I'm thinkin' Bora Bora. Maybe the Bahamas. Surrounded by hot chicks in bikinis."

I looked at him with shock. I couldn't believe he was willing to abandon the life that my father created for us; the only way out is in a box.

"Don't act like it's a bad idea," he said as if he could read my mind. "Fuck it. Fuck Juan, fuck Pie. Let's grab Wes and get the fuck outta here. I got a hundred thousand in my duffle bag under the bus. maybe I can finally find me a man who isn't scared of a boss woman with fire running through her veins . . . I mean there has to be one on whichever island we run away too!"

He pointed at something behind me with a smirk, while I was left staring at Axel and trying to guess what trick he had up his sleeve to get me to look the other direction, he was always playing games. I did have one thought before I gave into his game, I was a little disappointed in myself for thinking that I would throw this life away over a little hiccup, I knew we were just talking shit about the night we were having. We were in this cartel till the end.

"I'm telling you to look behind you, fucker," Axel half-shouted as he took a step to the side, maybe to avoid a slap from me but was grinning the whole time.

I gave in and turned and was happy I did! The merch tech and a team of about ten building cartel members were pushing cases toward the truck. Approaching me and out of breath, the merch tech said, "I'll never be late again with the gear, boss!"

All I could do was turn to Axel and punch him in the shoulder for messing with me. It was time to finish this fucking load-out.

On a side note for all the viewers—there are rules for a reason in life, in nature and even in the cartel. We operate like our own government to keep order and make sure the system continues to exist. The number one rule is always to be on time. The second is to make sure the money stays moving. So, one of my last jobs every night was ensuring the cut product or money got to the truck safely. I thankfully had Wes and Axel help with the process, but the building cartel members are the check-and-balance system on top of the touring cartel members. Just because The Roadie Cartel production manager said the product left the arena does not mean the building cartel manager is in the clear if something isn't up to weight or if a dollar amount is screwy. So, each night I stand there with the cartel's building manager as we put our stamp on the product. Now if something is missing after that stamp of approval—well, you will never see that driver again. Once the truck door lock with the red (cocaine in the truck) or green (money in the truck) "X" goes on the truck, it can only be cut on the delivery side now. The x was small and only noticeable if you looked at the bottom of the lock, but it was a quick reference for the cartel guys at the drop location.

Look no cartel member wants to lose their life or even a friend's life over something as simple as being late, so we try to help the other members out for a reason, The Butcher. Rumors float throughout the buildings and on the buses about the man they call The Butcher and the spine-chilling murder stories of roadies who crossed the cartel. Most of these stories are told to keep roadies in check. Yeah, we're all criminals, but if we don't keep our word to the cartel, we know who's coming. It's rumored that a while back, a roadie cartel production crew's shipments kept showing up skimpy and always not the right cash amount. And here's the thing—we can get a little baggy of free coke from time to time from the lab, but it's in our best interest to keep it at that. But this crew took it upon themselves to take bricks from the trucks and lab. So, when The Butcher walked onto the bus that night and saw one of Juan's bricks sitting on the table in the front lounge . . . well, it didn't end well for them.

Now, not many people know who The Butcher is or what he looks like—I, on the other hand, know what Adolf looks like, so these clown shoes told him, "I think you walked on to the wrong bus, old man," laughed in his face and finished with, "time to beat it, gramps." In response, The Butcher made the production manager cut up his team into pieces, right there in the front lounge of the bus, as the next victims watched in horror. Adolf has always been a calculated man who had been around the block a few times. So, before the crew got on the bus that night after the show, The Butcher had drilled shut all the windows in the back lounge so no one could escape. Then in the end after it was all said and done, The Butcher helped the production manager shoot himself to indicate a murder-suicide. This tale gives even the hardest roadie cartel member the creeps and keeps grubby little hands out of the stash.

Stamping the product and ensuring the lock with the X went on the back of the truck doors was insurance that my and everyone's lives that had touched the product up until then had done their job. The money handling was done similarly regarding the stamps and shipping. Having arenas and stadiums to help clean money was one of the cartel's best choices. We have an in-house "bank" that the money goes through once it reaches the venue. Then the building accountant shuffles it back in with earnings anywhere from concessions to the luxury suites sales and, of course, high roller booze for players and artists. That in-house markup on booze is a beautiful trick hidden in plain view for anyone questioning a sale; all they have to do is look at the settlement at the end of the night.

Okay, back to the story. It was time to complete my last little duties of the night . . .

After the idiot checks around the buildings and the tour's rigging truck has closed its doors, we were almost finished with the day.

01:00:55 PRODUCTION OFFICE

Wes, Axel, and I always ended the night with shots of tequila and a couple smokes before a post load-out shower. We all didn't shower together for obvious reasons, but we did all use the same locker room so we could finally have friend time together. Also, since we were the last ones working, it was also our time to catch up before the bus talk with everyone else. They are my boys for life, and being on tour with them was awesome, but sadly it wasn't all fun and games. There was a lot of work each day, but if we timed it right, we might catch a coffee in catering together. Unfortunately, it was more likely for us to stand backstage together waiting for the artist, and just as we would start to have a great conversation, the show would ruin our fun. That's touring, I guess. So as fun as it sounds, the post-show locker room hangs were our little getaways when we joked about the other departments, gossiped about who pissed us off that day, and we poked fun at each other. Anything could be said, and no one would hold back their feelings, not like any of us had them anyway. And on this night, we could only make fun of the merch tech running toward the truck as if Leather-face was chasing him. Overall, for such a bummer of a load out, we made it work, and it was time to finish the shower and move on to the next city.

02:00:00 BUSES ROLL

2 a.m. and not a second later. That was our rule for the buses rolling out of the parking lot and on to the next venue. Tonight's bus ride from one city to the next wasn't the longest I've been on when going into a show day, but the drive was going to be tight and would make for a tighter load-in. Part of my routine venue check this upcoming morning dealt with the building cartel manager and I going over all the ins and outs of the day. We made sure the building was ready to ship money or cut cocaine that night. The tour riggers marked the floor to hang motors from the ceiling for the show's audio, video and lighting junk. I should sleep tonight seeing that it is a long day tomorrow, but we know how it goes when you have something do to the next day . . .

02:01:01 BUS 1 ON THE HIGHWAY

When a drive is longer than a few hours, you have time to get a good sleep in your bunk before load-in, but that is never how it goes. The best bus parties start with one beer. Add in one more, followed by a cigarette, and then sprinkle in that high-grade blow. And then before you know, it is only an hour before you have to start the next day of work . . . that is when you are left with a nap, not a good night's sleep.

03:30:01 EMERGENCY TRUCK-STOP DETOUR, LOCATION, SOMEWHERE, USA

"I'll take massive diarrhea for 1000, Alex." The merch tech shouted from the front lounge couch.

"Things you shouldn't consume on the bus if you don't want to make a pit stop," the sassy production assistant said in tears, laughing at Wes, Axel, and me.

"What are blow, cigarettes, and old pizza? *Ding-ding-ding!*" Our driver shouted at us as we ran down the stairs of the bus.

Even though there's a toilet on our half-million luxury coach, it's a glorified urinal. It's standard etiquette to keep poop and toilet paper out of that bad boy, or else the crew suffers from a biological warfare attack. So, truck stops are a sanctuary after destroying our bodies while the driver fills up the gas tank.

And the toughest of roadies—you know, the tattooed, burly dudes—somehow transform into giddy five-year olds during this magical time of the night. Keychains, knives, ceramic figurines, tasteless T-shirts and "As Seen on TV" products produce a carnival vibe. Rolling into a truck stop we take full advantage of the facilities, you'll witness a gang of drunkards grabbing handfuls of junk food and trying on pink cowgirl hats and unflattering sunglasses while stumbling to the register. By the time we leave, the truck stop has profited hundreds of dollars thanks to their random, overpriced trinkets.

03:59:59 BACK ON BUS 1 AND BACK ON THE HIGHWAY

"Okay, losers. I'm off to bed," I said as my merch guy and Wes' second security member sat together on the small front lounge couch. They tipped their pink cowgirl hats at me and continued to chow down on junk food.

05:30:00 BUS 1, VENUE PARKING LOT, BOSTON, MA

As my alarm's incessant tone furiously beat its sound onto my eardrums, I rolled over and slapped it a few times. I knew where I was, but I questioned myself a few times if this was hell.

I did it again. I drank way too much and felt worse with each movement as I struggled out of my bunk. I don't think I'll ever learn my lesson, but I continued my routine. Piss, brush my hair, put it in a ponytail, brush my teeth and then chug some water. I grabbed a sugar-free Red Bull to wash down a handful of Advil. I turned on the coffee machine and waited impatiently. I did find half of an Adderall in my pocket; this should help the brain today.

05:45:00 BUS 1, FRONT LOUNGE

Black coffee brewed. Time for a smoke. I grabbed my bag from under the bus.

05:49:00 VENUE BUILDING

I ran behind today, sluggishly making my way to the cartel building manager. Out of all the buildings the cartel owned, this was the worst of the worst. It would be one thing if we had two semi-trucks backing into this gem of an arena, but we had thirty semi-trucks plus buses to be put somewhere. This building also needed loading docks, so it was another fucked up truck-loading party tonight. It was time to go meet the cartel building manager. Wes, Axel, and I would walk the arena with the building manager to make sure everything had stayed the same since the last time we were there. We would check the best route to the cutting lab for the cocaine and any possible Plan B situations that may have to happen. If it was a money day, we would do the same, but walk toward the "bank vault" instead.

After discussing The Roadie Cartel's needs, the show production needs take precedence. We schedule the department heads to be on the arena floor thirty minutes after we start our walk so that they never interrupt our conversations about the dope and money. These talks are for the crews to be able to come in and hang the speakers and other production elements that make up the show. Axel and Wes usually break off at this point to look at the best paths for the artist and gear that would be rolling in shortly. At the same time, Axel is sniffing out the local crew's steward to talk stagehand work.

Simultaneously, the "smiling" roadies slowly make their way into the building to find catering for coffee and a nice bathroom. My team has been in the building since I walked in the door. They have tasks like meeting the lab techs and finding the boxes of shirts shipped that come from Mexico. The always-amazing production assistant has been hard at work hanging signs on walls for the tour crew coming into the building, so there's a road map of locations. This mini city gets pieced together quickly, especially if the tour has been out for a while.

07:00:00 LOAD-IN BEGINS

Watching the gear roll into a building is an exciting thing. It can look like the bulls running the streets in Spain if you have a local crew methed-up and ready to go. Otherwise, it can look like the dinner rush at a retirement home—so slow that you have to remind the elderly folks pushing the cases that the show is tonight, not in a few days.

I was waiting to spot two cases out of the sea of hundreds that would roll into the arena today. Both of my cases were hand-me-downs from Ivan. It was awesome to keep his legacy alive; plus, he kept most of his stuff in them since he was the tour manager out on this tour. He just didn't want to deal with setting up anything, so I would have his little world set up for him when he leisurely walked in with the band at 2 p.m. Most of the time, there'd be a tour management office for him, but he liked to be next to me. He still liked keeping tabs on what I was planning and doing.

After setting up my production desk and Ivan's desk for our computers, I added a clock for mine and candles for his, which he liked in his old age. Two big cocaine movements had to happen on this specific day. The first shipment traveled from Texas, which had to be flipped and out of the building ASAP. The second shipment had been in the lab overnight with the chemist. Once the Texas truck was unloaded, we had to load that right back up for its little drive up to Maine and into Canada.

The boxes of T-shirts for the lab were marked, but they needed to be packed together. So, it would take a minute to sort and get them to the chemists. The time was ticking, and even though things looked promising, those shirts had to be dipped and dried for sale later that night. Remember that the coke still had to be baked and cut, so by no means were we in the clear. The last thing that needed to be done that night was getting the cut coke back into the right merch truck and on its way. I had two merch trucks out there. The band killed it on merch each night, so it was nice to be able to have both trucks as options; I rotated trucks in and out constantly, they all were running different routes. One of them was a decoy, and one had the blow. It was a constant dance of revolving trucks and drivers for the merch side of things.

08:09:10 TIME FOR SOME FOOD, CATERING

We traveled with our own catering team, and they were brilliant! Donuts, thick-cut bacon . . . each morning, the spread looked like it was out of a culinary magazine. Hell, somedays it felt like Top Chef in that kitchen. They had a fun pun posted on signs as you walked in like, "What puts a big smile on our faces in the morning? Our big sausage in your warm bun." It really is the little things in the morning that can brighten a sour day when you travel like we roadies do. I love food, but as the days continued, I usually ended up busy and missed lunch and dinner. So, I took full advantage of the sweet egg specialist making omelets to order that morning. This was my quiet time while the trucks got dumped and the roadies did their thing with the gear. I ate and waited for my merch truck to back into a spot.

But my radio never stops.

"Axel for Wyatt."

"Go for Wyatt."

"Yeah, I need you to take a look up-stage right. We can't fit the giant–"

Static now blared through the radio. This usually happens when an impatient party changes channels without listening for radio chatter.

"–stupid door."

"Copy, stupid door. Heading your way."

I usually sit for another second or two, waiting for the next issue to come over the radio before I address anything. This is always how it starts: enjoying my meat lover's omelet with extra bacon, a side of bacon, and my glazed donut when an issue arises. Today, I took an extra few bites of my omelet and the donut was for my walk to Axel.

Some of the older venues weren't made for the extra-large gear and set pieces we tend to tour with nowadays. Juan had spent millions renovating many of the first arenas he purchased, but it all went to the cutting laboratories, the bank safes, and later the luxury suites. We've dealt with it a lot, but hey, that is why we tour with saws and grinders.

09:11:01 SMOKING BY THE TRUCKS

Smoking isn't a good habit, but it's preferable to murder when you're having an irritating day. Today felt extra annoying; there weren't enough smoke breaks in the world to combat the stupidity floating around in the air.

Checking on the trucks introduced sunlight into my life, usually seeing that most of my days were spent inside a large concrete box. When Axel radioed for me, I told him I was still with the catering team.

"10-4," he replied irritably, and I could hear him mutter, "Lazy motherfu–" before he released the push to talk button.

Standing between two trucks, smoking, I watched Axel stomp over, too peeved to notice me. I jumped out at him, and he nearly fell backward.

"That's payback, you lazy bitch," I snarled with a smirk.

I let Axel take my cigarette. I lit a new one for myself.

09:20:00 MEDITATION ISN'T ALWAYS YOGA

Upstairs, not far from the arena floor, standing amongst the sea of road cases and gear flowing into the venue, I got lost in time. I don't usually have deep thoughts on life or the meaning of it all, but Ivan crossed my mind. Ivan always reminded me I was his special little dude-ette—female version of dude, so I hated seeing him down lately. I was looking forward to our day off to catch up and, hell, maybe share a feeling or two, even though that's not who he is, and I am not your typical sensitive girl. In a daze, I was rocked back to reality when Wes walked by and flicked my ear.

"You okay, sis?" Wes asked as he stopped for a moment to knit his brows at me and wait for a quick reply.

Still in thought, I didn't say anything. I uncrossed my arms and started to walk toward him. I gave Wes a pat on the shoulder and headed back to my production office. I wasn't really sure.

10:50:13 THE ARENA FLOOR

Every tour claims to have the best roadies, but honestly, this was the first time I looked at the whole crew as family. They were the best in the business. The non-cartel roadies worked as hard on this monstrosity of a show as the guys who knew it was a life-or-death career. I appreciated the daily, hard-working "ain't nothing gonna stop us" attitude.

One of the main guys who showed such dedication was my head carpenter, Mayhem—and yes, that was his legal name. He checked that the stage was built flawlessly and rolled it into place perfectly. He also kept the floor running when Axel was outside or on the loading docks dealing with whatever the issue of the hour was each day. I would go have a mid-morning smoke out on the floor with Mayhem to see how the day was going and if we had to keep our eyes open for any obstacles. As I walked toward Mayhem to wish him a good morning, Axel came over the radio about the merch cases making their way into the building. This was huge. Finally, they could start the hydrocainizing process for the shipment tonight.

11:33:55 UNLOADING TRUCKS WAS STILL PART OF MY LIFE, SOMEDAYS. . .

"Roll that case inside and down the first hallway to the right," I articulated loudly to a stocky stagehand kid with orange hair pushing a stack of T-shirt boxes on a handcart.

"Where?" he asked as if I had just spoken Greek to him.

It didn't matter. Before I could repeat myself, the guy continued on his way. I shook my head with a hard, slow blink of disappointment. But I was impressed by his determination to choose where the road case went. Invested, I made a quick hundred-dollar bet with Axel that the case would end up back by the trucks after an hour. Axel bet the kid would get it done within the hour. I called Mayhem over the radio to see if he wanted in on the bet too.

Luckily for me, the case didn't have a red "X" on the side for the lab chemists. This kid was so high that he stopped mid-arena and stood staring up at our lighting rig. It was a mesmerizing sight hanging sixty feet in the air, the lights blinking and spinning as our lighting crew chief tested the rig. Mayhem won the bet; he had said the kid would get stuck and never leave the arena floor.

All the T-shirts were in, and the truck was reloaded with the cocaine that was cut from the night before, heading to the great white north.

11:45:00 THE PRODUCTION OFFICE DID SMELL GOOD . . .

The smell of fried chicken made its way slowly down the hall, into my office, and snuck inside my nose as the caterers close by prepared lunch. *Fuck, that smells good!* I thought, but I had to turn my attention to Dick as he barged into the office. I never knew him in his younger days, but I can only imagine he has gotten sleazier over the years. There he stood in front of my desk, telling me about an update from Pie, immediately upon his arrival. There were no cordial salutations. He was all business.

Dick played other pivotal roles within the cartel, but he loved to take credit for deals that weren't his. So, when handing down orders from Pie, he loved to take control. No one in the chain of command traveled into the states as much as he did, so it was easy for him to do so. Pie was done with the touring aspect and now flew to private islands and made difficult business choices with La Reina about the cartel's future.

Now a little hangry, a lot more hungover that I liked, oh and with Ivan on my mind, I didn't pay attention to what Dick had to say. At the end of the day, I worked for Juan, and I had no choice in any of the jobs they put in front of me. With each slurred word that flew from his foul mouth, I somehow got hungrier and started to believe my checkered Vans looked appetizing, so I told Dick we'd take care of whatever the great Pie wanted to be done. Go ahead and send the extra trucks.

12:12:12 PRODUCTION OFFICE, OKAY TIME FOR LUNCH

Before I could head to the catering room, my production phone rang. Ivan loved calling me with the archaic device, leashing me to my desk. I knew he'd have bad news for me, so I stood there like prey waiting for danger to pass. But Ivan knew Dick had come to visit. Dammit, I had to answer.

"What!" I shouted in a semi-playful way into the phone.

"Do I have to remind you where I found you, little lady? You yell at me again like that, and I'll throw you back into that damn dumpster."

He wouldn't. He was a teddy bear that talked a big game. Before I could respond, Ivan informed me the old rock artists were in a bad mood after a botched guitar solo on stage last show. The old guy split his leather pants as his ass hit the stage, I wouldn't have felt bad; but he fell during the legendary part. Now, after months of shows, they would like to rehearse on stage today and demanded we do something to fix the "slippery" stage. They couldn't have picked a worse day to decide they cared about the show, but I had no choice but to agree. Otherwise, it would be more hell to pay down the road. I sometimes wished Ivan would get his sadistic brother to murder them all. The call was interrupted by someone calling him, and he cut me off with a quick, "make it right."

Click. . .

Well, shit, I'm sure he is in an even worse mood now.

13:14:15 PRODUCTION OFFICE . . . STILL

The third time's the charm. I hated my office and getting cornered with small talk when food was on my mind. Paralyzed in my chair, the audio system engineer busted into the office, telling me some jaw-slapping nonsense about speakers, seats, scoreboards and *blah, blah, blah*. I was forced to call the local cartel building manager to take over the situation. I just couldn't handle any kind of nerd talk at this point in my day.

13:33:12 LUNCH TIME, MAYBE?

Strolling into catering with a big grin, I saw the buffet of joy. I must have arrived after they restocked from the local stagehand cram down. Talk about a group of men and women who can shovel food down their throats. The time had come, and I could see the fresh batch of fried chicken calling to me. Close by were potato wedges and cheesecake at the dessert table. When a fellow roadie walked past me with a few slices on his plate, I was determined to follow suit.

The building's power flickered erratically as I picked up a plate to load it with food. Suddenly, the lights went out, and the emergency flood lights kicked on. This wasn't good. Not good at all. In these situations—and especially on cutting days—you can't mess with the hydrocainizing process. The solution can't break its temperature and cool until the chemicals have boiled for the allotted time. With no hesitation, I rushed down to the lab, I was met by the lab techs, the merch tech, and the building manager.

"Why don't you have power from the backup generator, damn it?"

All three looked at me as if I had seven heads. The generator had to be serviced at least once a year for this exact reason. The building manager and I sprinted up the steps, down several hallways, and down a few sets of stairs. We made it behind the arena where the backup generators resided.

I had Wes on the phone with the power company and Axel calling for portable generators big enough to power a small city.

"Axel, Wes—wait!" I hollered through the radio.

Opening the side panel where the switches lived, I found a simple fix. I switched the generator from manual to automatic, and the generator after a sputter or two, turned on, and purred.

14:10:00 OUT BACK BY THE ARENA DUMPSTERS

I lit a cigarette as I contemplated the lack of common sense surrounding me. For my sanity's sake, Wes joined me. Tragically, he didn't bring me the fried chicken I wanted, but he told me the city power should be back on within an hour, but the lab is up and running.

I reached for another Marlboro Red in my pocket, but I was fresh out. Talk about being kicked in the dick when I was already down.

"Maybe I'm having a bad day because I'm too focused on Ivan," I said as I turned to Wes. I was surprised to find Axel next to him, who handed me a cigarette.

My cell phone vibrated. It was Ivan.

I was happy to hear back from Ivan seeing that our last talk ended pretty abruptly, but nevertheless I was glad to see he still had a sense of humor over text.

15:56:30 BACKSTAGE

The power kicked back on. The three of us headed backstage and heard noises penetrate the radio airwaves. First, the sound of an elephant. Next, a lion's roar. I chuckled.

"Why does Ivan make animal noises whenever he gets close?" Wes asked.

"Just to be funny. He's done it ever since I was little."

"Weird. Hey, have you had that bomb-ass chicken yet?"

Asshole. He knew I hadn't. And I bet he's the one who told Ivan about the chicken too.

15:59:59 THE ARTISTS' SUV ROLLED UP

I wasn't in the mood to go meet the band backstage, but it was part of my gig. Ivan loved to wind me up, so he tossed me his empty bag of McDonald's as he exited the SUV and asked how my lunch was. I truly think Ivan's guy in the sky, this higher power he speaks of, is working against me today. With the empty bag in one hand and an even emptier stomach making crazy noises, I walked Ivan and the band to the stage.

16:15:00 ON STAGE

My crew was ready for a run-through, but they glared at me because I told them to be in position an hour ago. As I walked the artists around the stage, I explained that the carps had laid down a new, super tough hybrid silicone composite, double poly-mono grip, and anti-slip marly that would help improve "guitar solo dance moves." I tried to not laugh as he walked from one side of the stage to the other; I was full of shit about the new flooring, but I needed to make myself smile.

The thing about the middle of the day on tour is everyone really does have a better place to be than on a stage waiting for the artist. I personally could be in my office eating, but I was waiting—again—on someone else. This time, I was on stage waiting for them to locate the band members who had wandered off the stage for who knows what reason. Maybe they needed a cup of coffee, or a quick pit stop in the bathroom . . . or maybe they were like cats and loved to roam the arenas. Talk about a hard job. Ivan's hands as tour manager of this old band were full.

17:01:01 MORE REHEARSALS . . .

It was a miracle the whole band was on stage, and, more importantly, the runner was back with my smokes. Damn, I need a smoke, but it was time for the VIP audience and band's fan club guests to come see the band in a staged/produced rehearsal. I hated it, but this little 45-minute act brought in millions of extra dollars for the cartel and some extra change for the band. There was even a small tour where lucky guests could see the backstage bathrooms and roadies sleeping on empty cases. Ha! Yeah, no one gets to see the dressing rooms.

Before the small backstage tour, there was a quick Q&A. The same questions would be asked from city to city, especially, "Is there a new album coming out soon?" Whenever I hear that question, I want to shake the asker and tell the truth: "They can barely tie their shoes or tell time. I'm scared to let them walk and chew gum. So, no. No, they will only play the hits from now until the end." Sadly, Ivan won't let me, so this is the opportune time to have a smoke.

17:46:00 THE STAGE

Crunch time was on. The artists finally got off the stage, and we were left with fourteen minutes to get the opening act on stage, set, and sound checked. I don't stick around for any of this fun, ever. That is what I have Axel for. I have never heard the opening act; I don't know their names, nor do I stick around for complaints about their time on stage. I feel like they know I won't show too much sympathy for their demands, I would only say, "tough titties, kiddos!"

18:00:00 DOORS ARE OPEN

At the time, I didn't understand the hype over music on a phone, but this old band had a big resurgence in their career thanks to a phone app where people put music to videos for the world to see. Kind of funny how things work out; thanks to this tour and hearing how these old dudes were rediscovered, well this is how I knew to come here to put my video diaries on the Internet.

My point is, these young juveniles needed room to jump and sing, so we are a general admission show for the guests on the floor. The youth run through the doors hysterically, especially if they're new to the concert experience. The older crowd like to meander in with their old merch shirts the cartel sold them thirty years ago. Hopefully they'd buy another shirt tonight.

Ivan and I used to place bets with Wes and Axel on how many would fall running to the barricade. If you couldn't tell, we loved to gamble. Wes had won the last three cities, so I wasn't happy when he took it again tonight. He has an unfair advantage; he scopes out the crowd prior to the stampede.

18:36:52 PRODUCTION OFFICE

It was finally dinner time. I got everything done. I even swung by the local building cartel manager's office for a quick talk about numbers on my way to catering. Tonight, I went for steak. I am curious to know how the chef knew I was in the mood for red meat after my day. With two huge slabs on my plate and three slices of cheesecake, yes, I know you typically don't see a 110 pound girl eating red meat like a cowboy who just won a rodeo, but what can I say, I love steak and cheesecake days in catering! I made my way to my desk in my production office where no one could bother me.

I was in my own heaven scarfing down my two favorite things, and I started with the cheesecake tonight. Then it happened. My radio went off. I paused. A very long pause.

It didn't go off again. Maybe they answered their own question.

Nope, it went off again. It was Ivan looking for me. I quickly shut it off to teach him a lesson for throwing his trash at me earlier. This was my moment to have just dessert on a day far from over. I had to have a little "me" time.

18:55:00 BACKSTAGE RAMP

After eating, I had to have a smoke to settle my gut. The best part was my radio was still off, so I was in peace for ten more minutes. Life was on the up, so I would take it all in until the downhill came with all its rage. The opening act was just about to take the stage. Although it had been a long day, the night was inching closer to my favorite song, the last one in the band's set.

With my Marlboro Red almost to the butt, I decided I could turn my radio back on. I felt a little lousy ignoring Ivan since the guy had been down lately.

19:50:00 PRODUCTION OFFICE

On occasion, I let the fat girl in me do the talking, and today she won. I slid through catering one more time on the way to my desk and got one more slice of cheesecake. Any time there was cheesecake around, it automatically turned into a "treat yourself" day in my eyes.

We were ten minutes from show time, and the halls would be filled with band members, friends of the band, and the artist's entourage at any second. It was their time to horse around pre-show while I'd have a smoke with Ivan in the closest dressing room bathroom, as he waited to walk the herd of cats to stage.

I hadn't seen him since the stampede of fans when the doors opened. Damn, he was probably calling me to talk about what the hell was wrong. I called him on his channel a couple of times.

Nothing. Great. Now he was playing the game of "if she didn't answer, then neither am I."

I walked down the hall and still didn't see him in the accountant's office, where he hangs out some days. I came back into the production office, and there he was—doodling designs on my computer like a bored twelve-year-old in school. He smiled, flipped me off, and told me we had to talk.

"Let's do it alone on a day off in New York." He grinned, thinking about the upcoming visit.

I smiled, flipped him back off, and took that as a sign that we were all good from earlier.

21:15:00 UNDER MY DESK

Beep! Beep! Beep!

My alarm sounded louder than this morning. Music was still playing. Okay, good. I didn't oversleep on that nap.

21:20:20 PRODUCTION AND DRESSING ROOM HALLWAY

I was filled with joy because the night was almost over. Pacing around the road cases that sat outside my office door, I did my last-minute load-out checks in my head. The show was closing in on a third of the way through. Check. I have my two drivers lined up for the coke drops. Check. The coke was cut and ready. Check. Cash was being counted and taken to the bank. Check.

21:30:00 THE DOCK

Wes, Axel, and I would always meet backstage by the exit doors to make sure we had the local cops in place to escort the band out of town. I got a kick out of cops in our building next to hundreds of thousands of dollars' worth of cocaine. Although I know we have a lot of crooked cops on our payroll, I also know there were plenty of good men and women just trying to do the right thing for the people in their communities. We totally don't make that easy, though, for sure.

Axel, Wes and I used this time to chuckle and tell dirty jokes, but we also have to have some real conversations about any hang ups we might see with getting the band out the back door or getting the blow to the trucks.

21:50:01 BACKSTAGE

There began my favorite song of the night—the last one. There is no greater song. It had been a long-ass day, and there was still so much that could potentially go wrong, but I was ready to G.O.!

22:15:15 BACKSTAGE HALLWAY

It was the same story every night. The band's friends stayed around longer to enjoy the free booze and a small army of after-show punters who had to see the inside of a dressing room. Some nights, it was fine. They would be on the other end of the arenas or stadiums, but tonight wasn't that night. I was in an extra foul mood; I had just discovered that the elevator we used to bring the dope up from the lab had stopped working. So, I did what I knew would bring a little joy to my night. I called Wes to come kick all the punters and radio "hang-arounds" to the curb. We were going to need every inch of that hallway tonight and the backstage general-use elevator; we didn't need some punter taking our lift when we needed it.

23:00:00 THE TRUCKS

Even without loading docks, tonight went exceptionally well once we got the elevator running. Thankfully, the building dude hadn't sent his maintenance guy home yet. It was an hour until midnight, and we were flying compared to the night before. I loaded my first truck full of cocaine-filled boxes slated for next-day delivery to the next arena. I watched Axel running between trucks, screaming into his radio at other departments who sent audio, lighting, and video gear to random trucks. All I could do was laugh at people who think we have some glamorous job where we hang with the artists in dressing rooms, snorting coke off mirrors and chugging champagne out of gold pimp cups. Instead, these hard-working roadies wake up and strive to put out the best work during their eighteen-hour days. They show up and pull off the impossible every day.

00:44:40 COKE TRUCK 2

My night was done as I watched the last three road cases full of coke get loaded into my last merch truck. I shook the local building cartel manager's hand, thanked him for the amazing cheesecake, and asked him to blow the building up before I came back—or I would. He smiled. I smiled. And with an uncomfortable laugh, he wished us a great night and safe travels as I put the lock with the red x on the trucks' doors.

Looking down at my Rolex, I realized we had shaved almost a half-hour off the load-out tonight. Time for fine tequila and a shower. And after one or two beers on the bus tonight—said no roadie ever—I'll wake up feeling refreshed and ready for a day off in New York City.

I was ready for an amazing day with my favorite human ever: Ivan.

>>>STOP RECORDING<<<

I am glad I went back through that day; I realized two things. One, I really do love my friends and even though we still aren't talking . . . I am glad that I can leave this world knowing we did have a few last good days together. Second thing is, I am so grateful to have had Ivan in my life too. He has shown me so much love and this day, although challenging, I felt like it was the day I could see I made him proud of the job I do. It isn't easy being his daughter and also a female production manager, in a highly competitive world of male roadies.

I think it is time I get out of this venue . . . I will finish up my last story tomorrow before I make it to the west Texas town I was born in, El Paso.

CHAPTER 18

The Robbery

>>>START RECORDING<<<

This is video diary #17 November 5, 2009, 13:41:00.

Phoenix, AZ

Hey, I am in the production office before the show and well . . . (I pause and look away from the video camera on the phone).

I remember this day as though I am still living in this nightmare, and can't find my way out . . .

When I was younger, Ivan would tell me the grueling tale of how he and his siblings arrived in America on one of the great ocean liners of the time. He told me stories about the farm he lived on with his brother and sister, but his nostalgia for his parents was particularly moving. On drunk occasions, Ivan would tell me about the butcher shop that his grandpa started from nothing. Bewildered, I used to ask countless times as a child why he'd leave something so amazing—a town with all he ever needed. He would just laugh and tell me I asked too many questions. When I became a teen, he would change the subject or distract me with a tall tale from the road about a drunk fan or some crazy roadie I knew. Look, I am not a roadie because I had an action figure of a long-haired tattooed guy in short-shorts smoking a cigarette on the side of a stage I got at the toy store. Most kids don't grow up wanting to be a roadie. But I did, I wanted to be like my hero. I am a roadie cartel member because of Ivan and his passion for life he would share with me. He was the only superhero I knew growing up and he lived a very dope life full of adventures. Sure, going out and seeing the view from the bus or standing side-stage with him, helped. He should have told me the story behind leaving Czechoslovakia, maybe then I wouldn't be in this mess. By avoiding the question and the real reason they started this cartel for so many years and using epic roadie tales to distract me, well, that is what made me who I thought I wanted to be. I don't blame him, just kind of wish I did do something different, maybe then I would still have my father.

I guess the old saying is true, "be careful what you wish for in life." Ivan was a good person, which made it difficult to believe his siblings came from the same bloodline. Yeah, they were my family through "association," but I didn't see a killer in Ivan like his brother, Adolf. I didn't see a lick of Zora in him either. He didn't worship money or the limelight. Instead, he resembled the stories he would tell me of his paternal lineage. Some of the stories he told me inferred he was getting used by the other two for his work ethic. Isn't that how most honest guys are treated? I mean I have been known to have used a few over the years. To me, it always seemed like his family was hiding something deeper and darker that terrified my father to the bone. And he was willing to sacrifice his happiness for whatever he was trying to keep hidden from the world and even me.

Ivan never seemed to enjoy the drug trafficking part of the work, but he lit up with joy when speaking of the shows and traveling. Although he regretted introducing Adolf to Pie, he would do it all over again because those experiences led to finding me. Like he would say there are no coincidences in life.

Over the years, though, we had grown apart in ways. We worked non-stop and rarely saw one another. We were both looking forward to the upcoming day off to take full advantage of the time together, great food, and hopefully a few adult bevies.

Coming back to the Big Apple for Ivan was a big deal, even though he did it regularly, it gave him butterflies to think about seeing the city. Not only was this the spot where he first got a shot as a roadie with Pie, but this was his first home after he left Czechoslovakia. At this point, Ivan was a multi-decade roadie for multiple bands. There are many in the touring world who needed an external validation to what they do or did, Ivan was not part of that group. He stuck it all out and loved the hard times just as much as he loved the easy-going times. Through all the shit, he never cared what anyone thought about him, he loved to do the work for the smiles he saw in the audience. Those smiles on the audience and bands' faces validated all the drug dealing bullshit he had to do to bring that joy. Okay, so my superhero was not your typical one, but his worldliness and love for life have given me the courage I need to stand up and do the right thing, finally.

He had seen so much over the years from cities around the world—their history, nature, culture, and life. Ivan and the family had made a career out of being really good criminals that not only saw the world but got to truly experience it. It is hard to believe Ivan was a multi-millionaire because he just didn't act like the others. For instance, one simple thing he loved about all the travel and places was getting a slice of cheese pizza in New York City and people-watching. The money stashed in his safe at the house would indicate he could fly anywhere, eat anywhere, and buy just about any item he wanted but he didn't. He would buy that large pizza and as he walked to a park, he would be handing out slices along the way, until he got to his last one. I dug that about the man. He was different from all the rest. Maybe that was why I never understood why he was here in an industry built on money, drugs, power, and sex. Adolf and Zora fit into those categories . . . and then there stood Ivan, a man who would give his shirt off his back to anyone on the street in need of it.

Looking back, in my mind all I wanted to do that day was to help Ivan. This year has been a tough one on us both. Don't get me wrong—work was work. We made money, and we had to grind daily. Big deal. The true downfall was that I was on tour with my best friend of all time, but we barely got a chance to really hang out because we were so slammed. This day off was a rare one for sure; he would usually have to spend the tour's days off babysitting the band and all their personal needs, plus all the appearances they might have to make in a city. Ivan was at the top of the game when it came to touring. So, when he barked an order, he expected it to be done. We have worked together for a while, some years less than others—and some years not at all—but we were back and with his long-time rock band, so I was all his on this tour and this day off, no matter the request. I have been around the man my whole life, so to say we haven't had an argument would be fucking crazy, but lately we have been at each other's throats. I have been denying some of his requests and putting the cartel needs before his band's needs, which we all know is part of the game, but I think that is making him agitated. But because of all of this going on, this day off was more than just a slice of pizza and a beer. It was for us to reconnect again as father and daughter, even see him again as my best friend. I still can't put a finger on his melancholy demeanor lately, and

I just wanted to help him get back to Ivan who loved to smile even on the bad days.

The city had changed since the days of Pie and Ivan hanging in the makeshift front lounge of the old, beat-up school bus they called their tour bus. Even though it had been decades since they met at that little club down in the Lower East Side, Ivan always walked by it when he was in town. New management had kept the name of the old club, but the place had a facelift. Regardless, it would always hold a special place in his heart. That's where he got his big start; it was Ivan's tale of losing his virginity to the temptress called the open road.

As for the man who gave him that shot at roadie fame, Pie had surpassed everyone in the business. Before his exit from the road life, he skyrocketed to the top of the cartel and touring industry. He was the godfather, the man who wrote the rules that still run all the tours crisscrossing the globe today.

Not to mention, Juan and Pie owned more real estate around the world than any roadie could ever dream of. Pie and Ivan, two men who met in a dirty backstage parking lot, had been running the whole industry from ticketing to merchandise and everything in between. Pie gave Ivan life again after leaving home at such a young age and was his first real best friend, so I think it was hard that he never got to see him anymore. So, visiting the old building to see where it all started was, I think, Ivan's way of saying thank you to that man upstairs he was always talking about.

It had been years since the last time he had walked me down there and told me more stories of the road as we walked the city streets. He took me there on a few occasions when we were out on the road, young child me and teenage touring me, but one time stood out the most. It was when he explained that standing and listening to music there was his happy place to get away from Zora and Adolf when they first arrived in America. He couldn't stand to be in the tiny apartment listening to them speak of how much better it was now that they were in America and the hustles they were doing.

Before our last show, I was able to catch him and discussed my interest in going back to the old club for more story time. I suggested we start the day with a slice of pizza and a cold beer at a hole-in-the-wall bar. We were also giant fans of the great Anthony Bourdain, so maybe we would belly up at one of his favorite hangouts and partake in an all-day beer fest followed by some drunken late-night street food. I think Tony would have highly approved of that decision. Whatever poison we chose to partake in, we would have one full day off to recover, so it was time to truly enjoy this day off to its fullest.

I had put the crew up in a nice hotel not far from one of the most iconic sports arenas we ever did business in. This building wasn't owned by the cartel, but let's just say an old friend of the cartel ran the show in there. Bobby had always kept business flowing for us in that part of town. But we stayed in town to avoid bringing our tour buses back into the city on the day of the show. Not only was it annoying for the drivers to deal with the Big Apple traffic in the morning but there was no parking for the buses at the venue anyways. Ivan stayed with the band, so he was at some posh hoity-toity, heated toilet seat kind of hotel not far from us. He wasn't slumming it in any shape or form. I crack up when I say we were "slumming it" in a hotel that cost more than what some people make in a week for a one-night stay . . . but, compared to Ivan's room, ours were made for peasants. So, instead of trying to meet in his lobby where they probably wouldn't let a tattooed messy haired female roadie like myself even glance through the window without chasing me off, we met at our second favorite day-drinking establishment. And trust me, I didn't start this tradition either, it was all Ivan and his obsession with cold beer and chicken wings. After dropping off my bags and taking a quick shower in a bathroom the size of a shoe box, I made my way to meet Ivan at Hooters. They do have ice cold draft beer! I have to laugh each time we go in there, we tend to get a few stares.

The Big Apple is unique. You cross so many different characters while walking the streets of New York, so instead of a cab, I opted for a nice walk. The sun was out and no wind, which was a great start to the afternoon seeing that I didn't put my hair up this day for once. The street peddlers and performers were in full swing. The hotdog stands were busy and even after a rough few days, I was in a great mood. I wasn't far from the cold beer and wing establishment when the strangest feeling came over me. It started just above my neck in the back of my brain almost. Take the most intense sensation of goosebumps and multiply that by ten—followed by a thick, almost painful chill that glided down my spine, bringing me to a standstill.

One thing you have to know about me is I don't believe in superstitious shit at all. I don't think aliens are real, keep your crystal off me, the devil never went to Georgia or wears Prada, the palm of my hand doesn't tell you squat, and the only people making good wine out of water are the Italians. But today there was something that I couldn't explain. This something had a hold of me there at this moment, this force was big and had to be standing right behind me; for I felt its cold breath panting down my neck.

I slowly turned. There was nothing; the street was completely empty. This was weird and extra fucked up. In New York City, there's always someone on the streets, but not at this second, I was the only one. I was frozen in place for a few more seconds—hell, maybe a minute or two. I moved my eyes back and forth studying everything, looking for any movement. I even slowly turned my upper body enough to look back in my original walking path. I straightened myself out, closed my eyes, and shook myself out physically and mentally. I felt normalcy again when I witnessed a woman in high-heeled boots walking her Shih Tzu while talking on her cell phone.

As I started walking again and reached the corner. Poof! People were everywhere, and the typical noises were back. It was like a weird glitch in the matrix and time. If I didn't already have a specific focus today, I'm sure Ivan would love to hear all about this experience. He loved to talk about the nuances of the world, and he loved to debate me on his man in the clouds. Most of all, he loved philosophy. He loved to talk about thoughts and dreams and the universe. But this could all wait, I needed to hear about Ivan and how he was feeling lately. He did say he had something big to tell me, so I look forward to hearing about whatever he has going on. As Ivan got older, we grew further apart—not in a bad way. We were just busy like I have said. I was sad we had become distant, though I never said it to him, it was on my mind lots. Ivan had always been the man I looked up to in life, the ideal that deep down I wish I could be and all the love to Mary for helping raise me, I was a daddy's girl deep down. Today was my day to care about him for once and not my own selfish needs. This was going to be the day I helped the man who always helped me in life.

Walking through the front doors of Hooters, I could see Ivan bellied up at the bar as usual. Yep, there he was, already making jokes with the girls behind the bar. I would say his mood had improved. But then again, what man wouldn't be happy with two, giant . . . ice cold beers in front of them, one for each hand!

As I approached, I studied the grey hairs that replaced Ivan's once-dark full head of hair. It was funny to me; I had just seen the man, but he looked like any typical older man without the all-access pass around his neck and push-to-talk-radio in his right hand. He kept his hair trimmed short these days, revealing a spot on the brink of balding at the crown of his head. His smile was deep—the kind that promotes all wrinkles on the forehead, under the eyes, and around the mouth. As he lifted his glass to take a sip between chuckles, I noticed that he was still fit, but his arms had lessened in mass over the years. His chest was smaller than it was a decade ago, which made his stomach look particularly bloated as he slouched over the bar. The fanny pack wrapped around his midsection didn't help the visual I was looking at. It was a bittersweet moment, reaching this bonding moment as a young adult while acknowledging that Ivan had aged. For all intents and purposes this man, Ivan, who fucking pulled me from a dumpster and gave me a life—a life well-lived at that—deserved lots of love from me today.

A few tables away, I impersonated Mrs. Doubtfire loudly enough for most patrons to hear. "Hellooo!" I followed obnoxiously with, "cute purse around your waist."

He looked down at his fanny pack and then glanced over at me. "What do you keep in there?" I continued. "A second set of dentures, some Viagra and your AARP card?"

I had hoped to embarrass the old guy. "One of those is a must these days," he countered as he winked at the Hooters girl. Ivan always knew how to take a joke thrown at him and laugh.

I sat down next to Ivan after ordering a beer. I was still a little shaken by my little episode out on the street. Even though we just had a nice little cut-up at Ivan's expense, it was crickets now. He had his eyes fixed on a TV that had some English Footie Ball on—not my cup of tea but he was also into wrestling. Ivan liked a lot of things, but football was his favorite. But soon it went to halftime and still nothing from him. This was not typical of Ivan. By now, he usually would have given me hell about my two best friends and how we all still partied a little too hard, but he was just fixed on the television.

I had to break the silence and asked, "Everything okay? You usually have a little more to talk about."

Before Ivan could respond, he reached into his fanny pack and pulled out his ringing cell phone. With hesitation, he slid it back into hiding. But once again, it rang. He retrieved it and reluctantly answered. I caught hints of Czech on the other end; over the years, Pie, Dick, Juan, and some of the upper levels in the cartel learned to mix Czech with Spanish. I was always too lazy to learn, so I watched Ivan intently, trying to piece together the conversation, which wasn't sitting well with him. He fidgeted, and his demeanor shifted.

Ivan reached for his wallet and threw a couple hundreds on the bar. He thanked our bartender, and like that we were out the door. I wanted to ask what happened, but I felt that now was not the time for any questions. Plus, he didn't seem to be in a talkative mood even before the call came in. Ivan was never a big drunk or smoker like me, so when he turned and asked if I had a pack of Reds on me, I knew it would be an interesting night. I never cared to know or look up to see if there was a full moon, but there was a certain feeling in the stale New York City air that day. I had a feeling that both of us would probably not remember much about tonight. We jumped on the D-train heading south toward Little Italy. Ivan wanted to go spend time around his original stomping grounds.

The train ride down to the old 'hood was quiet—not one word was spoken—except for the track noise and the off-key chords of the breaks doing their job. Once we exited the subway and got back onto the street, Ivan still hadn't spoken a word since he asked if I had smokes. It was getting so awkward that I finally nudged him with my pack of smokes to see if I could get a reaction, but he was lost in thought. That was the philosopher and overthinker in him, analyzing the phone conversation repeatedly in his mind.

We stopped in front of an older building that appeared to be apartments above a trendy wine bar. I really wasn't paying attention and then suddenly he spoke, "This is where my brother, The Butcher, went on a fifty-person killing spree in the '70s."

After I picked my jaw off the ground, I stood there in disbelief. For one I was not expecting those words to be the first he spoke to me and secondly, I figured Adolf had killed fifty or so in the lifetime but holy shit. As I stood in horrified amazement, Ivan continued, trance-like.

I stood there listening and processing and even trying to relate to Adolf. I know that sounds crazy, but I wanted to know why Ivan stuck around with this irrational man for so long. He could have just run never to be seen again after he met Pie. To be frank, it didn't matter, we were in the cartel for good. Property of Juan. I slowly got my mind back on track and rejoined Ivan as he finished that story of The Butcher coming back to NYC in the '70s.

Ivan continued to tell the story. "In the earlier years of The Roadie Cartel, I was on a tour that had been stopped by the police. We all got arrested and thrown in jail; it was a bad look at the time. Thankfully, Dick got us all off without a single mark on our records. Juan and Adolf instantly blamed the Italians, but they didn't have a fucking clue if they had actually snitched on us. But it didn't matter. This was a brewing war and a great excuse to attack."

Ivan looked down toward my feet and beckoned for a cigarette. I followed suit as he strolled away from the building still sharing this horrific story. I hoped we would find a bar along the way. I was parched and ready to sit and listen to Ivan.

"Juan had wanted this territory all to himself," Ivan declared after blowing a puff of smoke away from me. "No middleman, at least not one that had their own dreams of running the show too. So, he sent Adolf on a mission to beat, torture, and extort information from one of the sons of an Italian mob boss. This went on for days. The kid was still clinging to life when they found him and his boat floating in the Hudson River, but by the time they got him to land, he had perished. Adolf got all the info he needed to start the rampage against the mob. He and his cartel gunners followed Juan's orders to tear through their enemies like wolves . . . to scare the hardest of criminals and mortify every cop in the country and anyone else who wanted to take on Juan.

"I'm sickened to this day, knowing my own brother could do something so vile. I was disturbed when I heard about the crimes on every street corner and on the TV in my hotel rooms. The gruesome attacks stretched out to the suburbs to finish off the women and children of the mob boss after Adolf had made his way through the males doing work in the city."

Ivan stopped walking and looked up at the sky, inhaling the last drag of his cigarette as if it were his last and mumbled under his breath. It sounded like he said, "They are watching," but with a line of clamoring cabs and other vehicles, I couldn't make it out. Nervous about having him on the streets, engulfed by his dark thoughts, I shoved him gently around the corner to find a place to drink.

Not more than twenty steps after turning the corner, there was a bar. The sign was spray painted on the door and the little chalkboard out front read, "Choose Beer because no great story started with 'Hold my salad.'" The bartender was slick and slid two draft beers our way like in an old Western movie. We chugged half of the golden liquid from our mugs, and Ivan patted my shoulder as he wiped his mouth with the other hand. I knew what he wanted. I stood up and pulled a few bucks out.

"Anything but the Beatles," Ivan said as I walked toward the jukebox. By the time I returned next to him, two shots of tequila were waiting for each of us. He clinked the first shot glass against mine. But as I got ready to touch my glass to my lips and put this shot to bed in my belly, Ivan sat there with his slightly dirty glass a few inches from his mouth staring at it.

"Not feeling tequila all of a sudden?" I said in a half-joking tone.

"I . . . it doesn't matter. Here is to not fucking up the next life God gives me, if I am even that blessed," he said seriously. I shook my head, gave him a little side eye after taking down the tequila and sat there in silence trying to process what the hell he was talking about.

I picked up the next shot glass, slid his a little closer, and tried to cut the tension with a more lighthearted cheers this time around. We clinked shot glasses again and I gave a toast: "Here's to honor . . . wait, chance. Yeah, chance. I wouldn't have had a chance at life if it weren't for you, and it's by chance and chance alone that you have assholes for siblings, and if God is listening, then He or She can strike me dead on this bar seat. But if by chance I live to see another day then I will say it was all by chance I am not in hell." Ivan chuckled, rolled his eyes at my comments, and titled his head back as the liquor trickled down to his belly.

"Assholes, for sure." He took a long pause and turned his whole body toward me. "It was so beautiful there, Wyatt. I miss the smell of the mountains and the sounds of animals around Father's barn. If He doesn't strike you dead for that comment, make sure to spread my ashes on a mountain top not far from my hometown one day . . . if they ever find my body."

He chuckled, a little shorter this time and then stopped like he always stops. "God, I wish I never left."

"So, with all this money you have, why not go back?" I turned and said to him.

Ivan gazed up the ceiling as if the answer was written up there with a Sharpie.

I felt uneasy. Did I even want to hear the answer? Was I ready for this? This was about to open doors maybe I didn't want opened. Wanting the truth sounds reasonable, but it can tear down the walls of fragile mistruths we have built over the years. At the same time, I was ready to understand Ivan more—I wanted to know why this guy was in a business so cold and criminal? I flashed back to a merch tech I once had, who told me if I wanted to understand life, I would have to go to the darkest place to find it. My mind was a very dark place at times. I was willing and ready to travel to that dark place with Ivan.

"Two shot glasses, please. Your most expensive tequila on the shelf. Lock the door and say your closed." Ivan placed a dozen hundred-dollar bills on the bar. These weren't unreasonable requests considering we were the only ones in the facility, and the kid behind the bar seemed about as interested in serving people that afternoon as he would getting a tooth drilled. The bartender placed the items in front of us. After a long inhale, Ivan held his breath for what felt like an eternity. I had no idea what he was thinking. Never had I seen Ivan frozen in time like this.

The music stopped and other than the bit of street noise bleeding through the walls, silence took over the room. Still, nothing had been said, and it wasn't long before the bartender raised his eyebrows at me and exited from behind the bar. I heard him lock the front door and when he came back behind us heading towards the bar, he swiftly disappeared into the manager's office that wasn't far from the back door.

We could have been anywhere, but we were here in time at this little bar not far from where it all started for him as a roadie. This was no coincidence. This was meant to happen. I had to let Ivan work it out in his own way. We had nothing but time on this already eerie day off. Ivan lit a cigarette and took one long drag. And then another. And one more. In a matter of five drags, it had burned down to almost the filter, and with the last inhale, he finally exhaled the cloud of smoke through his nostrils. He looked like a fire-breathing dragon who had been awakened. Brooding. Fierce. The words flowed out of his mouth as he put the cigarette out in an ashtray not far from his left hand.

"I've lied to you about your mother. I met the young woman in a hallway one day when I was down at the Mexican farm on a business trip with Pie. She was crying, not far from his room in a study that was hardly used. With the little Spanish I knew, I asked her why she was crying and if I could help." A tear fell from Ivan's face. "She told me she had gotten pregnant and that if her family found out, they would kill her, for she was not married. As the daughter of a high-ranking soldier in the Juarez chapter of Juan's Mexican cartel, she knew the shame would be brutal. She could not visit any doctors in the area for they would tell her father."

Ivan paused and lit another cigarette. He rolled his shoulders as if a heavy weight burdened him. "When I was a kid, Wyatt, my father told me that the butcher shop and farm would be mine one day. He knew Adolf wasn't interested, and it was all I had ever wanted and dreamed about. Of course, those dreams were shattered, and I selfishly felt having my own child would fill that void." He poured tequila from the bottle and made a quick movement with his eyebrows. "So, I told the young woman to stay hidden in Juarez until she gave birth and to let me raise you. But on the night of your birth, your mother became enraged with guilt and had grown emotionally attached to you during the pregnancy. She felt that if she couldn't have you, no one could, so she tried to murder you and if she would have seen me take you from that dumpster, she would have tried to kill me too."

"What the fuck?!" I blurted out. Silence as I took my shot and processed. "So why not let her keep me—have her escape and never return? Why bring me into this crazy shit with the cartel, knowing how dangerous it'd be for me? I don't understand. Why be so selfish to take me away from my mother?" The questions wouldn't stop coming out of my mouth.

Ivan's silence darkened the room. He answered slowly as his eyes pooled with tears, "I am trapped in this business. I thought I was doing the right thing by keeping you close to me on the road. At least on the road I could try to protect you from them. I never wanted to lose anyone again."

"But why me? You could have just left me and had a kid with Mary to start a family . . ."

He bolted up from the bar stool. I had never seen him shake his head, smoke, and talk in Czech so much all while pacing the floor behind his bar stool, but he was searching for something. Then like a punch to the gut it all came out at me in one burst and knocked me to my knees.

"Because I want MY DAUGHTER AROUND ME! I can't trust anyone, and I thought I was doing the right thing with you. I couldn't let her take you away, knowing that my blood runs through your veins!"

My father fell back into an open seat behind him at a table.

I sat on my stool, too shocked to react. The man who I thought was just a nice man who saved me turns out to be my biological father! Anger started to build deep in me, wanting to know why he made that lie up. Why did he put me through this? But before I could give him a piece of my mind, something came over me, and I lunged right at him, jumping from my stool and wrapped both my arms around him as my true father for the first time. Not my stand-in father anymore. Not just a father figure either. My real blood father. No words could be said as we shed tears of joy. I had never felt a true love for someone more, ever.

We made our way back to the bar stools, and after a few pulls of tequila straight from the bottle and lots of tears, I regained the ability to put words together.

"Why did you think you needed to hide the truth?"

"In my mind and in my heart, I hoped you would never go looking for your mother."

I wasn't content about his reasoning because I knew we had a deep bond, but all this time, I could have known him as my legit father.

"What is it about my mom that compelled you to come up with such an extravagant lie? Was there romance between you two at all?"

"She became a different person as soon as I tried to help her. She threatened to harm you and inflict rage on everyone if you lived. If anyone were to find out you existed, she would have you killed right on the spot, she didn't want you in the cartel family. So, I did what anyone in my shoes would do: I hid you in plain sight, just like the cartel." He swiveled to face me, and I turned to meet his eyes, which were kind and pained. "Stop asking about her, please. Accept that she is a lost cause. And never ask around or inside the cartel; if she's still alive, she is crazy and dangerous."

Nothing good can happen when you're full of tequila and coke. Ivan wasn't as coked up as me, so I knew he wouldn't be in the mood if I started badgering the man, but I wanted answers. The conversation shifted, and I hit him with more questions about me. I was selfish with our time; I thought I deserved all the answers now.

Ivan being the philosophical man said, "Wyatt, in life, you aren't deserving of anything just because you feel like it is owed to you. Let it be and know I did it because I love you and didn't want you killed."

I shook my head like a spoiled brat would, but he was right. There were certain things I didn't need to press him about, especially at this point.

"I do, however, feel that I owe you the truth about my life, now that you know about yours." My eyes shot up at him, too scared to say anything for fear he might change his mind.

My father continued. "When Zora first approached me by the barn, I was just a kid. My size was needed for a brewery job that would help clear up some money issues in the family. When I told her no, she kicked over the bucket of milk and stormed off out of the barn. Zora has always been a spoiled girl when it comes to demanding what she wants.

"Not long after I cleaned up her mess and finished my chores, Adolf appeared from around the back of barn and stopped me. He's always been smaller than me, but I've constantly feared him. He has a way about him. You never know what he'll do if you cross him. When he calmly told me to join him and Zora, it was an order. I nevertheless told him I had things to do with Father early in the morning and didn't want to be involved with getting in trouble again. As a response, his shoulders stiffened, and I could feel the hairs on the back of my neck tingle because I couldn't see a soul when he looked me dead in the eye and said there would be no morning for me otherwise.

"This was a first for me. He had beaten me and yelled in my face, but he had never threatened my existence. I laughed uneasily, but as I went to walk around him, he put his hand on my chest. There was no force behind it, but the energy that transferred to me rendered me helpless. Physically, he couldn't hold me hostage, but he had a force I will never be able to describe. I was terrified of whatever was possessing him and didn't want to call his bluff, so I conceded.

"That night, the three of us walked toward the brewery and sat across the street in a small alley that dead-ended into warehouses. As we waited for our victim, I asked what this guy had done to deserve our attention, but Adolf told me to shut up and keep a lookout for his briefcase. In my mind, I imagined candy and crackers inside. Hell, at the time, I had no idea what men put in those things. If anything, they look like a squished lunch box, so I figured they contained food.

"'Are you hungry or something?' I asked half-jokingly. 'What do you want from this guy?'

My brother wanted to take everything; there was no remorse in his goal. I felt bad for the stranger, and I thought I could make sure nothing bad happened to him. It was one thing to take his things, but I didn't want Adolf to hurt him.

"I remember asking Adolf and Zora if they planned to hurt the man but received no reply. I was worried I would mess this up, and we would all get in trouble. I tried to tell myself it would be over soon, and I would be able to help Father in the morning.

"Father. What if the man had a wife and kids? The more nervous I grew waiting on this man to appear, the more I thought about him as more than just some businessman. Adolf and Zora were discussing their hustles, but I interrupted them to make sure we were only going to take the case and not hurt him. The scariest part about Adolf lately was that his blow ups were replaced by a low, commanding voice. It was bone-chilling. When he growled that we'd do whatever it takes to get the money, I was done. I got up to leave toward the farm. But as I turned, Adolf pulled me down and whispered into my ear something that haunts me to the core—that if I betray him, he'll make sure I burn; but first he'll burn the whole farm. Mother. Father. Every animal as I watch and then me.

"The sound of a door closing from across the street at the brewery pulled Adolf's attention off me. The stranger appeared. Adolf looked at Zora and then at me.

"Three, two . . . run. We stood up and sprinted across the small two-lane street and through the unguarded gate. Adolf had told me to grab the man and hold him, so I did my job. I rushed off to the side while the man's attention was on my brother. I was able to grab the man from behind in a bear hug. His arms were down by his sides while he struggled free. He was strong—maybe not like Hercules—but the man had power in his movements. It almost looked as if we were dancing while I did my best to tame him.

"Zora and Adolf had taken the keys to the stranger's sports car and were riffling through it, looking for who knows what. Empty-handed, they approached us to beat the shit out of the man I secured, but he broke free and pulled a gun from his trench coat pocket.

"I had one choice, Wyatt. I stepped forward with a punch and heard the bones in the side of his face shatter. The adrenaline from seeing the gun must have taken my strength to a new level. Even though I hated Adolf and Zora at that moment, I couldn't watch my siblings die. Besides, I was only trying to give us enough time to leave before he came to. But as his unconscious body went limp and fell sideways, his neck fell directly across his convertible window.

His neck cracked like a branch broken against a knee, and gravity dragged his corpse to the ground.

"My brother and sister fled after they watched his head angle unnaturally against his shoulder. I dropped to my knees, crying. I held the man's hand and begged God to bring him back as I looked into his bloodshot eyes that stared blankly ahead. And then right before a dribble of crimson came trickling from his mouth one last breath of life left him, his soul was gone, there was no bringing him back.

"I was mortified. I still am. I killed a man because I gave into my fear of Adolf's evil ways. I cried to the skies for mercy. But he was gone. It was futile.

"Suddenly, I was pulled up from the back of my shirt. It was Adolf. He screamed at me that we had no time. We ran—ran faster than I ever had in my life. But here's where my life truly fell apart. Once at the barn, the safest place I knew, the two planned our next move. To run again. To run away from our life.

"When I tried to protest, they belittled me. We all had to escape, for if we stayed, we would all go to jail and soil the family name . . . all because of me, they said. I was a scared young boy, and all I could do was cry. I close my eyes, and see that man dead next to his car.

"As Adolf and Zora slipped into the house through a side window, I rolled up into a ball on the barn floor near my mule. What Adolf and Zora did, instead was rationalize, pack up what little money they could steal from the family home, grab a bag of supplies, and return to the barn for me.

"They didn't say anything. They just dragged me off the floor and forced me into the openness. We headed on foot toward the train station, never to return.

"I wasn't even twenty and had committed the most heinous crime. I cried for months. Sometimes there were no tears, but my heart ached unbearably for that man. Then came the heartbreak of leaving home. I wanted to go back and face my worldly consequence in prison. I wanted to tell the truth so bad. At least then, I would have had my mother and father to comfort me in that cold, dark jail cell meant for people like me, but Adolf and Zora never allowed me. They said they would have to go to jail with me, and that was not an option. And Adolf reminded me daily for years how he would kill everything I loved if I dared cross him.

"They have held me hostage in my own body and mind for decades now. I have been a slave to their needs because they made me believe that I was the horrible one. That I would be responsible for placing the whole family in jail for my wild actions that night. I was naive and too scared to be alone, so I stayed with Zora and Adolf to have some family in my life and to save the lives of my mother and father. Hoping to see them again before death came for them. That is all I ever wanted, was my own family. Then when you came along, Wyatt, I wanted out of it all. But again, they struck me to the core. They have threatened that if I ever leave or talk about the cartel, they will kill you. So, to keep you alive, I've kept up the touring and transporting of coke for them.

"But I have messed up once more. This time, it's big. I have really done it this time, Wyatt. The Butcher is hunting me, and it's only a matter of time until he catches up to me . . ." Ivan dropped his head into his hands and started to weep.

I was at a loss for words. I had always wanted the truth, but now that it was on the table, I didn't want to know. Sure, I was completely shocked that the man I had never seen hurt a fly had actually killed a man, but I also knew it wasn't like he set out to do it that night. There was one thing I was more shaken up about—that I now knew this family's deepest secret. And with all the weird shit that has been going on today, I wished he could take it back and be somewhere other than in this bar. I wasn't ready for all this information.

Oh, how the time seemed to disappear in what seemed like a blink of the eye; it was dark outside. Up until now, I never believed the old saying nothing good happens after the sun goes down. Tonight, I felt it in my bones that nothing good could come of this hang. I wanted to believe in my heart that I was happy discovering Ivan was my father, but even that was tainted by the cartel.

I took a second to get out of my own head and looked over at the man who I never saw rattled, and sadly all that sat there was a man shattered, waiting for his brother to come for him. I poured him a drink and lit us both a cigarette. Staring at the shot glass full of tequila, he nodded his head defeatedly. I knew my time would soon be coming, as well. I wanted real answers about why the hell this psycho was out to kill his brother and potentially me.

Ivan had either hit his limit on booze or had left this world for a new dimension. He mumbled snips of phrases from prophets and poets while I stared at him, frustrated because none of this felt right—the day, this conversation . . . and that fucking crazy feeling I had earlier.

I was just drunk and irate enough to throw my shot glass against the wall. When it shattered to the floor at the other end of the bar, Ivan snapped back to life and started to blurt out his financial issues. Over the years, Ivan had made millions off The Roadie Cartel with his insane end-of-tour bonuses and kickbacks from the cartel and bands. He looked me dead in the eye and told me he had kept zero. Juan had paid for the El Paso house, and he kept just enough scratch around to keep Mary and me fed and happy. I was shocked! Where did all his money go?! Then he shared with me something I never would have guessed. Ivan would send hundreds of thousands upon hundreds of thousands back to his parents, their business, and most of all the church in his little town under an anonymous name so they would never look him up. This blew my mind. I couldn't express how gracious, but foolish, this was. How could he be sure that the cash even went into the hand of the intended recipients? How did he even know if his parents were there, blindly sending funds like that?

When he told me in the darkest moments coming to America and traveling alone, the only one willing to forgive and listen to him was God, I laughed with spite. "You should have given me the money," I sneered drunkenly. "I would have shown you a better miracle. Mine would involve tequila, blow, and a vacation to clear the mind. *Boom!* Magic. The worm at the bottom of the bottle saved you!"

"What does it matter, Wyatt?" Ivan slurred.

I didn't say anything this time. We sat there in silence . . .

One minute passed . . .

And then five . . .

And then . . .

"I finally got the courage to return to Czechoslovakia and face my darkest fear, I went back to see my parents in their dying years. I also wanted to introduce Mary to my parents. From the moment we touched down, my stomach started to hurt. As we made our way through the airport, I saw familiar faces: Mexican cartel hooliguns. I locked eyes with one of them as they started to board their flight. He smirked at me. We rushed out to the area I could remember where the farm was located. We showed up to nothing. The farmland, house, and barn were smoldering from a fire that burnt it to the ground. Every memory burned to a crisp. I remembered the church, but when Mary and I got there, that too, had been torched.

"Standing in the town's square, no one would explain what happened to me. A weight was on my shoulders . . . a chill ran down my spine. The feeling of an evil presence took over the air. There was nothing left to do. My town had been forever marked and scarred by this tragic loss of life and history. And once again I was left thinking I was the issue.

"When we arrived home in El Paso, the house had been searched and trashed. As we rounded the corner to the main dining room, we saw the present left on the kitchen counter. There was a note . . . "

Ivan shuddered.

". . . and the note had been stabbed into a severed head with a fucking knife."

He pulled out his wallet from his back pant pocket. Opening the trifold, he pulled out a worn piece of paper that had stains of red on it and was almost falling apart at the folds. He handed it to me slowly, dropped his head, and grabbed the bottle of tequila.

I KNOW WHAT YOU HAVE BEEN DOING. FOR YOUR DISOBEDIENCE TO THE CARTEL, YOU, YOUR BITCH, AND THAT KID WILL DIE. YOUR TIME WILL COME, BUT I DECIDE WHEN. BE AFRAID FOR ANYONE ELSE YOU ASSOCIATE WITH.

Anyone he'd have talked to would simply be killed before anything could be done about it, and it's not like Ivan could go to the police. There was no way to know who was a part of the Mexican cartel and who wasn't these days.

I told him to take my money, grab Mary, and run until he hit fucking Antarctica. "Live with the penguins in peace," I joked mildly to preserve my sanity.

He shook his head and placed it into his hands as his elbows rested on the bar. Tears started to flow as he apologized. He had led me to death's door as he did to his mother and father. I had a target painted on my back and doubted I would ever get to share these stories with anyone other than my bunk buddy at the morgue.

But here we are, seventeen videos in and trying to make each of my last seconds count not just for me, but for the world and everyone who is being manipulated by this cartel.

The bartender slipped back into the room and politely asked us to leave as we sat now in drunken silence and our tears in small pools on the bar.

Nothing but Ivan's lips moved in response. "Adolf told me in Czechoslovakian he's going to cut me and everything I love apart . . . and I told him I'm ready to stop running in fear. I am ready to meet my maker."

Looking back at the conversation, it made sense. Before we left the bar, I pulled out another eighth to keep myself conscious, and Ivan passed me an old small key from his pocket and then mumbled at me. I dipped the tip of the key into the bag and took a bump before we stood up to leave. I almost felt a sobering effect taking over, a feeling that it would all be okay. The bartender walked us to the door, wished us good luck, and locked the door behind us. We stood looking into the streets of New York City, hazy with emotion and liquor. My father dropped to his knees. My heart told me to respect his moment to—to puke his brains out. This was going to be a fun walk back to Ivan's hotel.

Being drunk in the bar was one thing; we were by ourselves. Now, out on the open streets of the Big Apple, anything could happen. I quickly went into survival mode; everyone was now a potential enemy working with Adolf. Ivan and I had a bounty on our heads; we had to stay alert. Each person who passed and glanced at us looked like a cartel member. I imagined guns and knives in everyone's hands. My drunk eyes and mind were playing horrible tricks on me.

I started to lose it. Everything was moving and spinning. I called the hotel and told them to send security up to check my room for suspicious people who might have broken in. I realized quickly, though, we have cartel members that work at the hotels we book for our tours. This was not good. The world suddenly got so very small, and I was going down a rabbit hole into my own fiery hell.

Hell. Should I believe in hell? Was Ivan right about God? Could He be the only one who saves me tonight? What am I talking about! I was drunk and needed to get Ivan back to his hotel, fast. I reassured myself that this would be over in the morning. Life will go back to normal. It was all going to work itself out.

Have you ever been in a dream so real that you almost forget you're asleep? At any moment, I believed I would drunkenly wake up and have to rush to meet Ivan on the day off. This had to be a dream . . . the day was just too weird.

Ivan was so damn wasted. It felt like I was pulling us both through the streets of New York City with weights on our legs. Trash collected around his feet as I practically dragged him from one side of the street to the next, trying to find the hotel.

An older fellow, huge in proportion compared to us, walked up and asked if he could help get Ivan into a cab. Looking up at him my eyes were suddenly flooded with a bright light from a bodega next to us, my squinting hindered me from viewing the man's face. As I started to move my vision back down to Ivan, I caught out of the corner of my eye one glinting, red eye. It had to be a light trace playing tricks on my vision, then, I noticed his hands were covered in snakeskin that shimmered under the shops florescent lighting.

I quickly told this oddity I had it covered, but he flung me to the side, and picked Ivan up like a rag doll. Helpless, I watched in horror as the man grew, hovering over me like a mountain. The red-eyed man tilted his head upward and snarled to the sky. He lifted my father above his head and launched him into the street. Amazingly, Ivan made it to his hands and knees, and when he looked up, his last sight was the headlights of a yellow cab. The clang of flesh meeting metal warped my ears, but I could see Ivan, still breathing. As my feet hit the asphalt to reach him, I turned and looked to my right as a bus barreled down on me at a rate that only gave me time to close my eyes and clench my fists . . .

I was jolted awake in the front of the plane when the wheels touched down in Seattle.

"Are you okay?" asked the flight attendant from her jump-seat. I was soaked and confused about what was going on in my life. I rubbed the sleep out of my eyes and began to look for my water when she asked again gently, "Are you sure you are okay?"

I really wasn't, but I looked at her and said, "Yeah, thanks. I had a long night, and—I think I am getting a cold." I didn't know what else to tell her. I was done with sleep for a minute; every time I closed my eyes, the memories from my last night with Ivan played like a broken record, round and round. Once my memory focuses on leaving that bar, my nightmares kick in, and I envision this devilish man attacking Ivan.

I know I could have shared with you, the viewers of my diaries, the main day off with Ivan but sadly this version with that devil creature is my new reality of that day with him. I can't close my eyes and not see that nightmare of a man, and I don't know why. It is like I am being hunted in two worlds. Neither of those worlds, real or dreamed, will I ever make it out alive. And the saddest part, is that in the end, I will just miss time with my father and even our last day together is now a tainted memory. Although I have to relive that version in my dreams, I still am able to hold on to the memory of the final goodbye we did share before he vanished.

That night after we left the bar, we returned to the hotel and Ivan's room in one piece. I was so freaked out from what he had told me about what his brother had done and threatened, that I stayed with him that night. We didn't leave the room for anything. I had the couch, and he had the bed. Room service was our hero, not only for the hangover but also because I didn't want to be in public on this day off. We laid around the hotel room that next day without speaking much.

"You know," I finally decided to break the tension in the air, "I could finish the tour without you if you choose to run. I'm proud to be your daughter and you know I will support you with whatever you decide. If you want to battle against the cartel, let's fucking go, we'll go down in a blaze of glory together."

"It'll be fine," he said with a slight smile. "I'll make a phone call and get everything sorted out before I leave the hotel tomorrow for the show."

When it was time to go back to my hotel later that day, I hugged my father so tight and didn't want to let go. I didn't want the feeling in my heart and gut to be right, so I knew if I let him go that it might be the last. We eventually separated and as I stood a few feet from him, I just smiled so big—I gave him the same smile I would as a little girl seeing her dad walk through the door when he was home from tour—he smiled back and blew me a kiss. "I love you, Dad. Thanks for everything you've done for me. See you tomorrow! Oh, and don't eat my cheeseburger this time." I added, trying to spark one last laugh for a man who so needed a win. He gave me a wink, put his hand on his heart, and smiled at me again. As I turned to walk away, I felt that old little key in my pocket, I turned, took a few steps, and pushed the door before it closed. "Hey you might need this," as I went to hand my father the key.

"Put that in your sock and keep it there until I tell you differently," he said.

"My sock?" I said with a silly look on my face.

"Yes, just trust me, Wyatt." Ivan stated as he kissed my forehead and told me he loved me one last time.

I didn't sleep that night. Ivan never showed up the next day. Sadly, I knew this way before Dick called me that afternoon—I had sent my father a message in the morning, but when I didn't hear back from him I knew his brother had come for him. Dick told me Ivan had been targeted by another gang, but there was nothing the cartel could do and to expect his replacement later that night. He was so insincere and heartless.

In the seconds that followed Dick's phone call, my blood boiled, I hated him. I hated the cartel. And I loathed Adolf! In those heated moments I had no idea what I wanted to do, my world had just crashed around me and I, well, I wanted to watch the world burn with me. . . especially The Roadie Cartel.

Here I sit in my production office, fighting, because let's face it, I have nowhere to run, and I have nowhere to hide. So, I am talking into this camera, looking for YOU, the one man my father told me to contact before his disappearance. I was told you could help me. I don't know exactly how to find you, but Ivan and you know each other, apparently. If you're out there, Officer Michael Gabriel Hernández, I am heading to El Paso, Texas tonight! I need to bring justice to the men who killed my father, it is time to bring this cartel DOWN!

>>>STOP RECORDING<<<

I launched my phone across the table the second after I hit the red button to stop recording. After letting some tears pour down my face, I picked up the phone again and hit the upload button. Unexpectedly, I get a foreboding feeling—goosebumps and chills that run down my back to my toes. It was that same feeling I got that last day on the streets of New York; I think The Butcher is closing in on me . . .

CHAPTER 19

The Ride Home... Continued

November 6th, 2009 - 07:05:00 Milepost 80 Highway 9,
Columbus, New Mexico

Lying on the floor of the bus

In one ultra-bright flash of light—it was like I was falling off a cliff and then suddenly jolting awake before hitting the ground—gravity and reality kick back in. My out-of-body experience was not just vivid, but I relived each and every moment up to this nightmare I am still stuck in. My vision is hazy, sounds are muffled, head and body throbbing. But here I am, alive.

I think.

I must have been stuck between living and dead. I am uncertain how long I was knocked out. I last remember making great time on our way into El Paso when suddenly our bus was over taken by a giant man . . . my skull twists as if someone is putting a cigarette out on my face. I realize I am lying with a foot the size of a small car smashing my head into the front lounge tile. I am so badly beaten I can feel my body shutting down and my brain going back and forth from unconsciousness to consciousness. Everything about my life is an absolute shit, a living nightmare.

I try to beg audibly for my executioner to end me, but as the first word exits my mouth. One of my lungs collapsed. As air rushes from my chest, I am left coughing and gasping for air. I squirm a little to get weight off my chest, but the gunman applies more pressure. My vision came back, I thought I had lost it, but when the behemoth reapplied his boot to my head, the sole moved from off my eye. It is not a desired result, but I have one of my senses back. FUCK. Now when I open my eyes, I am forced to stare at my dead friends in the face. My field of vision is quite sparse.

Besides the horrific view of Wes and Axel, I can see the clock on the wall and that is about it. Time at this point is irrelevant, hell, it feels like I have been on this floor for days now, and time is also not on my side, but I continue to shift my body for a different view. The pain is almost unbearable, and I am terrified of passing out from it. At times I wish I didn't have the fight of a tiger built into my DNA and though eternal sleep is starting to sound nice, I haven't come this far to just come this far. I have to keep pushing, for my father. When the heavy-footed gunman shifts his boot again, I am going to see if I can get it to move from my head to my upper back. After a few wiggles and a lot of pain, he moved it just far enough down to where I had a little more neck mobility but more importantly, I regained some hearing. I can hear the men speaking in broken English intermingled with Spanish. Another man is rummaging through the bus area behind me and from the sound of it he is repeating the phrase, *"no hay llave aquí."*

If the little Spanish I know is correct, then he is looking for a key. *BANG-BANG!*

Two shots ring out in the bus; the man in the back is also doing his due diligence and making sure only I am kept alive. They are clearly waiting for someone to arrive or I would have been shot a long time ago.

While the ringing in my ears slowly subsides, I get lost staring at Axel's lifeless face, the pain from my wounds lessens, heartbroken that they have taken my friends' lives because of me. I knew we would eventually leave this world, but not like this. Anything would have been cooler than dying in the front lounge of our tour bus. As tears slowly fill my eyes and my vision begins to blur again, to the point I cannot see Axel any longer, I begin to do something I never had done. I begin to pray. I prayed that wherever Ivan was that he takes these guys with him. I prayed that they knew how much they did mean to me. I prayed because I had no other options at this point . . . most of all, I pray for death. "Get off your ass and come take me," I screamed silently to myself as I closed my eyes in broken-hearted pain.

There for a split second all the noise, even the man in the back somehow shuts up, and then a giant weight pulled me down. It wasn't gravity or a feeling I had ever felt but I think my broken heart was coming to the end of its show, there were only so many more beats left in my set list of life. I might not be going to where Ivan is, and my destination may be a tad bit hotter, but at least I will burn knowing I put my whole heart on the line to try and take these fuckers on! I am pulled down more . . .

In my years of hearing people on daytime TV talk shows speak about near-death experiences, I have never believed the yahoos for a second. They talk about visuals, reliving moments, and then their entire life flashes before their eyes. Well, hell—I have had all that and looks like I am going to get a second run through it all again; the time had come, I had to be on my way out. The hype of death is strangely true. A sense of numbness overtakes my pain when visions of old start to play from my memory. They are young memories, fun times of me as a kid. Memories of Ivan and me out back playing by the pool followed by memories of my first time with friends on the playground. My brain is calm.

This sense of dying is not painful, if anything, shockingly I am very relaxed, but I find it weird that out of all that is happening, I can still hear. And quite well at that, considering that my other senses appear to be shutting down. The bus was back to the ordinary noises the other men had been making, then, out of the blue two new voices joined in, and—they sound familiar. The voice closest to me sounds, like Ivan—I was not all there obviously, so it took a second for my brain to catch up to my ear—but . . . could it be? Now the other I knew right away, Pie. My mind using what power it had left started questioning itself, running through reasons why either of them would be here on this bus. My dad, but he was dead. Then it hit me, was this whole thing a setup? The day off in New York, the story about being my father, his death . . . and now this bus massacre?

I am confused as to what in the hell is going on. The more I listen, the more I realize it is Ivan's accent, but the tone and inflections are off. I have to see, but my body is so heavy, my organs feel weak, and there is very little energy left in my tank. It is almost impossible to tell if I am moving anything, even though in my mind I am trying. I still feel death's cold hands making their way across my body in waves, but I am not dead, so I must keep trying to move my head. I know I prayed for death but at the moment, I don't want to move on to hell, I want to see who this is. I keep trying to move my head but with zero energy I am burnt bread in a toaster waiting to be thrown out. Just as I was throwing in the towel, I started to feel a muscle in my neck start to twitch. Then my face started to tingle—as if it had been asleep and blood flow started again—but this was not just blood flow to my foot after sitting on it for twenty minutes, no this was life being pumped back in.

Who knows why, but I was getting another go at life once again. I am not sure if my prayer was or was not answered, but as the blood started to pump through my veins again, the two men transitioned to slang Czechoslovakia-Spanish. With what little energy I have left, I began to squint and un-squint my eyes, hoping to fully open them. My right eye obeys enough to see hazy colors. The left eye follows. But I am sadly facing the wrong direction of the men talking. I hope to get my neck moving with that same positive mentality. I work my neck muscles just under the jaw close to the earlobes. I flex a couple times and prompt a sharp, excruciating pain that shoots down my spine. As I inch further out of death's abode, I can begin to move my shoulders. Then my feet and I just fucked up. In my slow movements, the behemoth of a man feels me shift and moves his giant boot back on top of my head. The other hitman from the back comes forward, and all four men talk casually in a mix of Spanish and English about the carnage they had just committed. They laughed and mocked the dead. All those years of giving your life to a cause only to find out they never cared about you in the end.

Someone—something—hell, maybe it is that man in the clouds Ivan loved so much—is on my side because the giant assassin sneezes, causing him to readjust his foot ever so slightly. I free my head and roll it over for a better view. It *is* Pie with a man that I cannot fully see, but from what I can make out, it isn't Ivan. This man has a much smaller frame with his arms marginally spread from his torso, attempting to make his physique look larger than his natural size. My sigh of relief must have been felt by my oppressor because—just as fast as I got free to take that peek, the beast placed so much pressure, I felt some of my brains seep past my ear drums. My head felt like a watermelon with a hundred rubber bands wrapped around it, waiting for that last bit of pressure to pop it. I am so torn as to why I must keep suffering for something that I am not going to win! I keep asking Ivan and his God to either give me a sign or fucking please kill me. My brain, beat up body and heart can't keep this up. But all I keep getting in return is more fight, more fight in me but also more resistance from them . . . "just give me a sign, please for the love of GOD!"

As the men chit chat, Ivan's voice comes to mind with wise words he once told me, "We humans are so breathtaking; each one of us has so much potential built deep in us that if we want to move mountains, we can. A person just has to dig deep, build high and if your path gets washed away, start a new one while everyone else is complaining." If I am going to get out of this fucking bus, I will need more than my eyes and ears. I try and flex other parts of my body. Arms—not much movement yet. Fingers—the same as the arms. But my toes—my toes just moved!

Wait. What the fuck is in my sock?

Holy shit. It is the key Ivan had given me that final night in New York when I took a bump of coke at the bar. They probably came looking for this object that night when they killed my father, but I had it. This bus massacre is the consequence.

I hear the bay doors open and rummaging through our bags. As the thrashing under the bus subsides, the sound of a helicopter emerges outside. The thick, pulsing sound of the blades and sand blasting the side of the bus were shortly followed by heels tapping up the front stairs of the bus and then on to the tile floor. There is another woman suddenly on the bus and she has a very strong and seductive Spanish accent that instantly takes over the room. Everyone is silent while she speaks. There is anger in her voice, and the man with Ivan's accent responds in broken Spanish. Then, with each click of the high heels, the woman's voice moves closer to me.

When the man rants in Czech, my thoughts jolt to Ivan on the phone at the Hooters in New York City. It is Adolf! If I could move, I would jump up and choke him to death with my bare, weak and blood covered hands.

Someone hastily steps across my back as they made their way toward the back of the bus. And the smell that follows sends me to a panic. Gasoline!! The whole bus now reeks of gas. Ivan was right about them the whole time; they were hunting him and now me. I do not have much time left, and the man from my nightmares, Adolf, has finally hunted me down. They are clearly going to torch this bus to the fucking ground with me in it, but what the hell are they arguing about? I can only guess it has to do with the key that is nuzzled against my little toe.

I have been so curious why Adolf would be mad enough to kill Ivan for going home to the farm. I am sure at this point their parents would not care less about their children's dealings and would be glad to know their baby boys and girl were at least alive. I feel there must be something Ivan had told Adolf along the way to send him into this rage—to erase Ivan, whatever this key will open and whomever Ivan crossed paths with. I highly doubt it will unlock any happiness for Adolf, but I hope it can bring rest to Ivan wherever he may be. In all my pain, it is suddenly made very clear why Ivan gave me this key. I still have one job to accomplish before my death: to take the cartel and this evil man down, the murderer of my father and the man willing to destroy lives for this key.

Now that I can feel it, I can't stop thinking about this key. It is an old small key, no longer than a pinky-finger but it did have a magnetic strip on one side. Maybe it wasn't so old after all. The top part had a four-leaf-clover and a gothic cross stamped in the middle with one small hole for a key ring. Looking back, I can see images of Ivan wearing it around his neck on days by the pool and even around the house. He never took it off, but I always assumed it was a fake key he had picked up at a thrift store or something from his hometown that came over with them.

I think back to our last interaction. My mind went blank. Shit, I can't remember what my father told me when he handed me the key. I was too overwhelmed with the secrets revealed at the time. I only remember the phrase "no one but you."

My equilibrium is off. I open my eyes to stop the dizziness, but small, black dots and beams take over my peripherals. The man above me eases his boot, and I spin my head over to see Axel and Wes again. I don't know why—maybe to build up anger. Maybe it is my reminder to survive. We might not have been on speaking terms when they were murdered, but damn it, I want to live for them too.

The man prepping the bus for incineration makes his way to the front, stepping on Axel's head as the strong smell of gas follows behind him; I hear my friend's teeth crunch between his jaw and the crackling of bone. Heavy footsteps follow the pyromaniac down the stairs and off the bus. The man above me gives a good stomp to my brain and trails behind the others. The woman's heels click down the steps next, and Adolf hollers at her from outside before she exits. "Don't worry. I will do what you couldn't do. I will kill your no-good daughter and then clean up your mess in Italy."

Ivan was right about my mother! She didn't want me to be found and from the tone of The Butcher, she must have been on the hunt for me for a while. Perhaps even before Ivan spilled it all to me recently. By the way things are looking, I am not making it far from this spot, and it looks like she is finally getting her prayers answered today. I can only imagine that soon this fiery hell I have heard about will quickly become a reality inside this bus.

The door slams shut, and it immediately feels like someone has thrown me into an oven. The bus fills with flames in a flash, literally. As the temperature rises, I am shot with a small burst of energy suddenly—or maybe it is that my legs are on fire—I roll to one side and then my back. Flames are everywhere . . . in the back lounge, the bunk area . . . above me! With a rush of adrenaline, I do a semi-sit-up and push my head up as far as I can and look out the front windshield. Those pricks surrounded the bus with fire. Flames dance along the glass of the front lounge windows.

Death by fire is the least appealing way to go and my biggest fear. As the seconds tick by, my life slowly creeps away as my lungs fill with smoke. At this point, a spectacular drowning would have been acceptable; falling from the sky would have sucked, but at least it would have been fast. The metal treasure in my sock blisters my skin as the surrounding fire intensifies. I better figure out this walking or crawling thing and fast because if there is one dominant trait of mine, it is to prove others wrong.

First, I need to get my head pointed toward the front of the bus and start army crawling in that direction. I do not have the strength to physically move my friends out of the way, so I try to slide over them. I spin myself around without help from my legs, and that burning key, yeah, that provides further motivation, so I manage to get my two elbows on top of my dead friend, Wes.

I can see someone lying close to the door, crammed up against the front wall of the bus. It is hard to see through the thick smoke now consuming the cab of the bus and pushing my lungs to the max. I cannot catch air that is not contaminated with burned byproducts. As I move my right arm off Wes to make my final push toward the door, I fail. I am a noodle of a woman again. Everything of mine is in excruciating pain!

I want to scream, but that is useless. I do not think I am close enough to a living soul to hear me. I never in all my years would have imagined it would go down like this, but I chose this life and now I get to die here in my own hell truly surrounded by fire. The Roadie Cartel might have got the win, but I know that I at least have informed the world of them. Hopefully, and even if it is not for ten years, my voice will not be censored, and they, too, can burn in a fiery hell soon enough.

I see black. The fire's illumination behind my eyelids dissipates slowly, much like the sounds around me. The inevitable eternal darkness, much like what I imagine a black hole to be, is sucking me in as I have one last thought of Ivan. I can hear him in my head, telling me, *"that no matter where I go, he will be there for me."* At the moment, I thought it was the cheesiest thing my father could have said in my mind, but it was a truth he had said to me since my childhood. He always showed up for me at just the right time, and now more than ever, I want him to show up like he did so many times. But I know he is gone, and I feel like I let him down as his daughter. But dammit, I wish I could have him here to help me or even just to hug me once more.

My heart was telling me something as darkness engulfed me. I must speak to the one person I thought might actually listen. "Okay, Ivan. You said you would always be here for me, and . . . well . . . I am in a bit of a predicament, and I would love to live. I need to bring down this cartel for what they did to my great-grandparents, Wes, Axel and you. Regrettably, I think your big guy has other plans for me. And since I never bought into that place "heaven" you always spoke of, I am hoping you are there enjoying a margarita. Well, I am going to a different place now, but I want to say thank you for life, and thank you for being the best father I could have. I love you!"

I know nothing will come from this, but I will leave this world on a positive note, at least. Everything for so long in my life has had hints of negativity, but as much as this sucks, the last thing to leave my mind will be love for my father. As the feeling of my last breath was creeping upon me I—

Darkness. . . and then all that was left, a dwindling heart beat . . .
lub dub, dub lub,
lub dub,
lub,
dub . . .
BANG! BANG! "Wyatt!" *BANG! BANG! BANG!*
LUB DUB, LUB DUB, LUB DUB, LUB DUB LUB DUB, LUB DUB! My heart rate shot up as, as . . . I hear banging in my head. No. Wait that's not in my head . . .

That is on the passenger side of the bus?

What the hell is going on? I am paralyzed from the smoke in my lungs. Am I playing games with myself? But the banging continues. A female voice. Then nothingness . . . is death playing a game in my mind. WHAT THE FUCK IS GOING ON!

Nothing . . . again but the sound of the bus being ripped apart by fire. Then abruptly and violently, two hands wrap around my forearms. I am yanked across Wes. Sliding headfirst. Down stairs. Sand and brush. Shock. Blind.

My open wounds get a taste of sand, the morning sun and a cold desert wind. I am reminded that life is full of pain. My wounds scream. An explosion. *BOOOOOOOM!* I fly across the desert landscape. I scream in agony as I hear bits and pieces of the bus landing around me. I lie there in pain, but alive.

November 6, 2009 - 07:23:13, Milepost 80 Highway 9: Columbus, New Mexico

The sound of sirens approaches the scene in the morning air. I still lack vision and cannot feel my legs. As tears make their way down my cheeks as I lie on my back, I wonder who I will see when my sight returns. As much as I want it to be Ivan, I am left emotional because I know it cannot be. Regardless, I feel in my heart that he pulled this miracle off. Instantly, I start to think about how I am so grateful for this second chance—or more like the hundredth chance—at life. Lying in pain, it is hard to think about the future, but I know I have a job to do if they can keep me alive. Voices are searching for survivors, and I hope my rescuer did not fall into death's hands when that explosion occurred. I feel guilty that I might have been the only one who survived. But the pain in my body quickly takes emotion away, feeling as though I have razor cuts covering my body and submerging in rubbing alcohol.

The sun has made its way over the mountains and into the light blue sky as the first responders' voices approach. The sun is bright and blinding to my damaged eyes but I can see a prominent shadow in my vision now. A man's silhouette contrasts sharply against the sun's yellow hue and enormous blue sky. With my blurred vision, it looks like an angel from a Michelangelo painting Ivan had in his room next to his bed.

I mutter a faint help as the image comes closer and down toward me. It grabs my hand with warmth, and says, "Wyatt, I am Officer Michael Hernández. I was contacted by Ivan. He told me you would lead me to the man wanted for the murder of a businessman in Czechoslovakia and the leader of the Mexican cartel. You might have a key; it will unlock the cartel's deepest secrets. I know this is all overwhelming now, but this is my partner, Detective Lulis Ramirez, we are here to help you. She has been tracking you, thanks to your videos. That is how we ultimately found you."

As the two detectives cover me with a jacket, Lulis asks puzzledly, "Who was with you when the bus exploded?" I had nothing for her. "Wyatt, who pulled you from the bus?" I tried to shrug my shoulders for I had no clue.

I was loaded into an ambulance sometime on the morning of November 6th. I had been saved on my birthday, no less. The medics informed me that we would leave soon, and Officer Hernandez quietly noted that he and his partner would ride along. I could hear them climbing into the ambulance and felt my stretcher sway slightly.

"Wyatt, we are here to protect you," Ramirez said softly. "We will take you to an undisclosed location. We need you to recover because soon we will need your help taking down this criminal organization we have been chasing for far too long." She paused when I coughed. I hesitated, wanting to speak. "You shouldn't say anything right now," she continued. "Rest your head and mind. We will get more of your story soon enough. The last transmission we had with Ivan is that you have the key to a lock box in his homeland where he hid important documents that will lead to the apprehension of Zora, Juan, Adolf, La Reina and so many more in the roadie cartel who are so deeply embedded in, not only American society, but throughout the world." She smiled at me then yelled to the driver, "We need to get to the jet immediately!"

And just like that we were off. I didn't have much energy left in me, but I was able to break a slight smile for the detectives. But before I passed out from exhaustion and pain, I reached for the last thing of my father's I had, but as I went to feel for it, Officer Michael took my hand. Grasping my hand tightly between his, he started to gently whisper. At first I couldn't make out what he was saying. The ringing in my ears paused and his words cut through clear as day, he was reciting a child's prayer. It was the same one Ivan used to say to me when I was on the road with him and as he came to the end I could hear my father's voice finish with him, "Be at my side, to light and guard, to rule and guide." There was silence in the ambulance after he finished, not even the machines keeping me alive beeped, then he whispered once more, "Papa is here *mija*, please help guide me in protecting her now." Tears poured down his face as he began to loosen his grip on my hands to wipe them from his eyes. I didn't have time to think about how he had been hurt or who hurt him, but I knew he was clearly talking to his little girl. So, I did the only thing I could at that moment, I clutched Officer Michael's hand more tightly and slowly coiled my toes to grasp Ivan's last gift to me, one of liberation and one of vengeance . . . these two keys are going to help me bring down The Roadie Cartel.

CHAPTER 20

The Only Cop . . .

Exhausted . . . physically, mentally but most of all emotionally and not really sure what the next move is going to be other than get this girl to safety, we boarded the private medical jet. Wyatt headed straight for her spot in the hospital room with wings, while Lulis and I headed to the front of the jet to find a drink, a comfy chair and most importantly, sleep. "Ha, sleep," I chuckled to myself as I reached for the tequila bottle on the mini bar. My fingers wrapped around the neck so tightly as I went to lift the premium drink to my lips, but I slid the bottle to the side and grabbed something non-alcoholic for myself today, a simple bottle of water. I wasn't ready to silence my mind with my favorite numbing potion. My soul needed a second to decompress a situation so akin to a time I had already lived once before. Seeing that girl lying on the ground bloodied, burnt and beat tonight took me back to that stormy night where I crawled through the mud to my little girl and held her lifeless body. A night that has haunted me for exactly twenty-seven years to the day in that same Southwest desert. There is not a day or night that goes by that I don't feel and see her shell of a body lying across my blood-covered arms. And up until recently I had been a fall down drunk trying to erase those memories of her, but as I slid that bottle of tequila a little further away from me the images of me once again holding a hurt young woman in my arms flash into my mind. I have cried to Him before, "why," but I get no response as to, why me . . . why am I going through this. What I am supposed to fucking do? I have tried—twice now—and each time people get hurt! So why me, what am I supposed to do?

I stood there looking at my unkempt self in the mirror at the little bar on the jet, looking down at my beer gut and then up to my tired eyes. I started staring deep into my own eyes. I asked myself again, "What am I supposed to do?" My mind stayed quiet like it normally does. I ask again, nothing. Internally each time I ask I can feel my blood start to boil with thoughts of The Butcher doing this again. "WHAT AM I SUPPOSED TO DO!" I asked internally again. Then with a rush of adrenalin my hands clenched into fists, the closed water bottle top blew off and water came shooting out of the top, and I screamed, "WHAT THE FUCK AM I SUPPOSED TO DO?" while falling to my knees in tears. I could feel a few hands on my shoulders comforting me and telling me not to worry about the mess. I didn't stay down on the ground too long but instead got to my feet and asked the flight attendant for some towels to clean my mess up. He answered me and I got up. I got to my fucking feet instead of like last time where I became a fall down drunk. I don't know exactly what I have to do but I know that I have to try and I have to go after this asshole differently than ever before.

After I cleaned my mess up from the floor and bar, I decided it was time to get my ass into a seat. I hadn't even changed clothes or washed my hands as I sat down with my new bottle of water. My mind was racing trying to comprehend how I was right back to where it all began with The Butcher. Sure, it was a little different but here I was once again on the hunt for a man I have been chasing almost my whole career. A wicked and evil man who will stop at nothing to hurt and brutalize anyone who crosses his path. Sitting in one of the first-class style chairs toward the front of the plane, I could hear the doctor and nurse checking Wyatt's vitals behind me. Lulis sat down just across the aisle from me, "Are you sure you are okay, Michael?" she gently asked.

I had no idea if I was "okay" but shook my head up and down, then I turned slightly, smiled at her and said, "I am ready to put an end to this cartel once and for all."

The plane finally started to move after all the medical supplies had finally been loaded. I didn't fly my whole life and up until I met Lulis, I had only ever seen a plane. So, as she snuggled into her reclined seat, I was left gazing out the window as we took off into the blue sky. Leaving El Paso, you can see the true awe of the two cities in two different countries butted up next to each other and the only thing separating them is some arbitrary line. A border line that only matters to a few and even then, that line that is drawn on paper will never be able to hold back a force like Juan's unless the Hydra loses all its heads. As the plane crept up over the Franklin Mountains and past a few random clouds, it started to make it's turn to the east, but

I was able to see far enough into the distance the spot where the day and my nightmares all started twenty-seven years ago.

Looking into the beautiful blue sea that is the sky I was left with a feeling of grief suddenly. I wish my family was alive to see this. They always called me their superman, and here I am flying through the sky in a jet. Life is so strange; one minute you are a falling down drunk cop who could give two shits about life or the city I once cared so deeply about, to being sober and going after the man who for all intents and purposes changed my entire life and all the dreams I once had. I have only recently become sober and not for really any reason other than Agent Lulis saving me from my ultimate demise as a suicidal alcoholic. Since that fateful night on November 6th, my life has never been the same. The love-filled dreams I once shared with my wife soon turned into night terrors, even my daydreams became vile reenactments of the events that led up to my family's horrific deaths. But now here I am sad because I am alive and finally have a chance to be my family's superhero. The Butcher has not only taken my physical life from me over the years, but now looking at it with a sober mind, he took my mental life too. He left me with survivor's guilt but would never let me take my own life. He owned me.

Watching the sky slowly change from baby blues to darker shades of blue as we cruised across the times zones to our first stop, I started to think back to the day I met my wife . . .

We were two young kids playing on the jungle gym in elementary school when we met. I would say it was love at first sight, but at that age I think we just enjoyed the simple giggles we shared. She moved to my small town not knowing a soul and I wasn't a very popular kid so when she asked me to play that morning, I knew I would do anything to keep her in my life. And as the years went on that promise became more and more real. Our innocent platonic friendship soon blossomed into a beautiful romantic garden by the time we were ready to leave our sleepy little town deep in the heart of Mexico. Shortly after we graduated high school, my love decided she wanted to become a teacher. She was passionate about the sciences and wanted to share her knowledge with all the kids of Mexico. She hoped to inspire a student who would one day walk on the moon or find the cure for cancer. She wanted to create a new style of hero the kids of Mexico could look up to. My wife was my hero for that pursuit. I, on the other hand, chose law enforcement. I know that sounds silly, but I wanted to help clean Mexico of its crime and drugs to make it a safer place for the kids of our little town first and then the country. Being a cop is a very underappreciated job in Mexico, but I still believed I had a shot at making a difference. Looking back at the feeling, it is the same feeling I got today when I crushed that water bottle in anger.

A few years down the road, we made our dreams a reality. She taught at a local all-girls school for the underprivileged, and I was moving up in rank at the local police department. We had a family dog, a small house, a crazy black cat (Officer Merlin was his name; he was always on the lookout for a snake in the grass), and a chicken (we named Archie) that would find its way into the yard each day to peck and chase Merlin. Not long after my promotion into the special unit for the drug task force in Mexico, we found out my beautiful wife was also pregnant with our first baby. The promotion and the little bit of extra cash that came with it would be an enormous help with the new mouth to feed. The day had come, and God had brought us a daughter—I still crack a smile from ear to ear each time I think of this day. She was everything you could ever want in a little girl. She was healthy, had a giant smile like me, and had great looks provided by her mother.

Not long after the birth of my daughter, the police department asked if I would move closer to the border for reassignment to help the never-ending, worsening drug trafficking problem and to fight against the illegal guns coming back into the border towns from the United States. We knew it was going to be tough, mainly because whoever was supplying the guns was paying the U.S. government a pretty penny to stay out of the way. We both jumped at the opportunity to see something new and for me to face the organization that could be so daring; Juan's Mexican cartel. We wanted to make a difference in life, and this was our shot.

After the long drive and then many months of digging our roots into the new town, we were blessed with the news that another child was on the way. At first this was a tiny bit stressful too, but soon my beautiful wife found another teaching job but this time it was a coed school for wealthier children in the area. Like any teacher, she was excited to play with newer equipment provided by the school and have new students to help open their minds to the world. I too, was lucky with a new team, and my patrol duties came with a partner; I loved the idea of having a friend to hang with daily. In the past, I patrolled by myself. Life was grand and everything we had dreamt of was coming true. My first true taste of success as a cop came when cocaine became the new gold in North America, and the white powder was everywhere. In the new town I was quickly promoted to the head of this region in Mexico's drug police unit, it was our version of the DEA. This was huge for my family and me . . .

The jet hit a little turbulence and an alarm sound on one of Wyatt's machines in the back took me out of my daydream, so I decided to get up and go check on her. I don't know what it is, but I am drawn to this young woman as if she is my own daughter. Lulis had been following her for quite a while longer than I had been, obviously but every time I looked at her profile with Lulis, she just reminded me of my little precious Alicia. After a while I couldn't watch her diaries without tears running down my face at the sound of her voice. There was a certain ring in her words that took me back to my own little girl calling out for me in the backyard when we would play after work. And then when I found out her life was saved the night my sweet girl's was taken . . . I had no words for days. Walking quietly past my partner who had passed out with a bag of chips in her hand I needed to go see Wyatt and make sure that alarm was just a fluke. But as I got closer to the back of the jet I heard the doctor shout to the nurse, "Grab the crash cart!" My stomach sank as I approached the door. I could see the doctor giving her chest compressions as the nurse readied the paddles to jolt her heart back to life. Looking through the window I was left in tears watching Wyatt's already badly burnt and cut body be pushed on more. Her lifeless arms and hands shook violently with each jolt. I cried harder as her face soon became my sweet Alicia's face. The tears flowed down my face and pooled around my feet as I could do nothing but shout, "PLEASE NOT HER, NOT AGAIN!!" Then a single sign of hope emerged from the chaos suddenly, the heart machine beeped, then again and then in rhythm. Her heart started up and she began to cough. With the deepest sigh of relief, I put one hand to my heart and the other to the door. I stood there, a mess of tears, snot and emotions, but she made it and she was fighting. The same thing I had to do for her and my Alicia.

I left eventually, but not before I saw her move her hand. It took so much anxiety away.

Once back in my seat the flight attendant brought over a warm towel to clean my face and to inform me that we would be making our one stop soon and to just sit back and relax. She informed me that we would be on the ground for a little while and there was a small room on base where I could go and get a coffee, but to be back before six o'clock. The jet we are on was a pretty high-tech plane, but we were going to have to stop and get fuel before we made the longer push over the ocean. We also had to pick up a backup doctor and nurse so they could have sleeping shifts. We landed at an undisclosed Air Force base on the East Coast and after a couple hours on the ground, and a small walk around the hanger with Lulis we started to wrap up our talk on what the plan was going to be when we landed. She had a whole team ready and from the sound of it a great place for Wyatt to go into a witness protection program, where Lulis was sure no one would look. I thought it was a little out there, but I wasn't running the show, Agent Lulis was.

With a full tank of gas and some extra gear, we all sat there in anticipation waiting for the pilots to throttle up the large-winged beast. Gazing out of my window, I got lost in a beautiful tree-lined view just past the runway. I had never seen trees like this, ever and I sure as hell had never seen where we are going, France. I had only ever had a French fry from a fast food restaurant so I am in for a small cultural shock. You could hear the two engines begin to wind up and in a blink of the eye, the pilots let off the brakes and we were gone down that runway. As the jet's tires left the ground and my eyes fixated on the sky, which was now a rich dark blue, I thought back to my buddy Charlie. We only ever met after dark when the sky was this same color, he was the first to tell me about The Butcher.

When I first met "Charlie," my life was in a steady routine, with most days starting and ending the same way. I did not live far from my station, so I could wake up and spend time with my family first. I liked to wake up early and make a cup of coffee before the rest of the house began to stir. Some mornings I would go for a little run so I could stay in shape for not only my family, but the job. By the time I would get back from my run my little girl would be there waiting with the cat. She loved to let him out and watch the animals play in the yard. After that it was breakfast for us all, because every once in a while the job called for me to go on special assignments late into the night. We did this so for at least one meal we all sat down together. Once I arrived at work, I had the same morning tasks. I would look at reports from the night before, usually sifting through to see if there was anything cartel related. But more often than not it was just the standard shit. It didn't take me long to realize my small town was a large front for the cartel's hub into the US, but no one wanted to rat anyone out, because they were all on the payroll. I just did my job the best I could to keep these criminals safe from other criminals.

Most of the time, petty crime kept the station busy, which sucked. I was built for a good challenge, so boredom did sadden me from time to time. But what could I do in a town that feared the mysterious cartel that worked from the inside out—cunning, sly, sleek—so I confronted radio silence with dismay. I spent most days preparing the team for the big drug or gun bust I hoped would one day come. I tried to be proactive, wanting to stand a chance against a cartel that most of these guys never dared to face. I was warned many times to leave them be, to just focus on tourists and the other drug runners but leave Juan's men alone. I was hooked on finding that dragon one day and slaying it. I was too cocky in my approach. All I wanted was to be the knight who walked back into town after taking down the Hydra and dropping its lifeless heart in the town square for all to see . . .

My life and focus changed when I woke to a call at my house, it was a tip about a snitch leaking information to Juan's cartel within my precinct. I was so mad to hear someone was leaking info to the enemy from one of my guys that I skipped my normal morning routine and headed right into the station. I was looking over my shoulder to reverse out of my driveway when I was startled by a *gringo* hiding in my back seat.

This man, who I knew only as "Charlie," talked to me the whole ride in to work and he tasked me with digging into Mexican and American local and state agencies. Before he exited my car swiftly at a random stop sign, he asked me if I was ready to take down the biggest cartel and if I was not, that I needed to forget him and to keep driving once he exited. I told him my reason for becoming a police officer in Mexico. Once he knew my heart lived for justice, he told me that he would be in contact soon. Charlie and I met intermittently for months, exchanging information that slowly built a case against members of Juan's cartel and we even had a trail that led to men in Congress, the Department of Justice and a few Federal Banks. We learned the complexities behind this global operation. Our hearts were set on enlightening the world with the truth and vast reach of this cartel, which would ruin the sinful lives of many prestigious people in America and Mexico, but we did not have enough to pin the mastermind yet, so we dug more and more.

Then radio silence fell on the case. A few weeks went by, and Charlie had gone quiet on me. I got to the station one morning, and a few of my fellow colleagues (who knew I had been pushing back against Juan's cartel harder than they wanted me to) shared some news. "I needed to remember who I was going after," one said under his breath as another began to approach me. They handed me the El Paso Times newspaper and there on the front page was the article. The headline read, "American Undercover Agent Murdered." Police found the agent's naked body hanging off the roof and above the front steps of the El Paso Federal Court House by one leg and he was also missing his head. The agent had his tongue stabbed by a dagger into his right lifeless hand and dug into his chest were the words *"listo cochinillo."* Charlie had warned me that I would be signing my own death certificate if the investigation went south, but I wasn't scared of their "ready piggy" comment. My wife pleaded with me to stop my daydreams of being a superhero. She would say, "These men aren't playing the same game you are; they are playing a much darker one, where rules only apply to one side."

Staring into the dark sky outside the plane I can only replay her words and wish I would have listened . . .

Regardless of everyone's counsel, I continued to dig, in honor of

Charlie and to ensure the best future for my family. But without my powerful ally, I asked for help from the only other person I could trust. I had never gone to him before because Charlie didn't want a third party involved, but I needed a second set of eyes, especially now that there was a bounty on my head. Plus, my partner had witnessed most of the process and watched me look through countless files at my desk. I had even slid one across the desk a time or two to see if he had ever heard of some of the men we wanted to go after.

Our little town was small and quiet, but illegal action took place outside its perimeters always. With open land and few obstacles—other than the brutal dry heat during the day—the terrain was simple to trek across. Since the cartel had invested in U.S. military technology, our Mexican police force didn't have the resources to slow down products coming and going. Like I said before, it was going to take way more than just cutting off the head of the snake to shut down activity successfully. We were going to have to get both sides of the border involved. The cartel had technology and a code system that was too hard to break even if we did get some intel. We had been in the process of getting someone to snitch on them, but it was almost impossible. Juan gave hope to the poor and they were willing to fight to the end for the man. He is one of the most calculated leaders I have ever read up on.

I had not gone and checked on Wyatt in a while, so I decided it was time. My eyes for the first time in about a month actually got a little heavy and I didn't want to fall asleep without making sure she was still fighting a good fight back there. Looking through the window into her little hospital room I could see her heart beating on the screen and at one point I even think I saw a finger move, so because of that I think it is time I go actually try and close my eyes. It has been a long six or seven weeks, I don't actually know, and tonight is the first night I don't have any of my sleeping pills. No drinking and no sleeping pills; ha, I don't see this being a restful night.

Making my way back to the front of the jet I smiled, one because Wyatt was alive and two because I was alive. I haven't been a cheerleader of my life in a very long while because for the last twenty-five years I have been a fall-down drunk who hated my life. Just a few short months ago I would leave my favorite bar and go stand in the street praying that the city bus would mow me down. I prayed the driver would see the desperation in my face, push the gas a little harder, and plow me down like a dirty street rat. Sadly, or maybe thankfully, it never went that way. There was one bright side to my daily suicide attempt: I was not far from home when it failed.

My room was above a popular whorehouse that doubled as a tor-ta shop during the day. I don't bother with either, but I would say both businesses got many visitors regularly. My daily routine had changed since my years as a good cop. I spent most of my days finding the will to care after Juan's cartel had taken all power away from the local police department, but especially me. The only action I would see is when the federal police threw some weight around for the cartel; all we could do is sit back and watch them push through town and across the border maybe even block a street for them to move fast through town. I was just a space filler for when the actual government does come through, which they never do, and needed us to do something, but again they didn't and still don't care to go to that little border town.

My days were pretty simple then. I would wake up and have two decisions to make. Cheap tequila or cheap beer to start the day? And should I even show up at the police station or work from the bar? During the random chances when I would go into the station, I usu-ally ended up drinking there too. Then after my shift, more drinking. Drinking was the only thing bringing me closer to death. It is a slow one, but it beat having to deal with reality and the memories in my head. I wished so many times that I could find the strength to pull the trigger, but it is not something God ever let me do. Seeing it from this seat that I am in now, what I thought was Him torturing me was him trying to get me to hold on to a tiny sliver of hope.

Talk about perspective, not long ago my seat looked very different. I would sit in the only chair in my apartment, which is next to my bed most days. The chair allowed me to look outside my room's one grime-covered window. Alone in that hell, I sat looking at the only two items left from my previous life that didn't burn in the fire when the cartel torched my house. I used to go between staring at the badge and gun on the table, and only taking breaks when I would take a sip of my cheap tequila that resembled gasoline as I would peer out of the dirty cracked window. Deeply gazing at that badge that I once wore with pride and swore on the Bible of justice and duty. Now, it was a symbol of the government's lies which would lead my shaky hand to grab the gun, two, three, four times a day and shove the barrel deep into my mouth.

But a voice always spoke to me from out of the darkness that was my life then. I never could tell if I was just drunk. I hoped it was my wife speaking to me, but more often, it was my crazy neighbors, the hookers, making enough noise to distract me and all my suicidal tendencies. Hell, I know it sounds crazy even thinking back about these memories, and maybe it was the booze then, but there was a voice. Who was it; then I had no idea. But it was there every time I would go to swallow that extra handful of pills. It was there when I would grab the gun off the table. It was there when I didn't want to be on this planet or anywhere any longer. At the time I figured it was God or my guardian angel trying to tell me something. But now I know it was my sweet Alicia, telling me I had a job to do. I never thought it would be for that girl at the back of the jet.

I smiled and looked over at Lulis. She is a good sleeper.

I took a peek to my left and it was pitch black, I couldn't see anything out of my window except a little blinking light which would illuminate the window for a second . . . So, I decided to do something I really didn't like to do sober, sleep. I even decided I was going to turn my overhead light off. I hated the dark now-a-days, hence why I used to drink myself to sleep every night. I drank till I passed out so I didn't have to worry about turning off the lights, because that is when he would return. The Butcher and his men visited me every time I closed my eyes. When I was drunk beyond fucked up could be, I would still see him but only for a few moments as the booze took me to another planet. There was one other part to me turning that reading light off, it cast a spotlight on me that made me question if I was made for this mission. That single beam of light shining down, well, it felt like I was in the police limelight again. The one cop who Wyatt was trying to find to help her avenge her father. It felt like I was the one who was going to take the weight of the world on my shoulders, again. I was torn, sit in the dark and sulk or, was I finally ready to try and face my darkness. Face my own obscurity that might allow me to sit in the light one day. Clearly, I was going to have to if I wanted to keep this young woman alive on my end. I hadn't cared for someone in a very long time, and I knew the man I needed to become was going to have to face all his fears, even relive a few. Without a single grain of sleeping powder in me or an eye dropper of booze, I was ready to voluntarily walk into my worst nightmare. I buckled myself into my chair and even told the flight attendant to not wake me . . . this was my detox; this was my first step into becoming the superhero I always promised my little girl I was.

With a little heavy blinking I zoned out and took myself right back to November 6th, 1982. It was a semi-typical day around town. A few college kids were locked up for fighting the night before and our town drunk at the time was looking for a warm bed and a bean burrito for breakfast in his cell. A little time had passed since Charlie's death but that didn't give me a reason to not keep an eye on what was going on. Workdays for me would never be routine again, but I was moving forward in my pursuit for justice and in no time the phones would be ringing again. Not long after I sat down at my desk to look over some new activity, I had got a lead on, a call came in, a call about suspicious activity near an old, abandoned farm on the outskirts of town. Nothing felt off about the call, but it was late in the afternoon, and I didn't feel like it was worth the drive today. My partner, who was not married, insisted that he go so I could be home on time. As he headed to the squad car, I read over old police reports about the cartel to see if any of this new info had any similarities. Today's reports had revealed a pattern of calls about the cartel's activity into our local police system coming from a specific location in Juarez. This was not far from our headquarters.

The leads, I discovered, were purposeful. The caller created a never-ending load of police work focused on a Mexican cartel competitor who was tiny compared to Juan's operation. Also, this cartel would never cross into Juan's territory, that was certain death; they operated where Juan's men told them to operate. I stared at the grainy photos and paper trails that led to dead-end leads of a few houses in El Paso and Juarez Charlie had given me months earlier. Gutted, I sunk into my chair. I felt defeated. It was all a big cover up to keep guys like me busy. I was so frustrated when lead after fucking lead kept taking me down a road to nowhere. I wanted justice for the crimes the cartel had committed. I wanted justice for Charlie and the other men who died trying to bust these *pendejos.* I wanted justice for all the men and women who were addicted to the cartel's junk. I was sick of letting down the Mexican people and my family by not being the hero cop I wanted to be for them.

That day and time had gotten away from me. I was late for dinner, so I kept sorting and looking over some older files when I realized I had not heard from my partner. It did dawn on me that the drive was a little way out of town and our normal patrol radius. So, I returned to my research for a new clue or hidden anything in all these files. As time ticked away that afternoon and with my partner now on my mind, I started to justify the situation with rational thoughts. When he didn't answer his radio, I figured he was out of range. When he didn't call, it was because there was nothing to call about, yet. I had finally worn my eyes out for the day, and my gut feeling was eating at me. Perhaps he got stuck or fell. I did not connect his disappearance with the cartel because they notoriously worked under the cover of darkness, which was now only barely settling in.

I didn't leave the station because I didn't want to miss his radio call, my house wasn't always welcoming to radio waves finding my antenna. More time had passed so instead of his radio, I called my partner's house from my desk phone and like his radio, there was no answer. I couldn't go home knowing my partner had not returned. That is not how we were with each other. Since the first day we rode together, we had each other's back. He came to family dinners and we even had him join us at church some days. He wasn't my best friend, that was my wife, but he was the next closest thing I had to a best friend.

Sitting here reliving this story, I can feel the blood in my veins starting to pump faster. There is a certain weight being pushed down onto my shoulders and the hairs on my neck are starting to stand on end. This feeling of sitting in the dark with just my own thoughts is so strange and realistic.

Vividly remembering when everything in my world suddenly shifted came sprinting across my memory as if it had just happened.

But my ship sank that late afternoon when I called my wife to let her know I had to investigate a work matter and would be home as soon as I finished. The phone rang for what felt like an eternity, I prayed for her to pick up but there was no answer. I hung up and sat back in my chair, pondering the strange sequence of events unfolding, a new bigger ball of tension started to build in my stomach. I was starting to panic inside with each growing second after hanging up the phone. I decided to call my partner's house again just for good measure. Nada. "What in the fuck," I blurted out. I looked around the station, but everyone was gone. I picked up the phone and called home incessantly.

I threw the phone across the desk and kicked the chair out of my way. I bolted out the door and ran down the stairs to my cruiser. I drove my old, worn-out Ford cruiser like I was in the Mexican Grand Prix, the lights flashing, I pushed the siren button so hard my finger pushed it through the dashboard. I prayed for a distress signal to appear and summon a true superhero, but I knew it was going to have to be me to go and save them. "Oh God," I begged, "please let my wife and kids be okay. I will do anything. I will be a better man just please spare them for me." I cried that day on the way to my house and sitting here in the dark, I can feel the tears falling down.

As I rounded the corner, sliding sideways against gravel, I could see her car with open doors. When I got closer, I could see the gate and front door both open. I jumped out of the car, and when I reached the front door, I witnessed carnage, even from a criminal's standpoint, they would have said it was caused by barbaric savages. They had slain my animals as if they were trying to paint my walls red with their deceased bodies.

I ran room to room searching for human life, but the house was a ghost town. I ended up in the master bedroom last, so before leaving, I took the only other item I would need that night. I grabbed my own judicial system; it had nine big boys plus one mean girl sitting in the chamber ready to deliver that final verdict. Rushing back out to the car and not trying to trip on a dead animal, I got a glance at a recent family photo and as much as I wanted everything to be ok, my gut told me differently. Back in the cruiser, rather than head to my partner's house, I pushed the gas pedal through the floorboard as the tires hooked up with the pavement and the car straightened toward the abandoned farmhouse.

Making my way to the out skirts of town was not going to be quick but I knew a few old farm roads to help me miss driving straight through any congestion. Anything that could flash or make noise on my car was, I did not have time to slow down as I blew past another intersection. I saw flickering lights the closer I got to the property, but out of the blue, *BAM!!!* The force of an SUV hitting my passenger side sent me in every direction opposite of my destination. The impact sent the car flying, flipping me upside down so severely that when my head and the cruisers roof met the ground the force knocked me into a new world. I blacked out for who knows how long.

When I awoke from the accident, I came to with a couple men dressed in dark army fatigues—but I knew they were both cartel men—talking loudly above me. I felt a man next to me move, before I rolled my head to see who it was. It was my partner. We were both hogtied in the back of a rusted-out pickup truck. His tear-filled eyes said it all. He was the insider Charlie and I had been chasing. He was the one giving us false leads to chase. I heard muffled words, but I could only make out the word "sorry." I hated to hear that and hated him in that moment. Another bigger man climbed up in the truck bed, but before a second word could be said back there, he hit my partner and then me with the butt of his shotgun.

The sounds of men yelling and gun fire going off not far from me, jump-started my heart and jolted me from a knocked-out state of existence. I was deep in a dream for what seemed like years and not a good dream either. For one split second, right before I was rocked awake, my conscious mind gave me a sliver of hope that my nightmare was merely that. The hope was that I would wake up, look over, and there my beautiful wife would be. That was not the case, and this is not the bed I thought I would be waking up in. My body aches as if I had just fallen off a cliff and used the jagged rocks at the bottom to break my fall. I had no idea where I was this time, but I knew my life was soon coming to an end as the smell of burnt gun powder overtook the usually soothing smell of desert rain. The distinct smell of the creosote bush during a big rain used to signify growth and rebirth in the desert. Tonight, there was only destruction and betrayal. Being a cop in Mexico came with a very short life span, sadly. I couldn't see but I knew I was facing the sky by the way my eye lids would fill with light each time lightning danced across the sky, and the way the rain drops crashed into the open wounds on my face.

I felt as though I was slowly drowning laying there on my back unable to move. It was hard to focus. My eyes were getting more swollen with each drop of rain pelting down on them, millimeters from being sealed shut. Raindrops the size of baseballs fell from the sky this night, it was as if God had broken His promise, so He worked laboriously to flood and cleanse the Earth of evil now surrounding me. Lightning, one strike after another, continued to add to the ominous night sky as I prayed for one to strike me dead. Thunder rolled as I gained full consciousness and realized I was hogtied and gagged with an old gas rag. I was dying, but not dead.

My ears perked up when I heard my wife's voice just outside the truck bed. The gas-soaked rag in my mouth stopped me from calling to her. The zip ties that bound my hands and feet rendered me immobile. The only thought I had that second was that I had failed my family. I failed to protect my kids. And, I had failed to be the husband I promised my wife I would be. There was no superhero in me, just a man reduced to a hogtied pig starring up at a goliath-like butcher. I cried for God to come and rescue her and the kids.

"TAKE ME!" I screamed through the rag stuffed in my mouth. I tried with all my might to push that rag out, but at times I felt myself swallow that gasoline rag more than anything else.

With what little vision I had from swollen eyes and the rain coming down on me, I could see a taller man with dark features appear with a woman. They rested their arms along the side of the truck bed and looked down on me. The man held a knife, a big cleaver, that he tapped against the metal of the truck, and he grinned with wickedness as he, tap, tapped his friend on the bed. He spoke to the Mexican woman in an unfamiliar accent. He was not from the area. He casually explained to her that he was about to define real pain for a cop who didn't understand. The kind that would haunt me daily for trying to derail a system he worked so hard on. "Juan and the cartel will get what we want," he said to her.

Cringing with anguish, I pleaded through that rag for them to let my family go and take me instead.

The man signaled at someone behind him. "Grab the cop that showed us where we could find everyone. I want him first."

As blood-encrusted hands grasped my partner, I could hear my children and wife screaming my name, crying in fear and begging for their lives. Their cries became high-pitched shrieks as a man yelped and screeched in pain. Gurgling. Gasping and drowning. Silence.

Even though it has been almost thirty years, I can't unhear those voices that night. Sitting in my dark seat with my eyes fixated on a tiny speck of light hitting the cockpit door, I try to stay calm as sweat beads on my forehead. My throat tight, so tight it is hard to swallow as I grip the arm rests so tight I can feel the bones in my fingers starting to bend, but the pain of what comes next starts to elevate my heart rate and I can feel my breathing shortening . . .

After the man who sold my family and his soul to the devil was no longer a part of this world, my life ended too. My wife spoke her last words to me soon after his last breath. I don't have words now and I didn't have words then. To say that my tears soaked my face in the rain would be an understatement; they drenched my face. My wife and children would soon be gone. Feet from me and I couldn't do a thing to help, I couldn't even be a coward in those moments and cover my ears to shelter my soul from hearing their screams . . .

"I love you," came across that truck bed one last time, what used to be words of hope and light for me sadly became a goodbye memento.

I screamed to the heavens for my wife and children. I had to tell them I love them. I tugged on my restraints, feeling my wrists ripping out of their sockets. But my physical pain was nothing compared to the blood-curdling cries belted out while the Butcher and his men hacked off their limbs. I was forced to listen as these animals laughed at my suffering.

The sounds of death drowned out my pleas, and I was left alone with shame, disappointment, and disgust for myself. I could not stop the cartel as a lone wolf fighting a never-ending uphill battle. My opponent has been in bed with the same government heads who have paid me to supposedly keep these criminals off their streets.

My fight was null and void.

Crying in that truck bed I prayed for someone to shoot me in the head but that would be too merciful. The Butcher is not human, but a demon, a sick and twisted grim reaper walking amongst us. He is my mortal enemy who has massacred my colleagues and now my family. I once considered myself a man of justice and fairness. A man of unwavering faith. He has made me question it all.

I heard footsteps heading back to the truck. I remember tilting my head upwards, and The Butcher grabbed me by the face and hair, lifting me just above the truck bed. He spit at me in disgust. "Your ignorance caused this to happen. Look! LOOK PIG! Now look at me, you fucking swine!" I shuddered, hearing the voice of impiety for the first time.

His cartel throng pushed me out of the truck bed, and the engine started. I felt the back tires cross over my lower legs. I laid there praying to die. Instead, the truck stopped and pulled forward again, skipping across my muddy body, and the red taillights slowly faded away into the dark, rainy night. Looking back out into the night sky from the jet's window, I am reminded of the emptiness I felt that night on my back in the desert. God had betrayed me; He spared my life when I begged for death. He took my everything and then took more. I managed to slide my bloody body closer to the mangled pieces of what was my heart and soul. The war with Juan, his sister and the man they call The Butcher has left me with nothing but mangled flesh to cry on.

Dry, warm and alive, my grip loosened on the arm rests as stars appeared in the sky outside my window. *Hmm.* I know for a fact that the only visible light I was able to see just a short while ago was the blinking light on the wing. I have never been up this high in the sky so I had no clue what I could or could not see. But for the first time in a long time, I saw something so very beautiful in front of me. I can't help but think back to lying on my back with my wife staring up into the billions of little dots that scattered across the sky. We would try and count them from time to time and some nights we just laid there quietly peering into a vastness neither of us could explain. We trusted that no matter what happened to us in life that we would end up in these vast heavens together. I know she is not here with me but seeing that I am closer to the heavens than any time ever before I can hear her, "I love you." There was a weight hoisted off my shoulders in that instance and hope came back into my heart. After everything I had witnessed and the long painful nights alone trying to kill myself, I always kept a tiny ounce of hope hidden behind my dead heart. I knew my baby girl Alicia would give me another chance to be the father I promised her I could be.

"Michael."

"Michael."

I jumped to my feet!

Lulis and the flight attendant stood, waiting for me to come back to reality.

"Sorry, sorry, I didn't see you standing in front of me." I said as I rubbed my eyes.

"We just walked up Michael, you have been dreaming pretty hard for the last few hours." Lulis said with a confused look on her face.

"No, I was gazing out of the window at the stars and galaxies, a few minutes ago."

"No, you were sweating, swearing and fighting something in your dreams, whoever it was, I think you might have finally won."

I stood up to stretch and look around, a little confused, I turned to look behind me. Ok I was still on the jet, I then bent down a little and pulled the window shade up. There he was, the sun, shining so bright and miles into the blue sky as we started to make our descent into France. I sat back down for a quick second and then hopped up. I headed back to check on Wyatt. I had to see her; I had to see if she was doing better than when I left her. Walking up to that room was not easy for me, the emotion of seeing tubes and probes hooked up to her didn't sit well with me. Hell, looking into that room with all the machines was like opening an old book written in Latin, it made no sense but when I got my first look at her this morning, my heart filled with joy. Her general position seemed to be the same, but her head was turned away from me. It appeared that she was looking out of the windows of the plane. Not only did I feel my heart open up again, but that feeling of hope came alive in me knowing that not long ago she was in a dark place, she was circling the drain on that bed. Now, now she is looking at a new sunny day. We made it through that dark night together.

I turned and headed back to my seat with a new found purpose in life. The attendant approached me in the aisle not far from my seat and offered me a coffee. I smiled and said, "I would love a cappuccino." My ass hadn't even hit the cushion.

"You drink those now; well you sure aren't the same Michael I met in September," Lulis said with a grin. But she was right. Today marked the first day I woke up feeling joy in a very long time. The day Lulis found me, was going to be my last day on this planet.

I looked over at her, smiled and began to share a little memory of that day with her . . .

"You might not know this, but my phone had a broken bell inside from being thrown across the room so many times in that shitty little trash dump of an apartment. So, when it rang, it was more of a clanking sound than the traditional ring. That morning, I wasn't sure what time of day it was or what day it even was, but someone, you, kept calling me and waking me up. I wasn't in the mood to get out of bed or answer that phone for anyone but you wouldn't stop!

"Clank. CLank. CLAnk, CLANk, CLANK!!!! It was like one of those cartoons where the rabbit is trying to make the other character go crazy, so they have him do something silly, like call until they pick up and then phone explodes. I just wished it exploded.

"I was still in my clothes from the night before or maybe even a few days before and hiding from the sun, the phone and life at this point under my shitty blanket. It wasn't the best blanket; in fact, it was about as thick as a piece of notebook paper, and it did about as good of a job as the ripped and cigarette-burned curtains hanging over my grime-filled window. The clamorous phone would not shut up, you must have called a million times."

"Three," Lulis said sarcastically.

I squinted my eyes and raised one eyebrow.

"Anyway, I did what I had done a few times before; I went to reach for it so I could launch it across the room. But it wasn't there. Confused and pissed off that I moved the phone I sat up. There it is, in the middle of my floor, with a white envelope leaning against it. Now I was super confused. 'Charlie sent me, answer the phone,' was written on the front of that piece of paper. I was speechless.

Seeing his name sobered me up and dropped me to my knees, I even crawled over to it on all fours because I didn't think I could walk. I remember the phone was still clanking and carrying on while I sat there on the floor with my hand suspended for at least another five clanks as I stared at the envelope with my friend's name on it.

"I picked up the phone and the voice said, 'The whale is eating her young.' And there you were and your strong Italian accent. 'Read the letter and don't be late.' Then you hung up.

"I took that letter and scooted back over the bed. I was still in so much shock. Charlie? I didn't want to believe it. I totally thought it was a set up from the cartel, but why now . . . they had already killed me. It took me a second, but then I remembered he always called Juan and his sister the whales of the cartel business. After making that connection I couldn't open that envelope fast enough! I can picture that exact second, taking my index finger I ripped down the side of the envelope and slid out one single paper with a typed message:

```
There will be an unmarked dark blue car for
you. It will be cattycorner, parked at the
stop sign from the bar you frequent most.
Meet in one hour from that phone call. Get
in the back seat and bring everything you
value.
```

"I had so many questions running through my mind. Biggest one, how the fuck did this letter get into my apartment? Then I gazed over at the door and there it sat wide open, with my keys stuck in the lock. My gut told me after seeing that, if they were going to kill me, they would have just done it last night.

"I was still torn about going. 'What did Charlie or this person want with me now?' I kept asking.

"I almost didn't go—pulling myself up off the floor revealed one big thing to me. When I went to climb back in bed, there sat my wallet. It must had fallen out of my sweatpants at some point in the night. It was open and there sat the last remaining photo I had of my family. Fuck, I had not looked at that photo in years, it always drove me into a deeper depression. I was the furthest thing from a superhero I had promised them I would become. After the pain hit me again, Lulis, I rolled into that shitty bed and tried to hide from my moment to avenge my family. I had no idea what was actually going to happen with anything, but I was so scared. I was so scared I was going to hurt more than I already did and also scared to have to be looked at as someone who was going to do something important in life.

"I laid under those covers shaking with fear. Then I heard my little girl Alicia's voice talk to me; she didn't say much more than my name, but it was the voice that always helped me take the barrel of that pistol out of my mouth. I slid the photo out from behind the stained and yellowed plastic sleeve. There we were trapped in time. I was in my uniform, holding my baby boy and kneeling next to our little girl and the love of my life. She was down on one knee next to us—so elegantly with her hair blowing in that desert wind. The faded photo brought back so many memories that I thought I had snuffed out over the years. I couldn't remember the year but then I recalled, my wife used to date every photo so that we could always go back to check dates. When I flipped it, I was not expecting anything more than a date. But of course, my beautiful wife wrote more, 'El día que conocimos a nuestro Superman, mayo de 1982.' If only I had become their superman. After reading that I heard Alicia's voice again, but this time she was reciting a child's prayer I used to say to her every night. The night before she was murdered, I kissed her forehead and she said, 'Daddy, I want to guide and protect you from the bad guys.' I softly chuckled and said, 'How about we leave all that heavy lifting to your guardian angel sweetheart, good night, I love you always.' I didn't think alcoholics had enough water in their system for tears but that morning I must have because the tears fell like a summer rain storm as her voice gently spoke to me.

"I don't remember much more after that hard cry in bed but as I locked the door to that old room, I did pause to take a deep breath. I wasn't sure if I was ready for this adventure as I pulled the key from the lock but when I got to the sidewalk, I dropped that key in the trash can just outside the front door. I bet that bottle of tequila I left sitting on the rackety folding table missed me whe'n I didn't come home, but you gave me a new assignment in life . . ."

Before I could finish my thought, the sudden feeling of the plane touching down, followed by a pretty intense jolt forward as the engines roared us to almost a joggers pace.

Lulis looked over, "You signed yourself up for this new assignment, I just dropped the note off."

I smiled.

"Well, are you ready to go take down the whales, Officer Michael Gabriel Hernandez?" she said with a giant grin on her face.

With love in my heart, not only for my family but that girl in the back, I looked at Lulis and smiled. I smiled a smile that I hadn't had since the day that photo in my wallet was taken and in that moment before the doors opened to the plane, I nodded my head yes. Yes, I was ready! I was finally ready to wear my badge again. I swore on a Bible to protect the people of my country, but this time I will stand up for the good, the beautiful, and the truth in this world.

If only it were all so simple! If only there were evil people some-
where insidiously committing evil deeds, and it were necessary
only to separate them from the rest of us and destroy them. But the
line dividing good and evil cuts through the heart of every human
being. And who is willing to destroy a piece of his own heart?
— Aleksandr Solzhenitsyn, *The Gulag Archipelago* 1918–1956

. . . may be the title of a Fall Out Boy song but it is the truest way to start this thank you page. Every thank you I have said up until writing this is now a memory of a person and place. Some are of friends who gave me praise for taking a chance at something new. Some are memories of even a harsh critique I didn't really want to take at the time but thankfully I shut my mouth for once and listened to only watch it work out in the end. And some are from strangers who just liked what I wrote. So, for all of that I truly do thank you all for the memories and it is only fair that I now try to share that gratitude in writing so that generations might be able to imagine some of the faces that have been so kind to me on the road to becoming an author.

Here I go . . .
I first want to thank **God.** He gave me this dream of writing before I ever believed it was possible and then He gave me the strength every day to see it through.

He also gave me **Berkley,** my incredible wife and manager who has put up with me for several years at this point. You have been with me through the thick, thin, good, bad, ugly and pretty parts of our relationship but no matter what you always had faith in me. So, for that you deserve a medal of some sort when you reach Heaven. You were also the first person to ever hear me say the title of this book and the first to tell me to follow my dream. Now, I couldn't imagine life any different.

Maverick, Mace and any future children you all will never know the long nights or sleepless days. You'll never know what it was like writing on my lunch break in that dusty and somedays arctic cabinet warehouse I once worked at to make some extra money to help us get to this point, but I am sure I will remind you plenty. I get to live out one of my favorite childhood movies because of you all, Stand By Me, about a stay-at-home father who was also a writer. Because of you I finally have my dream life.

Archie, Merlin, Freddy and Goose ... you were the animals who drove me crazy during those late nights when I needed to concentrate but all you wanted was extra attention. In the end, you truly helped me relax on days when a cold nose to the calf would brighten my long days of writer's block.

My Parents, cheers! You both are completely different humans and for that I am most thankful. Dad, you showed me work ethic and drive. I also know more about cars than I ever will need in my life but most importantly, you gave me a very dry sense of humor! I thank my mother for taking me to my first concert and giving me many other life experiences, which helped shape my life.

Now there are obviously so many family members who have supported this journey. Some are still here today and others may never know the impact they had on me but each one of them gave me encouragement along the way.

Ok, these next people are new and old friends, but each played a very direct role in this book getting published.

They say be careful what you ask for and when I asked this next person to give me her thoughts on one of my early drafts, I thought she was going to call me and tell me I was the next John Grisham. Boy, was I wrong but because of her honesty, I was able to not change but mold my novel into the work it is today. **Laurie P.**, thank you!

Fitzy, Ashley Fitzgerald, you introduced me to JuLee, the most wonderful publisher a first-time writer could ask for, you rock girl!

JuLee Brand, owner of W. Brand Publishing, thank you for taking a chance on me and this wild ass story. You have given me the creative steering wheel to the car and let me stomp on the gas pedal, literally and we haven't looked back yet.

Without this next person, I would not have had the confidence to send this book to JuLee because although it was a good "story" it needed a true editor. **Desi Yost** came into my life in high school and over the years I watched her blossom into one of the most badass females I know but there was one thing she crushed the most grammar and spelling! Ok she loves saving animals too, but the point is, Desi picked up her phone one random day and listened to me ramble on about some novel and at the end of our conversation she said yes to being the novels first true editor.

Thank you, ladies, for believing in me.

Now there is a very long list of close friends, friends, roadies, co-workers and acquaintances who flood my memory from around the world I must thank as well. Many of them have supported me on social media, listened to my podcast and even texted me randomly to say kind words and for that I will always hold a special place in my heart and mind for each one of you. But two specific dudes have been around listening to me talk about how one day I was going to write a book since we were kids, (eleven to be exact) **Neal** and **Andy**. Thanks for picking up the phone every time I called to tell you how I threw everything out the fucking window and was starting over in life . . . neither one of you questioned me or asked if I was going back, ever.

I must also give a big shout out to two special humans who without their generous donations I might not be here. Thank you, **Zach Farley and Eric Roccaforte**. I will pay you back with fine tequila one day.

To **"the road"**. You deepened and darkened my imagination more than I ever thought possible. Maybe it was the countless hungover days lying on my hotel floor dying and trying to think about what I may or may not have done the night before or maybe it was the millions of sleepless miles spent looking into the beauty that is this world only to be followed by another dark soulless music venue. Either way, I do know you made me stronger for all the days and nights spent alone wondering if there was something cooler than being a roadie. But also thank you to every job I had until I had a career as a roadie, you all impacted my imagination and my perspectives on how humans all interact. From my first job at Team MR in El Paso, Texas to my last official job at the cabinet warehouse with a kid named AJ who had to listen to me ramble on about life while out doing deliveries. Special thanks to Clair Global for letting me travel the world on someone else's dime for well over a decade which resulted in me unknowingly doing research for a book I never knew was in me.

Thanks **Joe Rogan** and **Jack Carr** for the podcast that changed my life forever. Jack you told me that you can stop doing something you have done forever, shift and then start over and then rise to the top of a new adventure!

To my amazing team: **Berkley Kriz, Jamie Wendt, Alissa Endres** and **Lauren Koops** who worked tirelessly on the book trailer. Kickstarter, design, one sheets, book tour, and so much more Y'ALL SLAY.

Milestone Publicity: Jessica, Taran, and **Mike**, you all have believed in this story since day one and have been fighting to get it out there!

The Talking Book, a.k.a. the best audio book recording studio ever. Kris and team, you brought me **Melissa** and I am blown away at your love for the audio book world.

I could go on forever, but I would like for you all to get to the real story, so I am going to end this with one last paragraph. I will start with these famous words.

"We have multiplied our possessions but reduced our values.
We talk too much, love too seldom and hate too often.
We've learned how to make a living but not a life.
We've added years to life, not life to years." – George Carlin.

He always had a very special way with words. He was right in many ways, and I use this quote because I truly thank everyone, I have encountered in the forty-one years it took to get here. Every good and bad moment carved my river to getting here and becoming an author. So, to all who I have hurt along the way I am sorry and to those who hate me because of my actions again I am sorry, but I thank you for your time in my life. And to all those who have played even a fraction of a part, thank you for your time. Since the day I decided to take this leap of faith into a world I knew nothing about, I have only added life to my years and for that I am truly thankful, grateful and appreciative of every single person who has spent their hard-earned money to allow me to follow my dreams.

Cheers and LOVE!

PHILLIP J KRIZ

Watching Guns N' Roses from the side of the stage in London, standing on the set of Saturday Night Live with Paul Simon, receiving a signed skateboard from Carrie Underwood, and mixing front-of-house sound for Kiss . . .

These are just a handful of experiences in the rearview mirror of Phillip Kriz's extraordinary journey in the music industry as a sought-after "roadie" tech and trusted tour confidant.

Born and raised in El Paso, TX, Kriz is influenced by his Spanish, Mexican and Czechoslovakian heritage as evidenced in his debut fiction novel *The Roadie Cartel*. He discovered music through his parents. Beyond spinning classics by Led Zeppelin and Bob Dylan, playing Howard Stern on their drive to school, his mom predestined his future in the business by buying tickets to his first concert, U2 and Public Enemy at the Sun Bowl. However, a Pink Floyd gig would be the point of no return.

After a stint in San Antonio, he graduated from Full Sail University in Orlando where he also worked his first production gigs. Eventually, he landed his "dream job" at production powerhouse Clair Global. Coming full circle, his first assignment placed him on a jaunt with Guns N' Roses in 2010. He hit the road for the better part of the next decade. Clients included Alicia Keys, The Scorpions, Justin Bieber, Florida Georgia Line, Paul Simon, Carrie Underwood, and Queen & Adam Lambert, to name a few. At the onset of the Global Pandemic, the business shutdown, and Phillip found himself at home in Nashville.

After hearing former Navy S.E.A.L. and bestselling author Jack Carr guest on the *Joe Rogan Experience* podcast, he decided to write a book of his own and follow in his grandmother's footsteps of writing.

In addition to being an author, Phillip is a happily married stay-at-home dad with two adorable little kids, three cats and a dog.

https://www.theroadiecartel.com/